SIX WINTER DAYS

A Novel

by

Kevin Montgomery

International Standard Book Number 13: 978-1-60452-088-0
International Standard Book Number 10: 1-60452-088-4
Library of Congress Control Number: 2014936004

BluewaterPress LLC
52 Tuscan Way Ste 202-309
Saint Augustine Florida 32092

http://bluewaterpress.com

This book may be purchased online at -
http://www.bluewaterpress.com/sixwinterdays

Printed in the United States of America

Cover Artwork by Monica Meza, San Francisco, CA

SIX WINTER DAYS

Prologue

Hundreds of Hessian prisoners marched down a muddy Philadelphia street with their heads down. Many were wounded. They glanced secretly at the American residents who lined the road, careful to avoid eye contact, in case they should attract the attention of one of those small, but dangerous, rock-throwing boys.

A mother, father, and their thirteen-year-old daughter watched the procession. The father drank from a jug. The mother complained, "Oh, how I wish you'd stop drinking that awful stuff."

"Aw, leave me alone."

They watched a particular Hessian with a bandaged head. The father nudged his daughter, handed her the jug, and motioned toward the wounded man. The daughter went over to the Hessian and helped him drink.

An American soldier rode up on a horse. "Get back. These men are Hessians. They're dangerous."

The daughter looked up at the rider. "I was only helping him. My father said to."

"Go back. Go back to your home."

"Father?"

"Get out of here or I'll strap you."

The soldier pulled a leather strap out of his pocket and waved it in the air. In cowering submission, the daughter covered her head with her arms. The father leveled his musket to his side, cocked the hammer, poured the powder in the pan, and watched.

The mother mumbled, "What's going on over there?" She raised her petticoat and marched through the deep mud toward the soldier, her eyes growing more fiery the closer she got to the young man. Sensing movement from the crowd, the soldier turned away from the girl and stared at the approaching mother.

The mother shouted, "Stop that. Right now. You put that away, Billy Reed."

"Mrs. Bedford?"

"You'll be sorry, Billy. I'll tell your mother. I'll tell Frances you raised a strap to Lydia. She'll tan your hide red."

"Oh, my God, Mrs. Bedford. No, don't do that. Don't tell mother. I didn't mean to do that. I didn't know she was your daughter."

Billy backed his horse up slowly. Another Hessian guzzled a long swig from the jug and then passed it along. The Hessians chuckled.

The mother stomped up to the horse, stabbing her finger through the air. "Now you take your horse, and your gun, and your strap, and your sorry behind, and you get the hell away from my daughter."

Billy backed his horse up faster, turned around, and galloped away. The Hessians laughed hysterically.

The father eased the hammer down onto the pan and shook his head. "It's a miracle."

A neighbor asked, "What is, Tom?"

"That they took Trenton, with fools like that."

People went into their homes and came out with food, fruit, water, and whiskey. The Hessians scooped it all up like starving dogs, then slogged away down the long road west.

The Battle of Trenton was over.

Chapter One

Day One, Sunday, Dec. 29, 1776

A muffled argument simmered in a house three miles east of Princeton, New Jersey. Maggie, the mother, yelled at her older son, Isaac, seventeen years old. "No, you can't go. You can't do that to me."

"Becalm yourself, Ma. You're getting hysterical again."

Maggie was an attractive thirty-five-year-old woman, but strands of greasy hair hung down into her face. The living room was cluttered with pieces of cloth and half-sewn dresses strewn all over the tables and chairs.

"I have bills. Your father isn't here any more. What am I to do with the children? You always do this to me, Isaac. You always want to go off and fight someone. Why, I know not."

Isaac said, "I can't stand working in that shop. All those old women. I'm going to get out."

"No. You'll be killed. What about your brother? Who will care for him? I don't have time to run the shop and care for everyone."

Maggie's other son, Toby, heard the yelling from the kitchen and came into the room. Toby was a little small for his age.

Isaac said, "He's fourteen, for the sake of Christ. Why do I have to care for him?"

"Because he's your brother, that's why. And don't you use the Lord's name like that. I won't have you talk like that in my house."

Isaac rolled his eyes. "I'm joining the Tories. The rebels are going to be destroyed. The Reverend says so."

"No, no. There's rebels everywhere, or British, or Hessians. Everyone's gone mad."

Maggie paced around the living room. Her dirty apron had large rips in it that caught the banged-up furniture as she walked by. She cried, turning away from the boys so that they wouldn't notice her eyes, and rubbed away the tears lightly.

Toby said, "Ma, don't cry."

Maggie said, "Hang those rebels. I had a home and a family. Now there's people with guns all over killing everybody. You'll get killed, Isaac, and Toby, too. No, you can't go."

Toby walked over to his mother. "Ma, it'll be all right. Isaac, you're staying here."

"Don't tell me what to do, you little runt."

Maggie turned toward Isaac, her eyes puffy from crying. She scolded, "You boys stop that! I didn't bring you up to fight with each other."

Isaac said, "Ah, Ma, he's such a baby."

"Am not." Toby looked at Isaac, who gave him an icy stare. Toby turned to his mother for support. "Ma, make him stay." He looked back at Isaac. "You're staying."

Isaac said, "Damn you," and rushed at Toby. Toby ran around the table and faked a dodge to get away, but Isaac didn't fall for it. Toby shouted, "Ma, Ma!" Isaac grabbed at his brother across the table and barely missed. Toby ran into another part of the room. Isaac caught up with him and clutched Toby around the neck, but not too hard.

Isaac said, "Hold your tongue."

Maggie wedged herself between her sons. "Stop that! Stop it! You're to take care of each other. You're brothers. This is a very bad time." Maggie cried again as she pulled Isaac and Toby apart. "You don't have a father anymore. You have to take care of each other." Isaac released Toby reluctantly.

Toby rubbed his neck. "Ma, he hurt my neck."

"Ah, hush up. Ma, I have to get out of here. I can't stand it."

Heavy footsteps stomped up the porch outside. Maggie, Isaac, and Toby turned toward the door at the violent knock. "Open up in there, ya blimey rebels. Open up, I say, or I'll break down this door."

Maggie whispered, "Isaac, get in the kitchen."

Isaac went into an adjacent room through a doorless opening. He stood around a corner, out of sight of the living room, and listened closely.

Maggie said, "Open the door, Toby, then get away."

Toby opened the door. A British soldier, Nigel Lawrence, entered quickly. With a black patch over his left eye, he sneered scornfully at Toby. "You a rebel?"

Toby was shocked at the sight of a one-eyed soldier. "No. Ma?"

"Got any more rebels in here?"

Maggie moved over to Toby and touched his shoulder. Facing Lawrence she said, "He's not a rebel. He's only fourteen."

"Old enough to die. I'll shoot you right now."

The soldier backed up two steps and leveled his musket at Toby's nose. Toby jumped back. Maggie shouted, "No, I told you, he's not a rebel." She reached into her pocket and felt for a small paring knife, then looked threateningly at the soldier. "You put that down or you'll lose something you don't want to lose. Toby, move away from the officer and go into the kitchen."

Lawrence lowered his gun and glided up to Maggie. He eyed her lewdly with his one good eye and ran his hand through her hair and down her neck. His hand approached her breasts. "I ain't no officer, bitch." He smiled wickedly. "I ain't that polite."

Isaac peeked around the corner of the room and saw Lawrence close to his mother. Maggie spotted Isaac and shook her head slightly, "no."

Lawrence leered at Maggie, up and down, then glared at Toby. "Get out of here, rebel." He smiled back at Maggie. "Your mum and me want to be alone."

Toby's eyes welled up with horror. Isaac slinked out of the kitchen, crouched low, and slid into the living room, behind Lawrence and Maggie. She and Toby could see Isaac, but Lawrence faced the other way. Maggie tolerated the soldier's hands tearfully, but twirled the paring knife in her pocket to get a good grip. The soldier continued to run his hand lightly over Maggie's breasts.

Toby shouted, "Isaac."

Lawrence turned his head, searching for danger from an unexpected rebel, but he looked toward the living room, not the kitchen, and Isaac plowed into him hard, smashing Lawrence into the table. Lawrence wasn't able to judge distance well with one eye, so Isaac had a slight advantage. Isaac rushed again, but Lawrence held his fist in the air, and, as expected, Isaac ran right into it. Lawrence pushed Isaac against the wall with only one strong arm. Isaac tripped backward and fell forcefully against the door, which slammed shut with a loud smack, sending a message of conflict through the silent, Sunday-afternoon neighborhood.

Chapter Two

Sunday, Bristol, PA

Geneeral George Washington sat at a table in a small tent. Three other officers were present. Washington wore a clean red uniform, but his demeanor was haggard. He was pale and tired, his normally robust physique thin and worn. Captain Warren Murphy, a forty-year-old captain with the First Pennsylvania Riflemen, saw Washington's hands tremble, almost imperceptibly. The strain of the last few months had obviously affected him.

Washington said, "We're going back."

Captain Murphy could see that Washington expected a reaction from his generals, Hugh Mercer and Roche Fermoy. The hesitation in Washington's voice indicated that it was a plea, or a suggestion, not an order.

General Mercer frowned and said, "We scored a great victory, sir. I respectfully recommend we go into winter quarters here."

General Fermoy spoke up. "Sir, I agree with Hugh." Fermoy was ragged and unkempt, with a scraggly beard that hadn't been trimmed in weeks.

Washington said, "It was a raid, gentlemen. We caught them sleeping. What do you think the enemy will do if we stay here?"

Mercer said, "They'll try and cross the river, but we can defend it from here."

"Who? Who's going to defend the river, and the city, when the whole army is gone? A division of regulars and three hundred riflemen, against the whole British army?"

Murphy's attention rose with the mention of the word 'riflemen,' his own regiment.

Washington glanced at Murphy. "Sorry, Murph." Murphy nodded. The great man had just apologized to him.

Fermoy said, "It's crazy, sir. It's suicide."

Mercer admonished him, "Sir, please keep your advice on a military level."

Fermoy's voice rose higher. "We can't make it over there. We'll get slaughtered. Besides, we don't have the supplies, the guns, the powder and shot. It's just crazy."

Mercer said, "That's enough, General."

Washington glared at Fermoy. "We just took ten wagons of powder from the Hessians. Where is it?"

Fermoy stammered, "Well, sir, it's, uh, it's spread out. I don't know. Even with that, we don't have enough guns to go back there."

Washington said, "We have the men, though, don't we? We have the men. But we won't for very long. Don't you understand, gentlemen? We can't stay here. We won't have the men."

Captain Murphy spoke up from the rear. "I'll find the powder, sir."

Washington's hands stopped shaking. Murphy hoped that it was because of his statement about finding the powder. He respected Washington and Mercer, but he always wished that his commanding general were anyone but Fermoy.

Washington said, "You want to know the real reason? Why we're going back?"

The generals and Murphy stared at him, expecting a revelation, and they got it. Washington took a deep breath. His eyes focused on Fermoy. "This army is going home when their enlistments expire on Wednesday." Washington's gaze shifted to Mercer. "I'm going to get another fight out of them if I have to march 'em to New York on Tuesday."

Mercer straightened to attention. "Yes, sir."

Fermoy rubbed his forehead, which Murphy surmised was at the prospect of another disaster.

General Henry Knox stooped low through the tent flap and joined the group. "We've got the prisoners shipped out." Knox studied Washington's face, then looked at Mercer. "What's happening?"

Washington said, "We're going back. Caldwalater's at Trenton. Get the men back across, Henry. You have more time, but you can't take two months like you did at Ticonderoga."

Murphy smiled to himself. In the greatest achievement of the war so far, Henry Knox had dragged the cannons of Fort Ticonderoga from upper New York to Boston last year in the middle of the winter. Murphy knew that Henry Knox would take Washington's criticism far too seriously.

Henry was shocked. "There were no roads. It was woods, rivers. It was freezing. We couldn't even see through the snow."

Mercer and Murphy laughed. Fermoy didn't.

Washington smiled. "I'm joking, Henry. You have more time than last week, but no later than tomorrow night."

Washington turned to Fermoy. "Send an officer over there. Tell Caldwalater to stay put. Have him send some men up to the ferry and help unload. I'll be over tonight."

Murphy said, "I'll go, sir."

Everyone left the tent except General Fermoy and Captain Murphy. Fermoy wrote an order and took a long drink of whiskey from a flask. He said, "This is the biggest mistake he ever made, which says a lot."

Fermoy handed Murphy the order, and then sucked another swig. He emptied the flask, but some of the last drops of whiskey dribbled into his beard. Fermoy wiped his face and casually licked the alcohol from his hand.

Murphy shook his head and left.

Chapter Three

Sunday, Near Princeton

British Major Steven Derring, on a horse, led a detachment of troops west toward Princeton. They heard a door slam in one of the houses. Not knowing which one, the soldiers readied their muskets. Derring listened closely as he passed each house.

Inside, Maggie took the paring knife out of her pocket and held it in Lawrence's path as he rushed at Isaac, cutting Lawrence on the neck. Toby kicked Lawrence in the leg, but the seasoned soldier swatted Toby away like a bug. Toby fell sideways against the table and fell to the floor.

Lawrence sneered casually at Toby with nothing but contempt for small rebels. In that instant, Isaac rushed again, but Lawrence was a veteran, strong and quick. He braced his shoulder against Isaac and slammed him against the wall. Isaac grabbed the doorknob for support as he fell. The door opened. Lawrence picked up his gun and aimed it at Isaac. Click, went the hammer, back, loaded, ready to fire. Then Lawrence saw Derring on the horse outside, staring at him through the open door.

British Major Steven Derring saw only Maggie and Lawrence inside the house. Derring wondered at the situation, an American woman and a British soldier seemingly alone. Derring quickly gathered the scene in his mind. Something was amiss here, and both Derring and Lawrence knew it.

Lawrence lowered his gun as he gawked at Derring. Unauthorized presence in an American house was strictly forbidden in the British Army, except for officers, of course. Sadly, for Corporal Lawrence, that wasn't the case. Also forbidden was even a consensual relationship between British soldiers and American women, again, except for officers. Lawrence gazed into the eyes of real trouble.

Maggie saw opportunity in the momentary confusion and kicked Lawrence hard in the rump. Lawrence plunged through the doorway, onto the porch, skidded down the steps, and sprawled at the hooves of Derring's horse. Derring reared his horse back quickly, not for the sake of Lawrence, but for the horse. A horse in 1776 was worth a lot more than a scalawag British soldier. God forbid the horse should break a leg stomping on a man's head.

Maggie stood openly in the doorway, defiant of the presence of several armed soldiers. She gripped the open door with her right hand.

"And stay out, you damn bastard!" The door slammed shut, and almost fell onto the porch from the force. The troops smirked, but not Derring. He steadied his horse. "Calm down there, girl." He peered at Lawrence with disgust. "What's your name, soldier?"

"Lawrence, Corporal, Welsh Fusiliers."

"Figures. I never thought much of the Fusiliers, anyway. Now I know why, beat up by a woman."

"That woman has rebels in there."

"Get in line. We've got real rebels to fight, not their mothers."

Lawrence got up out of the mud. With his hand, he rubbed his neck, then looked at the bloody symbol of his humiliation. He wiped his neck again and turned toward the house.

One soldier said, "Cut himself shaving."

"No, stabbed himself with his own bayonet. He's a Fusilier." The soldiers all laughed.

Derring stifled a grin, "Belay that."

The closed door, the soldiers' laughs, Derring's hardness, all of these things suddenly ruined Lawrence's plans for a pleasant evening of shooting a rebel or two and perhaps even getting intimate with an attractive American woman.

"I'll get you. I'll get you, you rebel bitch. You and your rebel boys. I'll burn down your house with you in it. You'll see."

Derring spurred his horse forward angrily, then instantly pulled back on the reins. Lawrence lunged backward at the slight movement. Derring turned the horse sideways to the road to get a better angle, shifted his body in the saddle, and kicked Lawrence hard in the back. Lawrence fell again to the road. Derring moved the horse closer, threateningly, but carefully. Lawrence looked up in terror at the huge horse hovering over him. Derring stopped. The horse stopped, watching. Even the horse seemed to recognize that this was a dangerous man. It snorted hard, spraying horse mucus all over Lawrence.

Lawrence wiped the scum off his uniform and looked up at Derring, high on the menacing horse. "Don't you understand? There's rebels in there."

Derring inched the horse up closer to Lawrence. The horse stretched its neck, eager to go forward over Lawrence's cowardly torso, but Derring held the horse back. Lawrence scurried backward to avoid the deadly horseshoes.

"I was at Lexington. They wouldn't even let us surrender. The Americans are devils, all of them, rebels or not."

Derring steadied the horse and said, "Get in line. I'll kick your behind all the way to Princeton if you don't fall in."

The other soldiers laughed. They all moved down the road toward Princeton.

Inside the house, Maggie searched for her sons. She saw Isaac holding his arm, slumped against the wall. "Oh, Isaac. Oh, no. Are you hurt?"

Isaac faked a momentary wince for sympathy, then breathed deeply. "No, I'm all right."

"He'll come back. Oh, God, I know not what to do. He'll kill you boys. Toby? Where are you?"

Toby rushed to his mother's side. "Is he gone?"

Maggie put her arm around Toby's small shoulders. Isaac picked himself up. Maggie said, "Now you boys have to get out."

Isaac said, "Good. What I wanted all along."

"No. You won't fight. I won't have it. You'll get killed. If he comes back, they'll hang you both."

Maggie paced around the room, thinking, worrying. "Hang those rebels. Hang that Washington. Hang the whole lot of them."

Isaac said, "I'm leaving in the morning."

Maggie didn't hear him. She paced nervously. "Franklin, too, that scoundrel, that traitor."

Toby butted in, "Be calm, Ma." He held his breath against the expected tirade.

"Don't 'be-calm' me. Poor Richard. Yes, Poor Richard. Did his stupid almanac say we'd all get killed by the British? What about poor Maggie? Hang him, that Franklin, and Washington, all of them."

Maggie turned and peeked out the window to see if the British were still there. She held her face away from her sons and wiped her teary eyes with the curtain. She regained some composure, but with that came anger.

"They did this to us, put the British against us. Hang 'em all."

And with anger, came resolve, and there was no dissuading Maggie from anything once she had her mind fixed.

"You boys have to get out of here. He'll come back."

Toby looked at Isaac, then over to his mother. "No, Ma, he won't come back."

Maggie picked up a plate from the table, just as a distraction, to get back to reality. She rubbed its surface fondly in a daze, her hands trembling. "I had so many beautiful things." She tried hard to control herself, but the plate crashed to the floor. She sobbed into her hands. "Oh, Lord, dear Lord, why did you do this to us? Why did you send the British here, and the rebels?"

Isaac stared at her. He'd seen her this way before, many times, rising anger, uncontrollable emotion. Sometimes she recovered quickly, but more often, not. Occasionally she'd get a gun and point it at someone, but there was no one to shoot at any more, no more husbands around.

Maggie stopped crying. She wiped her eyes with her sleeve and focused with resolve on Isaac. "You have to go to Allentown."

Isaac absorbed the words in shock. "What?"

"Aunt Rose and Uncle Bernie can take you."

"You can't be serious."

"You know where it is."

"I am not going to Allentown."

Maggie searched the street again through the window. "Get Toby there, and the two of you stay there until this is over."

"No, I'm not going, especially not with this fool."

"Do as I say, Isaac. Take your brother there. Do it."

Isaac couldn't believe his life was wrecked like this, just when he thought he was getting out. "No. I'm going to fight the rebels. The war'll be over before I... I can't go. No, I won't. The Reverend is waiting for me."

"Hang the Reverend, too. Do what I tell you." She stomped into the kitchen.

"Oh, no, I can't do this. I have to get out." Isaac sat down at the table and put his head in his hands. He looked up at his annoying shrimp of a brother who was ultimately responsible for this catastrophe.

Toby asked, "Where's Allentown?"

"Pennsylvania, you fool. Now you've done it to me again."

Isaac rubbed his left arm, which was still sore from Lawrence's punch. He stared into the table for a long time, held his head, and moaned, "Oh, my God, no." Then he raised his head from his hands. "Wait. Wait a minute. Sure, I'll go. It'll get me out of this hell hole."

Toby asked, "You want to go? You're going to stay there, too, right?"

"No. As soon as you're there, I'm coming right back here and fight the rebels. This is the last time I'm taking care of you."

Isaac got up and shouted into the other room, "All right, Ma, sure, Ma. I'll take him to Allentown. I'll take him to Virginia if it'll get me out of that shop. All right by me, but you won't be seeing me again."

"You can't leave me there. You have to stay, too. Ma says."

Isaac looked at Toby with the most intense hatred he'd ever known. "I'm going to get you there and then come back, or wherever the Reverend tells me to go."

"No, you can't. You can't do that. I can't stay there by myself."

Isaac almost cried, "I'm going to come back and shoot all the rebels I can find. And I'm not coming home again. And I don't want to see you again, either. You've ruined my life for the last time, Toby." He walked away.

"Isaac. Isaac. I can't stay there by myself. Isaac!"

Chapter Four

Day Two, Monday, Dec. 30, 1776
Delaware River, NJ Side

General Henry Knox's boots sank four inches into the mud with every step. A lighter man might have had less difficulty walking toward the boats if it were dry ground, but a lighter man might not have been able to pull his boots out now. Henry's immense strength allowed him to move along the Delaware River's shore with seemingly little effort.

He shouted orders to the boats coming up. "Stop. Let your neighbor in there. You, turn left. Come ashore over there. That's it. Easy now. Get a rope out there."

Henry sloshed up the Delaware to a tangle of boats and men who strained to lift cannons out of boats and drag them to dry ground. Boats collided with each other as they made for the small area of beach. Men yelled at each other, "Get away from here. Watch it, get away." Officers and sergeants on shore struggled in the mud.

As one boat made it to shore, another plowed into its stern and tipped over. Sacks of supplies fell into the river. Men spilled out of the boats and waded up to shore. Some men reached under water and picked up the bags, but most of them just tried to get out of the freezing water. Another boat approached fast. Henry pointed and motioned for it to go to his right. Men jumped out of the boats and waded up the bank.

Captain Murphy rode up on a horse. He addressed General Henry Knox without a salute, because it would never occur to Murphy to salute Henry Knox. Henry Knox was just 'Henry.' Murphy said, "Hello, Henry. The General sends his regards."

Knox replied, "How are ya, Murph?"

Murphy watched the confusion. A small, flat-bottomed boat to the left was almost to shore, but a rope holding the cannons snapped. Two cannons careened to the left, causing the boat to list. Men on the right side leaned out over the gunwale to try to keep it balanced, but two of them fell overboard. They struggled in the icy water and tried to climb back in, but it was too deep, so they just hung onto the side.

The boat listed more to the left. The force pulled the two men right out of the water as their side of the boat shot high in the air. The cannons spilled out of the boat and sank into the river.

The boat turned over. All the men found themselves underneath an overturned boat as they found their footing in the mud, standing upright in five feet of water with a boat for their roof.

Henry Knox and Murphy watched the bottom of a boat creep toward shore. Henry shook his head. Men from shore helped get the boat off the tops of the men underneath. Everyone on shore and in the boats was soaked.

Murphy asked, "So, how's it going?"

"All right, so far. Do you know how many times these guns have crossed this river? Four times in the last month, back and forth, back and forth. I wish I'd get to shoot these once in a while."

"You might get your chance pretty soon, Henry. Sorry, I mean 'General.'"

"Ah, that's all right."

Murphy recovered from his embarrassment at addressing a senior, highly respected officer by his first name. It was just that Henry Knox, plump, gentle, friendly, smart, competent, and brave, didn't fit the 'yes, sir, no sir' military demeanor of most generals.

Murphy asked, "So, what do you think?"

"We should be in Trenton tonight, if nothing goes wrong."

Murphy surveyed the confusion. "What could go wrong?"

"Ha. Indeed. Any word on the enemy?"

"Nothing, so far. We have sentries all over, so we'll know if anything happens."

"Tell the General I'm sending Sullivan's division into town."

Murphy said, "Yes, I passed Sullivan on the road."

Henry moved to the side to get a better view of an overloaded vessel that was stuck. "Excuse me, Murph." Henry trudged up to a group of men who sat in the mud. He pointed at them, "You. Get those boxes out of there. Yes, you, you heard me." The men got up, groaned, and unloaded the boxes.

Ropes flew through the air from the shore and from the arriving boats. Henry picked up a rope and pulled hard. The men in the boat fell backward and out, into the cold Delaware, but the boat came fast to shore from Henry's pull. Henry turned toward Murphy. "It helps to have a little oomph."

Murphy saluted with a smile. Henry Knox returned it.

"See ya, General."

* * *

Murphy continued down the shore on his horse toward Trenton. He approached an officer on horseback directing a group of men trying to unstick a cannon from a ditch. Just as Murphy arrived, the officer yelled to his men, "Push. Harder. Jackson, take the wheel. You have to push harder, damn you."

Murphy looked at the men, then at the officer, and asked, "What are you doing?"

"Trying to get this gun out, obviously. Jackson, no. Push on the wheel, for the sake of God."

Murphy watched the struggling men sympathetically. "Why don't you help them?"

"I am helping them. Satchel, put your weight into it, you stupid imbecile."

Murphy asked, "Why don't you help them push?"

The officer's eyebrows went up. "I'm an officer. I don't push."

Murphy glanced at the officer's horse and noticed a rope looped on the saddle horn. He slipped his right leg out of the stirrup, swung it over his horse's back, and deftly touched down. Walking over to the officer, his eyes stayed focused on the rope. He took the rope off the officer's saddle and swung one end down to the men quickly, before the officer could tell what was happening.

The officer covered the saddle horn with his hands. "What do you think you're doing?"

Murphy tied the near end of the rope to the officer's saddle horn. "Trying to get this gun out, obviously. Turn your horse." Murphy pushed the officer's hands aside and continued to wrap the near end around the saddle horn.

"Get out of here. I outrank you. Who do you think you are?"

Murphy finished tying the rope. "Captain Warren Murphy, First Pennsylvania Riflemen. Turn your horse, Captain."

The officer said, "Murphy?" He hesitated, but then turned the horse.

Murphy slid down the bank to the men and the cannon. He tied the end of the rope to the axle, placed himself next to Satchel, behind the gun, and shouted to the officer, "Go," then to the men along side, "Push."

Murphy pushed as hard as he could. He slipped, fell in the mud, got up, and pushed again. The gun skidded sideways twice, but ulitmately became unstuck. Murphy followed it up to the road, making sure it wasn't going to fall back, and then diverted to higher ground. Jackson followed him. Satchel and the other soldiers untied the rope and pointed the gun toward Trenton. Murphy and Jackson rested on dry ground.

Jackson asked, "You're an officer?"

"Yes, Captain Murphy."

"You think we'll see any British?"

"I reckon we will, son."

"Good. I didn't join the army to serve in the navy."

Chapter Five

Same Day, Monday

Isaac and Toby walked west toward Princeton. The air was calm, the sun up. It was a beautiful, cool winter day. A light snow covered the ground, but it felt like springtime, warm for that time of year.

Toby walked behind Isaac, kicking a stone. Isaac reprimanded him, "Toby, come on. Keep up. Stop dawdling."

Toby caught up, although not as quickly as Isaac would have liked. Toby asked, "Why do you hate everybody?"

"It's only you I hate."

"Me? Why? What did I do?"

"Aw, you're such a coward. You're always afraid, crying like a baby. Always 'Yes, Ma. No, Ma.' Just like John."

"And why did you call him 'John?' I called him 'Father.'"

"He wasn't my father."

"He was, so. You know, the little ones noticed you never called him that. They asked me. I couldn't explain it to them."

"My father left a long time ago. I hate his guts, too."

Toby stepped on a piece of frozen ground. His right leg shot forward, and his gun arm flew up in the air, but Toby didn't let go. A backpack in his left hand went out for balance. Toby sailed into the air, almost horizontal. "Whoa, Nellie." He smashed his left foot onto the ground in a little dance, splattering mud all over Isaac, and then skidded backward on one leg, but recovered without falling.

Isaac wiped the mud from his pants. "Come on, Toby. Stop that. Stop playing around." Isaac shook his head at his brother's agility. "I tell you, Toby, I've got to do something. I'm not going to waste my whole life in that dress shop."

Toby slugged ahead. "I miss him. The first one, I mean. He taught me how to shoot. Pa, I mean."

The boys walked. A four-story building with twenty windows per floor appeared to their left. An elegant mansion next to it blocked the sun. Isaac looked at the building. "That's the College."

Toby said, "I'm hungry."

"All right, we'll stop here."

Isaac opened his pack, took out some silverware, a bible, a knife, and a coil of string. "What the hell did she pack all these things for?"

Isaac looked amusedly at the coil of string. The boys dug further into their packs and found some bread, butter, nuts, and dried fruit. They stuffed everything else back into the packs and ate, then got up and continued their journey.

They walked down the road a mile and a half and came to a bridge. It was forty feet across and spanned Stony Brook Creek, which was thirty feet wide and ten feet below the bridge.

Isaac said, "Here it is, the Princeton Bridge. Haven't seen it in years."

It was a wooden bridge. Two pilings on the east, two on the west, and two in the middle supported it. Logs and boards made the road. A wooden railing on both sides made the pedestrians' walk a bit easier. The bridge on the eastern side was far enough out of the water to go under without getting wet. The boys were on that side.

They put their guns and packs down on the ground. Toby went under the bridge first. Isaac followed. They looked around. Toby examined one of the logs and rubbed his hands along its side, the smell of paint and varnish still permeating the cold air after all these years. Water below lapped gently at the pilings.

Toby said, "Remember we used to play soldier under here? Look, here's your initials, IM. Here's me, TM."

Two sets of initials were scratched into a log, right next to each other without even a space between them, IMTM. They faded into the wood, but they were large and deep enough to have a few more years left in them.

Isaac inspected a different log. "And this is where you hit your head. What a dummy you were. I thought you were going to take the bridge down. Ha." Isaac rubbed his hand along the log, a little farther down. He barely made out two letters, carved into the bark, 'BR.' "Look, here's Billy Reed. Gosh, Billy Reed. I wonder what ever happened to him."

Toby moved over to Isaac's log and looked at it closely. He remembered the pain of hitting his head, many, many years ago, 'many' being relative in terms of a fourteen-year-old's life. He remembered the good times, when Isaac didn't hate him so much. He remembered shooting the make-believe Indians who tried to cross the Stony Brook Creek and attack the settlers. Toby, Isaac, and Billy Reed had to protect the settlement from almost certain annihilation.

Billy Reed, he was Isaac's friend, always kind to Toby. Toby remembered Billy throwing Isaac into the cool Stony Brook Creek one summer's day. Isaac was furious for a week, but then everybody got over it. He also remembered the game they were playing that day he hit his head. "Yeah, let's play 'charge.'"

Isaac said, "No, that's ridiculous. We're too old for that now. We have to get going." He stooped low to get out from under the bridge.

"Aw, why not? You be the charger."

"No, I don't feel like playing."

Toby followed Isaac out. "That's because you'll lose."

"That's because you cheat. No, I won't play. We have to go."

From years of playing charge and other games of their childhood, Toby knew Isaac's hot spots. "You afraid?"

"Afraid of what? You? Ha. That's ripe. No, you cheat. I'm not playing with a cheater."

"You're afraid I'll beat you, right? That's it, isn't it?"

"Yeah, right. You're going to beat me at 'charge' without cheating. Ha. Good one, Toby. Remind me to tell that to somebody who cares, if we can find an old fool around here. Let's go."

"All right. If you're afraid, that's all right. I understand."

Isaac said, "I'm not afraid, of you, or anybody else, or anything."

"So?"

"So what? We have to go."

"Sure. If you're afraid I'll beat you, sure."

"Ah. All right. You're the shooter. And don't cheat. You can't load faster than thirty seconds. And after this, you have to keep up. I'm tired of your straggling. One game, then we go. Get a stick 'cause I'm coming."

Toby smirked. He retrieved a long stick in the weeds next to the creek. Isaac walked south in the field along the east bank of the Stony Brook Creek.

Toby placed the two muskets in the grass pointing toward Isaac. He watched Isaac go deeper into the field, but since Isaac was still walking away, Toby had time to pick up the two guns quickly and point them at Isaac, testing the feel of retrieving them quickly. He laid them back down as Isaac got to his designated distance.

Isaac, twenty yards away, crouched down in the grass. Toby turned his back to Isaac, according to the rules of the game. Isaac rose up and charged. "Whoop, Whoop, here I come." He shouted as he ran and held his right hand in the air as if he had a knife. Toby turned quickly, aimed his stick, and yelled,

"Pow. Got ya."

Isaac clutched his shoulder with his right hand, reeled in simulated pain, spun around, fell forward, and tumbled into the snowy grass.

Toby reloaded the stick. He poured in the powder, pushed in a bullet, and smashed it down with a ramrod. Isaac rose up and charged again. He'd been dreadfully wounded, and was in terrible anguish, but determined to take out his foe. Toby fired the stick again.

"Pow. Got ya again. Two for me."

Isaac kept going, shot in the leg this time. He clutched his leg with one hand and his shoulder with the other, suffering, limping in theoretical pain.

Toby smiled at Isaac's antics. Isaac always was the best charger, and this was looking to be his best performance ever.

Isaac slowed, stopped, turned, and fell to the ground on his back, struggling in agony. But, he miraculously got up again with the last ounce of his mortal strength. As soon as he did, "Pow."

Isaac said, "Ah. You didn't have time to load. I'm taking that back."

Toby said, "I know how to load a gun."

"You couldn't load that fast. That doesn't count. Now play right, and don't cheat."

Isaac rushed again, "Whoop, Whoop." Toby watched him come with the supreme knowledge of a sure victory. Isaac was seconds from plunging the make-believe knife into Toby's chest when Toby reached down and brought up both real guns. He held them tight against his hips. Isaac's face turned pale.

"Pow." Toby shook the left gun.

"Pow." He shook the right gun.

Toby grinned. Isaac stopped, relieved, and then said, "You cheated. Where would you get two guns, anyway? And you could have killed me, for the sake of Christ. I won. Let's go."

"I didn't cheat. I had two guns. They wasn't loaded."

"And where would you get two guns? I'm not playing with you anymore."

The boys walked up to the bridge, Isaac in front. Toby trailed with the two guns under his arms. "Pow, Pow." Imaginary bullets slammed into Isaac's back. Toby laughed.

"Grow up, Toby."

The boys crossed the Princeton Bridge. Just as Isaac walked off on the Trenton side, he paused and rubbed the right railing of the bridge fondly. "So long, old bridge. Don't know if I'll ever see you again."

Isaac crossed. Toby followed. Toby rubbed the railing in the same place that Isaac did. The road curved into the woods after thirty yards. The boys rounded the bend toward Trenton.

Chapter Six

Day Three, Tuesday, Dec. 31, 1776

The last day of 1776 dawned cold and gloomy for Corporal William Jackson and his men, the soldiers who unstuck the cannon at the Delaware River with Murphy. A soldier in bivouac would have the comforts of a warm tent and plenty to eat if he were a good scrounger, but a soldier on the move was not so lucky, especially in winter.

Jackson woke up at dawn and roused his men. Five soldiers groaned as they stirred out of their blankets. One didn't. A soldier sniffed the air, "What's that smell?"

The other men smelled it, too. Jackson turned toward his brother. "Oh, my God, Satchel." Jackson dashed over. "Satchel, Satchel." Beads of sweat poured down Satchel's face. "Satchel." Jackson touched his brother's face and neck, which were burning hot.

Jackson's eyes filled with doom. "Help me get his pants off."

Satchel was a robust boy, seventeen years old, and not easy to lift. The men diligently helped Jackson remove Satchel's pants, careful not to breathe the foul air of his soiled clothes.

A soldier restarted the fire a few yards away. "Give 'em to me." Jackson walked the pants over. The soldier held his nose against the smell and stirred the embers to get a good fire going. Satchel's pants hit the fire with a flaring whoosh that momentarily lit up the road.

Another of Jackson's men got a blanket and wrapped it tightly around Satchel, spittle and drool pouring out of Satchel's mouth. Jackson rushed back to help. "Easy, Satchel. Let's get him to a tent."

Jackson and another soldier dragged Satchel in their arms, struggling from the weight. The other soldiers assisted as they could. Four soldiers carried Jackson's brother, looking for a place of safety and warmth, anywhere to get him some help. The soldier at the fire stirred the embers of Satchel's pants.

Jackson stared in horror at his brother as they moved. The other soldiers avoided Jackson's gaze while they dragged Satchel away. Harry, one of Jackson's men, looked up. "Jack, it'll be all right. He'll be all right."

Harry let go for a moment, retrieved a canteen from his belt, and held it to Satchel's lips. "Satchel, drink. Drink a little." Harry gently forced the canteen against Satchel's mouth with one hand while supporting his head with the other. Satchel tried to drink, but the water dribbled down his chin. Satchel's eyes floated backward in his head. The men stopped and put him down in the road while they stretched their backs for a minute.

* * *

Their captain, their "stuck-in-the-mud" captain, trotted up on a horse. The polished bars on his cap reflected the light of the upcoming sun. "What're you doing?"

Jackson said, "He's sick. We have to get him some help."

"Leave him."

"What?"

"You heard me, leave him. God, damn, he stinks." The officer turned away in disgust. He waved his hand in front of his nose to dissipate the smell, then turned to Jackson. "He's tetched, anyway. Leave him here. You men are on ditch-digging duty. Right now."

Jackson pleaded to the officer, "I can't leave him, he'll die."

The officer pulled a pistol out of his belt and fingered the barrel, casually gazing into the small opening, as if making sure that there was a bullet in there. He aimed it at the sky and looked along the barrel with one eye, practicing his aim, to make sure that these insignificant fools knew that he knew how to shoot a pistol. Jackson saw the officer's squinty eyes slowly come around until the officer stared at Jackson's face.

"Which one of you do you want me to shoot, Mr. Jackson, him or you? Makes no difference to me."

Jackson froze. He looked at Satchel, then at the officer, then at his men. They didn't know what to do either. Jackson tried to reason with the officer, "Oh, no. Please. I just have to get him some place warm. He'll be all right. Please. Let me get him to a tent. He just needs to rest."

The officer cocked his pistol and shook it at Jackson, angrily, then at Satchel, and then back to Jackson. "Your choice, Mr. Jackson."

Harry retrieved his musket and leveled it at the captain. "Say the word, Jack." The officer was between Jackson and the soldier at the fire, who still slowly stirred Satchel's pants. Now that there was a fight brewing, the fire soldier didn't want to miss out. He stopped stirring. He cocked his musket with a click and called over, "Say the word, Jack."

The other soldiers picked up their muskets, click, click, click.

The officer saw five muskets pointing straight at him. "This is mutiny. I'll have you all hanged."

The soldier at the fire asked, "This ain't mutiny, is it, Jack? Ain't that when you throw the captain overboard?"

Harry replied, "No, this ain't mutiny. That's only on a ship. We ain't on no ship. This is just a simple shooting."

The officer turned his horse to get away, but Harry snatched its reins and steadied the horse. "Whoa, girl, settle down there, girl."

The officer panicked. He was surrounded by yokels who didn't seem to understand that he was an officer, of respectable authority, and that they had to obey him. They just didn't understand. Not only that, but they were pointing guns at him. The effrontery of these vagabonds. "I'm an officer," he said, "I'll have you all hanged."

Harry said, "We didn't elect you our officer, so ain't nothing you can do but get shot. Them's the rules."

The soldier at the fire crept up and stuck his musket in the officer's back. The officer's hands trembled in fear and rage. All of Jackson's men now crowded around the horse. The officer looked quickly at each one of them, and at the pointing muskets. "You're on report."

Harry jabbed his musket barrel into the officer's butt. "You better not point this behind at me if we get in a fight."

The officer turned his horse and faced Harry. What's your name, soldier?"

Harry said, "Harry Hairy Horse." The men snickered. Harry was at the horse's side now. He raised his gun and pointed it at the soldier's eyes. Harry asked the officer, one eye squinting down the barrel, "What's your name, soldier?" The men roared.

The officer looked at Harry, then at Jackson, seeking some way out of his danger. Jackson raised his eyebrows and glanced at his brother lying in the road, then turned toward the officer. The officer tried to turn his horse and get away, but the men were too close.

Harry grabbed the horse's reigns again. "Whoa, girl, steady, girl. You ain't going nowhere." He stroked the horse's side to calm her down. "There, there, girl. You know, Jack, we could sure use a good horse, long as there ain't no officer on it." Everybody laughed.

The horse was immobile, but the officer turned his body toward Harry, his nearest threat. He stared fearfully at the men, his life expectancy only a few more minutes. He was trapped on the horse with nowhere to go.

Harry said, "Say the word, Jack. I'll blast his brains across the river." All the men raised their muskets at the expected word, 'fire.'

The captain got it now. He made a mistake, a big mistake. You couldn't push these men too far. You couldn't even push them a little. But it might be too late. All it would take now was one short, four-letter word from a distressed corporal, his dying brother lying there in the road, one word, 'fire,' and the officer's life would be over. Sure, they'd be hanged. The generals would see to that, but what good would it do him then? The captain closed his eyes in anticipation of the deadly word and the shot.

"Put the gun down, Harry."

"Ah, Jack, let me shoot him."

"Put it down, Harry, all of you."

Harry lowered his gun. The captain spurred his horse and galloped off. Harry reached down, picked up a rock, and threw it at the galloping horse. It went nowhere near the officer, but for Harry it was a great boost to his stature. The men laughed, "I hope you can shoot better than that, 'Hairy Horse'."

Jackson shook his head. "You can't do that. He's an officer. Now we're in deep trouble."

Harry said, "Ain't my officer."

Jackson shouted, "You can't shoot no officers."

Harry said, "You're our officer." The men agreed.

Jackson exploded, "I ain't no officer. How many times I tell you that? I'm a corporal. You're privates. Then we have lieutenants, and captains, and generals, and a bunch more in between. Ah. They're officers. Damn. He's an officer. We're in big trouble." Jackson wagged his head. His men ignored him.

The soldiers picked up Satchel and carried him away. Harry mumbled, "Ain't my officer."

Chapter Seven

A farmer opened his barn door slowly. He peered inside, pushing his musket through the opening, his finger on the trigger. He looked suspiciously at the hay drifting down from above. "What're you doing up there? Git down here." He aimed the musket at the loft.

Isaac whispered to Toby, still asleep ten feet away, "Toby, Toby, get up."

"You git down here, or I'll blast you full of lead."

Toby opened his eyes when the sound of a musket shot startled him awake. Buckshot ripped through the floor of the loft. Loose pieces of hay flew through the air and fragments of metal scattered into the air nearby. Isaac scooted along the beams of the loft to a small window on the other side of the barn, yanking Toby up by one arm as he passed. Toby reached back and picked up the two guns while Isaac snatched up the backpacks. The farmer reloaded, his eyes following the sound of footsteps above.

"Toby, shhh. Come on. Hurry."

Isaac pushed the backpacks out a small window. He looked down, but it was too far to drop. He threw the guns out the small opening. The guns clanged against each other as they hit the ground, causing the farmer to run outside toward the sound.

Isaac heard the farmer go out and said, "Toby, get back. Over here." Toby scrambled down a ladder, inside the barn. Isaac followed. They ran out the barn door where the farmer had just gone. The boys slinked around the corner of the barn to get their guns and backpacks, but the farmer, near the backpacks, aimed and fired. He missed. The boys bolted toward the opposite corner as the farmer reloaded.

The boys scurried all the way around the barn, hugging the sides, no guns in their hands. The farmer crept behind them, out of sight. As the farmer got to each corner, he peeked around carefully, not wanting to get too close to a couple of teenage boys without a loaded weapon. He loaded it.

The farmer thought about his options for a moment. One shot, that's all he'd get. Could he take out two quick teenage boys with one shot? No. Even with buckshot, never. He'd have to go for the taller boy. If the little boy were hit, the taller boy would almost certainly charge him in a rage. That could be bad, very bad. Hand-to-hand combat at his age against a strong and angry teenager could be fatal, quickly fatal.

If he shot the taller boy, the little boy probably wouldn't be able to do much except cry, so it wouldn't be right. And then he'd probably have to fix the tall one up, lots of trouble. The farmer reconsidered, be sure not to hit either one of them, but scare them to death so they'd never think about sleeping in his barn again.

The boys spotted their backpacks and the guns ten feet away. Isaac shouted, "Get the guns. I'll get the packs." The farmer heard Isaac's voice and charged around the barn toward the sound. Isaac picked up the backpacks and ran toward the road. Toby stooped down near the barn and picked up the guns, but he had to choke up on the left-hand gun to find the center of gravity while holding the other one against his shoulder. Meanwhile, Isaac got farther away. The farmer aimed his gun at Toby and backed up five feet to get a better angle. He could kill Toby right now, and the taller boy wouldn't be able to help, but the taller boy could easily turn around, charge, and attack him in ten seconds if he heard a shot, and it was thirty seconds to reload.

The farmer had to think. He needed to fire, but he couldn't hit the smaller boy and risk enraging the taller one. He could fire into the air, or at the ground, but that wouldn't cause enough terror. He'd have to fire at his own barn. Ah, a good plan. The wood was rotten there, anyway. He'd get to it in the spring. Toby now had both guns securely in his hands.

The farmer fired. Buckshot smashed into the side of the barn, barely missing Toby. Toby ducked his head instinctively as splinters flew through the air and tiny pieces of wood smashed painfully into his face. He clutched at his nose and cheek and shouted, "Isaac!" Toby's face drew blood as he scratched at the protruding needles of wood. Blood dribbled down. The farmer studied Toby carefully as he reloaded, and glanced over at Isaac. Toby cried, "Isaac. Come back."

Isaac got to the road with the packs, but looked back to see Toby rubbing his face. The farmer, twenty yards behind, was nearly finished loading, but there was a hitch in the farmer's plan, because Toby wasn't running away. Isaac heard Toby's plea to come back, dropped the backpacks, and headed for Toby. The farmer pointed the gun at Toby for another shot at his barn. Toby still scratched his face hysterically, unaware of his danger. Isaac yelled, "Toby, run! Toby!"

The farmer was ready to shoot, but noticed his own gun wasn't cocked. He lowered it, cocked it, and leveled it again. Toby still rubbed his face. More blood came out as Toby aggravated the wounds. Toby cried, helpless, frantically clawing at the splinters. Toby was wide open to the farmer's next shot.

The farmer crept closer to Toby to get a better angle. His plan was working, but only barely. The taller boy wasn't rushing at him with violent anger. That was good, but the smaller boy also wasn't running away in terror. Damn, and breakfast was getting cold.

Isaac went back to the road and searched through his backpack, but there was nothing in there he could use. He picked up a rock from the road. "Hey you, over here, ya damn rebel." Isaac threw it. The rock hit the side of the barn and caused some more rotten wood to splinter away.

The farmer turned and faced Isaac. He aimed his gun high on purpose. Slugs of buckshot blasted a tree above Isaac. Isaac ducked. "Toby! Toby! Get over here! Now!"

Toby ran toward the road. He cried, still picking at his face. Isaac yelled to Toby, "No, no! The guns! Get the guns!"

Toby stopped, turned around and picked up the guns. The farmer reloaded slowly, allowing Toby enough time to get away. "I'll get ya, ya little rascal, say yer prayers." Toby turned around and sprinted to the road near Isaac. The farmer aimed his gun high again. Another blast hit the trees. Isaac and Toby ducked as they ran.

Toby turned right on the road, heading the wrong way, toward Princeton. Isaac picked up the packs and shouted, "Toby. Turn around. This way, Toby. You're going the wrong way."

Isaac dropped the backpacks and ran after Toby. Isaac was light now, with no backpacks. Toby carried two guns, stumbled, stopped, ran, stumbled again, and rubbed his face. Isaac finally caught up with his swift little brother and pushed Toby to the ground. It didn't take much force, just a light touch, and Toby was down. Isaac grabbed Toby by the back of his shirt, picked him up, and turned him around. Toby cried. Isaac gently picked the splinters out of Toby's face with his fingernails. "Wait. Hold still."

Isaac finished extracting the splinters, then picked up some snow and rubbed it on Toby's face. "You're going the wrong way."

They walked down the road, picked up the backpacks, and continued toward Trenton. Toby rubbed his face, smooth now, no more splinters. "Thanks," said Toby.

Isaac shook his head, "Aw, you're such a baby."

Chapter Eight

George Washington had a lot on his mind. The fate of the nation hinged on what would happen in the next two days. He didn't know where the British were, or how many. Did they have the hated Hessians with them, or the feared Grenadiers?

Washington sat at his table, alone in a tent, and stared blankly at a map. The old cautions haunted him again. "Was it a terrible mistake to come back?"

"What about the Grenadiers," his cautious side asked. He remembered them at Fort Lee, in November. There was no way his troops could sustain that kind of assault again. The British officers had lit the fuses, and the soldiers threw the bombs into the fort, the first exploding shells in history. He thought, "These men can't go through that again."

Washington constructed the looming disaster in his mind. The Grenadiers would throw their bombs at the struggling Americans, already in retreat across the Trenton Bridge. The Americans panic. British cannonballs tear up the field, mowing down men, friends, brothers, and fathers. The men get to the Assunpink Bridge just ahead of the Grenadiers. Bombs explode into the Assunpink. Thousands, thousands of British rush to the bridge. The Americans all run away. The war is over.

General Hugh Mercer opened the flap and entered the tent. Washington glanced up and said, "I'm giving a speech tomorrow, Hugh. Have the men lined up, will you?"

Mercer raised his eyebrows. "You're giving a speech?"

"What, I can't give a speech?"

Mercer smiled. "Of course, you can, George. What are you going to say?"

"I'm going to offer them money, a bounty."

"Oh, no, I wouldn't do that. You know Congress will never pay. Then the men will blame you. I'm sorry, George, I think that's a bad idea."

"We have to keep them in the army. If they go home, we've lost. It was probably a mistake to come back here, but here is where we are. I expected another fight before now."

Mercer smiled again. "Damn British. Can't even count on them to show up on time." Washington looked at Mercer but didn't smile. Mercer became more serious. "All right. But not money. You can't offer them money. You have to appeal to the cause."

"I don't think they'll stay for anything but money."

"They'll never get the money. They know that, George. It's a hollow promise. They know that. You know that. Everybody knows that. Congress won't pay. Hell, Congress hasn't even paid them for what they've done so far."

Washington bellowed, "Then I'll pay them myself."

"Ah, George, you can't do that. It'll ruin you. No, don't offer them money. Go for the patriotism."

Washington stared at Mercer. Mercer stared back. Mercer averted Washington's gaze, but quickly faced Washington again.

"All right, the speech. What do you have so far?"

Washington recited from his hand-written notes. "My fellow soldiers, you have done all that I've asked you to do. But the country is at stake."

Mercer interrupted, "How about, 'My brave fellows.' It's more fatherly. And that's how they think of you, George, as a father. And use *your* country, not *the* country." Just a thought." Washington crossed out his words and rewrote the text.

Washington continued. "We have a cause that is worth fighting for, and we know not how to spare you. That's all I have so far."

Mercer added, "That's good. I like that, 'We know not how to spare you.' How about their friends and brothers who have fallen? Their fathers, their sons. I'd change that word, 'cause.' They won't understand that. It's good, though. Just don't say anything about money."

"Thanks, Hugh. You're a good friend." Washington put his head down and scribbled some more text.

Mercer said, "Good night, George." Washington nodded his head. Mercer saluted, but Washington was busily absorbed. Mercer turned around and left the tent.

Chapter Nine

Isaac walked in front. "Let's get off the road for a while. It's too muddy. Maybe the woods'll be drier. Keep up, will you?"

The boys scooted under some underbrush to the right, into the dense woods. "We'll keep the road in sight on our left. It'll be better, easier going than the mud."

They came to a clearing. Isaac said, "Let's stop here to eat."

The boys rummaged through their packs again. Isaac had to remove the string to get an apple. He got one and stuffed the string back into the pack. Toby found some bread in his own pack and pulled it out. He asked Isaac, "Tell me why you hated our father so much."

"What?"

Toby swallowed hard. "Our father. Why did you hate him?"

"Which one?"

"The last one, John."

Isaac took a bite of the apple. "I didn't really hate him. It's just that he was so, so, I don't know, so unmanly, I guess, or something. He never stood up to anybody."

"He was always nice to us, to everybody. He wouldn't hurt nobody, not even a bird."

"I don't want to talk it about it any more. I'm going to just rest here. We'll go in a minute. Stay here."

Isaac slumped against the tree and fell into a light sleep. Toby put a blanket around him from the backpack and sat down in the road. He chomped on his bread and looked around at the tops of the bare trees. Finished with the bread, Toby retrieved an ear of corn from his pack and wandered down the road toward Trenton, marveling at the towering trees. He sat down on a comfortable log, settled himself into a nice indentation, and listened to the faint chirping of the birds, then threw the corn cob into the woods.

* * *

An hour later, Toby looked up the road toward Princeton. Isaac slept against the tree off to the left side, his head tilted, but the blanket still covered him. Isaac had taken both guns and put them behind him for support, then went back to sleep.

Toby studied the trees, noticing a clump of thick leaves high in the branches thirty yards away. It was a bird's nest, vacant in winter. Toby walked up to the tree. He looked up at the bird's nest, considered it for thirty seconds, and then walked up the road toward Princeton and Isaac. He carefully removed one of the guns from behind Isaac, shifted Isaac's head so he wouldn't wake up, and then walked down the road toward Trenton and the bird's nest.

The tree was fifty yards away from Isaac, ten yards from Toby. Toby stood at the bottom of it, looked up, pointed his musket, and then lowered it. No, the crotch of the tree was in the way. He stepped into the woods to get a better shot with his unloaded musket. He took aim and whispered to himself, "Pow, got ya." Toby frowned, "No, too easy."

He came back to the road and pointed his gun at the tree, still too easy. Toby back-stepped toward Trenton, ten yards, twenty yards, thirty yards from the tree, seventy yards from Isaac, pointing his unloaded gun at the birds' nest. "I'll get you, you rebel," Toby laughed to himself. Apparitions of rebel birds peeked out from their decaying home.

Toby glanced back seventy yards at Isaac, still sleeping. He hesitated, but not for long. Toby poured the powder down the barrel, dropped in five bullets, smashed them down with the ramrod, leveled the gun, cocked the hammer, poured the powder in the pan, and fired.

Half of the nest fell to the floor of the woods, but the other half remained, daring Toby to take another shot.

Isaac wakened to the sound of a gunshot and searched the road for Toby. Behind Isaac's tree, seventy yards south, Toby stood in the middle of the road, target practicing at far-off abandoned birds' nests high in the bare winter trees. Another shot, and more of the bird's nest drifted down. Toby reloaded and fired again. Isaac shouted, "Toby, what're you doing?"

Branches high in the air disintegrated at thirty yards from Toby. Toby took another handful of bullets out of his pocket and poured them down the barrel.

Isaac shook off the sleep and walked down the road. He mumbled to himself, "Jesus Christ, the whole world's going to be here in a minute."

Another shot came from Toby's direction, but that one didn't come from Toby. Toby ducked. The bullet hit a branch next to him. At the sound of the gunshot, Isaac fell down quickly into the grass and hid behind a bush.

Major Derring, the British officer who humiliated Lawrence on the street at Maggie's house, came out from the woods on the right side and trotted slowly toward the road. Toby looked around and behind, down the road toward Trenton, but he knew he could never outrun a horse. Maybe the woods on the other side, he thought. Toby's eyes drifted peripherally left.

The trees were packed like a wall, evergreen trees and thick bushes, impossible to even see through. Derring pranced his horse over a slight ridge on the right side and spurred the horse onto the road. Derring faced Toby, blocking any chance of Toby's running north toward Isaac.

Toby and Derring faced each other in the middle of the road, Toby with a musket, Derring with an unloaded pistol. Toby glanced up the road to where he thought Isaac should be. At the eye movement, Derring said, "What are you looking at, boy?"

Toby was startled. "Nothin'."

Derring's words were slow and deliberate. His voice was calm and deep, low and steady, not gruff or shouting. It was just a question. Even with a British accent, Toby sensed no anger in Derring's words, tone, or behavior, no danger, except for that pistol in his hand.

Isaac, twenty yards toward Princeton, slunk further behind some bushes and watched in horror. Toby was awe-struck at a towering man on such a huge horse.

Derring waited for Toby to move. The two faced each other, Toby in the road, a small boy, Derring a professional soldier. Derring loaded his pistol. He was a seasoned veteran, able to load without even looking at it. He stared at Toby hypnotically, mechanically loading, holding Toby in his gaze. The powder went in with only a couple of fingers guiding the powder horn, a bullet, a small ramrod, guided by the deft hands of an expert, smashed the bullet down the barrel.

Toby watched Derring load the gun. He was more amazed than afraid, curious at the facility at which this man loaded a gun without even looking at it. In a few seconds, the pistol would be loaded, and Toby would be dead. Toby gripped his musket hard and put his finger on the cock, ready to pull it back. For an instant, Toby's rational brain said, "Shoot this man." But then his conscience reminded him of his inner revulsion at killing any living thing, especially a man. Besides, in that intimate confrontation, Toby sensed that Derring was not going to shoot. There was something about the man with the steely eyes that made Toby think, hope, pray, that maybe that imperial soldier up there, on a high horse, with the power to kill, maybe that man would somehow feel the same way that Toby did about killing.

Isaac slipped behind a spruce tree and watched with increasing dread. He carefully retrieved his gun and backpack from a few feet away.

Three soldiers came onto the road. Corporal Lawrence said, "Caught a fish, I see. Cheery-ho." Toby recognized Lawrence and bolted toward Princeton, but the three soldiers clustered together and formed a wall of red uniforms. The soldiers raised their guns.

Toby stopped and looked left and right at the closely packed bushes. A soldier read Toby's mind. Toby dove for the underbrush on the right, but the soldier intercepted him and smacked Toby with the butt of his musket. Toby tumbled into the bushes to the right side of the road, fell down, and sprawled face-up at the British soldier pointing a gun at his head.

Lawrence shouted, "Shoot him. He's a rebel."

Toby cried fitfully, his face splattered with mud. There was no Isaac. The soldier looked up at Derring for an order, hopefully any order except "fire." Derring knew the boy was too young to die. He shook his head, no. The solider said, "Over there, boy." He got behind Toby and ushered him slowly back to the road. Toby looked north and south for Isaac, but Isaac was nowhere to be seen.

Derring slowly walked his horse up to Toby and put the point of his sword one inch from Toby's throat. "Drop it."

Toby stared at the many soldiers facing him. He looked again in Isaac's direction, as now a terrible fear welled up in his mind. Danger and dread loomed before him where there was hope before. Toby dropped his gun, powerless now. Derring grabbed Toby by the hair and dragged him forcefully but gently toward Lawrence and his cronies. "Take him back for questioning. Don't hurt him, he's just a boy." Derring let go of Toby as the soldiers clutched his arms. Derring turned his horse and galloped off toward Princeton.

Three miles west, at Five Mile Run, Sergeant Borg Swanson trotted onto the road. Four soldiers came out of the woods on each side. Swanson addressed them, in a German accent. "I hear from Colonel Hand. The regiment is be here tonight. Orders is no shoot. Anybody hear, see, back to camp. No shoot. Orders is report, no shoot." The soldiers acknowledged and returned to their positions in the woods.

Chapter Ten

Lawrence watched Derring ride off, then turned toward Toby. "You're that rebel from Sunday night. Ah, you're going to get it now." Lawrence twisted Toby's arm up his back and grabbed him by the hair. Toby screamed. Lawrence forced his arm even farther. "Think ya can get away with that, rebel? Huh? You and your rebel brother? Where is he?"

Lawrence released Toby and slapped him hard in the face. Toby fell to the ground on his knees, sobbing into the mud. Lawrence put his boot on Toby's backside and shoved as hard as he could. Toby slid two feet up the road on his stomach, crying fitfully.

In all of Toby's short life, he could never remember being slapped in the face. He'd been punched a couple of times, by Isaac, but that was in play, and usually by accident. Isaac would call him a baby, until Toby charged to avenge himself. Isaac would always dodge backward, out of Toby's path, laughing, and when Toby fell to the ground or into a tree, Isaac would always pick him up by the shirt and say, "Aw, you're such a baby." Not this time. Nothing ever hurt so much as that angry slap and the fear that more was to come.

Isaac sneaked down toward the scene of Toby's peril. The heavy shrubbery kept him from the British view. He moved in the direction that the British faced, toward Trenton, so the British didn't expect anyone to their right or behind them. But now, Isaac was directly next to the soldiers. Toby and Lawrence were ten yards down. Isaac couldn't just shoot. He'd be dead almost instantly. He might hit one of them, but that would be the end of his attack, and the end of his days. He stopped at a spruce tree to get a better look. He had an idea.

Isaac carefully weaved his loaded gun through the branches of the tree and lined up the barrel at each soldier one at a time. He balanced the gun on two branches and let it rest there, then stepped back to make sure the gun wasn't going to fall.

Toby picked himself out of the mud and turned toward Lawrence and Princeton. Lawrence and his three soldiers faced Trenton. All the British had their backs or partial backs toward Isaac, so they couldn't see him. Toby also couldn't see Isaac through the trees, ten yards up.

Lawrence screamed at Toby, "Where's your rebel brother?"

Toby cried, "We ain't rebels."

Lawrence slapped him in the face again. Toby fell down. "Where's your damn rebel brother?" Lawrence picked Toby up by his hair.

Toby said, "We ain't rebels. We're uh, you know, uh, Tourneys."

"Tourneys? Ha. What's that, a circus clown?"

Lawrence slapped Toby yet again. The other British soldiers laughed nervously.

"Maybe you're one of them jousters, you know. They stick each other with them poles. So, Mr. Tourney..."

Isaac reached into his backpack, took out the string, and studied it. He cut the string with his teeth and tied the barrel to one tree branch and the butt end to another branch.

Lawrence fixed a bayonet to his musket and held it against Toby's neck. He ran his fingers along the length of it. "You ever get stuck with a knife, rebel? I've done it a hundred times. The blood is all over, boy. You can't believe how it squirts out all over the place."

Isaac went back to the tree and aimed the musket at Lawrence, but Lawrence was too close to Toby. He swung it back to one of the soldiers, but a branch was in the way. Isaac steadied the gun at that position and quietly tied the branch back with another piece of string.

From farther down, Lawrence said, "I once stuck a Frenchie in the ass. Man, did he howl. Would have took him days to die."

Isaac's aim was too high on the soldier. He adjusted the string holding the butt end of the gun, raising the gun and lowering the aim, and then tied it off. One of the soldiers looked quickly to his right. The branch of the spruce tree shook slightly. Isaac froze at the fear of being seen, but thankfully the branch stilled. The soldier turned back to face Lawrence and Toby.

"Bleeding all over the ground. I had to stomp on his face 'cause he wouldn't stop screaming. And he wouldn't stop bleeding. Ha."

Isaac tied a string around the trigger. He cocked the gun carefully, and watched the soldiers closely through the branches of the tree to see if they heard the click of the hammer, but they didn't.

"And as soon as I get that brother Tourney of yours, it's going to be his turn. I'll stick him right in the ass. 'Course, you'll be dead long before that."

Isaac crouched down and meandered through the brush, moving south. A small trench followed the road, so he could slide low and out of sight. He passed the soldiers to his left without their noticing him, letting the string trail behind, but he held it firmly. Too tight, and the gun would go off, and an accidental slip of his leg against the string would be his end. He needed to be near Toby, with the soldiers behind him.

At a bush, Isaac had to decide to go toward the road or away from it. Toward the road would be easier, but might expose him to the soldiers. Away from the road, his string might get caught on the bush and not work. Isaac took a chance. He slanted away from the road, around the bush.

"And after all you rebel bastards is stuck in the ass, then I'm going to go back and see that pretty little mum of yours."

The soldiers laughed again reluctantly. They didn't enjoy the cruelty they were seeing, but they'd be hanged if they interfered.

"You should see this bitch. Wild as a hornet. Man, I'm going to like stickin' that bitch. Ha."

Isaac was near Toby and Lawrence now, but still obscured by the dense overgrowth. The bush that he went around was five yards back. He pulled on the string. The bush moved. A soldier, alarmed, turned toward the bush.

The soldier shouted, "Who goes there?"

Lawrence turned around toward Princeton and looked at the bush. Everyone now faced Princeton, but Isaac was farther down, nearer Trenton, and right next to Toby and Lawrence. Isaac tugged again. Both soldiers saw the bush move.

"Mr. Lawrence?" The soldiers backed up north, toward Princeton. Their muskets pointed at the bush. "Mr. Lawrence, come here."

Isaac whispered to himself, "Go off, please go off."

Isaac tugged again, harder this time. The bush moved noticeably. Both soldiers aimed their guns hastily and fired at the unfortunate bush. Isaac's gun fired from the spruce tree, ten yards farther up from the bush, and slightly behind the soldiers. The bullet splintered a log on the road.

Isaac sprinted toward Toby and Lawrence. The soldiers were shocked. They saw smoke from the spruce tree to their right, a bush swaying five yards toward Trenton, and a figure running through the woods ten yards farther down. Lawrence didn't see Isaac running, trying to understand the mysterious smoke, the moving bush, and the splintering log. Still out of sight of Lawrence's vision, Isaac held his right arm high, with a fisted hand, as if he had a knife in there. The soldiers shouted, "Aaieee. Rebels. All over."

The soldiers ran up the road toward Princeton. Lawrence called to them, "Get back here, you cowards." Lawrence turned slowly to his left. "Aaieee!"

Isaac was five feet away. He shouted, "Whoop Whoop." His right arm was high in the air. Lawrence noticed the threatening fist, but with only one good eye, and Isaac's speed, and the fury of Isaac's charge, and his other men running away, and the slipperiness of the road, Lawrence didn't have time to figure out if there was a knife in there or not. Too late.

Isaac plowed into Lawrence at a full run. Lawrence sprawled into the woods on the other side of the road and dropped his gun. Isaac tumbled and fell, but he wasn't hurt. He yelled, Toby, run."

Toby ran down the road toward Trenton, Isaac following closely. Isaac looked behind him and saw the two soldiers running in the opposite direction. He stopped, ran back to the gun and picked it up, then quickly went over to the dazed Lawrence and ripped the powder horn off his chest.

Isaac ran down the road toward Trenton and caught up with Toby after fifty yards. Lawrence recovered and walked over to the spruce tree. He saw the string on the gun, pulled on it, and saw the bush move. Lawrence shook his fist in the air. "Damn rebels. I'll get you, and your rebel mum, too."

The tree rustled in the breeze. Lawrence hustled off toward Princeton.

The boys stopped running. Isaac fell to his knees and stooped, panting, out of breath. Toby cried, "I want to go home."

"Well, we can't go home. How could you be so stupid? You damn near got us killed." Isaac got up and wiped his pants. "Shooting a gun in the middle of the road. Stupid. Now we have no packs, no food, one gun, and a long way to go."

"I want to go home. We can just go home."

"No. We can't. And we're not Tourneys, we're Tories."

"But what if that soldier goes back to the house? Ma's there. He'll hurt her. And the little ones."

"Hush up. You have any bullets?"

Toby reached into his pocket. "Yes, I have some."

Isaac handed the gun to Toby.

"Load it. I can't wait to get rid of you in Allentown."

They walked toward Trenton, Isaac in front. Toby wiped his eyes. He stopped crying and asked, "How'd you do that with the gun?"

"Do what?"

"Shoot from there."

"I used the string."

Toby thought about that for ten seconds, but Isaac got farther ahead. Toby caught up and asked, "Isaac?"

"What?"

"We've got to get some more string."

"What? Why?"

"'Cause you shoot better when you ain't got a gun."

"Aw, hush up."

Toby smiled through his tears. Isaac smiled too, but careful not to let Toby see him.

Chapter Eleven

On horseback, Washington faced the men with officers at his side. In a field south of the Assunpink Creek, the men were lined up for a speech. Washington moved to a point half way between the men and the creek.

"My brave fellows. You have done all that I have asked you to do. But your country is at stake, and we know not how to spare you. If you go home tomorrow, the war is lost. All your friends and comrades who have fallen will be forgotten.

"I'm asking each of you to reenlist for another six weeks. In six weeks we can put this campaign behind us and raise a new army for the summer."

Washington rode back and turned his horse toward the men. The soldiers looked at each other nervously. Some mumbled. Many kicked the ground or hung their heads to avoid the gaze of the officers. Nobody stepped forward. Washington rode out again.

"We don't have to win. We just have to not lose. But we have to have an army. As long as we have an army, we can't lose."

Nobody moved. Washington recalled the conversation with Mercer about not offering money, especially Washington's own money. It would ruin him. Four thousand men would cost him $40,000. Washington's entire estate was worth about $45,000, a huge sum in 1777, but it would indeed ruin him.

Washington spoke. "I'm authorizing a bounty of ten dollars for every man who will reenlist for six weeks. And I'll guarantee it with my own personal fortune."

Washington turned around and trotted slowly to the officers' location. Some men came out slowly, then others. The unsure soldiers looked behind them at their friends, nodded to each other with a "why-not" shrug, and stepped forward. Eventually all of them did.

Washington motioned to an officer, "Sign 'em up, Lieutenant."

Washington trotted up the field, accompanied by General Fermoy and Colonel Edward Hand. "Fermoy, you have men on the Princeton Road, right?"

Fermoy said, "I believe we have pickets at Five Mile Rum, I mean, 'Run.'"

"You believe? Don't you even know where your men are, General?"

Fermoy sputtered, "Uh, uh, the riflemen are in Trenton."

To avoid an outburst from Washington, Colonel Hand spoke up quickly, "All the men are up front, near the Run. Sergeant Swanson's at the point. He's a good man. I'm going up now."

Fermoy said, "I ordered you to pull everyone back to Trenton."

Washington thundered, "You what?"

Hand shook his head, because he expected that reply from Washington. Colonel Edward Hand, of Lancaster, Pennsylvania, had just turned 32 years old this very day, but he was not inclined to celebrate. Hand wore the ragged jacket and cap of a Pennsylvania Rifleman, but his men were up there, and there could be trouble at any minute. Washington forgave their improper attire, because they were riflemen, one of the best regiments in the army. Colonel Hand was their leader. Murphy reported to Hand. Hand reported to Fermoy.

Hand's horse snorted and kicked the ground, perhaps startled by Washington's bellow, perhaps just from the cool air. Nevertheless, Hand reached down and stroked the horse's neck, ever aware of the comfort and safety of the soldiers in his charge, even if one was a horse. "Easy, there."

Hand stared straight into Fermoy's eyes as he patted the horse's side. "I thought it better to get authorization on that order, sir." Hand turned to Washington for acknowledgement of his decision.

Washington said to Fermoy, "You, sir, are not authorized to pull back to Trenton."

Fermoy saluted hastily. "Yes, sir." Washington galloped away. Fermoy pulled the flask out of his pocket and took a long swig. "God, he scares me."

Hand gently pulled his horse to the side, looking carefully at how the horse's hooves struck the road. Hand nudged his horse toward the Trenton Bridge.

Fermoy shouted after him, "Come back here. Where are you going? I have orders for you. Get back here. Don't you dare embarrass me like that." Hand ignored him.

* * *

The fighting force of the British army was headquartered at New Brunswick, New Jersey, twenty miles east of Princeton. General Charles Cornwallis was commander of the British detachment there. With the winter campaign over, and the rebel army all but annihilated, he expected a pleasant trip back to London to see his wife before the spring fighting season began, if there even were to be another fighting season. The raid at Trenton foiled those plans.

Cornwallis steamed at his officers, "If Howe hadn't held me back, the rebels would all be dead by now. He sits up there in New York and thinks he knows how to fight these people, these traitors. Damn him. And damn those Hessians. I'd have cut the Fox off at the river if Howe hadn't interfered." The officers looked at him cautiously.

Cornwallis shook his head. "Fools. I'm plagued with fools at the highest levels." The officers turned away, avoiding the wrath of the general. "And now I'm stuck in this miserable swamp of a country called 'New Jersey,' of all things."

An officer corrected him, "It's a colony, sir."

"I know what the hell it is."

The officer slinked behind an aide so Cornwallis wouldn't see who said that. Cornwallis looked up from his rant. "What's the situation in Princeton?"

A brave officer stepped into the tirade. "Mawhood's there. The King's Fourth is on their way."

Cornwallis asked, "How many rebels in Trenton?"

"Maybe four thousand, about that, near as we can tell."

"Puny. Disgraceful."

"Sir?"

"It's a disgrace that the Hessians got beat by a rabble mob of traitorous cowards. If Rahl hadn't died last week in Trenton, I'd have him shot. I may still have him shot."

"Sir, he's already buried."

"So dig him up and shoot him again. Then send his miserable carcass back to London in a box. Let the King see what contemptible incompetence our money buys these days." The officers fidgeted anxiously. Cornwallis said, "Tell Mawhood to move the 17th and the 55th to Trenton."

"It might take some time to get the guns up, sir. The roads are muddy."

"Damn the mud. And the Fox. I want 8,000 men in Trenton on Thursday morning. Keep two more regiments at Princeton, 1,400 in reserve."

"Yes, sir."

"The Fox made his biggest mistake this time, coming back. Huge mistake. Now I don't even have to cross the river."

Cornwallis scribbled an order and handed it to one of the officers. "What a fool he is to come back here. And only a fool would miss this chance to crush him. And I, sir, am no fool."

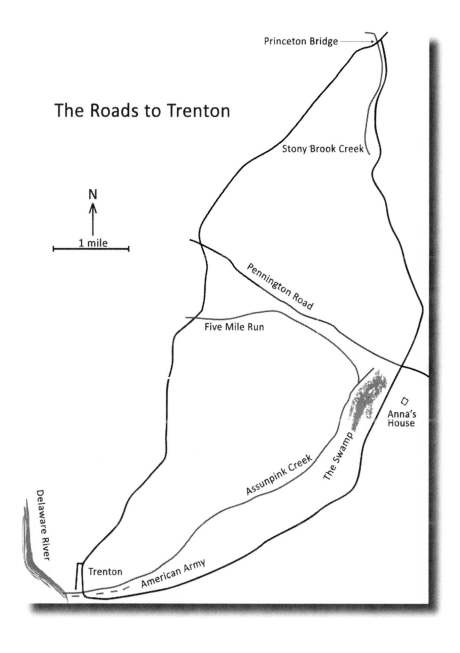

The Roads to Trenton

Chapter Twelve

Isaac and Toby came to a crossroad. Toby looked down the road to the left. "Is that the back road?"

Isaac said, "Now how can that be the back road? How can the back road go off in the wrong direction from the front road? Jesus, you're stupid. That's the Pennington Road."

"Where does it go?"

"It goes to the back road, and it's not the back road, it's the Quaker Road."

"I thought you said it's the Pennington Road."

"This! Is the Pennington Road. The back road is the Quaker Road."

"Why don't we take the Quaker Road?"

"'Cause you're too stupid, that's why. The back road... Ah, the Quaker Road, goes below Trenton. We can't cross the river below Trenton." Isaac mumbled, "Stupid."

The boys passed the Pennington crossroad, walked another mile, and arrived at a small stream called Five Mile Run. It was ten feet wide and only inches of water. They sloshed across.

A hundred yards down, Sergeant Swanson's rebel soldiers sat in the road. Swanson arrived on horseback. "Off road. Watch. You see, run back. No shoot." The men went into hiding in the brush on both sides.

At the boys' location, Toby whined. "Isaac, I'm tired."

"Stop complaining. I'm tired, too. We have to keep going. Damn. It's going to be dark soon. We're probably going to have to stay out here all night. Damn."

The sun on the southwest horizon nearly blinded them as they walked directly into it. Isaac shielded his eyes. Toby ducked behind Isaac and used Isaac's body as shade.

Toby dragged his feet as they walked another twenty yards. "How much longer?"

"That was Five Mile Run, so it's five miles to the ferry. Come on, keep up."

A soldier strained his ear toward Princeton. "Did you hear that?"

"Yes. Somebody's coming." The soldiers hid themselves more securely.

"Isaac, can't we stop? I'm tired. I can't walk no more."

"What do you want me to do? We have to keep going. Come on."

"Halt. Drop your weapons."

Six soldiers appeared on the road. Toby turned to run, but fell down in the mud. A soldier fired. Toby heard the sound of the bullet whiz past his ear as he fell to the ground. Isaac grabbed their only gun from Toby's hands, stood in the road and cocked it, but there was no powder in the pan, and no time for loading. Isaac aimed his unloaded musket at the rebels coming slowly toward him. "Toby, get up, run." Another shot from the Americans missed Isaac by inches.

Sergeant Swanson came out from the east side of the woods on his horse. He deftly maneuvered it onto the road behind the boys, so Isaac and Toby were trapped between Swanson and his men with nowhere to go. Toby took off into the woods to the east, behind the horse, just as another bullet hit a nearby tree. He turned left, parallel to the road, toward Princeton, and zigzagged like a rabbit. Toby splashed across the stream and fell into the mud on the other side of Five Mile Run.

Toby looked behind him, no Isaac. He got up and faced Trenton. "Isaac, Isaac." A three-shot volley from the other side of the creek spelled death for Isaac.

Isaac lunged for the west woods, but Swanson was ready, and spurred his horse to intercept. Swanson had to duck a low-hanging branch, but his horse completely blocked Isaac from escape, and Isaac slammed right into the horse. The unexpected touch caused the horse to quickly swing its head toward the danger. The horse snapped at Isaac's hand and just missed. The turn of the horse caused Swanson's head to smash into the branch. Swanson turned his horse straight, and then raised his hand to his head. There was some blood. Isaac stooped low, slid under Swanson's horse, and ran up the road toward Princeton. Swanson held his stricken head and dismounted slowly. The horse blocked the soldiers, too, but they fired anyway, wildly high. Swanson shouted, "No shoot."

From thirty yards up, Toby heard the shots. "Oh, no! Oh, my God, no! Isaac! Isaac!" Toby waded across the stream, crying. "Isaac, Isaac." Tears rolled down his face as he searched the woods for his brother, but he expected the worst. "Oh, no, what did I do?"

Toby saw some movement ahead. Isaac rounded a turn in the road and ran fast toward Toby. Toby's face brightened. Isaac slipped in the mud and slid off the side of the road, but got up again and yelled, "Turn around. Go back." Toby turned and ran back to the stream, slowing enough to let Isaac catch up. The boys crossed Five Mile Run and stopped on the other side to rest.

Sergeant Swanson touched his head again and looked at the blood on his hand. A soldier took a cloth and tied it around Swanson's head. "Sorry, Sarge. Should we go get them?"

Swanson tightened the bandage. "Nein, let them go. They know we here now. Now we be very careful. You watch very careful. And no shoot no more."

The soldiers looked at each other sheepishly. "Sorry, Sarge," and went back into the woods.

Chapter Thirteen

Isaac walked toward Princeton, puzzled at what had just happened. Toby followed silently, carrying the gun. As they arrived at the Pennington crossroad again, Toby asked, "Now can we take the back road?"

"Aw, hush up."

The boys went to the right, down the Pennington Road. Isaac walked quickly, but Toby lagged behind. "Come on, Toby, keep up." Toby hustled up, and walked side-by-side with Isaac.

Toby asked, "Who were those men?"

"I don't know. Probably some militia, or stragglers or somebody. I don't know."

Isaac stared at the ground, walking slowly now, trying to figure out who those men were. Toby changed the subject. "What do you think happened to our first father?"

"What? What does that matter?"

"I was just wondering."

"You were wondering that now? We almost got killed."

Toby said, "So, what do you think?"

"About what?"

"About our first father."

"I hope he's buried in the ground."

"Why? Why do you say things like that? It wasn't his fault. Maybe it was Ma's fault. You know how she is, always screaming and yelling. I can't stand that myself. Maybe he couldn't either."

"No, it was his fault. He shouldn't have left. He should have stayed and taken care of us or taken us with him."

Toby's pace slowed again. "I could never leave Ma."

"I could. Instead, I was stuck with 'Cowering John' for a father."

"John was nice. You know that. And if you went with Pa, we wouldn't be together."

"So what? Then I wouldn't have a stupid kid hanging around me right now and forever and for the rest of my goddamn life."

Isaac stopped and turned around. "I didn't mean that. Come on, keep up."

"I miss him, I think. The first one, if I remember him right. He taught us how to shoot. Me, anyway, not you."

* * *

The sun had set long ago, leaving the boys in near-pitch blackness. Toby held onto Isaac's belt like a plow on a mule. The trudge down the Pennington Road was slow and difficult. Even the moon couldn't help, not due for another four hours. Isaac had to feel his way to keep to the road. He clutched at the trees to the right, careful not to stumble and fall.

Isaac was afraid. It was cold. It was dark. The trees bent their deadly tentacles across the road like menacing monsters, perfectly willing to poke out a boy's eye at the least provocation. Only the stars gave the faintest glimmer of light. There were no houses, no barns, no fields, no smoke, no signs of life anywhere. It was almost eleven o'clock. Isaac searched desperately left and right for somewhere, anywhere, that they could find some shelter for the night.

They peered into the sky ahead. There was nothing but darkness, except for the stars. A particularly bright one, just to the left of the road, cleared the high trees with no trouble at all. Toby asked, "What's that star?"

"I don't know. Maybe a planet. Maybe Jupiter, or Venus, or something, I don't know. We're in trouble here, Toby."

The star was the brightest in the sky, rising higher over the trees as they walked.

Toby asked, "Is that the 'love' star?"

Isaac shouted, "Toby, stop asking fool questions. We're in trouble. I don't know if we can find any place to stay. Damn. We could freeze to death out here."

Toby said, "We can build a fire."

"And how are we going to build a fire? You lost the packs, remember?"

"I can shoot the gun. That'll start a fire."

Isaac thought about that. Yes, that could work. Complicated, but it could work. "All right. Let's get to the Quaker Road. Maybe there'll be some houses there, or something. If not, we'll build a fire."

The boys arrived at the junction of the Pennington and Quaker Roads. The Quaker Road ran southwest toward Trenton. Isaac said, "Here's the Quaker Road. Hurry, Toby, keep up. We have a long way to go, especially now."

The boys turned right, walked another mile, and heard a honking sound to the right, the cry of a winter goose. Isaac went off the road to search for it. "There's dinner. Here, goosey, goosey, goosey."

Isaac disappeared into the darkness. Toby went over to the west side of the dark road and searched for movement. "Isaac, come back. Where are you?"

Isaac ran toward the honking sound but slipped in the mud, fell on his back, and struggled up. He slogged another ten feet, but his left foot got stuck and he fell down again, this time on his hands and knees. He lifted his left leg and stood up, but his right foot was trapped in the deep ooze. Isaac tumbled backward and fell on his rump. The goose ignored Isaac, flitted past him, and rushed toward Toby on the road.

"Toby, shoot the goose. Shoot him."

"Isaac, where are you?" Toby raised his gun to his side and watched the big bird come at him. The goose slowed to a walk but marched straight at Toby, honking. Toby poured the powder in the pan with one eye on the goose. He pulled the hammer back, pointed the musket at the goose, and took careful aim.

The goose walked up to Toby, its neck slinking forward and backward with each threatening step. Toby pointed the loaded gun right at it and backed away slowly. His gun shook more with each snake of the goose's neck.

"Don't you come any closer."

Isaac watched from the other side of the road, too stuck in the mud to get out, and too amused at his brother's predicament to even care about it. "Toby, shoot! Shoot! Ha!"

The goose attacked. Toby backed up, but the goose's beak clung to his pants. Toby dragged the goose backward into the field. "Ah, ah! Get away from me! Ah." The goose let go, but charged at Toby again.

Toby kicked at the goose but didn't hit it. He fell down on his back, kicking. Instinctively though, he held the gun parallel to the ground so the powder wouldn't fall out of the pan. The goose avoided the kicks and charged again. Now it pecked at Toby's face. Toby held his free hand in front of his eyes and jumped up.

Toby ran away from the road twenty yards into the field. The goose chased him all the way, pecking. It was smashed-down cornstalks, dry terrain.

"Isaac! Ah! Get him off me! Isaac! Isaac!"

Isaac laughed. "Shoot the goddamn dinner, Toby."

Through the darkness, Isaac saw Toby running fearfully from the bird. Isaac shook his head and struggled to stand up, but swayed sideways because one foot was still six inches deep in the mud. He fell onto his back, tried to get up, and fell again, this time face-forward. Both feet were now stuck solid.

Isaac steadied himself upright. He slowly picked one foot out of the mud and placed it in what appeared to be a more stable location. He tried to withdraw his other foot, but the suction of the mud drew him back. His shoe came off. Isaac reached behind him to retrieve it, but in doing that, he fell on his face again. Isaac carefully stood up and lifted his shoeless foot out of the mud.

Toby managed to distance himself by ten feet from the enemy goose. He had a military advantage now, a death-at-a-distance weapon, a loaded musket, no match for a crazy bird. Toby aimed his gun again. He checked the powder in the pan. Loaded, but the goose just wouldn't quit.

Toby jogged to the side, but the goose followed him with every movement. He backed up into the cornfield and looked behind him, careful not to trip. Toby stopped and pointed the gun. No, he wouldn't shoot. He pushed the cock down onto the pan so it wouldn't fire. He flipped the gun and held it backward against the goose, pushing the stock away from him like a bayonet. The powder poured out of the pan.

Isaac had a shoe in one hand and a foot stuck solid. He carefully extracted his foot from the stuck shoe and reached backward to get the other shoe out of the mud. Now he had two shoes in his hands, but his feet were deep in the mud. Still, he could move more easily that way. Isaac trudged slowly toward the road.

Isaac spotted Toby and the goose facing off deep in the field. Both the goose and Toby stopped, daring each other to attack. Toby jabbed the stock of his gun at the goose. The goose ignored the threat and charged. Isaac mumbled, "Ah, Jesus Christ."

* * *

A musket blast pierced the silent night air from twenty yards away. The goose was obliterated, feathers all over the place. The boys turned toward the sound of the gunshot. Isaac stopped struggling in the mud and stood still.

A figure strode quickly and confidently toward them through the darkness. Both boys froze. Closer, closer, closer, then to Toby, "Give me that gun."

It was a girl in baggy men's pants and a bonnet. She took Toby's musket from his hands, dropped her unloaded gun on the ground, and walked onto the road. She looked at the pan of Toby's gun, no powder, but no matter. She cocked the gun and pointed it at Isaac's head.

Anna was seventeen and attractive. "Get out of there," she said.

Isaac struggled out of the mud. He dropped one of his shoes and stooped to pick it up. At the movement, Anna backed up suspiciously and narrowed the aim of Toby's unloaded gun at him as he inched along toward the road. Isaac looked at her closely as he passed. Anna stared back, but gripped the gun tightly. "Hands up." Isaac and Toby marched as prisoners in front of Anna, their hands in the air.

A woman called out from the distance, "Anna, Anna. Where you? Whas you do? Who shoot?" Isaac and Toby were startled by the voice. A small house appeared a hundred yards away.

"I'm here, Momma, I'm all right. We have trespassers."

Toby looked behind him and saw Anna following them through the field. Anna stumbled slightly on the corn stalks, but she never took her eyes off Isaac. She stooped to pick up her own gun, so now she had two unloaded guns. She kept Toby's musket at her hip, continually pointed at Isaac's back, and said, "Go. Over there. Now."

Isaac was in the way of Toby's backward view of his captor until Isaac moved to the side. Anna tripped again. She went down on her right knee, but her gun maintained a perfect angle on Isaac's back. Her left arm went out to support herself. She recovered without even looking down.

Toby asked, "Where we going?"

Anna said, "To the house. Momma's there."

"You have anything to eat there?"

Chapter Fourteen

Murphy adjusted his glasses as he read papers by lamplight. He crossed out the number "150" on a requisition, scribbled a new number, "75," then scratched that out and wrote "50." He threw the paper onto a stack and sighed heavily as he pulled out the next one. Jackson entered Murphy's tent timidly. "Sir? Can I talk to you?"

"Ah, you're the kid who was stuck in the mud. What can I do for you, son?"

"You've got to get us out of there."

"Out of where?"

"That company. Captain Hawkins is crazy. You saw him. He's crazy. He was going to shoot me. Or Satchel. You've got to help me. Us. Please, Sir?"

Murphy shook his head at the difficult breech of military protocol that Jackson just asked him to perform. "I'm sorry, son, I don't know what I can do."

"We want to fight, me and my men. We want to join your regiment."

"I don't know as you'll see much fighting with me. I mostly push papers, not cannons."

"I heard you can do anything."

Murphy smiled at the compliment, but there were other difficulties. "I don't know. You're not riflemen."

"I can shoot. So can Satchel. He's my brother."

Murphy hesitated, thinking. "Shooting a rifle is different than shooting a musket. It takes a long time to load."

"We can learn."

"I don't think we have the time."

Murphy stared at Jackson for a moment. "How old are you, son?"

"Eighteen."

"I have a boy about your age, two boys."

"Are they here?"

Murphy paused a long time, shook his head, and looked down at his papers. "No, they live with their mother. I haven't seen them in years."

"Can't you get us out of that company, sir? We'll do good. Captain Hawkins will kill us, and we won't even be fighting. Please, sir. You can do it."

Murphy couldn't refuse the plea, but replied without commitment, "I'll see what I can do."

"And Satchel, too. Not just me. He's sick right now, but he'll get better."

Now it was even more complicated. Murphy didn't want to discourage the young man, but it was better to let him know the chances right away. "I don't know if I can get you both out."

"He's my brother. He has to go where I go. And my men, too."

Hopeless now, almost impossible to pull off, Murphy cautioned, "I can't promise you. I'll see what I can do."

"You can do it, Cap. Thanks, Cap. Thank you."

Jackson exited, pulled the tent flap closed with bright hopes, and disappeared into the night. Murphy watched him go and returned to his papers.

Chapter Fifteen

Anna passed the boys a few feet before they got to the house. "Stay here." The boys stopped outside the door. Anna turned toward them and backed up to the door. She tucked one gun under her arm and held the other at her side with one hand, her finger on the trigger, which freed up her left hand. She reached behind her and turned the doorknob, backing into the house. "Get in here." Anna turned around, her back to the boys now. They entered behind her.

A matronly woman sat in a chair at a table with a gun across her lap. A curtained window was behind her, along with a door going out back. Several chairs in the room were neatly arranged, uncluttered by garments or contraptions, as the boys were used to seeing. A table sat underneath the window in a small kitchen area in the back, but there was no wall between the main room and the kitchen.

The slight smell of smoke and the warmth of a fire instantly lightened the boys' dread. Wisps of steam drifting out of a black pot hanging over the fire, with a smaller pot hanging down into it, carried the aroma of sumptuous soup throughout the house. A grandfather's clock in the corner chimed eleven o'clock.

The boys had little time to enjoy their new comfort. Momma screamed, in a thick German accent, "Eek. Whas you do, girl? Who this? Neina come in my house. Get out."

Anna put the guns on a chair. "Momma, they're hungry."

"We neina let strangers here, Anna. You father shoot them. Go away."

"Momma, they're just boys. They haven't eaten in days."

Isaac and Toby looked at each other with a 'what?' expression. Anna, Isaac, and Toby were lined up with their backs to the front door. Momma, six feet away, stood up from her chair, raised her gun, and looked down the barrel at Isaac's head.

"Whas you name, boy?"

"Isaac. He's Toby. We're brothers."

"Where you from?"

"Near Princeton."

"Whas you do here?"

"We're trying to get to Allentown."

Momma motioned toward the kitchen, "Sit."

The boys took places at the table while Anna sat in a chair in the main room. Momma put the gun to the side, retrieved some plates, butter, bread, and dried meat out of a cabinet and put them on the table. She fished some potatoes out of the small pot with a fork and put them on the boys' plates. The boys devoured the food ravenously.

Momma opened the door and lumbered out back to a porch. She walked over to a large wooden tub, upside down, circular, three feet in diameter, two feet tall. She wiped some light snow off the sides and turned it upright. The heavy tub would have been difficult to move for a woman with a slighter build, but Momma had no trouble. She came back into the kitchen without even losing her breath.

Momma opened another cabinet door and took out three large pots. "Take these, girl, get water."

Isaac jumped up from the table, still chewing. "I'll go with you." Isaac and Anna scurried out the back door.

Momma glared suspiciously at Toby, scooping food into his mouth faster than he could swallow it. Without even looking up from his plate, Toby asked, "Can I have some more potatoes?" Food spit out of his mouth and onto the table. Momma shook her head.

Momma speared another potato. She sliced it, buttered it, and slid it onto Toby's plate. "Why you go to Pennsylvania?"

"Our mother wants us to get away from the war."

Toby wolfed down the last of the food. "We're Tories."

"Eina Tory, Mas Niecht. Out. Get Out. I shoot." Momma picked up the gun and pointed it at Toby's head.

* * *

Isaac and Anna walked toward an outdoor pump ten yards from the house. Isaac carried the three water jugs.

Anna asked, "Allentown? Isn't that in Pennsylvania? What are you going to do in Pennsylvania?"

"I'm going to get Toby there and then come back here and fight the rebels."

"I see. So you're Tories. And why do you want to be Tories?"

"I don't know. Our mother doesn't like the rebels. She hates Washington. And Franklin. She really hates Franklin. I don't know why."

"Don't tell Momma you're Tories, she'll shoot you."

"I don't know who we are any more. The British are trying to kill us, the rebels are shooting at us, farmers... Hey, even you. I don't know anymore."

"You don't know too much, do you, Isaac?"

"No, I guess not."

Anna said, "My father's in the army."

"Gosh. Really? He's a rebel?"

"Yes. He fought here last week at Trenton. We saw him after that, but then he had to go back."

Isaac stared wide-eyed at Anna. "Gosh. He's a rebel."

"Momma and Papa and Grandma came over here from the old country before I was born. They wanted to get away from, you know, all that stuff."

"What stuff?"

"Never mind. Papa's a great patriot. He loves Franklin. He used to read to me from the almanac, 'Little strokes fell great oaks.'"

Isaac said, "I don't know about those things."

"No, I wouldn't think you would, being a 'Tory,' and all..." Anna raised her eyebrows for a reply to the challenge.

Isaac lifted both hands in the air and put his head down. "I don't know. I'm sorry, I just don't know any more."

"It's all right, Isaac."

Isaac gazed into her eyes. She stared at him without any judgment. She even smiled, a beautiful smile to Isaac, welcome on this terrible night and this terrible journey. Isaac was grateful for that smile. It could have been much worse when he told her he was a Tory, with yelling and screaming and shooting.

Anna said, "I miss Papa terribly. I hope he's all right. 'God helps them that help themselves.' 'No gains without pains.'"

"Yes, I've heard that one."

Anna smiled reproachfully. "Oh, you have, have you? 'It's hard for an empty bag to stand upright.'"

Isaac scrunched his face. "What? What in hell does that mean?"

Anna laughed. "Ah, Isaac, you're funny. We came here last summer from Germantown when Grandma died."

Isaac struggled for a reply to that, but couldn't think of anything smart. "I've never been there."

"It's in Pennsylvania, too. It's a very small town."

Anna took two of the three empty jugs from Isaac's hands. "We better get the water." They walked silently to the pump and put the jugs down. Anna said, "Hold that one under."

Isaac put his bucket under the pump. Anna pumped the water into it. Filled, Isaac moved it to the side while Anna fetched the next one. The water came faster, Anna doing very little pumping because of the suction.

The third bucket filled to the top, but Anna couldn't stop the bucket from overflowing. The water splashed all over Isaac.

"Aaieee. It's cold."

Anna reached into the bucket and threw a handful of water on Isaac.

Isaac screamed, "Ah, stop that. It's cold." He scooped some water out with his hand and threw it at her.

Anna ran away laughing, then came back. "Now don't you do that anymore. You got me wet."

"You got me wet, too. It's freezing out here."

Anna smiled. "Aw, it's not that bad for this time of year."

Isaac looked up at the sky. "Yes, not too bad so far."

Anna took the opportunity to douse him with another icy blast. Isaac lunged backward to avoid it.

* * *

Inside, Toby cowered against the wall. "Isaac. Help. Isaac, get in here. No, please, put it down. Don't shoot."

"You Tory, I shoot."

Toby looked at the back door, no Isaac. His eyes moved to the gun. The hammer was down on the pan, so it wasn't cocked. Toby's quick little brain seized the logic immediately, but he overlooked the practical convenience of keeping his mouth shut. He said, "I don't think it's loaded."

Momma was surprised, but recovered quickly. "You think I no kill you with empty gun?"

Momma held the gun by the barrel and raised it over her head. Toby searched around frantically. He was trapped in the corner between the grandfather's clock and Momma with nowhere to go. Toby sank down on his butt and covered his head.

Momma raged, "Get out. Out. You and that boy. You Tories, I kill. Out." Momma shoved the gun high in the air, threatening to strike the blow. The gun hit the ceiling, sending pieces of wood and straw to the floor.

Toby took advantage of the momentary extension of his life expectancy. "No, wait. We fought the British on Sunday, and again today."

Momma paused and glared at Toby, but the gun still hovered over her head like a bat.

"Isaac shot them, the British. He shot them with a string on a gun. I mean, with a gun on a string."

Momma raised the gun higher, ready to swing.

"No, wait. See, Isaac can't shoot. I mean, he can shoot, but he can't hit anything. So he... wait. They had a knife to me. They was going to kill me. Us, I mean. The British. Me and Isaac. Isaac shot them with a string on a gun."

"I smash your head."

"No, Isaac, get in here."

Outside, Isaac watched Anna as she wiped the water from her pants. Her blouse was soaked and her stringy hair dribbled drops of water onto her face. She wiped her sleeve across her brow. Isaac stared, entranced at her innocent prettiness, like no girl he'd ever seen, like an angel, a beautiful angel, but an angel who could shoot.

Isaac carried two buckets of water back to the porch and set them down. Anna set the other bucket on the porch floor. She glanced knowingly at the tub and took Isaac's hand.

"You know, Isaac, it's going to be midnight pretty soon. It's customary in the old country to kiss a person you like in order to bring good luck in the coming year."

Isaac panicked. "I, uh, uh, I never kissed a girl before."

Anna said, "Don't worry. You have a few minutes to get used to the idea."

A loud noise sounded from inside the house, followed by a muffled, "No, don't." Anna turned toward the back door. "Sounds like Momma and your brother have been talking."

Isaac and Anna rushed inside to see Toby huddled against the clock. Momma's gun was ready to swing again. Anna spotted pieces of a broken plate on the floor and shouted, "Momma, no."

"I kill all Tories."

"He's not a Tory, Momma, he's just a boy."

Toby closed his eyes momentarily, then exhaled deeply. Isaac and Anna sprang over. Isaac stooped low to take Toby's hand, but Toby withdrew it in embarrassment and pushed on the floor to get up. Isaac pulled him upright by the arm. On the way up, Anna rubbed Toby's head in consolation.

Isaac whispered, "Shhh. We're not Tories anymore."

"Yes, I know. Jeez, thanks."

Momma's face scrunched into a threatening snarl. "You. Take pot off fire."

Isaac looked at Anna for an explanation of what Momma wanted. Anna said, "Do as she says, Isaac. Take the pot off the fire. Don't get burned."

Isaac asked, "Why?"

"Just take the soup pot out of the water and put it over there. It'll be all right, I promise you."

Momma pointed to the kitchen chair. "Sit, girl."

Anna cleaned up the broken plate, and then sat in the chair at the table by the curtained window, next to the back door. Isaac picked the small pot out of the hot water, put it on the table, and moved quickly away from Momma.

Momma opened a cabinet and took out a very large knife and a brick-like object. She said, "Get pot. Out back."

Isaac walked toward the fire, careful not to get too close to Momma. Seeing the knife, he asked, "Anna?"

"Hmm?"

"Where are we going?"

"Out back. You too, Toby, out back. You'll be all right."

Isaac pulled the steaming pot off the fire and walked out. Toby followed. Momma came out last.

The back porch ran along the entire length of the house. The tub was to the boys' right as they exited. Directly behind the tub was a small bench, pushed against the house and underneath the window.

Momma said, "Put water down, here."

Isaac put the water outside the door. Momma scowled, "Over there."

Isaac asked, "What, the water?"

"No, you."

The boys backed up next to the tub.

Momma said, "Off."

"What?"

Momma moved between the boys and the window and faced them. She shook the knife in her hand. "Clothes, off, now."

The boys looked at each other, hesitating, confused. Momma shook the knife again violently. Toby and Isaac stared at her wide-eyed.

Anna called from the kitchen, "Better do it, boys."

They removed their shirts slowly, then stopped, as if that might be enough. Momma gestured toward the tub with the knife. "In there, clothes."

The boys threw their shirts into the tub. Momma turned, faced away from them, and poured some hot water from the pot into each of the cold-water jugs. She picked up the knife and sliced pieces of soap from the brick into two of the jugs, but not the third. Then she swished the knife in the jugs to make bubbles and faced the boys again. Their shirts were off now. They shivered against the mild chill. "Eicht. Off. All off. In tub."

The boys gawked at each other in disbelief. Toby gasped, "She's crazy."

From inside the house Anna said, "Better do it, boys."

The boys reluctantly removed their pants and threw them into the tub. Now they were in their underwear.

Momma put down the soap and knife and went back into the house. As she entered the kitchen, she glanced to her left at Anna, sitting at the table. Anna gazed innocently around the room. Momma turned to her right and went through a door into her own bedroom, off to the right of the kitchen.

Anna got out of the chair, pulled aside the curtain, and stared at boys in their underwear with their backs toward her. Momma's footsteps coming out of the room disappointed Anna in her peeping. She barely had time to scramble into the chair before Momma reappeared in the kitchen.

Momma emerged with towels and clothing under her arm, throwing Anna a cold stare as she passed. Anna feigned an admiration of her fingers with cool indifference.

Momma went back outside and dropped the clothes and towels on the bench under the window. The boys watched her warily as they held their shoulders against the cold. Momma picked up the knife, marched over to them, and shook the knife inches from their groins. "Off. All off."

Isaac and Toby were terrified now. They looked at Momma, then at the knife, then at each other.

"Off. All off. Off."

Anna watched through the curtain, but turned toward the room so Momma wouldn't hear a voice through the window. "Better do it, Isaac."

The boys took off their underwear and threw it into the tub, naked now. They held their groins so Momma couldn't see.

Momma said, "What, you think I no see boys before? Get in tub."

The boys stepped into the bucket, standing with their butts toward the window. Momma bent down and picked up one of the buckets and faced them with it.

Isaac and Toby knew what was coming now. They both backed up, but in the tub there was nowhere to go. Isaac stammered, "No, no. Don't you... Don't you dare. Don't. I swear, I'll..."

Whoosh. Momma threw the bucket of water on them.

"Aaieee. Cold! No!"

"Is cold, yes, is good for you."

Anna heard the screams, smiled, and gently pushed the curtain away. She positioned herself so that she and Momma couldn't see each other. Anna held the curtain by the bottom so that it wouldn't move, and peeked at the boys in all their nakedness from behind. She giggled. Another bucket of water hit the boys.

Isaac and Toby shouted, "Aaieee. No, please!"

Isaac's heart pounded in his chest. Toby's skinny little body shook with cold and fear, but Momma wasn't interested in their cries. "Scrub."

The boys stood in the tub, freezing and shivering. They scrubbed themselves all over as Momma picked up the last bucket of water.

Isaac pleaded, "Oh, no, no more, please, no."

Water on them.

Anna watched through the curtain. She giggled again and held her hand to her mouth.

Momma pointed to the towels and the clothes on the bench. "Dry off. Get clothes." She picked up the knife and faced the boys. They turned toward the window and stepped out of the tub to get the clothes.

From the turn, Anna now viewed the boys in all their full frontal nakedness. "Oh, my goodness." She turned her head away, but her eyes slanted back to the window. She watched the boys dry off and get into their clothes. They'd be coming in soon, and Momma too, so Anna scrambled back into the chair, straightened the curtain, crossed her legs, and shook her foot up and down.

The boys crashed through the door and into the kitchen, falling all over themselves. Momma stayed outside a minute to finish up, swishing the clothes around in the dirty water and hanging them over the bench to drain. Then she dumped the tub upside down and let the muddy remnants of the boys' dirt spill into the yard.

Isaac and Toby fell panting into chairs in the front room. Anna asked them, "Well, boys, have a good time?"

Momma came in with their wet clothes in her arms, water soaking her and dripping all over the kitchen floor. She hung the clothes over the fire to dry, meticulously arranging them over the potless frame. The fire crackled and spat.

Toby couldn't take it any longer. His eyes drooped. Anna looked over at Isaac, who stared straight at the ceiling, recovering his breath and dignity. Anna slipped over to Momma at the fire.

"Momma, they have to stay here tonight."

"Nein. They go. You father shoot them."

"Momma, it's late. You can't send them out in the cold. They'll die."

"They die you father find out."

"Momma, we won't tell Papa. It'll be our secret. Please, Momma? They can stay in my room. I'll sleep with you."

Momma shook her head in indecision. "Ah, Child, no. I no think..."

Anna kissed Momma on the cheek and turned to Isaac in the other room. "Come, Isaac. Let's get Toby to bed."

"Nein, you stay, they go."

Anna whispered, "Momma, I have things in there. I have to get them out."

Momma sighed in disapproval, then went back to drying the clothes. Anna and Isaac helped Toby out of the chair. They walked him a few steps toward the front of the house to a door to Anna's bedroom, to the right of the front door. Anna entered first.

Anna picked up some underwear on the bed and shoved it into her pockets. Toby fell into the bed and was fast asleep instantly. Anna went to a cabinet, retrieved two blankets, and plopped one on the bed. She spread the other one out and covered Toby with it.

Momma shouted from the other room, "Anna, come back here."

"Coming, Momma."

From the main room, the grandfather's clock chimed, "one, two, three..." Anna listened, then walked over to Isaac. She faced him and looked up into his eyes, their bodies barely touching.

"It's midnight, Isaac. You know what that means."

"It's seventeen-seventy-seven?"

"Yes." She took Isaac's left hand and wrapped it behind her back. Anna pressed herself against Isaac's body. "It's time."

They kissed. They kissed again, and again.

A voice crackled from what seemed like many, many miles away. "Anna, come here, girl."

Isaac closed his eyes. Anna took a deep breath and delicately extricated herself from Isaac's hug. "Coming, Momma."

Anna fixed her eyes on Isaac as she headed for the door. She sighed another deep breath. Before she left, she looked down at Toby, asleep, and rubbed his head. "Good night, Toby. Good night, Isaac."

Isaac was too stunned to reply. Anna left her bedroom, giggling.

Chapter Sixteen

Day Four, Wednesday, Jan 1, 1777.

The boys walked down the Quaker road toward Trenton. Through the sparse trees, they caught glimpses of an open field to their right. Toby asked, "We almost to Trenton?"

"The bridge is just ahead, then it's up through town and over to the ferry. We should be in Pennsylvania this afternoon."

"You think that British soldier is around here?"

"I don't think so. I hope not."

"What about them rebels we saw?"

"The rebels are in Philadelphia. Those were militia, I guess. The Tories will take care of them. Ha."

"I thought we wasn't Tories no more."

"Oh, yes. I forgot." Isaac smiled at the remembrance of Anna's kiss.

A stone bridge appeared as the Quaker Road curved north. The trees on their right became more and more dense, obscuring the field. Isaac frowned as he sniffed the air. "What's that?"

"What?"

"That smell, smoke. Maybe a fireplace, or something. See if there's any houses over there, but don't go too far."

Toby went three feet into the trees, looked around, and came back. "I don't see no houses."

Isaac stopped, nervously testing the air for the direction of the smoke. He could see that the trees cleared a little farther up. "Let's get up there. I don't like this."

Toby said, "It's probably just a house. That's Trenton up there, right? Over the bridge?"

"Yes. Probably the Trenton houses. All right, let's go."

The field came more clearly into view as they approached the thinning trees. Two hundred yards to the right, hundreds, hundreds of tents lined the Assunpink Creek. There was very little wind, so the smoke billowed high into the air from the many campfires.

Isaac peered through the trees in shock. "Holy Christ, the army's here. Damn." His voice turned into a harsh whisper. "Get down."

The field to their right was filled with wagons, cannons, tents and men. The boys crouched down, out of sight, scooting low to the last tree before the bridge. Isaac surveyed the field and whispered, "Damn. What are we going to do now? There must be five thousand men over there. Damn." Isaac looked over at the bridge and at the barren road that led to it. "Damn."

Toby glanced around at the road, the men, the bridge, and the road again. He said, aloud, "I don't see nobody on the other side of the creek."

Isaac admonished him, "Shhh." He scanned the area on the other side of the bridge. No, the rebel army was all south of the creek. Isaac searched the road for any signs of movement. "You're right. There's nobody over there, and nobody from here to the bridge."

Toby peered at the many men, so far away, but so dangerous if they were discovered. "Let's go back."

Isaac looked at him and said quietly, "No. We have to get to the bridge. There's nobody over there. If we can get to the bridge, we'll be all right."

Isaac peeked out a little more from behind the tree and whispered to Toby, "There's nobody on the other side, or to the left. Let's crawl on our bellies to the bridge. Maybe we can get under it and wade across, or swim, or something."

Toby shook his head. "It's all mud over there. We just took a bath."

Isaac raised his voice, "Hush up," then whispered, "Oops." He held his finger to his lips. "Shhh. It's our only chance."

The boys slid across to the left side of the Quaker Road on their bellies, Toby dragging their only gun. The ground was a few inches lower than the road on that side, so they were out of sight of any military eyes from the field. Isaac raised his head a couple of times to make sure that there was no unusual activity in the rebel camp. They crawled toward the Trenton Bridge, a hundred yards away.

A gruff voice boomed from behind them like the crash of thunder from an unexpected storm, "Get up!"

Isaac and Toby turned their heads backward and saw three muskets pointing at their backs. Isaac considered running to the bridge just as three more soldiers ran up and blocked the road with muskets ready. A soldier in front saw Isaac's eyes move toward their musket. "Leave your weapon on the ground, Tory, or you'll be in it."

Toby blurted out, "We ain't Tories no more."

The soldiers were startled by Toby's admission of being a Tory. One soldier grabbed Toby by his shirt and forcefully pulled him to his feet. Isaac yelled, "Leave him alone." Isaac rushed at the soldier. Another soldier jabbed his musket barrel into Isaac's side as he ran. "Oww!" Isaac clutched his ribs and plowed off to the left side of the road. The other soldiers ganged up on Isaac and pointed their muskets down, right at his chest.

Isaac got up slowly, holding his side. The boys were marched away.

Chapter Seventeen

Washington sat in his tent, going over the maps. Mercer, Fermoy, and Murphy stood next to him. "Fermoy, where's your regiment?"

"Colonel Hand's up there, at Five Mile Run. Colonel Hand, He's there."

Washington pretended to study the map. "Shouldn't you be up there also, general?" Fermoy reached into his pocket and felt for the flask of whiskey. Good. He glanced at Washington, who wasn't looking, but Mercer and Murphy saw the flask protrude from Fermoy's pocket.

Washington spoke without looking up. "General Fermoy, you know your orders?"

"Yes, sir."

Washington raised his head and held Fermoy in his gaze. "Send word back here the instant there's contact. Delay the enemy until we're in place."

"Yes, sir." Fermoy hoped the questioning was over. He focused peripherally at the tent opening as he stared at Washington. Washington went back to the maps. Fermoy was relieved. He headed for the freedom of the outside air, where he could take another swig to ward off the fear of commanding an army in battle. He got to the tent flap.

Washington never looked up, but said, "Make it cost them, General."

Fermoy's heart pounded. He felt Washington's steel eyes on the back of his head and turned around slowly. "Sir?"

Washington waited for Fermoy to face him directly. "I want them to know that it will cost them to cross that creek. Make them pay, General."

Fermoy saluted, "Yes sir," and exited the tent.

Mercer rolled his eyes and looked at Murphy. "We're doomed."

Washington heard that. "What?"

Mercer replied, "Nothing, Sir."

Washington gazed at two of his favorite soldiers, Mercer, a major general and a friend, and Murphy, another remarkable officer from another colony. Pennsylvania was far away from Virginia, almost another country, but Murphy was also a friend, in a way, if the commanding general could permit himself such thoughts.

Washington returned to the maps, his head down. "Hugh, tell Henry to put the guns behind us, on the road."

"Yes, Sir."

Mercer and Murphy turned toward the tent flap.

Washington said, "Don't go, not yet."

Washington stared at the two men again. He looked at Mercer first, the old friend from the Braddock campaign. What a disaster that was, twenty years ago, the last war, but Mercer was a Virginian.

"Hugh, we've been together for a long time."

Mercer looked curiously at the general. "Yes sir."

Washington considered asking the question, "Do you think I made a mistake?" But no, he was the General. Whatever happened, the blame fell on him. He did not ask the question.

Washington turned his thoughts to Murphy, a Pennsylvania Rifleman. What would he do without the riflemen? The Pennsylvanians were rough, tough, and uncouth, even a little dirty. They swore a lot, much unlike the men from Virginia, genteel farmers, or Boston men, educated merchants and booksellers, gentlemen all, who enjoyed a spring ride in the country. Virginia and Massachusetts were remarkably similar, given their geographical distance. Pennsylvania was different, like a different country.

Even so, the differences were apparent between Boston and Virginia. Boston men would fight anybody, any time, any place, no matter what the danger, especially if there was danger. They actually enjoyed the thrill of defying the most powerful military force in the world. It bound them together. Radicalism infected Boston and all of New England. The revolution would not have happened were it not for the men of Boston. Virginia, well, they were intellectual, rational, sensible men.

The Virginians had books. They could read. So could the people of Boston. Pennsylvanians, they were different. They had Ben Franklin, of course, the greatest scientist and writer of the New World, but he was the exception. Pennsylvanians were not considered the intellectual equivalents of Virginians or Massachusetts men.

But they sure could shoot. They seemed to know what to do without being told. They weren't radical, not intellectual. They were in the 'middle' colonies. They just did what had to be done.

Perhaps what made them different were the many whiskey farmers from out west, men who still fought the Indians. If a Pennsylvanian got into a fight with the Indians and lost, it would be very bad.

The men of Pennsylvania knew that. It made them tough and practical. Murphy had many of them in his command. Virginia and Massachusetts didn't have Indian problems. Pennsylvania did, so the Pennsylvanians had those deadly, long-barreled rifles. They needed them. The Indians didn't take prisoners, so losing and living was not an option for a Pennsylvanian.

All of these comparisons flowed through Washington's mind in a fraction of a second. Washington compared the competencies of these two officers intuitively with the general who had just left. He said, "That man scares me. I wish I didn't have to send him up there."

Mercer replied, "You have to, though. He's got the riflemen, and Congress will come down hard on you if you relieve him now."

"I know. I just wish I didn't know."

Mercer tried to reassure the General. "Colonel Hand's up there. He knows what to do."

Washington tried hard to accept the assurance that it would work out with Hand at the front. "All right. Murphy, you're with Hand, aren't you?"

"Yes, sir. I'm working on ordnance. I'm going up as soon as I can get away."

Washington rose slowly from his desk. He stared at the two men again. Mercer and Murphy watched his large frame rise and tower above them.

"Murphy"

"Yes, sir."

"I'm saying this to both of you. Hugh, you have to stay here. You know that, right?"

"Yes, sir."

Washington said, "This is confidential to both of you."

Mercer asked, "What is it, George?"

"I have something to say. Murphy..."

"Sir?"

"You're going up, right?"

Murphy said, "Yes, Sir."

Washington breathed deeply. "I can't order you to arrest a general, unless it's for treason or gross incompetence, and that would be very hard to prove."

Murphy and Mercer glanced sideways at each other, both knowing that something extraordinary was coming. Mercer added, "And he's a favorite of Congress, so you can't do that, George."

Washington nodded. "Murph, I'm sorry to put this burden on you, but if we lose up there, it's probably going to be the end. If you can get Ed Hand in charge, I'll be grateful. I'll support you in any way I can, such as it might be, if any of us are still alive."

Murphy got it. He could not let Fermoy cause a disaster up there at Five Mile Run. He said, "I won't let him lose it for us, sir."

Mercer and Murphy saluted. Washington returned. The two favorite officers stood silently. Washington said, "Make them pay, Murph. Send Ed Hand my regards."

Feelings of determination welled up in Murphy's eyes. "Yes, sir."

Washington said, "All right, gentlemen, let's move. The enemy is already late."

Chapter Eighteen

Outside the tent, Murphy looked around. Hundreds of men worked hard, feeding horses, loading wagons, and stuffing cannonballs into guns. A few men even drilled, ordered by officers to "Left front, right wheel." The men crashed into each other. Murphy shook his head at the chaos as a soldier approached.

"Sir, we caught some locals coming into camp. They could be spies. Over here."

Murphy and the soldier walked to another tent ten yards away and went in. Isaac and Toby sat on boxes. Another soldier guarded them. Murphy said, "Who are you?"

Silence.

"Who are you and what are you doing here?"

"One of them said they were Tories, sir."

Toby blurted out, "I didn't say we was Tories. I said we *was* Tories. I mean, we used to be Tories."

Isaac shouted, "Hush up, Toby."

Murphy couldn't believe he heard that name, 'Toby.' He stared intensely at the boys. "Toby? Your name's Toby? How old are you, boy?"

"Fourteen."

Isaac said, "Don't tell him anything."

Murphy's jaw clenched. His mind raced, calculating the present age of his two sons. He did the math, looking at Isaac. "What's your name?"

Isaac stared at the ground.

"How old are you, about eighteen?"

Toby said, "He's seventeen."

Isaac yelled, "Toby!"

"He was just asking, Isaac."

Murphy's gaze shot to the ceiling, wide-eyed. "Oh, no. Oh, my God." He walked out of the tent, his head low.

The soldier followed him out. "What is it, sir?"

Murphy kicked the ground. He shook his head, shuffled the mud around with his foot, and mumbled. "Oh, no, it can't be." He looked down at his left hand. It trembled a little, but he held it against his thigh so the soldier wouldn't see.

Murphy went back into the tent. The soldier ducked low under the tent flap and came in behind him. The other soldier followed Murphy with his eyes, glancing from Murphy to his friend. The soldier behind Murphy shrugged his shoulders, indicating that he didn't know what was happening.

Murphy stared at the boys in self-absorbed concentration and worry. "Your mother is Maggie?"

The boys gaped at Murphy.

"Your father is John Sinclair? Your mother runs a fabric shop or something?"

Toby made the correction, "It's a dress shop."

The two soldiers looked at each other. One asked, "Captain Murphy, what is it?"

Isaac jumped off his box. "Murphy? You're Murphy? Warren Murphy? I'll kill you."

Isaac charged at Murphy with his fist in the air. Murphy ducked to the side to avoid the punch. The two soldiers grabbed Isaac and threw him roughly back onto the box.

Isaac raged, "Why did you leave us? Do you know what you did to us? And Ma? I hate you. I swear I'll kill you."

Toby's jaw dropped. "You're our father? Pa?"

Murphy said, "Look, I don't have time to explain what happened with your mother and me. Is she all right, and John?"

Toby looked for Isaac to answer the question, but Isaac couldn't speak. Toby offered the answer. "He left last year, went back to England."

"I'm sorry to hear that. He was a good man."

Isaac choked out his contempt, "He was a coward."

Murphy asked, "What are you doing here?"

Toby said, "Ma says we have to go to Allentown, away from the war."

"Ah, yes, her sister."

Toby, ever the one to offer more information than was asked, said, "Then Isaac's coming back to fight the..."

Isaac slapped his hand across Toby's mouth. Toby struggled to breathe. Isaac relaxed his grip and whispered, "Hush up."

Isaac looked at Murphy. "The Tories. And the British. I'm coming back to fight the British."

"No. Nobody's crossing that river for a long time. Isaac, you come with me tomorrow. Toby, you stay here until the fighting's done, then I'll get you both home."

Murphy turned toward the soldiers. "Put 'em to work. And keep an eye on them."

Isaac shot a hateful stare at Murphy. "We're leaving."

"No, you're not. I can't take a chance you'll give us away, and there's nobody to guard you."

"You can't order us around. You're not our... well, you can't tell us what to do."

The soldiers gripped their muskets. Murphy said to one of them, "Shoot 'em as spies."

Isaac suspected a bluff, but he wasn't sure. He sensed something in that casual order to blow their heads off that wasn't really an order. He hated his father for leaving, but he never remembered his father being mean. The trouble was that Murphy wasn't doing the shooting. Would those soldiers know it was a bluff?

Isaac smirked, "Go ahead."

One soldier looked at Murphy for confirmation of the order. The other soldier, knowing Murphy a little better, and perhaps teenage boys also, calmly feathered the tip of his rifle. He blew a piece of dust off the opening and rubbed his finger over the barrel, stalling for time. The soldier then calmly raised his gun, clicked the cock, and pointed it at Isaac's nose.

The other soldier aimed his gun at Toby's head. Murphy didn't interfere. Murphy eyed the soldiers unemotionally. They looked back, but kept their rifles pointing.

Fear intensified in Toby's face as the bluff played out. Murphy said to the soldiers, "I gave you an order."

Toby screamed, "Isaac! No!"

Isaac folded. "All right, all right. Wait. All right, I'll go with you, but Toby comes with me."

Murphy, relieved, said, "I give the orders here."

Isaac paused. He decided to call the bluff again, if only out of self-respect. Two short words would tell,

"Ma says."

That did it. Murphy told the men, "Stand down." The soldiers lowered their rifles. Murphy left the tent. Toby breathed with relief.

Chapter Nineteen

T he life of a single mother in 1777 was difficult, as Maggie Murphy-Sinclair knew all too well. With two small mouths to feed, the product of her second marriage, she worried continually about what would become of her family, and now there was a war, and her sons were gone. Her conscience struggled to affirm that she did the right thing. There was Murphy in her thoughts, too, so long ago. She wondered what he looked like now, or if he was even still alive.

She sliced vegetables at the kitchen table. The children, ages four and five, sat at the table eating soup. Maggie noticed the one child staring at her. "Mommy, are you crying?"

"It's the onions, dear."

Maggie continued to chop with a small paring knife as the children watched her. Tears rolled down Maggie's face.

"Mommy, when are the boys coming home?"

Maggie gazed past the vegetables, past the table, through the floor and into the deep, dark earth far below. The knife cut slowly and by itself.

"Mommy, when are Isaac and Toby –"

"Ow." Blood poured out of Maggie's left index finger. Ow, Ow."

"Mommy, Mommy."

Maggie stuck her finger in her mouth and sucked out the blood, then recovered a little for the sake of the children. "I'm all right, children. It's all right. I just cut... I cut my - Just a little."

Maggie sobbed as she put the knife into her pocket. She examined her finger again, which was still bleeding. "Oh, my God, I can't. I just can't." She put her finger back in her mouth.

"It's all right, children. Just my finger. I have to just..." She ran out of the kitchen in tears.

In the bedroom, Maggie found a cloth, tied it around her finger, and held it tight against the wound. The bleeding stopped, but not the anguish. She stared into a mirror above the dresser. Her eyes turned red from crying.

"Oh, Isaac, Toby, Warren. Dear God, I'm sorry. I don't mean to send them away. I drive everybody away. I don't mean to. Please don't take them, God. Isaac, forgive me. Toby..."

She cried fitfully into her hands. "Please don't take them. Please, please. I'll die if... (Hiccup) I'll just die, God. I won't be able to live (gag, hiccup)."

Maggie pleaded to the pitiful face in the mirror, "I promise, God. I promise. I won't send them away anymore. Please don't take them (gag, gag, hiccup, gag). I promise (hiccup, hiccup, hiccup)." She grabbed a pan next to the bed and threw up.

Maggie wiped her eyes and mouth. She walked tearfully back into the kitchen where the children noticed her rumpled face. "Mommy, are you all right?"

"Yes, children. Eat your soup."

Chapter Twenty

Isaac and Toby lay in cots, half asleep. Murphy entered the tent and nervously sat down on a box. He set his gun to the side. They all looked at each other anxiously. "You boys all right? You get anything to eat?"

Isaac said, "Yeah."

"You know, I didn't just up and leave you mother. It was a mutual thing. We just couldn't get along."

Toby asked, "You knew about John?"

"Yes, of course. I liked him. I knew he could take care of you. It's hard to explain. Don't you remember all that yelling?"

Toby said, "Yes. That bothered me a lot."

Isaac watched. The anger was gone in his eyes but not the suspicion. Murphy continued, "Yes, me, too. And her. Always arguing, yelling, crying, but we really did love each other. Still do, I guess. I send her money whenever I can, even though I don't have much."

Isaac opened up, "I remember she pointed a gun at your, your, you know, your..." Isaac's gaze fell awkwardly to Murphy's crotch. Murphy followed Isaac's eyes.

"Ha. You remember that, do you? Ha. You couldn't have been more than ten. Yes, we sure had our battles."

Murphy picked up Isaac's almost imperceptible smile. Isaac asked, "You had sex after that, didn't you? I heard it."

"What? You heard us? No, that's not possible. You couldn't have. Did you? You heard us? Damn. I thought we were pretty careful." Murphy faked a faint annoyance. "How did you hear that? You couldn't have heard that. We were careful. Ah, never mind. Yes, we usually did make up, you know, sometimes, in that way."

Toby turned his head. "Eeewww."

Murphy said, "Where do you think you came from?"

Isaac agreed, "Yeah, ya little runt."

Isaac and Murphy chuckled. Toby stared at them in confusion. There was a long pause, but then Isaac's face turned from a faint glow to a frown. "You left us with John."

Murphy caught Isaac's change in mood. "I'm sorry, Isaac. I didn't know it would affect you so much. It just got harder and harder to make up. It's completely my fault, not your mother's. My fault. I'm sorry. I guess I couldn't handle conflict back then. Now, look. I'm in a war."

Toby listened to the conversation. "What do you do now? You married?"

"No, not married. I have a small hog farm in West Chester."

Isaac didn't smile any more. He remembered the hurt from losing his father, so long ago. "I bet that stinks."

Murphy looked at Isaac, searching for a little humor in his eyes. He was disappointed. It wasn't a joke, just a sarcastic remark from a bitter son. Murphy changed the subject. "Yes, well, I'm with the First Pennsylvania Riflemen. I report to Colonel Hand."

Toby frowned. "What do you mean, 'report to?' you give him reports, like in school?"

Murphy smiled, happy that he had a chance to explain a little military protocol to someone who seemed interested. He glanced at Isaac, but Isaac turned away. Murphy looked back at Toby. "No, I, uh, I like, I work for him. He's my commanding officer. Hand reports to, uh, Hand works for General Fermoy."

Toby was curious. "Who works for Washington?"

Murphy said, "We all do."

Toby said, "Ma hates him, you know."

Murphy asked, "Who?"

"Washington."

"What?"

Toby said, "Yes, she hates him. Right, Isaac?"

Isaac shook his head, "Yes."

Murphy was confused. "Why?"

Toby said, "He started the war."

What?"

Isaac stared obsessively at Murphy for the reply to Toby's statement that Washington started the war, but he didn't say anything.

Toby asked Isaac, for confirmation, "Didn't Ma say Washington started the war?"

Murphy repeated, "What?" He almost lost control. "Washington didn't start the war. Don't you boys know anything about this war? Ah." Murphy settled down and sighed the deep breath of an unintentionally neglectful father.

Isaac spoke now. "Then why are we in a war? Anna's mother damn-near killed Toby when he said we were, uh, you know, in a war."

"Who's Anna? And why does your mother hate Washington? She knows about the war. She knows what it's all about."

Isaac said, "I don't know. She hates Franklin, too. I guess she hates everybody."

Murphy lowered his head. "That could be because of me."

Toby asked, "So who works for you?"

Murphy was grateful for the change in subject. "I have some men who report to me. One of my best men is Sergeant Swanson. I expect you might meet him tomorrow. I'm with the Pennsylvania Riflemen. We marched 300 miles to Boston, came all the way back down here. Lost only a few men so far."

Toby tensed up at the thought of death. "What? You mean they died? How did they die? Did they get shot?"

Murphy brightened a little, enjoying the conversation. Even Isaac listened to what Murphy was saying. Murphy noticed Isaac's momentary enthusiasm and paused for a moment, careful to keep up the fragile momentum.

"Toby, in a war, men die. The point is, in my regiment, my group, we've lost very few men. We have an edge on the enemy. Sorry, the British. The British are the enemy. You know that, don't you?"

Isaac said, "Yes, of course we do. So why did only a few men die? You're in the war. Lots of men died so far."

Murphy reached for his rifle. "Because of this. We have a very special weapon."

Murphy held his rifle in both hands and handed it to Isaac. Isaac took it with one hand, but the unbalanced weight caused the stock to hit the floor of the tent. Murphy said, "Easy, Isaac."

Isaac picked it up and examined it. He moved it up and down in the air to test its weight. It was heavy, but not really different than every other gun he'd ever seen. Isaac shrugged, "It's a gun."

Murphy corrected him, "It's a rifle, a Kentucky Long Rifle."

Toby watched Isaac turn the gun around and around. Toby was fascinated. He frowned at Isaac's mishandling of it, treating it like a toy. Toby asked Isaac, "Can I see it?" Isaac handed the rifle to Toby. Toby fondled it carefully, looking down the barrel and cocking the flintlock back and forth. Toby looked up at Murphy. "It's not loaded."

"I don't keep it loaded, except if we're in a fight. To tell you the truth, there's no need for me to load it."

Toby inspected the gun further. "I heard about these. Gosh, a 'long' rifle. They can hit something from a long ways away, right?"

"Some of our men can kill a man at 300 yards. Trouble is, it takes a long time to load." Murphy pulled up the flap of his coat and displayed a long knife from a sheath. "The British like to charge. They love to charge. Scares the hell out of everybody. You can't be loading your rifle when the British charge. You need a big knife."

Murphy put the knife back in its sheath. "It's better to stay far away and shoot, as long as you have time to load."

Isaac listened thoughtfully. On Murphy's gaze, he pretended indifference, but he was curious about the guns and the British.

Isaac said, "Toby can shoot."

Murphy said to Toby, "I remember. You were a good shot. You used to shoot from your hip, didn't you?"

Isaac saw an opportunity to squeal on his little brother. "Yes, but he won't shoot. Not even a goose. In the swamp, he wouldn't even shoot a goose when we were starving. If not for Anna, we'd have starved to death in the swamp."

Murphy was surprised at Isaac's sudden enthusiasm. "Who's Anna?"

"She's the girl at the swamp. On the Quaker Road. She lives there. I mean, on a farm, next to the swamp. We stayed there last night."

"I see." Murphy saw a chance to leave on a high note. He got up from the box. "Get some rest, sons. We leave tomorrow for the point." Murphy left, satisfied that he had a good breaking-in session with his sons.

Toby removed his pants, getting ready for bed. He asked Isaac, "What's a point?"

"You know, it's a, uh, I don't know, it's a, well, a point, you know. Like on a map. Don't you know anything?"

Chapter Twenty One

Day Five, Thursday, Jan 2, 1777 1:00 p.m.
Five Mile Run

Colonel Hand sat on a horse, talking to Sergeant Swanson, who still had the bandage around his head. Ten soldiers stood around Swanson, listening to the conversation. General Fermoy was ten yards back toward Trenton. Hand asked Swanson, "See anything yet?"

Swanson replied, "Not since Tuesday, those boys. We have pickets, so we'll be warned."

Murphy walked up from the south, Isaac and Toby trailing behind. Sergeant Swanson faced Princeton, talking to Hand, so Swanson didn't see Murphy yet.

Murphy handed Fermoy a note. "From the general, sir."

Fermoy leaned down to take the note, but lost his balance. He clutched his saddle horn to keep from falling and slowly straightened up. His hands shook as he unfolded the note. Fermoy read the note once to himself, then again out loud so that Murphy could hear it, "Report back the instant there's contact." Fermoy looked down at Murphy, and then raised his eyes in expectation of a reply.

Murphy frowned. "What? So, report back the instant there's contact. What?"

Fermoy said, "Yes. Report back. The instant there's contact."

Murphy got it now. "Who, me? I can't go back. Send somebody else back. You go back. You're the goddamn general, not me."

Hand and Swanson heard the developing argument and stopped talking.

Fermoy shouted, "You can't address me like that. I'm your superior officer. I'll have you court-mars-r-aled. Marshaled. Court-marshaled."

Fermoy pointed his finger at Murphy, but the weight of his outstretched arm disturbed the torque of his carefully balanced saddle position.

Murphy watched. "Yeah, sure." Murphy walked away toward Colonel Hand and Sergeant Swanson.

Fermoy slid off the horse and fell into the mud. The horse galloped away a short distance, riderless, into the woods. Fermoy went after it, ducking low branches. He caught up and reached for the horse's reins, but the horse just wouldn't cooperate. "Steady, Rosebud, come over here." The horse pulled away. Fermoy gave up. He sat in the muddy road, took a flask of whisky out of his pocket, and sneaked a long swig. The horse snorted from ten feet away.

Fermoy got up, steadied himself, and fell against a tree. "Here, horsey, horsey." The horse grunted and slapped its hoof at the ground. Fermoy approached it slowly. "Here, horsey." The horse stood still this time. Fermoy breathed a sigh. "Good horsey."

Fermoy stroked the horse's side, hoping he was in charge again, but not so. He threw his whole body over the saddle again, belly-first, but the horse turned at the sudden assault and twisted its neck toward Fermoy's legs. Fermoy plunged over the other side of the horse, turned upside down, and fell to the ground on his back.

The alcohol numbed the pain. He got up and tried again. Foot in the stirrup, he threw himself over the saddle. Fermoy straightened himself and took the reins, in command again, of a horse. He reached into his pocket, pulled out his flask, and took another swig.

Murphy walked toward Colonel Hand, with Isaac and Toby following. Fermoy trotted up to Murphy, Swanson, and Hand, but stayed ten yards down, drinking. Hand faced Trenton. Swanson faced Princeton.

Murphy came up and addressed Swanson. "Borg, I need you to take care of these boys."

Swanson looked behind Murphy and recognized Isaac as the boy who ran under his horse the day before yesterday. He reached up to his bandaged head instinctively. "Ach du yungen."

Isaac recognized Swanson, turned and ran. Murphy grabbed Isaac by the shirt as he sidestepped to avoid Toby. "What's going on here?" Isaac stopped, so Murphy released his grip. Isaac stared at the ground like a guilty schoolboy.

Murphy asked Swanson, "You know each other?"

"He try and kill me. He give me this cut on head. I shoot this rascal." Swanson pulled back the hammer of his long rifle and reached for his powder horn.

"Wait a minute. Sergeant, wait. Borg, I don't know what's going on here, but these are my sons."

"You sons? What sons you have try and kill me? You no say you habben sie kinder here."

"It's a long story, Borg. I'll tell you all about it after the war. Right now, I need you to take care of them. Don't get them shot, all right? A favor for me, Borg."

Swanson glared menacingly at Isaac. "All's right, but they do as I say, or I shoot them myself."

Murphy replied, "That's fair."

Swanson looked at Isaac. "A word to the wise is enough."

Isaac said, "All right, sure."

"But many won't fill a bushel."

Isaac frowned at Toby. Toby shrugged his shoulders.

Indiscernible shouts came from the Princeton direction. Three soldiers appeared from ahead, yelling "British, British." Everybody turned toward Princeton. The soldiers stumbled into the company and fell to their knees.

Hand said, "What is it?"

"British! Hundreds of them! Five hundred yards up, coming this way."

Fermoy shouted, "I have to warn the general." He turned his horse and bolted toward Trenton as fast as he could ride. Everyone watched him go in shock and disbelief.

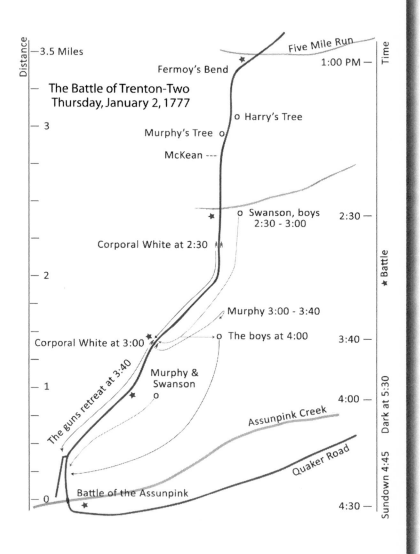

Distance

— 3.5 Miles

The Battle of Trenton-Two
Thursday, January 2, 1777

Fermoy's Bend

Five Mile Run

1:00 PM —

— 3

o Harry's Tree

Murphy's Tree o

McKean ---

o Swanson, boys
2:30 - 3:00

2:30 —

Corporal White at 2:30

— 2

Murphy 3:00 - 3:40

o The boys at 4:00

3:40 —

Corporal White at 3:00

The guns retreat at 3:40

Murphy &
Swanson
o

— 1

4:00 —

Assunpink Creek

Quaker Road

Battle of the Assunpink

— 0

4:30 —

Time

★ Battle

Dark at 5:30

Sundown 4:45

Chapter Twenty Two

Murphy glanced up at Hand on the horse. "I guess you're in charge now."

"Damn. Damn him. Hang him, that jackass of a general." Hand looked down the road to see Fermoy disappear around a bend. He closed his eyes tight and shook his head hard. "Damn him." The blast of his voice made his horse stagger to the side. Hand steadied the horse and moved to the right side of the road to get a better view north. "Damn."

Colonel Edward Hand had unexpectedly been thrust into command of one of the top five most important military engagements in American history, perhaps higher, perhaps even number one, because if Edward Hand failed to delay the British until sundown, there likely wouldn't be any more American military engagements.

The willingness of Hand's men to obey his orders had now been cut in half with the disappearance of Fermoy. An American soldier from Massachusetts, Pennsylvania, Virginia, anywhere, they'd obey any general, although reluctantly, no matter where he was from. The consequences were grave for disobeying a direct order from a general.

But a colonel had to be twice the leader of a general in order for his men to obey. A major had to be twice as brave as a colonel and be more persuasive, but not as much as a captain. For a captain to order his men to charge into fixed British bayonets, that captain would be better employed telling his men to retreat. That they'd do. The skill of leadership and persuasion for a successful officer must go up as his rank went down.

And now Edward Hand was in the fight of his life, and there was no general there. A general, any general, even a drunken fool of a general, would ensure that the men would do as ordered. No such luck for Colonel Edward Hand and the brave but simple souls he commanded.

Hand said to Murphy, "All right, go back and warn the others. Take charge 'til I get there. Get them off the road into the woods. We'll be there shortly." Hand dismounted. Murphy climbed up on Hand's horse and galloped back.

Hand gave an order, "Off the road, everybody. You know what to do. Keep track of the sun."

The road ran southwest at this point. The sun was two-thirds of the way across the sky, to the west of the road. The road curved farther south a half-mile away, toward Trenton, where Fermoy's dust still hung in the still air.

Swanson gathered his men. "Off road." Isaac and Toby listened. "You, boys, get here." The boys walked into the woods on the east side of the road with Swanson and several other soldiers. "Get down. When we fire, run back through woods. No road."

The British, lots of them, appeared on the road in file. The Americans on both sides hid behind trees and gripped their rifles. The British passed Swanson on the east and Hand on the west without seeing the Americans. Hand watched them go past from his side of the road. The British were only a few yards away, with just a few insignificant trees in the way. The Americans on both sides fingered their triggers. They wished they had some of those damned musket men with them, able to reload and fire every thirty seconds, but only Isaac and Toby were there today.

The British stopped, no doubt wary of a straight and deserted road under the circumstances. Hand stood up so all could see him.

"Fire." All the Americans stood up, on both sides. A British officer turned toward Hand's voice. Hand's rifle didn't miss. A puff of dust appeared in the middle of the officer's chest.

Bullets flew from both sides of the road, hitting the British with eighty-percent accuracy. These men had been around guns since they were ten years old, so they knew how to shoot. Swanson's group fired. Isaac hit a tree. Toby didn't shoot. More British fell as several riflemen held their fire to get a better shot, but no one fired twice. Hand's Americans ran back fast, all unloaded.

Swanson scolded Toby, "Boy, why you no shoot?"

Toby had a loaded gun. He froze, watching the British through the trees. Swanson took Toby's musket, fired, and hit a British soldier. He handed the musket back to Toby "You shoot, boy. All back."

The British fired into the woods on both sides and crept back warily. Swanson's group slinked through the woods toward Trenton. More British came up to retrieve the dead and wounded. As the Americans rounded Fermoy's Bend, they slowed and reloaded, still keeping to the protection of the trees.

* * *

South of the bend, Murphy halted his horse at another small group of riflemen. One of them asked, "What's happening?"

Murphy replied, "Our guests have arrived. Get ready. Hand's coming down."

Hand plowed out of the woods on the left side of the road with dozens of panting Americans. Swanson came out on the right with the boys, his men, and others. Two hundred yards now separated the two forces. Hand looked at his men. "All right. We have a few minutes. They'll bring the artillery up now. Everybody rest and reload, then back into the woods. Anybody hurt?" Nobody replied. "Good. Murphy, get some musket men up here. There's too many British for rifles."

The Americans reloaded and dispersed into the woods, their numbers augmented now with the additional riflemen. Hand went to the left. Murphy turned his horse toward Trenton and was about to head down when Isaac yelled, "Pa."

Murphy said, "I can't help you now, boys. I have other duties." Murphy galloped away. The boys went into the woods and joined Swanson heading east.

Murphy arrived at the next group of soldiers down the road. The men milled around, oblivious of the danger, even though they could hear shots closely north. Jackson sat on a log in tears and held his head in his hands. "Oh, no. Oh, my God, what am I going to tell my Ma?" His friend, Harry, stood by his side with his hand on Jackson's shoulder.

Murphy tightened the reigns of his horse and stopped. He sensed a big problem here, five men doing nothing but watching their leader sob into his hands in the snowy road, with a thousand British less than a mile away. Some of the men fought back tears. Murphy dismounted and slowly tied the horse to a tree, checking the knot to make sure it was secure. He checked the knot again, not because the horse might run away, but because he wanted time to think. He needed these men, and right now, they were not manageable.

Murphy looked toward Princeton at the first blast of British cannon fire. Sensing a disaster looming, he walked up to the group of men and stood next to Harry as another British cannon boomed from the north.

Jackson looked up, then cried again into his hands. Harry tapped Jackson on the head. "Jack, our officer's here."

Murphy asked, "What's happening?"

Jackson looked up at Murphy and cried, "Satchel's dead. How am I going to tell my Ma?"

Harry said to Murphy, "He died this morning. Consumption, they said. We just found out. Walter was with him." Harry motioned toward one of the soldiers nearby.

Walter came over at the sound of his name and said, "He just went to sleep, Jack. He said, 'Tell Jack I'm sorry.' Then he went to sleep. He was all right, Jack." Walter looked up at Murphy "He just went to sleep." Walter kicked the ground.

Murphy looked sadly at Jackson, still on his hands and knees in the mud. "I'm sorry, son. I'm very sorry." Another cannon blast and rifle fire came from the north, closer than before, which meant that the British had rounded Fermoy's Bend. "Jackson. Jackson, can you get up?" Jackson still cried, immobilized with grief. Murphy turned to Harry for help.

Harry said, "Jack, get up. He's our officer. Get up, Jack."

Jackson lashed out verbally at Murphy and Harry. "He was my brother. My Ma said to take care of him. Now he's dead. I sent him into the river. I shouldn't never have sent him into the river. How can I go home? I can't never go home no more. God, Satchel. Oh, my God, Ma, I'm so sorry."

Murphy whispered to Harry, "Get yourself and two men on the other side of the road." Harry motioned west to Walter and another soldier and the three of them went off to the left.

Murphy said softly, "Jackson, you need to get up. Can you get up?" Murphy reached down, took Jackson's hand, and pulled him up. Jackson struggled to his feet.

"I'll help you tell your mother. I promise you your mother will understand. Not right away, but she will. I promise. All right? That's a promise. She'll understand. Right now, though, I need you to get your men off the road to the right."

Jackson recovered a bit. He rubbed the mud off his pants and wiped his tears. Streaks of mud rolled down his cheeks, but he stopped crying.

Murphy looked at the remaining men on the road. "You men, off to the right. Jackson, you all right?" Murphy touched Jackson's arm.

Jackson sniffled, "Yes, I guess."

Jackson turned to the right, but Murphy grabbed his arm to steady him. Murphy called over to the other group of soldiers who ducked branches to go west. He held Jackson and called to Harry, "Wait a minute. Harry, that your name? Harry?"

Harry turned around. "Yes."

"Come here."

Harry turned around and joined Murphy and Jackson in the middle of the road. The two groups of men bunched up on each side, watching, listening closely.

Murphy peered seriously at the two young men. "Look, the British are going to try and outflank us on both sides." Murphy looked at each of the soldiers separately. "Get your men out there and stay low, about twenty yards up, fifty yards in. Harry, you're on the left. Jackson, the right. Blast 'em and run like hell back here. Keep the sun on your right."

Both boys said, "Yes, sir."

"Go."

Harry and Jackson went off to their respective sides of the road with two men each. A few quick words were all that was needed for their men to understand, and they all disappeared into the woods. Murphy looked north again, hoping that his orders came in time, that the British were not already too far into the woods for Jackson and Harry to get behind them. The sounds of cannons and gunshots all around worried him even more.

Colonel Hand stumbled out of the woods from the west side of the road with scratches on his face and torn trousers. He collapsed to the ground, huffing and puffing, at the hooves of Murphy's horse, then looked up. "Hi, Murph. Everything going according to plan?"

"You really shouldn't be on the point. You're going to get shot."

Hand said, "Ah, what's the difference?"

Murphy asked, "You want your horse back?"

"Nah, you need her more than I do. You're too old to walk."

Murphy laughed, "True."

Hand said, "Probably outlive me, though. We'll know by sundown."

"Ah, don't say that."

Hand smiled. "All right, get back down. Take care of the next group. I'll be sending British your way."

Isaac, Toby, Swanson, and others came out of the woods on the right side of the road. Other men emerged from the left. Cannon shots sounded from the Princeton direction, solid shot. Trees went down. Branches were torn away. Twigs, branches and leaves fell all over everybody. There was a twenty-second pause, and then another volley. Many Americans came onto the road from up ahead.

Hand said, "They've got the guns up." He shouted to Murphy, "Keep with the plan." Hand and others disappeared to the left. Murphy trotted away south.

Swanson looked at Toby. "Boy, you shoot, you hear me?"

Toby said, "I can't shoot a man, I just can't. I'm sorry, I just can't."

Isaac asked Swanson, "What's 'the plan'?"

"Stay in front and far away. Slow them down."

The Americans were 1200 yards south of the slight curve they now called, 'Fermoy's Bend.' Swanson looked toward Princeton. Red uniforms appeared around a slow curve to the left, but they were still too far away to hit. Swanson grabbed Toby by the arm and spun him around. "You load." He looked at Isaac. "You shoot."

Swanson, the boys, and others went off to the right, toward Jackson's location, but much closer to the road. Jackson and his two men made their way into the woods, keeping low, dodging trees, and moving east.

Isaac whispered to Toby, "'In front'? What does that mean? In front of what?"

Toby replied, "In front of them, I think."

Isaac nodded, "Oh, yeah."

Swanson told his men, "Wait. Stay still." The British approached slowly, bunched up in the road, but Swanson knew that firing through trees at that angle would do no good. Swanson repeated, "Wait."

On the other side, Hand had the same problem, but the plan was working well. Six hundred yards away, the British slowed to avoid any trouble, taking a full fifteen minutes to get that close. There was also sporadic gunfire from far up around the bend by American stragglers who didn't keep with the plan. For Hand, another half-hour would work out just fine for them to get about 200 yards away.

The wait was agonizing for the Americans on both sides, glaring at the dangerous sea of red uniforms through the trees, the enemy coming right at them, and nothing they could do but wait. Five more minutes, and five more, and then,

A gunshot from a jittery rifleman on Hand's west side hit a tree. Another shot from Swanson's side sounded from up ahead, and the faint but dreaded British order, "Charge!" was heard all through the American line. The British rushed down the road with fixed bayonets. Hand yelled, "Cease fire." Swanson yelled, "No shoot." All the Americans on both sides fired, at targets 600 yards away through trees. Isaac fired. Even Swanson fired, but not a single British soldier was hit. Billows of futile gun smoke climbed into the trees in the windless air.

Hand said, "Damn. Damn. Pull back. Pull back."

Every American zigzagged to the road and then sprinted south. Hand stepped onto the road and yelled, "Halt!" defiant of the British charge, which didn't matter anyway, because the British were too far away. The men slowed to a walk, ashamed of their momentary breech of discipline. The charging British saw only fifteen cowardly figures in the road in front of them, turned, and laughed as they walked back to their lines.

Jackson and his men lay down in the light snow, far into the woods and hidden behind trees and bushes, adjacent to Hand and Swanson. Fifty yards toward the road, Jackson saw Swanson's Americans running south.

A dozen British soldiers appeared in the woods. The British walked hunched over, looking to their right, being very cautious of any rebels near the road. One soldier loaded as he walked. Lawrence led the group. He ordered his men, "Forget the gun, use the bayonet."

Lawrence's men passed Jackson's position. They were ten yards to the left, far from the road, but they'd been outflanked themselves by Jackson.

Being flanked in a battle was bad. The enemy, Jackson, in this case, was east of Lawrence. Lawrence's men were in a line, tightly packed, perpendicular to the road. From Jackson's view, the British formed a narrow column, almost a single line, several men, only a few men protruding a few feet from the linear view of Jackson's sight.

Jackson's men were spread out to the left and right of the column, forming a "T" at the end of the British line. If Jackson fired, his men couldn't help but hit someone. Even if a bullet missed its target, the British were so clumped together that the bullet would still sail west until it hit another man, or another. On the other hand, if Lawrence's men tried to shoot, they'd likely hit one of their own men. When a soldier was flanked, he was in trouble, and likely dead.

Jackson rose up. He whispered to his men, "On four." The men stood up, concealed behind trees, and leveled their muskets. Jackson counted quietly, "One, two, three, fire." Two muskets fired at the same time, but Jackson held his fire. One British soldier was hit.

Lawrence looked to his left and saw shadowy figures looming among the trees. "Aaieee, flanked."

Then Jackson fired. He hoped that this strategy would conceal how many men he had. A soldier fell. Others crashed into trees to get away. Jackson yelled, "Reload. All of you," meaning 'both' of you. Jackson was proud of his newfound military skill and forgot about Satchel for a minute.

On Harry's side, a similar situation developed. Seven British soldiers were stalking the Americans, but they were closer to the road than Harry and his two men. Harry watched them carefully. At Jackson's blast, those British turned toward the road to see what was happening far on the other side. As soon as they turned away, Harry shouted, "Fire." Two British were shot, three others backed up toward the road, and two others fired at Harry's men. One bullet hit a tree, the other dropped leaves down on Harry from high in the air.

But now Harry was unloaded. He didn't know if he should run or fire again. "Load," he said.

Two more British shots didn't even go ten feet through the trees. Harry, Walter, and the other soldier backed up slowly as they reloaded. Harry's British hesitated, then heard commotion from the other side, Lawrence's solders running and yelling as they came back to the road.

Harry yelled, "Fire!" His men looked at him. They were nowhere near loaded. The British on Harry's side rushed to the road to regroup with their comrades on Jackson's side.

Harry raised his musket in the air as he ran. He looked to his left and saw Jackson running, far away, on the other side. Jackson turned his eyes to the right. He smiled at Harry through the trees and his tear-stained eyes.

Chapter Twenty Three

With Hand and Swanson retreating south, Jackson and his men were now the northern-most point of the American defense. Jackson looked south, slowed, and then shuffled west. Harry, on the other side, did the same, and then all of Jackson's men met on the road.

Harry walked over to Jackson. "You all right?"

"Yeah, I guess."

Harry laughed. "I guess we got 'em. They'll never come down here now. Ha."

Another soldier chimed in, "Jack, you see that big one? I plugged him good."

Walter, the soldier who was with Satchel when he died, said, "I got me a officer."

Harry said, "He weren't no officer."

"Yes, he was. He was a officer. I swear."

Harry laughed. "All right, he was a officer. Man, they sure ran like rabbits."

They all laughed. Even Jackson smiled. Harry said, "You sure you're all right?"

"Yeah. The captain says he can help me with my Ma."

"Yes, he can do that. He can do anything."

Musket shots sounded from the Princeton direction. They were from deep in the woods and there were no British on the road ahead, so Jackson didn't like the sound of that. He asked everyone, "Where do you think they are?" Harry shrugged his shoulders.

Jackson took command again. "We better get back into the woods, deep. Work our way south. Harry, get over there, across the road where you were, and don't get shot."

The men scrambled into the woods on both sides. Jackson went east, Harry west, but Harry paused at a tall tree on his side of the road. Walter said, "Harry, are you with us?"

Harry stared at the tree, up and down. "Go back down. I'll be there in a minute."

The rest of Harry's men continued into the left woods, but Harry stayed by the tree. He pulled on a low branch and looked up. Walter came back to the tree and said, "What are you doing?"

"Hold my gun."

"What?"

"Hold it a minute. I'm going to get up there and see if I can see where they are."

"Harry, no, you'll get killed."

Harry climbed the tree carefully. "I'll shout to you where they are. Listen for my voice."

Harry was head-high in a minute. He reached down to Walter, "Give me my gun." Walter sent it up to him.

"Harry, get down here. Come on. You'll get shot."

"I'll be fine. Get off to the left. I'll get down in plenty of time before they get here. I just want to see where they are. Go." Walter reluctantly headed off into the woods, looking back at Harry continually.

Harry slipped his gun between two branches, higher in the tree. He climbed up like a monkey, balancing his gun on two more branches above. This was easy. He climbed higher. The tree became thinner as Harry got thirty feet in the air. He wrapped his arms around the trunk as it swayed. "Whoa. Damn." His gun came loose from a branch, but Harry saved it in time and steadied himself in the shaky tree.

He positioned the gun so that it was level and secure between two branches, and pulled back the cock to expose the pan. He poured in the powder with his free hand. With his legs straddling the trunk and his feet on another branch, his arms were free to push in the bullet. He repositioned the gun on the branches so the powder wouldn't fall out.

The view from high above the road was captivating. Harry saw two British cannon far away around Fermoy's Bend. Many men pushed and tugged at them. Behind, through the thin treetops, he surveyed the American line retreating through the woods and along the road. He saw Murphy two hundred yards back, pointing right and left. To his right, Jackson and his men crouched down, hid behind trees, and loaded their guns.

"Jack, Jack, how ya doin'?"

Jackson looked west. "Harry? Where are you?"

"Up here. Look. Over here."

Jackson searched the road for where he thought Harry should be, but Harry wasn't there. "Harry, where are you?"

One of Jackson's men spied Harry in the tree. "Jack, look."

"Oh, my God."

Jackson said to his men, "Let's go," and headed for the road.

From far away, Harry laughed. "Hey, Jack. Whoa." He watched Jackson coming toward him as he swayed high in the cold air. Harry peered out at the frozen fields, woods, and roads. He saw red uniforms moving behind Jackson, deep in the woods.

Harry shouted, from the treetop, "Jack, behind you, British." Jackson turned around. The British were within twenty yards, deeper in the woods. Jackson stopped. His men turned toward the woods and fired a volley. Three British were hit. The rest of the British squad got down on their knees and aimed, but their shots went high. Bullets hit the trees. Jackson's men rushed toward the road. As they did, they saw two dozen British coming down the road toward Harry. Harry fired from his perch in the tree and missed. The British stopped and searched the trees for the source of the shot, high in the air. Spotting Harry, they crept down the road with their eyes focused on the devil in the trees.

Harry scrambled down, abandoning his gun high on a branch. He reached up to grab it, but his foot slipped on the snowy branch and became stuck solid. Harry fell backward, the gun tumbling through the tree, striking branches. Harry lunged for it as it passed him, but missed. The gun dropped between more branches and finally struck the road. Harry's ankle twisted sideways and snapped from the weight of his lunge for the gun.

Harry clung to a branch, almost upside-down, reeling in pain. He righted himself awkwardly, sat on the branch, and pulled out his leg using both hands. Harry was very low in the tree now. He considered jumping to the ground, but his ankle couldn't possibly stand the shock, and the pain would be awful.

Jackson and his men nearly made it to the road, but the British got to Harry first. Harry watched as the many British soldiers rushed toward him. He lifted his leg physically out of the branch, but it was too much for him. He stopped struggling, six feet up in the tree, and waited for the British to arrive. Captured. The British slowed. Lawrence sneered.

Jackson ignored the danger. "No. Harry." Jackson charged the two dozen British by himself. He plowed through many small trees and over bushes. One of Jackson's men rushed after him, grabbed Jackson from behind, and tackled him to the ground. "Jack, no."

Lawrence, on the road, looked away from Harry and heard the cries of the Americans. He ordered, "Get 'em." Twenty soldiers with fixed bayonets sprinted into the woods toward Jackson and his friends. Jackson's men ran. Jackson got up, and facing the British with tears in his eyes, he raised his musket over his head like an axe.

The soldier with Jackson turned around, grabbed Jackson and dragged him back. "Jack, no. We can't help him, Jack." Another soldier turned around and ran back to help pull their desperate and foolish leader out of danger. Jackson stopped struggling. The two soldiers escorted Jackson away, Jackson raging at the British.

"He'll be captured, Jack. It's all right. We can't help him now."

Jackson turned around and walked through the woods, angling toward the road, watching Harry over his shoulder. He caught up to his other men. The British stopped and returned to Harry's location. Hundreds of British came down the road and passed the scene of the rebel in the tree.

Jackson and his men stopped fifty yards south, joined by Harry's troops from the other side of the road. They all turned and watched the fate of Harry through the thin winter trees.

Chapter Twenty Four

S outh of Jackson, Murphy directed the riflemen back into the woods as they came onto the road. More men came up from the south. Murphy pointed, shouting orders, "Go. You, over there, over to the left."

Many shots were heard from deep in the woods both east and west. The British were clearly trying to outflank the Americans, going deeper and deeper into the woods. Colonel Hand limped over from up ahead.

Murphy watched him intensely. "You shot?"

"No, caught my leg on a branch. They're getting deep. We've got to bring them back here. Fan 'em out more. They're getting around us, and get everyone off the road. Make it look safe for them. I'm going to block the road, down near the guns."

"Yes sir."

Hand walked south, then turned around.

"Wait, Murph, send a note to the general. Tell him Fermoy is gone."

"Yes, sir."

"No, wait. Don't say he's 'gone,' you know, the general might think he's, you know, 'gone,' and then he'd show up. Wait, that could be funny. Your choice, Murph."

Murphy smiled. "Yes, sir."

Hand limped past Murphy and proceeded south.

Swanson, Toby and Isaac came onto the road from ten yards north. Isaac shouted, "Pa."

Murphy walked north toward the boys and Swanson. A break in the action allowed him a little time to talk. "How they doing, Borg? Boys?"

Swanson said, "All right. But this one no shoot, and this one no can shoot."

Murphy said, "Thanks for taking care of them, Borg. I owe you. You boys all right? Pay attention to the sergeant. He knows what to do. Be careful." Murphy called Swanson to the side. "You know the plan, right? Keep the British on the road so they have to cross the bridge."

"Yes, I know this."

"Well, they're getting deeper into the woods. They're not going to get to the bridge that way. We have to drive them back to the road and bring them to the bridge."

Swanson said, "We need get deeper in."

"Yes. Take charge on the right. I'll take care of the left. Don't let the redcoats get behind you. Colonel Hand will be south. You should be all right as you retreat."

Swanson said, "You boys, off right. Get going."

Swanson and his men went east. Isaac lagged behind for a minute and looked at his father for some assurance, but Murphy didn't see him. Swanson stopped, turned around, grabbed Isaac by his collar, and dragged him into the woods. Isaac and Swanson disappeared off to the right.

Deep in the woods to the right, Swanson's men could see British sneaking toward them. Isaac fired, hit a tree, fired again, and missed again. Toby reloaded the musket. Isaac shot another tree.

Swanson said to his men, "Shoot. Run back." His men fired, and even though shooting through trees, they scored some hits. Isaac missed yet again. He said to Toby, "Damn-near." Toby was terrified as he reloaded Isaac's musket.

British cannons went off now. Solid shot tore up the leaves and branches. The sound of the American reply could be heard throughout the woods, and caused the British cannons to retreat.

Fifty Americans came onto the road from the woods. Murphy, alone on the road, sent them into the woods on both sides with orders, "Stay deep. Push them toward the road, and keep going south." The sun was low in the sky to the southwest. "Keep the sun on your right as you go back."

Murphy walked his horse up to a soldier on the road. He wrote a note,

> *Fermoy is gone. Hand is in charge. 2 miles up.*
> *We are holding.*
> *W. Murphy*

"Take the horse and get this to the general." The soldier took the note, mounted Murphy's horse, and galloped off.

Murphy called together a few men standing around. "Go. Off to the left. Fifty yards in. Keep the sun in front of you. Drive them back here."

The soldiers stared blankly at Murphy. "What? What are you talking about? Who are you?"

The plague that infected the army had arrived again. Men wouldn't take orders from officers they didn't know. Murphy had very little time to persuade these men to go to the left. "Sorry, son. You the leader of these boys?"

"Yeah, they voted me." The soldier asked his men, "Right?" The other soldiers shook their heads, "Yes." The soldier turned to Murphy. "They voted me. We're looking for Jack and Harry."

Murphy brightened a little. Something he had in common with these men could be exploited. "Jackson's up there. He's off to the right. Harry's to the left. They'll be coming down here in a minute."

"They're up ahead?"

"Yes, but you can't go up there. Get into the woods, fifty yards. See any British, blast 'em and run south, stay off the road until you get to Hand. Harry should be coming your way, on the left."

Murphy sighed with relief as the soldiers dispersed into the woods. He was still alone on the road. Cannons blasted from the northeast and gunshots ripped through the trees deep in the woods on both sides. The smell of gunpowder pervaded the air. Wisps of smoke appeared all around, wafting up through the trees.

Murphy searched ahead for signs of activity. Either uniform coming down the road, British or American, would signal what was going on up there. A feeling of dread came over him as he went up a hundred yards. He paused several times to gauge the direction of the fight. The road was barren of men on both sides as Murphy trudged north.

He stopped and checked his rifle, loaded it, and then walked slowly up again, toward the expected British. Murphy called out, "Jackson. Jackson, you up there?" It was silent, except for the sounds of sporadic gunfire. "Jackson."

Chapter Twenty Five

A hundred yards north of Murphy, Harry sat on a branch six feet in the air. Two dozen British soldiers gathered around him. Harry held his sprained ankle and whimpered.

Lawrence retrieved a bayonet from a pouch on his belt. "What you doin' up there, rebel?

"I surrender."

"Oh, ya do, do ya? Wasn't you at Lexington?"

"What?"

"Lexington. Boston. Remember? Ya wouldn't let us surrender then, would ya?"

"I wasn't even there. I'm from New Jersey."

"You devil bastards just kept shooting. Even when we was down. Shot us when we was down. Bastards."

Lawrence turned to his men and pointed at the patch on his eye. "See this? Lost an eye on a tree dodging rebel bullets from rebel bastards we couldn't even see. Bastards."

Harry sensed danger. "I wasn't there, I swear." Harry tried hard to get out of the tree and jump to the ground, but Lawrence smashed Harry's bad foot hard against the trunk with his hand. Harry screamed.

Lawrence fastened the bayonet to his musket. He ran his fingers along the length of it, testing its sharpness and reveling in Harry's fear. "I think I remember you. At Lexington. Yea, that was you. You shot my men dead when they were already down. Wouldn't let us surrender. That was you. I remember."

Harry looked at the other British soldiers. They looked up at Harry sympathetically, but they couldn't help.

Lawrence touched the point of his bayonet to Harry's leg and pushed it in slightly. Harry's leg drew blood.

"Ah. Don't!"

Jackson and his crew watched from a hundred yards south on the Trenton road. Jackson whispered to his men, I'm going back there.

"No, Jack. No. We can't help him."

"I'm going." Jackson marched toward the British. Two of his men grabbed him again and pulled him back.

At the tree, Lawrence poked Harry again. "Ow! Stop that." Harry clasped a branch with his left hand. "I surrender. Let me down."

"Do you damn rebel cowards think it was right to shoot at us from behind stone walls?" Lawrence stabbed Harry through the hand, impaling his hand into the tree. "And now you're in the trees? Shouldn't be shootin' from the trees, Reb. Ain't sportin'." Lawrence pulled the bayonet out. Blood poured from Harry's hand. Harry closed his eyes at the pain.

Lawrence looked at his men, who were stunned at the brutality they were witnessing. Lawrence turned angrily to Harry. "We couldn't surrender then, so you don't get to surrender now. Take that, ya rebel bastard."

Lawrence jabbed Harry in the leg. "You cowards did this to me. Took my eye out." Lawrence lifted his eye flap to expose a horrible wound. The eye was gone with only a hollow socket remaining. "You hid behind them trees and the walls. You waited for us to come down the road, you rebel bastards."

Harry barely whispered, "Please don't..."

Lawrence plunged the bayonet into Harry's eye. The bayonet cracked off as it hit the skull behind Harry's head. He faded into unconsciousness with the half bayonet sticking out of his head.

Lawrence said, "Damn rebel. Broke my knife. You're gonna get it now."

The other British soldiers watched with horrifying alarm. They were not accustomed to that kind of cruelty, but there was nothing they could do. To question the actions of a superior would mean a short trip to the gallows.

Jackson and his men watched. They were tucked out of sight so the British couldn't see them, but at the sight of Harry's bloody body hanging in the tree, Jackson stood up. He walked onto the road and shouted, "No!"

The British saw Jackson and formed across the road, pointing their muskets at targets too far away to hit. Two of Jackson's men came off the road, tried to restrain Jackson and drag him to safety, but Jackson shrugged them off. He aimed his musket at the many British ahead, searching for a good shot at Lawrence. There was no chance he could hit anyone a hundred yards away with a musket, and he knew it, but he didn't care.

Dozens of British muskets went off. At Jackson's location, leaves fell. Branches splintered. None of the bullets came close. Lawrence pulled the broken bayonet out of Harry's head and took another one from one of his men. He shook off the broken knife from his musket and attached the other one, with his good eye steeled on Harry. Harry was unconscious, so the next plunge wouldn't matter, but Lawrence needed the 'death' blow. "This is for my good eye." He plunged the bayonet into Harry's stomach, twisted it, and pulled it out.

Lawrence plunged the bayonet again, again, and again.

Jackson cried, "No. No!" He aimed his loaded musket at Lawrence, ready to fire the innocuous shot.

Murphy came up from behind Jackson's men. "Don't shoot."

Jackson turned and recognized Murphy, as did the men, relieved now that their officer was with them. Jackson shouted, "They killed Harry!" Jackson turned north with a consuming rage.

Murphy clutched Jackson's arm. "No, you can't shoot. The British are already behind us."

Jackson cried, "I'm going to kill them."

"No, son, you can't. If they hear another volley from here, they'll come back and cut us off. Get back down, all of you."

All of Jackson's men walked slowly down the Trenton Road. They glanced behind them as they went, as more and more British soldiers came to the scene at the tree.

Private Harry Hairy Horse hung upside down. Blood gushed out of his many wounds and ran down his face and chest. The blood poured out of his mouth like a hog in a slaughterhouse, onto the roots of the winter tree. He quivered in spasm, twitched with his last breath, then became still. Harry was dead.

Murphy clenched his rifle tightly as anger welled up in his eyes. Jackson's muddy face was barely recognizable, the grimy dirt moistened by his tears.

Jackson wiped the mud out of his eyes. "Shoot him."

Murphy aimed. "Which one?"

Jackson squinted through the trees. "I can't see him. He had a patch on his eye. Shoot any one of them. It don't matter. Wait, there he is."

Lawrence turned from facing Harry and stared straight at Murphy with his one good eye. Murphy aimed his gun right at the patch, no problem for a rifle at a wide-open target standing defiantly motionless a mere hundred yards away.

Gunshots crackled from deep in the woods to the south. Murphy paused, thought about the consequences, and then lowered his rifle. He said, "No. It won't do any good to shoot one lousy British soldier. Let's go. If the British down there hear a rifle shot from here, they might think they've surrounded us. We have to get down to the regiment before they get to the road. Get your men back down."

Murphy, Jackson, and the men walked quickly two hundred yards south. Jackson's men walked in front until, looking behind them, they could no longer see the British at Harry's tree. More shots were heard from every direction. Murphy said to Jackson, "Wait a minute. Call your men back here."

Jackson motioned for his men to come onto the road. They turned back cautiously. One of the men said to another, "What's this all about?"

Murphy said to the men, "Stay here for a minute. Off the road, out of sight. I have to check their numbers." He scooted low, dodged to the western side of the road, and walked up ten yards.

Jackson's men sneaked up to Murphy's new position. Jackson motioned for them to lie off to the left side, and then joined them there. They could see Harry's tree now. Jackson whispered, "Keep down." They all lay in the grass and pointed their muskets north. Murphy stayed on the left side of the road, just out of sight of the British. One of the men mumbled, "What's he doing?" The men watched Murphy approach a large tree.

Murphy balanced his rifle against the trunk and gazed high in the air, calculating the height. He studied the branches, up and down the trunk, and lunged for a sturdy branch seven feet high, just out of reach, but the force of his jump pushed his boots into the mud and he went nowhere. Murphy fell against the tree lightly and steadied himself, looking up, gauging the distance to the branch again.

Jackson and his men were shocked. Jackson whispered, "Oh, no," and crawled up on his hands and knees. Murphy dug his foot into a protruding root at the base of the tree to get a better launch platform. He jumped up again and caught the branch with both hands. He dangled for a second, then wrapped his legs around the trunk. Murphy wiggled up the trunk and flung himself over the branch. He panted, a little old to be climbing trees. Another good branch was six feet higher.

Jackson got to the base of the tree and whispered, "Cap, Cap. Get down here."

Murphy looked down. "I have to find out how many of them there are."

Jackson turned around to his men. They shook their heads in disbelief. "Oh, no, not again."

Murphy clutched his legs around the trunk and climbed up to the next strong limb. His foot found a firm young branch protruding from the trunk, which was good enough. Murphy placed his right foot on it. The sapling, being young and a little green, it was best not to put his whole weight on it.

He reached up for his target branch, much more reliable than the one his right foot was on, but to get there, he had to rely on the small young branch and a little momentum from a good launch.

He moved his right foot slightly, distributing the weight toward the big trunk, so the young branch wouldn't take his full weight. Only by grasping the trunk with both legs and arms would Murphy avoid falling if the young branch broke. It was worth a chance.

Murphy held the trunk against his chest and exerted all his strength upward. The young branch held. Murphy breathed easy and clutched the large branch. He pulled himself up and stood upright on it with his arms wrapped around the trunk. He rested again.

Jackson looked up. "Sir, Cap. Get down. That's how Harry got killed."

"Harry had the right idea, son. God bless him. He just didn't have a company of brave fellows to help him get down. I'll be just a minute."

The tree was sixteen inches in diameter. Murphy carefully concealed himself so he could see the British two hundred yards away. He peeked from behind the trunk at another group of British a hundred yards north, coming down. The British at Harry's body were strangely complacent, milling around and staring at the body solemnly.

Murphy counted one group individually, twenty-one men. There was another group, a little larger, behind them, maybe fifty total so far. Behind those men were more, about the same density. One hundred so far. No, behind them were even more, maybe another hundred. He recalculated his densities, one-fifty total.

Gunfire sounded from the sides and behind, but it was still far in the woods. Murphy hoped it was just some jittery Americans firing at imaginary trees that looked like redcoats in the waning daylight.

Jackson whispered up, "Sir, come on. We've got to go."

Murphy stooped down a little and spoke to Jackson. "There's maybe a hundred, maybe one-fifty. About even for us, I think. They seem to be waiting for something. Wait a minute." Murphy climbed back up.

Jackson cringed and looked at his men. He waved them north, toward him like an orchestra conductor, pushing his left hand down gently through the air, indicating to stay low, but pulling them toward him with his right hand so they could get closer to Murphy.

Murphy climbed up a bit, twenty-five feet high now. He spotted movement behind the bend at Harry's tree. He frowned at what he suspected was emerging, and he was right. He saw one cannon, two, four, now six. Many men pushed them and even more men followed the guns. The cannons moved slowly, struggling in the deep mud.

Murphy counted them in groups. They were not hard to calculate because they were moving slowly and they stayed together, waiting for the guns, six guns and at least seven hundred men. Damn. Murphy waited a moment to see if anyone else followed, but no, not so far. The men at

Harry's location still didn't move, so Murphy had some time. The British faced north and watched the cannons arrive, so slowly.

An officer appeared on horseback. He barked an order to the men at the tree, but Murphy couldn't make it out. Only two faint words arrived at Murphy's ears, those words exploding from the officer's throat, "What? Get..." Two soldiers pulled Harry's leg from the branch. Harry's lifeless body was lowered gently to the ground.

The officer leaned from his horse. The British jumped back, away from his wrath. The officer shouted questions that Murphy couldn't understand.

At the tree, Major Derring looked around at the men. They shrugged their shoulders. Lawrence had disappeared into the woods, out of sight.

Derring gave an order, "Off to the sides. Twenty yards in."

Murphy heard that, "Off. Twenty..."

The British plowed off to the sides of the road, happy to get as far away as possible from this fanatical major's anger. Murphy watched them go into the woods. Jackson looked up again. "Cap, we got to get out of here."

Murphy said, "Another minute. They're moving. Send your men back down." Jackson stood up, still obscured from the British view, and waved his hand to the left. His men pretended that they didn't understand. Jackson shook his arm harder, faster, waving them south.

The men ignored the symbolic order again and continued to watch Murphy in the tree. Jackson poked his finger south, again and again, violently, in a silent and empty threat that his men had better obey him or there'd be hell to pay. He waved both arms in the air, never mind that the British might see him now, in the middle of the road, if they looked that way. Jackson wanted to yell, scream at his men, "Get back, now," but he couldn't. The British would hear him. Jackson's men watched his futile gestures with determined resolve from their hiding places behind the trees. No, they wouldn't go, not just yet.

Jackson looked into the eyes of his men. They looked back blankly with the eyes of a puppy that you could yell at for hours but still wouldn't do what you told it to do. Exasperated, Jackson dropped to the ground, counting on the lay of the land to cover him. He tried one more time to get his men to go back, waving his arm in the air, lying prostrate on the road. Walter shook his head, "no."

Murphy called down quietly, "Jackson, get back. Get off the road."

The cannons got to the British line at Harry's tree. Men pushing the guns dropped to their knees, panting. Horses grunted and stood perfectly still. Murphy kept a close eye on the British fanning out slowly into the woods on both sides as he climbed down the tree six feet.

He stared at the British coming toward him and held very still behind the trunk of the tree, in case the British noticed any movement high up. It wouldn't matter, though. Murphy could drop to the ground from that height without any danger.

Jackson scooted back to the tree and crouched low behind the trunk. "What are they doing?"

"They're coming this way. I want to see how far in they are." Murphy paused for what Jackson thought was a very long time. Murphy saw what he needed to see. The British were not going very far into the woods, instead staying close to the road. The farthest British soldier was only twenty yards in and advancing parallel to the road. Murphy scrambled down the trunk. He used the green young branch once again for support, and dropped to the ground. He shouted to Jackson and the men, in the loudest voice he could muster, "Go, go, go!"

Murphy turned toward Princeton, just in case the British didn't hear him, "Go, go, go!"

The British were startled to see rebels jump onto the road and run south. Jackson and Murphy followed them. Gunfire sounded from the north as dozens of British muskets went off. Jackson's men, five yards ahead of Murphy and Jackson, in the middle of the road, turned around in fear. Murphy and Jackson were between them and the British. Murphy yelled again, "Go, keep going!" Then he said quietly, "Don't shoot. That's an order."

Jackson's men ran fast. Murphy said to Jackson, "Don't worry. They can't hit a thing at this distance." Jackson and Murphy caught up to the men. They all slowed to a brisk walk, the men nervously looking back, but not Murphy.

Jackson asked, "Why didn't you let us shoot?"

"Because you couldn't hit them at that distance any better than they could hit you."

"Yeah, but you could've with a rifle."

"I could've hit one of them. And if there's British in the woods here, they'd hear a rifle shot. They'd get ahead of us. Now they'll run back there because they think that's where the fight is. I didn't want your men to shoot, but I did indeed want the British to shoot. Understand, son?"

"Yeah, sure."

"Now the British in the woods think the battle is back there. You have to trick the enemy, cheat them whenever you get a chance. Understand? You have to cheat."

Jackson shrugged. "Whatever you say, Cap."

Murphy, Jackson and the men proceeded south, staying to the side of the road to avoid the mud, but out of the woods. They heard more gunshots to the left and right, so they were passing the British advance position. Continuing around a bend, Colonel Hand and the rest of the Americans came into Murphy's view. Murphy and the men were safe now. He touched Jackson's shoulder. "You all right, about Harry, and Satchel?"

Jackson replied, "Yeah, I guess."

They crossed a shallow, five-foot-wide stream and came into view of the main American line.

* * *

Hand spotted some men coming toward him and noticed Murphy behind them. He waited for Murphy to catch up. "Murph. God, I thought you were dead."

Murphy said, "No, sir, not yet. Just doing a little scouting, sir." Murphy waived Jackson's men into the crowd of 200 Americans milling around in the road.

Hand said, "What's up there? God, Murph, you could've got killed."

"No, not me. There's about 800 of them, if I counted right, and six guns."

"Six guns? Damn. Eight hundred men? We can't handle that. What about the guns?"

"Small ones, six pounders."

"Six guns, eh? Well, they can't get more than two apiece on this road. Still, they'll use grapeshot."

Hand wiped his face with his sleeve, thinking. "How fast are they coming?"

"Not very fast. They won't get ahead of the guns. I saw that. We have at least a half hour, maybe an hour."

"Good. Good. You think the riflemen could slow down the guns?"

Murphy looked north at the bend. "Yes. They can take out the gunners. Some of them, anyway. That's a good idea."

"Get some riflemen up there. Then I need you to get back down again, and bring the guns up." Hand squinted to a point a half mile away, where the road bent west slowly. "Ah, there they are."

Murphy looked south. Two American cannons sat in the road just north of the bend.

"Bring them halfway up to here, halfway up from the bend, solid shot. But send their officer up to me. I need to talk to him."

Murphy's face dropped. "I should go with the riflemen, sir."

"They can handle it. One shot each and then back here. I need an officer down there who can get things done. Send their officer up to me."

"But sir, the riflemen could get killed. They'll be facing the whole British army, against cannons and grape. I need to be up there with them."

"Sorry, Murph, not this time. Tell them to shoot and run, shoot and run."

Murphy nodded sadly. He wandered into the crowd of two hundred men clumped in small groups. They leaned on their guns, sat, joked, talked, milled around, and waited for the next phase of the battle to begin. Murphy looked into their faces. He wondered to whom he could assign this dangerous task, a dozen or so riflemen to face the advance force of the entire British army. Murphy recognized many of them, some of them officers. A few were called the "regulars," men with muskets, deadly at short range, hard and experienced, men who wouldn't run away unless it was absolutely necessary. Murphy had great respect for those men also, but no, this was a job for the riflemen.

Murphy spotted Jackson and walked up. Jackson talked to his men, and didn't see Murphy approach yet. "Jackson."

Jackson turned around. "Yes, sir."

"You know a Lieutenant McKean?"

"Sorry, sir, no."

Another soldier from a different group overheard. "I know him. He's a rifleman, right?"

"Yes. You see him?"

He's over on the left, I think." The private pointed to the left side of the road.

Murphy walked over there and stood on the edge of the road, looking for Lieutenant McKean. He scanned the faces of the ragged men huddled behind the trees. Murphy spotted McKean, ten yards in, and walked into the woods. McKean saw Murphy approach.

"Hiya, Murph."

"Hello, Lieutenant. I've been looking for you."

"What for?"

"I need you to do something."

"Sure, Murph."

"Come onto the road, over here." Murphy led McKean back to the road and pointed north. "See that bend up there?" He had to move to the left to get a clear sight of the road, because there were so many men in the way. Murphy pointed again. "Up there, see?"

"Yeah. What?"

Murphy paused before giving the order. He knew there was a chance he'd never see this kid again. "Take your company up there. About fifty yards around that bend."

"Sure. You're up there too, right?"

"No. Well, uh, no. I have to get back down toward town."

"Then who's going to be with us?"

Murphy fidgeted. He looked at the ground, then at McKean. "You'll be by yourselves. But you'll be all right."

"Whoa, Murph, hold the reins. Ain't the British up that way? And we's by ourselves?"

McKean's ten men came out of the woods, curious about what their officer was discussing. They strained their ears to hear the conversation as they approached the road.

"Yes. You'll be alone. They have six guns. Your job is to take out the gunners, or their horses, or anything you can do. Shoot once and run back. Slow them down. It's important."

"Murph, you're a pretty good officer, but I ain't lookin' to get killed today."

"You're a good shot, and your men. You're the only ones I can think of who can do this." Sporadic shots sounded from the north. "Shoot once and run. That's all you have to do. Once. Shoot once. Take your best shot. Slow down the guns."

McKean looked into Murphy's eyes for a second and then walked away. McKean said to his men, "Let's go. We're going up."

Chapter Twenty Six

Murphy saw Isaac and Toby twenty yards in the woods on the right side of the road. Swanson and his men sat on an old rotten tree, Swanson rubbing the mud off his gun with a rag.

McKean's riflemen moved swiftly through the woods on the left side of the road. Murphy watched them go, glancing intermittently at McKean, then his own boys, then back to McKean. McKean disappeared around the bend.

Murphy walked over to the boys and Swanson. He slipped in the mud, but grabbed a branch and never hit the ground. Isaac saw Murphy coming and hopped off the log. "Hi, Pa." Toby's face brightened at the words and the sight of his father.

Murphy approached Swanson, "How they doing, Borg?"

"Better, but still no can shoot, this one." Swanson wagged his head at Isaac.

Isaac smiled. "I can shoot. I just can't hit anything."

Swanson said, "A waste of bullets."

Toby shook his head at Isaac. "Should've paid attention when we was learnin'."

"I could hit them if they'd get a little closer, and there's no trees in the way."

Murphy said, "We sure don't want that to happen. So you'll be all right, Borg? I have to go down again. I want you to stay here with Hand's men."

"Yes. We have orders stay here, in woods, shoot, run back. You think many feind come?"

"Yes. There's lots of them. I counted around eight hundred, be here in about an hour. Six guns."

"Oh mein Gott."

"Yes, but they're staying close to the road."

Swanson's face curled into a little grin. "Ah, the foolishness of these Europeans."

Murphy chuckled. "I have to go, Borg. Take care of them, and yourself." Murphy walked to the road, then stopped and turned. "Boys, stay with the sergeant. I'll see you on the other side." Murphy reconsidered those words. "Of the creek, I mean."

Murphy reached the road. Hand reached for his arm as Murphy passed. "Nice job, Murph."

"Thanks, sir. Good luck here." Murphy hung his head and walked south.

Chapter Twenty Seven

Hand directed the men to form a long line across the road, going into the woods on both sides. "Three deep." Officers walked along the line in front, straightening the men. An officer told Swanson to man the right flank, the eastern-most portion of the line. Swanson and his men were pushed farther and farther east as the line stretched with ever more soldiers falling in. Swanson ended up 60 yards from the road.

On the other side, the same stretching occurred. Men eased west until that flank was anchored at the same distance. Across the road were three lines of ten men each, but on the sides it was hard to tell, as men crouched behind trees and fallen logs. Two hundred men altogether formed the line. Every one of them looked backward more than once, calculating his escape route.

Hand stood on the road. He spoke to two of his officers. "Go right and left, get all the officers over here as soon as their men are in place." The officers hurried onto both sides, identified their commanders, and gave instructions.

At the road, Hand called everyone together. There were twenty officers. "Look, here's the plan. Hazlet's riflemen are on the road." Hand looked at Hazlet, a member of the group. Everyone turned to the thirty men behind them, then back to Hand.

"Nobody shoots 'till they do. Understand?" Hand pointed to a large tree five feet on the west side. "I'll be behind that tree. Now here's what you tell your men.

"First, you tell them that anybody shoots before they hear a shot from me, that your orders are to shoot them dead on the spot. And if they shoot, and you don't shoot them, then I'll shoot you."

That got the officers' attention. Hand continued, "There's a dozen riflemen ahead. They're going to fire once, then run back here. Number two thing you tell your men, don't shoot the riflemen. They shoot a rifleman, I'll shoot 'em myself, twice."

An officer spoke up. "Is Murphy up there, or is he on the road?" The officer looked over to the men on the road. The rest of the officers looked behind, at Hazlet's men, searching for Murphy.

"No. Murphy's down there taking care of your behinds when your men run away. Now be quiet and listen."

Hand cheated now a little on the numbers, "They have about five hundred men, and maybe four guns."

The officers groaned, "Oh, no."

"They can only put two guns on the road at a time."

"But sir, there'll be British in the woods."

Hand replied, "Yes, they'll move parallel to the road."

"Para-what?"

"Parallel. You know, next to."

The officers puzzled at that expression, "What?"

Hand cringed. "Side-by-side, to the road. You know, next to the road, parallel."

An officer turned to a comrade. "I once had a para-cats side-by-side. Wouldn't breed. Hated each other." The men laughed.

Another officer chuckled, "I had a para-keet. Got out of the cage. Pooped all over. Had to shoot it."

The officers all laughed again.

Hand shook his head in exasperation, but smiled invisibly at the jokes. "All right, I get it. Let's get back to the war, gentlemen. We're going to put up a big fight here, but we're not going to get killed. After the riflemen fire, the British will come down the road. I'm hoping there'll be infantry in front of the guns. The riflemen here will take many of them out. Then the riflemen are going to get off the road.

"I repeat, tell your men, don't shoot until they hear a shot from me. And don't shoot the riflemen. Got it?"

The officers shook their heads, "Yes," and disappeared to the left and right.

Hand said to an officer, "Hazlet, stay."

Hazlet was in charge of the riflemen who guarded the road. "Sir?"

"Come with me." Hand walked with Hazlet over to his men, and addressed all of them. "The British are going to be here in about a half hour. I'll be behind that tree." Hand pointed to the tree again. "Do not shoot until I give the word. Understand?"

The riflemen were tough veterans. They understood.

Hand continued, "I'm going to wait until their guns are ready to go off. But you're going to fire first, so don't get nervous."

Hand looked into the dirty faces of the ragged riflemen. He thought to himself, *"Well, that was a foolish thing to say."*

"Sorry. Wait for my order from that tree, fire once, then clear the road. Get off the road to the left and right immediately. As soon as you shoot, there's going to be cannonballs coming your way. Get off the road."

Hazlet replied "Yes, sir."

Hazlet consulted with his men. He designated which side of the road to go to after they shot, half to the right, half to the left. The riflemen acknowledged.

Murphy, walking south, arrived at the two cannons. He spoke to the lead cannoneer. "Get the guns up there, half-way to the line, and Colonel Hand wants to talk to you." The soldier gave an order to his men and hustled up on foot toward Hand.

Hand slogged south down to the guns to meet the soldier. He asked, "You in charge?"

"Yes, sir, Corporal White."

"All right, corporal. You see those men up there?"

The corporal stared ahead. "Yes, sir."

"You have solid shot in there?"

"Yes, sir."

Hand pointed south. "You're going to be half-way up from that bend down there, see? Maybe a little closer to the bend. We don't want to lose your guns."

Corporal White looked behind him, then turned his eyes to the many Americans north. He was nervous. He'd never spoken to a colonel before. "But sir, those are our men."

"They're going to be off the road. And if they're not, you shoot anyway. As soon as you have a bead on the enemy's guns, you shoot. Low is better."

Corporal White stared with confusion ahead, where dozens of Americans clogged the road. Hand sensed the soldier's dilemma.

"You're going to try and take out the British guns. They'll be right there on the road. Those riflemen will be out of the way. Load your guns and aim them straight up as if they were there, right there, right now, just around that bend, because they will be there. As soon as you see the British guns, you shoot. I'm hoping you can take out one of them and block the road. If not, you'll certainly give them something to think about."

Corporal White thought of another problem. "But sir, if the road is clear, the British guns will be pointing right at us."

"They'll have canister, son. Nothing to worry about at this distance through trees and down a narrow road. Fire once, maybe twice, if you have a chance, but don't endanger yourselves. Fire and get down back, fast."

"Yes, sir."

"Oh, one other thing, son."

"Sir?"

"When you go back," Hand pointed south, "About a half mile or so below that bend..."

White looked behind him. "Yes, sir?"

"Lob a single solid shot high onto the road behind us, far as you can shoot. One shot. It will signal to everyone where to go."

"Yes, sir."

"And keep firing a single shot every ten minutes until I get there."

"Yes sir."

Hand snaked his way up to his station at the riflemen's location. He dug out a place behind the tree, behind the stream, and said to Hazlet, the riflemen's officer, "This will work out just fine. Just keep your men steady and wait for my word."

Hazlet saluted. "Yes, sir." Then to his men he said, "No firing until I fire first, or on my order." The men nodded their heads, "Yes."

Chapter Twenty Eight

The road at the bend, north of Hand, curved gently right after four hundred yards. McKean's riflemen planted themselves off to the left, where the road dipped into a shallow ravine. Their job was to take out the British cannoneers, if they could, and slow the advance. They were ten men against almost an entire army with cannons, but McKean's men didn't know that just yet.

They peered over and around the natural barriers that separated them from the view of the enemy. Red uniforms came toward them. McKean's men hid themselves more securely behind trees and crouched down in the cold mud.

McKean's men saw the British cannons lumbering toward them, two, four, six guns in line, two at a time. Hundreds of infantry were in front of them. The riflemen looked at each other with rising alarm as more British came into view. "Oh, my God. Look at all of them."

The riflemen watched the many British marching toward them on the sides of the road, maneuvering around the trees and underbrush. The British stopped and aligned their ranks once, twice. British officers shouted orders. The cannons lurched forward, pulled by two horses per gun.

McKean watched them as they realigned. "Damn. The infantry is ahead of the guns. Damn."

He whispered, "Edward, can you take out the left horse on that left gun?" Edward spotted the designated horse, towering over the ranks of the infantry.

Edward readied his rifle. "Done."

McKean looked over at another soldier. "Little Ben, the left horse on that other gun. Shoot him in the neck. You'll have to stand up for a shot."

Little Ben stood up and concealed himself behind a tree. "Got him. Sorry, Clover, nothing personal."

McKean frowned at Little Ben. Little Ben shrugged. McKean glided through the mud toward three men who were five yards down. "Franco, Smitty, you, too, Pete." McKean told them, "Don't shoot. When the others shoot, the British will run straight here. Wait two seconds, until they charge, and then shoot. Pick out your man and take him out. Now. Pick out your man now. But nobody in the middle. They'll be dead. Pick out a man on the side." The men discussed their targets among themselves. Franco motioned to Smitty, indicating a target on the right side of the road.

McKean crawled forward. He got to Edward's location with Little Ben and the four other soldiers.

"Martin, you're the best shot. I want you to take out one of the gunners. Thomas, Larry, take out the two middle soldiers, right there." McKean pointed to two soldiers in the middle. "When they fall, they'll open up a hole. Martin, take out a gunner. I'm going onto the road. I'll try and take out another gunner. "I'm going to try and get us two shots."

Martin said, "I don't see as how we can get two shots. They'll charge."

"Franco will take care of that. Thomas and Larry, you'll fire first, then you, Martin, right after. We'll see. If we have time for another shot, we'll take it. If they hesitate, then maybe. Maybe not. We'll see."

McKean whispered to everyone, "No matter what, shoot and run back. I'll stay a little behind and see if we have time for another shot."

Chapter Twenty Nine

At Hand's location on the right side of the road, an officer approached Swanson's group. Swanson stood up and saluted. Isaac sat indifferently on a log. Toby sat next to Isaac and listened closely.

The officer talked to the men on the right flank, sixty yards from the road and could not see it that far away. "Sergeant, you're on the far right."

Swanson looked to his right, where there were no Americans. "Ya, this I know." Swanson struggled for an explanation of why this young man was telling him things he already knew.

The officer repeated, "You're on the flank." Do you understand? You and your men."

"Yes. What you do to protect us?"

"What?"

"How we know when go back. You stay with us? You send man to say, we go back. Else we get, what you say..."

Swanson became confused, searching for an English word in his German brain, talking to an American fool about a British attack. Swanson stopped talking, flustered, and looked at the ground, embarrassed, frustrated, thinking, searching for the word he needed. At the long delay, Swanson felt the officer's eyes on him. He knew he had to take care of his men himself. He couldn't rely on this officer.

Swanson repeated, "In case, in case we get, you know — "

Isaac said, "trapped."

Swanson looked at Isaac. His eyes thanked the young boy for knowing the language and having the courage to intercede. "Yes, trapped. And killed. How you tell us? You stay with us?"

"Stay with you? Ha. You're here to protect us, old man. You're the flank."

The soldier shook his head, "Foreigners. All over. Damn, what a war. Old men who can't speak English." The officer looked to the other soldiers for a laugh, but nobody laughed. The officer became angry and pointed his finger at Swanson. "You hold this flank. You hear me?" He tried for another joke at Swanson's expense. I mean, "Zhis flank. Zhees flank. Ha, see?" The soldier laughed again at the slur, but nobody else did.

Isaac stood up, as did Toby. The other soldiers all arose from sitting positions on the logs. They looked at Swanson, already standing, ten yards from the officer, and then shifted their gaze to the officer. They expected a good fight.

Swanson held his gun at a normal elevation for a man standing with a gun. It angled naturally toward the ground, the barrel being heavier than the stock. It was easier on the wrists that way.

But now, as Swanson stared straight into the officer's eyes, the barrel of his gun rose slowly, ever so slowly. The stock went down, the barrel went up. The gun never got above Swanson's hip, but in ten seconds, the barrel of the gun was where Swanson wanted it to be. The officer looked down the barrel all the way to the chamber, not a single portion of the barrel protruding in any direction. It was like looking into a telescope, right at the eyepiece. The gun pointed directly between the officer's eyes, an easy target for Swanson, because the soldier was so close.

"Whoa, whoa," said the officer. "Easy now, Fritz. Put that down."

Swanson lowered the barrel. It now pointed at the officer's stomach. The officer calculated the new trajectory. "All right. Easy. Easy now, Sarge." The officer backed up, turned around, and sprinted to the road, dodging trees.

Swanson said, "We all born ignorant, but must work hard to remain stupid."

Swanson's men laughed.

Chapter Thirty

McKean's men at the bend steeled themselves against the expected fight. Franco, Smitty, and Pete, five yards behind, clutched their rifles. The rest of the men lay in the mud on the left side of the road and peeked just over the rise to watch the British come toward them. McKean was with the forward men.

The British hesitated, sensing danger. If there was a bee's nest down there, they didn't want to get stung. They slowed down and proceeded cautiously around the bend. The six cannons lumbered behind.

The riflemen saw the cannons curve toward them. Two horses drew each gun. The cannons fit onto the road two at a time, four horses per row towering over the men in front of them.

McKean whispered behind him, "Hold fire 'till I say."

The men gripped their rifles nervously. The British stopped. An officer said something that the riflemen couldn't understand. Several British on each side went into the woods and waited. The British officer said something else, which caused the soldiers to move forward. The British soldiers on the sides kept pace with the cannons.

McKean mumbled, "Holy hell."

All of McKean's men pointed their guns at those British who were on the sides, off the road. The British were a hundred yards away, coming in a long line that protruded shallow into the woods.

The other soldiers on the road clumped up, barely an inch away from each other's shoulders. The fearful cannons, no doubt loaded with canister or grape, lumbered behind, but the horses were visible above the heads of the men in front.

McKean said, "Take aim." The forward riflemen stuck their guns out from behind their trees.

McKean had six men with him at the bend in the road. It was a slow bend. Franco, Smitty, and Pete were five yards behind. Franco's men were all on the left side of the road so that they could see around the bend.

McKean looked over at Thomas and Larry. Their job was to shoot first, take out the men in the middle of the road so that Martin could get a shot. McKean made sure they were paying attention. He looked at the British. Seventy yards, sixty yards, fifty...

"Fire!"

Thomas and Larry fired. Two British soldiers on the road, hit in their foreheads, fell off to the sides. Other soldiers tumbled into the snow as the crashing dead men knocked them out of the way. They plowed over themselves, tripping over their fallen comrades. A hole in the British line opened up. Martin looked down his barrel, but it wasn't his turn to shoot yet. His task was to take out a cannoneer, a specialized British soldier whose job was to aim the cannons.

McKean yelled, "Fire!"

Edward fired. He hit a horse in the chest. The horse swerved off the road to the right, pulling the gun with it. British rushed to the surviving horse to calm it down, but it was attached to the cannon with a harness. They struggled to detach the live horse from the dead one and get the cannon out.

Little Ben fired. He hit the left horse of the right cannon, a different cannon than Edward's. The horse collapsed straight down. Two cannons were now out of work, one living horse and one dead one attached to each gun.

On Little Ben's cannon, a British private tried to get out of the way of the falling animal, but he was too late. The British were packed too tightly and the horse fell on the soldier's leg.

British on the road went down on one knee, their muskets pointing at McKean's men. An officer gave the order, "Fire." Thirty muskets went off, but the British were fifty yards away, too far for muskets. They rose up and charged, but the mud caused them to slip and slide.

Martin leveled his gun carefully at the ferocious British coming toward him. A quick aim from a crack rifleman, and a cannoneer fell dead. Martin reloaded.

McKean walked onto the road. A couple more British musket shots smashed into the nearby trees, but McKean was not concerned about that. There was still a gaping hole in the British line sixty yards away. He aimed and fired. Another cannoneer went down.

McKean turned south and rushed back down the road. The British on the road readied their bayonets and went after the Americans with vengeance. McKean looked behind him and saw the British moving as fast as they could through the mud. He looked at Franco's group, five yards down. McKean nodded, "Yes."

McKean and Martin dodged out of the way. Franco, Smitty, and Pete fired at their targets. Three British soldiers took a bullet to their heads. The other British on the road slowed down, not knowing what evil lay ahead.

The British in the woods to the left and right had orders to stay straight with the main body on the road. They slowed down to keep formation and then stopped. The British crouched down, reloaded, and fixed bayonets, those few who hadn't done so already. Behind them, men pulled the luckless soldier from underneath the fallen horse. Other soldiers cut the ropes of the dead horses and moved the cannons out of the way. Confusion ruled in the British ranks as men furiously tried to get the dead horses off the road and the rest of the cannons pulled up.

McKean shouted, "Get back, reload," an order that wasn't really necessary, as the riflemen already ran fast through the mud. McKean trailed. He assumed that Martin was right behind him, and glanced over his shoulder as he went south, but Martin didn't follow.

"Oh, my God."

Martin, the best shot in the company, stood idly in the middle of the road, ten yards up, casually loading his rifle. He faced the British with either contempt, or courage, or just plain stupidity. McKean couldn't believe it.

"Martin!"

Martin didn't even turn around. McKean shouted to his men, "Keep going. Don't stop, go," and then rushed toward Martin. "Martin, Martin, get back."

Martin aimed his loaded rifle at the British ranks. The British on the road panicked. They knew they couldn't hit anyone at that distance with muskets, and Martin wore the ragged signature of a rifleman. The British crashed off to the sides of the road to get out of the way of the shot.

McKean was five feet from Martin when a British cannon came into view behind the dispersing British soldiers. McKean shouted, "Martin, get down." McKean reached for Martin's arm just as the cannon exploded.

Canister.

Thousands of loosely packed slugs traveled the short sixty yards to Martin and McKean in a fraction of a second. Martin took most of the damage, through his entire body, riddled with uncountable holes, but many projectiles went entirely through his sides and sliced McKean into shreds. No matter about those wounds, though, because McKean's face wasn't protected by Martin, and small bullets, stones, pieces of iron, tin, chain, glass, and nails smashed into McKean's face and head.

The force of the blast knocked Martin off his feet. He took McKean down with him. Both men were dead before they hit the ground, bleeding all over the muddy snow. Their bodies were not much more than lifeless pulp.

Lawrence came up to them and kicked their bodies into the ditch. "Damn rebels, you're the lucky ones."

McKean's men, twenty yards south, witnessed the death of their leader and Martin.

Lawrence looked up. "There. Get them." The riflemen turned and raced down the road.

Chapter Thirty One

A t the sound of the cannon blast, Colonel Hand stood up from behind his tree on the left. He walked up to the front of the line and searched the road in the Princeton direction. Thirty riflemen lined up behind him, Hazlet's company. Hand watched eight men rush toward him from two hundred yards up. "Hold Fire. Hold Fire!" He turned around to make sure everyone heard him. "Hold fire." The remnants of McKean's company plowed into the lines and fell down panting.

Hand asked one of the men, "Everybody all right?"

Franco looked up. "No, Lieutenant McKean, and Martin, no."

Hand shook his head. He motioned for McKean's men to go south. "Get behind those men." McKean's men shuffled behind. Hand turned toward the soldiers in the road. "Steady, everybody, steady. They're coming now."

Gunfire erupted on both sides of the road. The sounds got closer and closer. Hand saw men moving as the British cautiously rounded the bend. The Americans gasped at how tightly they were formed, four abreast. The British stepped in unison, each row moving at a set pace. Both forces could see each other now. The British proceeded slowly toward what they thought was a puny group of rebels blocking their way, their cannons following a dozen yard behind.

Hand turned toward the riflemen again. He looked carefully at each side of the road to be sure nobody was running away. "Get ready to fire." Hand went back to his tree on the left. The riflemen were completely exposed to the British now, but Hand knew that they were not going to fire their cannons until they could get a good shot, and there was nothing to worry about with British muskets at that distance.

Hand said calmly to the riflemen on the road, "Easy. Wait 'till I say. I'm not going to let them shoot. Just a little more. Easy, easy, aim." The exposed riflemen picked their targets. The British infantry came relentlessly forward, then stopped to let the cannons catch up.

The British cannons rounded the bend, stopped briefly at the sight of the American line, and then continued. There were no horses. The British knew better now. They couldn't risk losing more horses, so six British soldiers and four cannoneers pushed each piece. The infantry fell back behind the cannons. The British on the western-most gun maneuvered to get a sure shot, but the second cannon also readied its deadly missiles for a guaranteed kill. Less than three hundred yards separated the two lines. A British soldier lit a match.

Hand yelled, "Fire." He fired. His rifle pricked the cold air. The soldier with the match went down with a bullet in the middle of his head.

The riflemen fired. Of the ten British per cannon, only five remained standing. The British infantry immediately broke for the sides and the protection of the woods. Hand shouted, "Second rank, fire." Another ten American bullets flew up the road. Two British infantrymen fell dead. A bullet ricocheted off the second cannon and struck a cannoneer in the face. Three British gunners fell, shot in the head and chest. British muskets fired with no effect. Another volley from the third rank of riflemen took out four more British soldiers. The riflemen ran into the woods on each side of the road and headed south.

Swanson, fifty yards in, and half way to the bend, watched through the trees as several British tried to avoid the hail of bullets by rushing right toward him, but they didn't see Swanson. Swanson's group fired, and sent the British back to the safety of the road.

Even though Swanson had prevented a collapse of the flank, the British were still loaded, just waiting for another match on the touchhole. Other gunners and soldiers came up from behind, cleared away the dead and wounded, and aimed both cannons at an empty road, except for those two American guns pointing straight at them six hundred yards away.

Corporal White's two cannons held a single six-pound ball in each muzzle, solid shot. The road was wide open now, no Americans, few British, but there were two big British cannons sitting there directly ahead.

The British yelled, "Fire." Corporal White shouted, "Fire." His men got to the touchholes first.

The two American cannons went off together. Cannonballs sailed straight up the road. One sucked the breath out of a British soldier as it passed within inches of his face and smashed into a tree to the left side of the road going up. The fierce momentum carried the ball through one tree, the next tree, and the next one, without even deflecting. British soldiers dodged to the side, falling down and scrambling to get out of the way. Finally, the cannonball came quietly to rest in the woods.

The second cannonball had a different fate. It originated from the right side of the road looking north. White's cannonball plowed waist-high straight toward the eastern-most British gun. The attending British soldiers heard the roar of the two American guns, but thought nothing of it as they bent to light the fuse.

A British solider glanced casually south to get a fix on the American position when, to his horror, he saw a black object coming straight at him. Instinctively, he reared backward and out of the way. The cannonball smashed into the left wheel of his gun and ricocheted off the barrel. The cannon spun around and faced west, but the twisting turn caused the left wheel to fall completely off, so now it lay in the mud with the left axle fixed four inches deep, pointing in the wrong direction. The ball wasn't spent, though, not yet. The deflection caused it to veer to the right, around the bend. It took the head off a British soldier without the least effort, sailed over the heads of the cannoneers in the second line of the British guns and smashed into the wheel of the third set of cannons far behind. That gun tilted and fell onto the road.

Major Derring watched the cannonball destroy two of his guns and rise high, ten feet almost straight up. He inched his horse back as a precaution, but he knew the ball wasn't going to do any more damage. The ball plummeted to rest in the mud at the hooves of Derring's horse.

"Get that gun off the road, and the others ahead, get them back."

Incredible confusion sapped the momentum out of the British attack. Two cannons blocked the road, making forward motion impossible. Soldiers worked furiously to move the heavy guns out of the way, but since there were no horses present, the soldiers had to try to move it by hand. A 320-pound cannon stuck in the mud required a huge effort, and Derring assigned ten men each to the task. At the other location another ten soldiers moved the unstricken gun behind the bend.

Corporal White dragged his guns back toward Trenton.

* * *

Hand surveyed the situation. There were no British up there, only shots on both sides. He listened to the direction of the sounds. There was nothing behind him yet, on either side. He glanced around. The riflemen appeared to be calm, forming properly off the road, so there was no cause for concern.

An officer appeared from the right. "We seem to be holding them, sir."

"Good. As long as we stay off the road, their guns are useless."

But now, Hand heard shots in the woods getting closer. Not to him, but to Trenton. That would mean that the British were getting behind him. Hand turned his ear toward the fire from the left and right. He ordered the officer, "Get back down, quickly, behind that next bend. Listen for a single shot from our guns. Meet there. Spread the word."

From fifty yards west to fifty yards east, the Americans encountered the British. They could hear gunfire all through the woods as small single engagements took place. On the American left, far in, a group of twenty British soldiers isolated only five rebels. The Americans fired, but woods were harder to penetrate than air. The American shots hit the trees. The British charged. Fixed bayonets came fast as the few rebels ran back, reloading, but not fast enough. The British stabbed the rebels in their backs with those long, deadly spears.

The British congratulated themselves as they watched the Americans bleed to death. It was a momentary victory, though, because they weren't far enough in. They looked to their right, where two dozen figures bore down on them. Another ten Americans appeared behind those soldiers. The British scrambled toward the road, but they were cut off now. They turned and charged the Americans on the right. The Americans hid behind trees and waited for the British to arrive, and then fired. Only six British remained. The rebels knelt down, aimed, and fired. The two surviving British ran back, panting, stumbling, and crashing into trees.

Chapter Thirty Two

Murphy stood with a group of soldiers a half mile below the bend. At the sounds of the rifle fire and cannons, all the men looked north.

One of the men asked, "Should we go up, sir?"

"No, they'll be coming here soon. I expect Colonel Hand will want to make another stand somewhere around here." He mumbled, "If he's still with us."

The two American cannons rounded the bend and came into the Murphy's view. Murphy said, "Stay here," and walked up to meet them. As he approached, he noticed Jackson and his men helping push.

"Mister Jackson, what are you doing here?

"An officer sent us back."

"I thought Colonel Hand wanted some musket men."

"He said the British was too far away for muskets. Said we'd be needed when they get close. What does that mean?"

"I can't imagine, son." Murphy grabbed a wheel and helped push. "Corporal White, how did it go up there?"

"We took down one gun, sir, maybe two."

"Very good. That will slow them down."

Corporal White said, "Yes, but there's lots of fighting in the woods. The colonel told me to get down a half mile from the bend and fire one shot, high, then every ten minutes."

Murphy said, "Ah, yes, the 'Hand' signal." They approached the group of soldiers, several of whom came up to help. Murphy released his wheel to a rifleman and walked around the gun to talk with Jackson.

"Jackson, did you see Sergeant Swanson up there?"

"Who?"

"Sergeant Swanson, a bulky man, had a bandage on his head?"

"No, sir, I didn't see nobody like that."

"How about two boys, one is your age, the other smaller. You see them?"

"No, sorry sir."

At the designated location, the men wheeled the guns around and pointed them northeast. Murphy asked, "How far can you shoot these?"

Corporal White replied, "About a mile, more if I load up the powder."

"Let's not blow up the gun. How about a mile?"

"Sure." Corporal White and his gunners readied the powder, but Murphy stopped them.

"Corporal, I suggest, and this is only a suggestion, entirely your choice, but I suggest that you load one of them with grape."

Corporal White said, "Yes, sir, that's a good idea."

Finished loading, Corporal White asked, "Where to, sir? I want to hit the road. You were up there, right?"

Murphy looked north. "Hmmm. Let's see, I think it goes due north from the bend." Murphy pulled out a compass and studied it, peering at the road and calculating. "Swing it around to the left more." The gunners moved the gun so that it faced due north, at a steep angle to the road. "Now right. That's it. That should put the ball right on the road. But don't tell Henry Knox I'm aiming his guns."

Corporal White smiled, lit a match, and touched it to the hole.

* * *

Sergeant Swanson anchored the right flank. He heard the cannon blast from the Trenton direction. To his right, and slightly behind him as he headed south, he heard the tops of the trees shatter, and saw the cannonball plunge directly into the stream, a hundred feet away. Swanson said to his men, "Too far up. Get back quick, off road."

* * *

Murphy called Jackson and Corporal White together, "I figure we have about a half hour. Hand will be here soon." Murphy pulled a watch out of his pocket. It was 3:00. Murphy said, "Tell Colonel Hand I went off to the right to look for my men."

Jackson said, "You want me to go with you?"

"No, you're needed here. I'll be back in a half hour. White, every ten minutes correct? You have a watch?"

"Yes, sir."

Chapter Thirty Three

S wanson headed south. His men drifted toward the road, but Swanson pulled them back again. There was no activity that far north, so he was able to move quickly through the woods.

One of the men complained, "Sarge, wouldn't it be better to use the road? We can move faster that way.

"Nein, bad road. Many fiend in front, fiend behind. We stay away." A second cannon blast from White's gun indicated he was going in the right direction, and he checked the angle of the sun to make sure. The third cannon shot ten minutes later put Swanson due east of the bend, one hundred yards in, but the direction of the sound made Swanson nervous, because he knew there was a bend, but he didn't know exactly where it was. He couldn't see the road anymore.

"Stay here. No move, no shoot. I check where we are."

Swanson left his men with an admonishing stare, and walked alone to the road, due west. As he got closer, he could see British uniforms moving south. "Oh, mein Gott," he mumbled. He peered around the bend to where hundreds of British marched in unison, none missing a single step, and directly in front of him, about to make the turn, were two, four, five cannons in the rear of the infantry, only a few yards in front of him.

Swanson waited until the last of the cannons were past, and then sneaked back to his men. He was surprised, but pleased, to find them still there. He told them what he saw and said, "We go, follow me." Swanson gauged the angle of the road perfectly, and walked parallel to it, keeping a hundred yards from the British. He said to the men, "More fast, need get ahead." The men proceeded more briskly through the muddy woods, Isaac and Toby in the rear.

* * *

Like a collapsing, inverted triangle, the Americans in the woods converged south, toward White's cannon shots, focusing more concentrated strength as they gathered onto the road from the flanks. Corporal White's fourth cannonball at the designated ten-minute interval signaled the time, 3:30 PM.

Colonel Hand came onto the road, along with 400 riflemen. They could see the British coming toward them a quarter mile away, straight ahead, but now there was no time to arrange a proper defensive line. Hand shouted, "Form in rank, across the road, fan out shallow!" All the Americans scrambled to get into position. To the men on the road, Hand yelled, "Get behind the guns, everybody! They're going to charge!" Then to Corporal White, "Grape!" White's gunners loaded the second cannon with grape, the first being already configured that way, which saved some time.

Hand grabbed the arm of a rifleman, "You, you're with the guns. Get them back after we fire. Plow through everybody, shoot 'em if you have to. We can't lose the guns."

Franco, of McKean's group, motioned to Smitty and Little Ben. Pete and Edward came over to help.

Jackson asked Hand, "Sir, we're muskets. Where should we be?"

"Ah, soldier, thank you. Right here, right in front. Thank you. Get off to the sides, so you don't get shot by our own men. I'll stay with you."

Hand asked Smitty, "Can you hit from here?"

Smitty looked far ahead. "I don't think so, sir."

"Try," then to the riflemen on the road, "Wait, wait... Fire!"

McKean's riflemen fired at targets 400 yards away, but there were no hits. Just as White finished loading, the British came forward with fixed bayonets from a quarter mile away. Hand shouted, "Artillery, fire!" White discharged both guns straight up the road. Several British fell, but, unfortunately, the smoke from the cannons blinded the riflemen, obscuring the road for several seconds. Hand ordered, "Artillery to the rear." McKean's men and White's group dragged the cannons south, pushing riflemen out of the way. The smoke cleared to reveal two British cannons.

Hand said, "Damn! Off the road!" The riflemen and Jackson's men all jumped to the sides as the cannons went off. Trees, branches, and several riflemen were shattered by the blast. The British charged fast. Hand ordered, "Back to the road, fire!"

At 200 yards, the rifles were more effective. "Second rank, Fire!" More British fell at 100 yards. Hand shouted, "Fall back," then to Jackson's men, "Stay." The Americans retreated south. Most of the British stopped, being too far away for bayonets, but twenty British came fast for Jackson and his men. Hand was with them, and fired, with a hit at 40 yards. Jackson's group fired, also with good results, and only a dozen British lingered. Hand couldn't reload in time, but Jackson's men could, and did. Five

British remained. Hand and Jackson's men dodged to the side, rather than accept the charge. Luckily, several riflemen arrived from the east to put five bullets into the heads of the chargers.

Hand said, "Whew, that was close. Good job, boys, let's go."

Jackson beamed. The Americans headed toward Trenton, double-time.

* * *

All except Murphy.

* * *

Murphy shouted, "Swanson, Isaac!" At the 3:20 Hand signal, Murphy was already a quarter mile into the woods, or so he thought. With the sun in front, it wasn't difficult to gauge direction and distance, but with it behind, it was almost impossible. He was lost. He shouted, "Swanson," and listened. "Swanson, Isaac!" There was no answer. He turned toward the direction of the 3:30 cannonball blast. He was too far north, and a half-mile away.

* * *

Swanson was due east of the American force at 3:30, when the American cannon signaled the call to come home. Swanson said, "We go. Move fast."

Isaac laughed. "Coming, mother."

The men moved silently through the thin trees toward Trenton. Swanson watched them like a mother hen. He pointed at Isaac. "You boys, you stay with me."

To the right, Swanson heard White's cannons discharge, and he saw the British retaliation, with British bullets filling the air. Swanson was alarmed to see no one to his right as he moved south. No Americans covered his left, as was expected, since he was the flank, but he thought he would see a line of Americans facing the enemy, someone he could attach to for safety. He looked to the right through the ever-thickening trees. No British there, either, but Swanson was in danger of getting cut off. He didn't know there was no flank now, just every man for himself as the Americans retreated toward town.

He made a decision. It was a good decision, but it could have some serious consequences. Swanson abandoned the flank and moved his men toward the road, slanting southwest toward Trenton. The sun was directly in front of him. "This way." Swanson moved in toward the road. His men followed him, including Isaac and Toby.

Thirty yards from the road, a dozen British soldiers fired at a few stray Americans tucked behind trees. It was a stalemate, nobody winning, no one getting shot. Swanson changed that. The British fired due south at the Americans, but Swanson's men crept up from the British left. Now the British had the enemy on the left and in front. Swanson whispered to his men behind him, "Down." He moved up to a tree, a little closer to the British, who didn't see him yet. Swanson moved to another tree and fingered the trigger of his rifle. A British soldier looked to his left, "Aaieee!"

Swanson yelled, "Fire!" He fired. His men fired. Isaac fired. Isaac hit a tree.

Five British fell. The Americans in front of the British were relieved to see Swanson's men to their right. They fired their rifles and another three British fell. The rest of the British ran north through the woods.

The stray American group fell back toward Trenton, but the presence of those few rebel stragglers convinced Swanson there was indeed an American line, and he was still needed to be the flank of it. Swanson called to his men, "Back, back!" He wanted to get deeper into the woods to where he was before, the right flank, but his men knew better. They realized it was good to be close to the road, where there was safety in numbers. Swanson reloaded and marched east, to get back to the flank. Isaac and Toby followed him, but the other men didn't. Swanson looked behind him and saw his men moving west, ignoring his orders to follow him back to the flank.

"No, this way. You, come here." His men hung their heads and ignored him politely, as if they had never heard the order. Swanson turned around and headed west toward his men and the road. He didn't know that Isaac and Toby had been following him east. Swanson assumed that the boys were walking back to the road with his disobedient men. In the dark shadows of the woods, Isaac and Toby didn't see Swanson turn around and go west. Isaac and Toby continued east.

* * *

They were the flank now.

Chapter Thirty Four

The boys looked around and ahead for Swanson, but could not see him. Toby spotted an unusual lump, covered with leaves and dirt. He approached it slowly, but jumped back at the sight of a dead British soldier. "Oh, no!" Blood poured out of the soldier's neck, turning the snow a dirty red.

Isaac looked north. Five British soldiers appeared through the trees, cautiously inching through the brush. Toby continued to stare at the dead man. He felt the soldier's horrible pain at the thought of the bullet slicing his neck open.

Isaac watched the British come toward him. "Sergeant, over here. They're coming. Here."

There was no Swanson. Isaac peered through the trees. No one else was there, but Isaac didn't have time to go looking for Swanson, who surely had to be nearby. The British soldiers heard Isaac's voice and stalked closer, but the British didn't see Isaac and Toby yet.   Isaac   reached his arm backward to Toby, but he focused intensely on the approaching British, not looking behind him. "Give me a gun," he said.

Toby couldn't take his eyes off the dead man, blood dribbling down onto the soldier's musket. The soldier's eyes were wide open, but he was surely dead. Toby became scared. He picked up the soldier's right arm and draped it gently over the soldier's eyes, then took the dead soldier's gun and put it in Isaac's hand. Isaac aimed it at the British coming toward him. Isaac's movement caused the British to turn in his direction.

Corporal Lawrence noticed an American musket leveled at him. Another rebel, Toby, was only a few yards behind. Lawrence didn't recognize either Isaac or Toby through the thick woods. His men, though, sensed danger. They were far enough into the woods where there should be no rebels, but there were rebels there. There could be many more rebels nearby.

Isaac saw the hesitation in the five British soldiers. The British stopped and pointed their guns, but crept backward against the threat of a single musket in the hands of a lone rebel. Isaac yelled, "Sergeant, we've got 'em. Ha, Sergeant, over here!"

The British fell back in fear. Isaac looked around, but there were no Americans anywhere behind him. The British retreated faster. They disappeared into the tangled woods, not willing to risk a fight even with only two Americans visible.

Isaac turned around to Toby. He asked, "What are you doing?"

"I never seen a dead man before."

"He had it coming."

Now there were no sounds, no shots, no cannons, no voices, just eerie silence in the darkening woods. Isaac said, "Where are we? Where is everybody?"

Toby shouted, "Sergeant, Sergeant! Pa!"

"Stop that. You'll bring the British back."

The sun hung low on the horizon. Isaac and Toby searched the trees for some movement. They listened for a gunshot, or an American voice, or something, anything to indicate where the fighting was. Nobody was there, and the only sounds of battle were faint and far away. Isaac pointed toward Princeton. He said, "We should go that way."

Toby said, "No, that way. Look at the sun." They could only see the sun through the tops of the trees. It was low in the sky, forty-five minutes until sunset.

"You're right. Let's go."

Toby got up with Isaac's help. They walked south slowly and then stopped for a minute. Toby sat on the ground and loaded all three guns, the two of their own, and that of the dead British soldier. Toby handed one gun to Isaac. The shots now seemed to come from the southwest, but it was hard to tell.

Isaac said, "We have to get back to the road."

Toby said, "I don't know as that's a good idea."

Isaac thought about that advice, more than he had ever paid attention to his stupid little brother before. Coming on the statement of Isaac's saying they should go 'that way' toward Princeton, but the sun being behind them, and Toby realizing that it was the wrong direction, and saying, 'no, that way,' Isaac seriously considered Toby's remark. If the battle was south, where they wanted to go, then the road would be loaded with British. It was better to stay away from the road. Isaac said, "You're right again. Twice in one day. Good for you. We should stay in the woods, no road."

Toby managed a weak smile at the compliment.

Isaac said, "But we need to get to Trenton. We'll follow the sun, but stay in the woods."

Toby replied, "Maybe we should go off there, and just run, run away, go home." Toby pointed to the southeast, suggesting that they go deeper into the woods.

"I don't think so. How are we going to cross that creek? You saw it. I don't feel like staying out here all night, either. It's going to get dark pretty soon." He called out, "Sergeant, Sergeant!"

Toby shouted, "Sergeant, Sergeant Swanson, Pa!"

No answer.

Isaac said "We have to stay away from the road, get to the bridge. If the Sergeant isn't there, we'll follow the creek and get away."

Toby finished loading the last musket. He looked at the gun. He didn't want Isaac to see the terror that he felt. "Isaac?"

"Yeah?"

Toby wiped his face with his sleeve and looked up. "Are we going to die?"

Isaac recognized the dreadful fear in Toby's face and sucked in some of that fear. He didn't know what to do. They were lost. There was nobody to help. They were in a war, with the enemy probably all around. A single shot, whichever one of them it hit, from wherever it came, and they'd both be dead when the British charged. They were in terrible danger.

Toby begged, "I want to go home."

Isaac's eyes got blurry. "No, we can't go home." Isaac peered into the woods. He cried, but not so that Toby could see him. Isaac talked into the woods, "But I'll promise you this..." Isaac wiped his eyes with his hand. He turned toward Toby with a dirty, tear-stained face and said, "If we ever get out of here, we are not going to Allentown."

Toby smiled a little.

Chapter Thirty Five

Swanson had arrived at the battle just in time to put five bullets into the chargers. Hand was already heading south as Swanson counted heads. There were two missing. He asked one of his men, "Where the boys?"

"I thought they was with you."

"Oh, mein Gott." Swanson peered into the woods, searching for Isaac and Toby, but the British came at them again from up ahead, walking slowly, and formed across the road, all bayonets.

Noticing Swanson's bandage, Jackson came over. "Are you Sergeant Swanson?"

"Yes."

"Captain Murphy's looking for you."

"Where he is?"

Jackson pointed east. "He went that way. Been gone a half-hour. You think he's all right?"

Swanson hung his head, then recovered. To his men he said, "Go. Go with Colonel Hand."

"No, Sarge, we'll go with you."

"Nein, you go. Hand need you." Swanson turned to Jackson. "Give me your musket, and your bullets."

Jackson handed them over and received Swanson's rifle in return. Jackson looked at it with amazement, having just made the trade of his life. The rebels looked north at the approaching British. Walter said, "Jack, we got to go."

Jackson replied, "Don't worry, I'm a rifleman now."

Swanson loaded the musket with five bullets and went east. Everyone else ran south toward Trenton.

* * *

Colonel Hand formed for another battle a half-mile above town, but at 4:00, he had already fulfilled his mission, because the British could not possibly cross the bridge before sundown. His cannons were across, and only a handful of men remained, the rest wisely running through town for the safety of the American lines on the other side of the Assunpink.

Swanson was 250 yards east in five minutes. He saw a figure plowing through the woods, almost directly toward him, but slanting away to his right. Five British soldiers pursued Murphy, who smacked into a tree and crashed to the ground. Swanson fired. He took the bark off several trees, and clipped the finger of one of the soldiers. Swanson was reloaded twenty seconds later, with eight bullets this time, and a little more powder for 'oomph.' His blast was like a shotgun, scattering bark, leaves, and British.

Murphy said, "Borg, thank God you're here. I thought I was going to die. Where are the boys?" He looked behind Swanson, expecting to see his sons, and then realized that Swanson was alone.

Swanson hung his head, looked at the ground, and then reached for his powder horn. "We go."

Murphy held Swanson's arm in mid-load. "Borg, where are the boys?"

Swanson said, "I not know. I lost them. I am, how you say, 'sorry.'"

Murphy said, "It's all right, Borg. Are they dead?" Murphy cringed at the expected reply.

"Nein, I not know. I lost them. I came back to find them. I am sorry. You gave them to me, and I lost them. I am sorry."

"Borg, do you really think that I would hold you responsible for them, even if they got killed? No, Borg, I would never do that. They'll have to get home as best they can, if they can."

Swanson shook his head and said, "We go."

They made their way past the 4:00 battle, which was too far to the right for them to help, and arrived at the edge of the woods. Murphy shouted, "There they are!"

The boys were a half-mile away, running due west into town.

Chapter Thirty Six

Isaac and Toby stumbled through the trees and underbrush, keeping the sun almost directly ahead. Toby carried two guns, Isaac one. The gunshots were behind them now. Isaac looked through the remaining trees. "There's some houses over there. That's Trenton. Where is everybody?" They emerged from the woods and saw the town, an assurance of safety if they could just get to those houses.

Trenton was a sleepy village with two almost parallel roads running south from where they were. Twenty houses and shops lined the two streets. The fighting was on the western-most road and spilling over into town. Isaac and Toby were near the eastern road.

The end of the town in the distance gave way to a wide, flat, open field a hundred yards deep. The eastern-most road led to the stone bridge over the Assunpink Creek, a half-mile away. The American army was on the other side of the creek.

American soldiers poured out of the woods far to the right, running through the streets. The Americans rushed toward the bridge as British soldiers came out of the woods behind them. The British stopped, knelt, and fired. They did not hit any of the Americans, but British cannons appeared, pointed their deadly muzzles at the fleeing rebels, and fired.

Iron filled the air with invisible death, grapeshot. Six Americans fell. Three got up and limped slowly toward the bridge, but three others didn't get up at all. The British fired again. Four more Americans died. The rest of the Americans poured over the bridge and collapsed on the other side. Waiting comrades helped them off.

Isaac said, "Let's get to that house and work our way down."

The boys ran through a small field in the open, toward the house. Toby got there first. He turned around to watch Isaac come up. Toby's eyes widened in terror as three British soldiers came out of the woods and pointed their muskets right at Isaac from thirty yards behind.

Toby yelled, "Isaac, get down."

Two British muskets went off. A bullet broke a window and another blew a piece of wood off the side of the house near Toby. Isaac instinctively ducked at the sounds. He held his hands to his head and ran toward Toby.

But there was another soldier with a loaded musket. Isaac didn't even hear that one.

The third bullet shattered Isaac's left arm. Mangled bits of blood and flesh shot out the other side. A shock wave of searing pain leaped up from Isaac's arm and drained the blood from his brain, his whole body aflame in a fire of agony. Isaac spun around and plowed into the house, his face and body smashing into the building. Isaac sank to the ground, unconscious.

Toby screamed, "No! No! No! Isaac, No! Get up! Isaac, No! Help! Somebody help!"

Nobody was there.

Toby grabbed Isaac by his shirt and dragged him to the Trenton side of the house. He leaned Isaac against a porch, facing Trenton. Isaac slumped down. Toby ran toward the woods. "Help, help, somebody help!"

Three British soldiers came out of the woods. They spotted Toby and ran toward the house. Toby ducked back to the porch, terrified, and looked around for anyone who could help. The three soldiers split up, covering both sides of the house, and crept along the sides of the building toward the lone rebel hiding behind the house.

Toby spotted Isaac's gun in the grass, but it was too far away to retrieve. He remembered the game, Monday's Battle at the Princeton Bridge, with Isaac. He carefully balanced the two muskets on the railings of the porch and cocked the hammers. He clutched one gun in his left hand, the other in his right, holding each gun at his hip, but at the correct elevation, the only issue being the angle of the shot, if he had to shoot. Toby waited, facing Trenton. "Hold up, Isaac. Please, hold up."

One British soldier appeared on the left, running away from the house toward Trenton. Toby aimed from the hip and shot. The soldier fell. Another soldier appeared from the right, heard the shot, turned, and faced Toby. Toby shot him with his right gun. A third soldier rounded the house on the left, but Toby was unloaded. He flung his right-hand gun at the soldier. The soldier ducked. Toby flung the left-hand gun. The butt of the gun hit the soldier in the nose. The soldier clutched his face and went down.

Toby gripped Isaac's good arm and dragged him toward the bridge, a quarter-mile away, struggling through the mud at only a foot or two per minute. He dropped Isaac's arm, panted, and looked around. "Help! Help!" Nobody responded. Nobody cared. Men everywhere rushed to the bridge.

Toby got behind Isaac, cradled his arms around Isaac's chest, and staggered backward toward the bridge across an open field with British soldiers only a few hundred yards behind. Isaac was still unconscious. Toby looked at the British soldier he just hit with the musket barrel.

The dazed British soldier stood up and saw Toby dragging Isaac away. The soldier picked up his musket and loaded it. Toby dragged Isaac faster and yet faster to the distant bridge with all of his diminishing strength, getting more and more exhausted every second. The soldier calmly loaded his gun. He aimed, no problem for a musket at this short distance. Toby cried to Isaac, who couldn't hear him anyway, "It's all right, Isaac. It'll be all right." Toby expected a bullet in his head, or Isaac's, at any moment. He couldn't look at the British soldier. "Sorry, Isaac. Very sorry."

A shot sounded from thirty yards away, directly behind the soldier. Toby rubbed his free hand all over his body. No, there was no blood that he could find, and Isaac was the same as before. Toby looked up. The soldier fell dead. A bulky man with a bandaged head lumbered up as fast as he could run. Swanson took Isaac from Toby and laid him gently on the ground. Toby sighed with relief.

Swanson inspected Isaac's arm and frowned. Murphy ran up from behind. Swanson said, "Bad, very bad. We get him to bridge."

Murphy and Swanson carried Isaac through the town toward safety on the other side of the Assunpink. Toby followed. At the edge of town, the Americans fell over themselves trying to get to the bridge. Swanson and Murphy fell behind the crowd with Isaac in their arms. Toby brought up the rear of their group, with other Americans closely behind him. He loaded as he ran, then stopped and turned toward the British.

Colonel Hand was thirty yards behind. He saw Toby aim his gun directly at him. "No!" Hand ducked to the ground, his momentum plunging him into the field. Toby fired. Hand felt Toby's bullet whiz past his ear as he fell and heard an agonizing, "Ahhh!" five yards behind him. A British bayonet was only moments away from plunging into Hand's back. The soldier fell forward and sprawled into the mud. Hand glanced behind and saw the soldier fall, and then turned toward Toby, who was running again toward the bridge. Hand mumbled, "Damn," as he got up.

Halfway though the field, Isaac regained consciousness and raised his slouched head to see where they were going. A lonely Washington sat on a horse in the middle of the bridge fifty yards away from the boys and the men. Americans rushed past Washington in the distance. Washington said things to them and pointed. The sun was on the horizon.

Isaac and the group got to the bridge. Hand and his men were a few yards behind. Swanson supported Isaac but lost him in the shuffle as they crossed.

Isaac slid along the right side of Washington's horse. He turned, staggered, and caught the horse's mane in his good hand to keep from going down, but then spun backward and fell onto the hard road of the bridge on his back. Isaac looked up and saw Washington on the horse through fuzzy, teary, pain-filled eyes.

Hand was the last to cross. Washington pointed to his right. "Colonel Hand, form your men in that field."

Hand and his men went off to the right. Swanson and Murphy picked Isaac up and carried him off the bridge. Toby followed.

Chapter Thirty Seven

A ll the Americans were now across. Washington turned around and slowly trotted toward the lines on the American side of the creek. Eighteen rebel cannons lined the slight rise 200 yards back where men poured in the powder and smashed the balls down the barrels. Other men hurried to move the thirty wagons out of the way, up to the road and behind the trees, beyond the sight of the British guns, but not far enough away that the ammunition was unavailable. Three thousand American muskets pointed at the creek and the bridge. Many men lay down in the frozen grass to present a lower profile.

Hand's men were on the right. From Hand's angle, he watched thousands of British come out of the woods behind town and run toward the bridge. He estimated about five thousand British altogether. No doubt, there were others on the road, yet to arrive, along with their cannons.

The British infantry lined up just south of town. They crouched behind houses and trees in case of an American artillery attack. They waited. They loaded. Officers steadied them. A contingent of British grenadiers a hundred yards to the north of the bridge steeled themselves against the expected command.

The Americans heard the dreaded order from across the creek, "Charge!" Forty British soldiers charged fast for the bridge.

The bridge was sixteen feet wide and made of stone. It ran north and south. The railings were stone, three feet above the base of the bridge and nine inches thick. The British came onto the bridge with hatred in their eyes.

American cannons exploded from behind. Cannonballs slammed into the bridge and columns of water shot high in the air. American muskets mowed down the British from far and near. The British scrambled back to their lines. Many were wounded, and others never made it off the bridge.

The firing stopped. Other British came onto the bridge with no interference from the Americans and dragged away the dead and wounded. The walls of the bridge were still intact. Washington was fifty yards from the bridge now. He ordered some men nearby, "You. You men, cover the exit. You too, up to the bridge. You, over there, off to the right. Report to Colonel Hand, over there."

The British formed heatedly on their side for another attack. A British officer pointed to the bridge. Another fifty British charged with bayonets. The three British cannons, in place now, boomed from secure hiding places in town, aiming for the American guns. There were no hits.

The American artillery opened up again. Hundreds of American muskets went off. Two American cannons aimed for the British artillery at the edge of town and took off the top of a Trenton house, too high a shot. The British cannoneers moved back into the protection of the houses. Another American cannonball smashed the bridge's right, eastern, stone railing, creating a gaping two-foot hole in the side. Buckets of British blood poured through the opening and into the water below. British soldiers tumbled off both sides and into the creek.

Colonel Hand and an officer watched the battle at the bridge from the right. The officer asked, "Shouldn't we send some men over there, sir?"

Hand said, "That would be about the stupidest thing we could do."

The British formed for a third charge. To cover it, the British artillery opened up. Cannonballs flew overhead, striking the mud and scampering around through the American lines. Another fifty British charged the bridge. Cannonballs and bullets slaughtered them. They fell into the creek like cattle off a ravine. Simultaneously, a hundred British rushed to the Americans' right, Hand's men defending, and waded into the creek. Henry Knox, with the artillery, pointed them out to his gunners. Hand's men blasted them with rifles. Cannonballs splashed into the creek from Henry's guns. Arms, legs, and mangled bodies gurgled to the surface.

The firing stopped. British Major Derring waded into the freezing water to retrieve a wounded soldier. Hand took careful aim. Derring looked down the barrel of a Kentucky Long Rifle a mere thirty yards away and stared coldly at Hand for a long three seconds. Hand lowered his gun. Derring pulled the soldier out.

On the British side, General Cornwallis sat on a horse just south of the buildings, a hundred yards north of the creek. Another officer rode up on a horse. He arrived just in time to see the slaughter at the Battle of the Assunpink. The officer looked south at the many dead and wounded lying on the ground on the British side of the bridge. There was no more firing from there, because proper warfare etiquette forbade the shooting of wounded soldiers in retreat. The officer watched as several British soldiers dragged the wounded men back toward town.

Cornwallis's horse snorted from the acrid smell of gunpowder clogging its nostrils. Cornwallis patted the horse. "There, there. It'll be over soon."

The officer said, "We'd better hold off for tonight, sir. It's getting dark."

"Yes, I know. No matter. I'll bag the Fox in the morning."

The officer said, "If Washington is the general I take him to be, his army will not be found there in the morning, sir."

Cornwallis didn't reply. He only stroked the mane of his horse, indifferent to the carnage at the creek.

"Sir, how shall I report the casualties to General Howe?"

"There were no casualties today, my good man."

Henry Knox spied Cornwallis and the officer on horses 400 yards away. He pointed them out to Alexander Hamilton, nineteen years old, Captain of artillery.

Hamilton was one of those remarkable young officers whose age didn't seem to matter to anyone. Henry remembered him last week at Trenton when he pulled two cannons onto King Street just as the British were about to counterattack. Two shots from Hamilton's cannons sent the British reeling just in time.

Henry asked, "May I?"

Hamilton motioned to his cannons with a 'help yourself' gesture.

Henry aimed the gun himself. He crouched down behind the gun and lined his eye up the barrel. "Up." The men cranked the gun up an inch. "More." Another inch. Henry shoved the barrel around to the right and realigned it with his eye. He stepped away from the gun to get a better perspective, but Cornwallis moved. Henry went back to the gun. "Wait." He moved the barrel a smidgen to the right and looked up at Hamilton without a word. Hamilton lit a match. Henry took it and touched it to the hole.

The cannon jumped backward. A cannonball sailed over the creek and plowed into the mud three feet from Cornwallis and the British officer. The officer's horse whinnied and went up on its hind legs, so the officer climbed onto the horse's neck to bring it down and then slipped back into the saddle as the animal landed. The impact of the cannonball splattered the officer with mud. Cornwallis backed his own horse up to get out of the way.

Cornwallis looked the officer up and down. "For God's sake, man, clean yourself up."

Hamilton said, "Nice shot, sir."

Henry Knox shook his head, "Damn," and walked away.

Chapter Thirty Eight

Isaac lay on the ground, conscious, but writhing in pain. Swanson kneeled and inspected his arm while Toby and Murphy stood behind. "How is it, Borg?"

"The bullet go clean through. No hit the bone, I think. Maybe he be good. Maybe not. I wrap it up. We see."

"Not yet. I'll be right back." Murphy turned around and walked off quickly.

Swanson took out a knife and cut a piece of cloth from Isaac's coat. He forced it against the wound and said to Toby, "Hold tight. I get bandage." Swanson walked away.

Murphy entered General Fermoy's tent with contempt in his eyes. Fermoy lay on his cot, but got up, startled, as Murphy came in. Fermoy reached for his bottle of whiskey from a table and took a long swig.

Murphy stomped over to him. "Gimmee that, you bastard." Murphy took the bottle and stared threateningly at Fermoy.

Fermoy said, "All right, old chap." He reached under his cot, pulled out an open box with dozens of bottles, got another one, opened it, took a drink, and put the bottle on the table. The bottle wobbled. Fermoy eyed it suspiciously. The two men watched the bottle for ten seconds, spinning around and around on its bottom. Fermoy reached for it, but missed.

Fermoy fell to the ground, on his hands and knees, at Murphy's feet. He reached slowly for the bottle from his location on the floor, but hesitated before actually touching it. The wobbling caused his brain to wobble also, his eyes spinning in their sockets with each round. Fermoy pulled his hand away and sat up on his cot. He watched the bottle "whittle-whittle-whittle," and end up straight. Fermoy smiled. "So, how did it go, old chap?"

Fermoy tried to get up, but staggered against the bed and had to steady himself with his hand on the tent wall. It was a very flimsy tent. His right hand punched through the soft cloth and he swayed back and forth, his right arm wrapped in tent cloth. Fermoy reached in the air for something to grab, found the head of his cot, and clutched it with his left hand. He dragged the cot toward the tent wall as he fell to the right, but Fermoy was a pro at this drinking business.

He forced his right foot under the tent and shifted his weight left and right to keep from falling. "Whoa." Steadying himself, he turned toward Murphy, but the turn caused his left-right balance to fail, so he yanked his arm from the hole in the tent and sank down into the cot, all in one motion. Murphy looked up at the roof of the tent, in case the force caused the tent to collapse. It miraculously didn't. Fermoy picked up the uncooperative bottle and took another swig. "Sorry, old chap. How did it go?" Whisky ran down his face.

"Do you know how many men want to shoot you dead?"

Fermoy shrugged. Murphy took the almost-full bottle of whiskey and left the tent.

* * *

Swanson came back and took the cloth from Toby. He pushed hard against the wound. Isaac winced in pain. Swanson held him down with his leg and forced the cloth harder against Isaac's arm. Isaac screamed, but the blood stopped flowing. Toby, close to tears, held his hand to Isaac's forehead. "Isaac, don't die. Please don't die."

Murphy came up with the whiskey and knelt down next to Swanson. Murphy looked to Swanson for implied permission to pour. Swanson nodded, "Good. Yes, good."

Swanson removed the cloth. Murphy poured some whiskey over Isaac's mangled arm as Swanson reached into a bag, took out a roll of bandage, and wrapped the wound. "That will help."

Jackson came up with some other men behind him. "Hey, Cap, maybe we could have a taste of that, huh? Ya know, we fought all day."

Swanson recognized Jackson's voice, turned around, and said, "Give me my gun back." They exchanged weapons, Jackson reluctantly.

Jackson said, "All right, Cap? We could use a little."

"No, this is medicine."

Jackson frowned.

Murphy said, "But I know where you can get some more. Lots more." Jackson's face brightened.

Murphy looked down at Isaac, then at Jackson. The two boys were very close in age. Murphy remembered Jackson's brother, Satchel, dead now. Murphy thought what it would be like for Isaac to lose Toby, or for Toby to lose Isaac, probably worse.

Murphy said to Jackson, "Fermoy's drunk. There's a box of whiskey under his cot. Sneak around the back of his tent and drag it out underneath. Don't tell anybody or you'll lose it."

"Gosh, thanks, Cap."

Murphy watched Jackson disappear into the smoke, clutter, and tangled mess of a fighting army after a battle.

Swanson finished bandaging Isaac's arm. He lifted his leg off of Isaac's chest and said, "You stay still, boy." Isaac nodded. Swanson got up. "I get some water."

Murphy said, "Thanks, Borg."

Swanson nodded and walked away.

Isaac lay on the ground on his back. His eyes slowly closed shut. Murphy bent down, held Isaac's hand and rubbed his forehead. Toby knelt down next to Isaac and watched the blood ooze slowly through the makeshift bandage. Toby asked, "Pa?"

Murphy looked up at Toby, who stared in anguish at Isaac's gaping wound, the blood seeping through the bandage more each second. Murphy pressed the bandage harder against Isaac's arm. Isaac opened his eyes and shuddered in anguish.

Murphy picked up the bottle and placed it to Isaac's lips. "Drink a little. It'll take away the pain." Murphy tightened the bandage with another wrap of the cloth. Isaac drank, coughed, and drank again. He liked it. He drank some more.

Murphy withdrew the bottle. "Whoa, boy, a little at a time. There's a lot of fighting ahead."

Toby's tears streamed down his face. "Is he going to die?"

"No. We won't let him die."

Washington and Mercer rode by on horseback, talking. Isaac saw them and raised his eyebrows. Murphy faced the other way, but turned around at Isaac's expression. Washington recognized Murphy and trotted up with Mercer following. Murphy stood up and held a salute. Washington returned it.

Washington said, "Hi, Murph."

"Sir."

"These your boys? I heard about them today."

"Yes, sir. Boys, the General."

Isaac and Toby were speechless. Murphy raised another salute. He told the boys, "Salute, like this."

Murphy saluted. The boys saluted, even Isaac, with his good arm. They returned the salute before Washington did. Washington held his salute, then returned. Murphy returned.

Murphy said, "I'll work on that with them, sir."

Mercer smiled, as did Washington. Washington asked, "How'd you boys get here, anyway?"

Isaac's pain slackened from the whiskey. He said, "The Quaker Road."

Now Washington became surprised. He looked around and behind him to see if anyone was listening. "You took the Quaker road? Did you cross the swamp?"

Isaac replied, "Yes. I got stuck in the mud. I couldn't even get up."

Washington's face soured in disappointment.

Isaac continued, excited. "Toby got chased by a goose. You should have seen him, running all around, this goose quacking, biting him. Toby was running for his life. Ha. From a goose."

Washington spotted the bottle of whiskey next to Isaac. "Steady, soldier." He addressed Toby. "How were you running around if it's all mud?"

Toby still knelt next to Isaac. All this time, he'd been staring at the great general in awe. Now he was asked to speak. He eyed the two generals, Washington and Mercer, miles high, on two huge horses, wearing immaculate uniforms, peering down at him.

Silence. Everyone looked at Toby for an answer, but Toby didn't hear the question. He froze. He looked around at the faces of those present. Everyone stared at him, except Isaac, who sneaked another swig of whiskey. Washington's horse snorted. Even the two horses seemed to expect something of him. Toby looked at Washington in fear.

Washington leaned forward, his face at his horse's head. "How were you running around in the mud?"

That didn't make sense, because there was no mud on his side of the road. Toby thought, *what mud*? He panicked. He lost track of the conversation, and he didn't want to look like a fool in front of this great man. Toby's mind raced, trying to figure out what mud Washington was talking about "Uh, uh, what? I don't know."

Washington dismounted while Murphy held the reigns, and then Washington walked over to Toby. He extended his arm and said, "Give me your hand, son." Toby took it. Washington said, "Stand up, if you please." Washington pulled with what Toby imagined was the greatest force he'd ever felt. Toby rose, almost without his own effort, still in emotional shock and confusion.

Toby stood up, feeling a little better. Even though Washington was six-foot two, he was a little less intimidating than being on that giant horse high in the air.

Washington released Toby's hand. "This is important, son. How were you running around at the swamp when your brother over there was stuck in the mud?"

Toby was relieved. He understood now. He said, "I was on the other side of the road."

Washington's eyes focused curiously on Toby's face. "What's on the other side of the road?"

"Anna's house."

Washington was expecting a military reply, but paused, realizing that he had to get his information from wherever he could, even from a fourteen-year-old boy. "All right. Let me ask you in another way. What was the ground like? Was it mud on your side of the road? What was the ground like on your side of the road? You're a soldier. I expect you to remember things like a soldier does."

Toby liked that. He was a soldier. The great general called him that, a soldier, a real soldier. He was a soldier. Toby felt better, proud. He said, "The ground? No, no mud. Not on Anna's side. Corn stalks, I think." Toby looked at Isaac. "Right?"

Isaac nodded his head, "Yes."

Toby affirmed, "Yes, smashed-down corn stalks. We walked straight to Anna's house." Then turned to Isaac, "Right?"

Isaac nodded, and added, "Yes. We didn't have any trouble. I mean, we just walked."

Washington asked Isaac, "What about the Quaker Road, coming here?"

Isaac replied, "All right, I guess. We just walked."

Washington asked Isaac another question. "Which side of the road at the swamp was mud?"

Isaac replied, "Coming here, on the right."

Washington was satisfied that he had everything he needed. He looked at the boys piercingly. "You boys forget this conversation. If you say anything to anybody about the Quaker Road or the swamp before tomorrow..." Washington shook his head in stern admonition.

Murphy said, "You'll do five years on a prison farm just waiting for trial."

The boys indicated in their faces that they got the message. Washington remounted his horse. "Murphy, come here. Hugh."

Washington gently pulled the reigns left and trotted his horse into the field. Mercer followed, with Murphy on foot. The three men gathered out of earshot of the boys. "Murphy, get Sullivan, Greene, and Knox up to my tent."

Murphy saluted and walked away. He went back to the boys and said to Toby, "Take care of him for a little while. I've got something to do. The Sergeant will be back soon."

At the Washington-Mercer conference twenty yards away, Mercer asked Washington, "You thinking of taking the back road?"

"I've been thinking about it all day, but I didn't think we could cross the swamp. The enemy would come down the Pennington Road and that would be the end. Now it's different."

"The boy said the mud's on the left going up. You think that's true?"

"It doesn't matter. We know at least one side of the swamp is passable. We'll get some men out ahead."

Chapter Thirty Nine

Five hundred yards to the east of the American army, the Assunpink Creek was shallow enough to cross. Washington knew that. Cornwallis knew that. Everybody knew that. At 9:00 PM, Thursday night, an axe struck a tree on the American side. A few seconds later, another chop was heard all the way to the bridge. Then, to the west of the bridge where the creek was not fordable, chop, chop, "Tally Ho." A tree crashed to the ground. More axe chops filled the distance between the fordable locations far to the right of the bridge, and the unfordable locations to the left. Trees fell all up and down the American lines.

Sounds of digging chunked and clanged through the chilly air. The British, from their positions on the other side, saw dirt fly high. More sounds of axes and shovels picked up the rhythm. The Americans were very busy.

Far behind, almost to the American artillery section, the British heard more hacking and sawing. Trees went down. Several British crept up to their side of the bridge to see what was going on. The Americans hauled trees over to the bridge and piled them on the exit. The British watched as more trees appeared from behind and were thrown into the water.

An Aide entered Cornwallis's tent. Cornwallis was almost asleep. "Sir?"

Cornwallis choked awake. "Hrumph. What? What is it?"

"The rebels are fortifying, sir."

"So?"

"Well, sir, uh, should we open up, maybe, uh, maybe we could disrupt them, sir. A few cannonballs might distract them, keep them from digging."

"And put them to sleep? Are you out of your mind?"

"No, sir, I just thought we should break up their fortifying."

"Spread the word, leave the rebels alone. Have the men get some sleep. They'll need their strength in the morning."

"But sir..."

"Let them dig all night. Let them wear themselves out. Leave them alone. Now get out."

"Yes, sir. Sorry to trouble you, sir." The officer left.

Cornwallis went back to bed with the annoying sounds of clanging shovels and hatchets strokes in his ears. "Damn rebels." He smiled, though, as he pulled up the cozy blankets, thinking about the glory he'd have in the morning. The war would be over, and he'd have all of London at his pleasure. Even the King wouldn't dare deny him the riches he'd be due. Ah, the simple defeat of a rebel fool. "Good night, Mr. Fox. I'll see you in the morning. Dig all you want."

Chapter Forty

Murphy sat at a desk in his tent writing a letter. Done, he rose wearily and walked a few yards to another tent where two soldiers guarded the entrance. He said, "Captain Murphy, First Pennsylvania Riflemen." The soldiers acknowledged him and moved to the side. Murphy stooped at the opening. "Permission to enter, sir."

Inside the tent, Mercer recognized Murphy's voice. "Granted. Come in, Murph." Murphy pulled the flap out of the way. Washington said to Mercer, "It's a go, Hugh."

Washington sank down in his chair, put his head in his hands and mumbled, "God, so tired, so tired. And the men, so tired. How can we do this? God save us."

Mercer headed for the tent door, then turned. "It's a good plan, sir. God bless us, not save us." Washington's eyes drooped as Mercer whispered to Murphy, "Don't keep him long. We need him." Murphy nodded. Mercer exited.

Washington looked up from his desk.

Murphy said, "I'd like you to sign this letter, sir. One of my men. His brother died today. Consumption."

Murphy handed the letter to Washington. Washington picked up his glasses, put them on carefully, adjusted the arms around his ears, and read aloud.

Dear Mrs. Jackson:

It is with deepest regret that I inform you of the death of your son, Satchel. I can only say he died honorably and in the company of his friends.

Though it is of little comfort now, I promise you that one day we will all look back with fond remembrance of those who died, and look ahead to those who will die, and say solemnly, to them we owe our country.

God speed you through your grief.

Sincerely,
Gen. George Washington, Esq.

Washington read it again to himself and signed it. Murphy said "Thank you, sir," and turned to leave.

"Murph, wait." Washington looked up. The strain was evident in his face. "You know we need to keep up the charade, keep the fires burning all night."

Murphy waved the letter in the air and smiled. "I have just the man for it, sir."

Chapter Forty One

Toward the right-most flank of the American line, Murphy walked up to a group of soldiers who were laughing and joking noisily. He asked, "You men drunk?"

The soldiers came to attention. "No, sir." They hid their bottles behind their backs. Murphy stared at them like a father who had caught his children in a harmless lie. "You see Corporal Jackson?"

"Yeah, sure. Jackson, right? I think he's over there." A soldier pointed to his right. "I think. Yeah, I think I seen him over there." The men snickered. Murphy gave them a cold stare, not much he could do about the drinking anyway. "Yeah. Thanks for your help. I'll be back. Slow down on that whiskey." Murphy walked east.

Murphy walked around groups of soldiers, looking for Jackson. It was dark, not even a moon yet, and hard to recognize anyone. Many men had faces blackened with mud and grime. He peered into the eyes of several men as he went east. "You see Corporal Jackson?"

Expressions of "No, sir," and "Who?" disappointed him.

Murphy came to another group of soldiers, also drinking, but keeping to themselves. They sat on logs and on the ground, talked softly, and watched the fire. They passed a bottle of whiskey around openly. The men spoke calmly, softly, took a swig or two and passed it on, and then they saw Murphy walk up. One of them took another casual swig and handed off the bottle without even glancing away from Murphy's approach.

Murphy noticed their clothes, unlike any others in the army. The firelight flickered on their tattered shirts pulled out of their trousers, sleeves pulled off, heavy vests set against the cold, but their arms were bare. They were rough. They were riflemen. Murphy came up to them. One soldier watched him suspiciously. The others didn't care.

Murphy stopped in front of them. All the men were sitting, staring into the mesmerizing fire. He asked, "You men are riflemen, aren't you?"

The solider, not young, but not Murphy's age, spoke up. "Yeah, so what?"

Murphy turned his attention toward the man. "You their officer?"

The soldier said, "We ain't got no officer. You killed him, remember? Franco, quit hoggin' the juice."

Franco passed the bottle to Little Ben. Murphy froze. He looked through the dirt and mud on the soldier's face, where, even in the darkness, he could see the sour expression. He recognized the soldier, but he wasn't sure from where. Murphy was confused. "I killed him? Who?"

The soldier looked away and stared at the fire. "Ah, never mind."

Murphy walked away shaking his head. He heard the soldier ask his men, "Where'd we get this drivel, anyway?"

Franco replied, "Jackson, that musket corporal. Stole it from Fermoy. Ha."

Murphy turned around quickly and walked back to the men, thinking. He remembered the soldier's face now. The men stared silently at Murphy, coming back toward them. They thought this was all over, an officer intruding on their personal thoughts at a comforting fire after a terribly sad day. They all stood up, ready for a confrontation, and ready for some officer to get shot if this officer didn't leave them the hell alone.

Murphy said, "You're McKean's men, aren't you?"

The soldier replied, "Yeah, so?"

Murphy said, "I'm sorry. I didn't know he died. I'm very sorry." The soldiers hung their heads.

Murphy asked, "Who's your officer?"

The soldier said, "I told you, we ain't got no officer. Now leave us alone."

"I'm sorry. Who else do you report to?"

Franco piped up, "You."

Murphy looked at the men separately. "I'm looking for Jackson. One of you said Jackson."

The soldier pointed east, "Over there. Gave us this crap whiskey, damn musket man."

Murphy turned toward the east. "Where is he?"

Franco pointed to a particular campfire. "That one, I think, left of them trees."

Murphy fixed the campfire location in his mind, relative to the creek. He addressed the soldier and his men. "All right, I'm your officer. I'm Captain Murphy. I want you to report to Sergeant Swanson. He's a good man. He's a rifleman. He'll take care of you."

The men were relieved. The soldier asked, "Where's he?"

Murphy pointed to the bridge. "Just south of the bridge. Go there. Find him. Tell him I said you report to him. Sergeant Swanson. I'm Captain Murphy."

The soldier replied, "We know who you are."

The men picked up their stuff, including the whiskey, and walked ten feet toward the bridge. Murphy stopped them. "Wait." The men stopped. "Wait." Murphy walked over to them.

"Go that way." Murphy pointed south, perpendicular to the creek. "Then cut over to the right and get to the bridge. I don't want the British to see you marching toward the bridge." The men obeyed and trudged south toward the double distance to the bridge. At least they had an officer again.

* * *

Murphy went east, looking again into the faces of the men in the darkness, searching for Jackson. He heard some muffled yelling, "We have to stay here." Murphy thought he recognized the voice, but he wasn't sure. He stopped momentarily and turned his ear in that direction.

"No, Jack, We're too close to the creek."

Murphy picked up on the word, "Jack." He headed there, careful to avoid looking at the ground, in case he'd lose his fix on the position and have to start all over again.

Jumbled words sailed through the silent night. Murphy strained to hear another utterance of the word "Jack" again, but only mumbled gibberish reached his ears, mixed with audible shouts of, "Ah, you, piss off," and "Shift your fat ass." Murphy got closer to where he heard the name, where several men stood around a campfire like ghosts in the gloomy night. Their fire threw silhouettes onto the ground and into the creek. Murphy finally recognized Jackson talking to his men.

"Jackson."

Jackson said, "Yes, sir. Oh, Cap, How are ya?"

Murphy came up, thankful that he'd found his man. He looked around at Jackson's men. They were all standing, so Murphy calculated that they were not drunk.

"You boys didn't drink all that stuff, did you?"

Jackson said, "No. Some. We gave it away, bad stuff.

Murphy asked, "How ya faring, son?"

Jackson stared at the ground and shook his head slightly. "Still don't know how I'm going to tell my mum about Satchel."

The other men hung their heads. Murphy reached into his pocket, pulled out Washington's letter, and handed it to Jackson. Jackson held it against the light of the fire and read it. His face welled up with tears as he got to the end, 'God speed you through your grief.'

"Thanks, Cap."

Jackson's men stared at him. "What is it, Jack?"

Jackson replied, "It's to my mum, from the General."

"Really?"

Jackson wiped his eyes with his sleeve. "I'll show you later."

Murphy said, "In return for that, I need you men to do something, all of you. It's important. You're not drunk, now, right?"

The men replied collectively, "No, no, can't drink that stuff. Makes me sick."

"I need you boys to keep these fires burning, all night. Understand? Do not let the fires go out."

The men nodded to him.

"There'll be other men to your left and right, but some of them are drunk. I need you men to do this." Murphy looked straight into Jackson's eyes.

Jackson spotted a change in Murphy's usually paternal expression. Jackson's eyes drifted downward from Murphy's face.

Murphy tapped Jackson on the chest. "Look at me, Mr. Jackson. Do you understand, Mr. Jackson? Do not let the fires go out."

Jackson said, "Yes, sir."

Murphy looked seriously at all of the men, staring coldly at each one. "Do you all understand? Do not let the fires go out. Anywhere. If they go out, then start them back up."

A soldier asked, "Why do we have to keep their fires going? Why don't they do it themselves?"

"I can't tell you. Besides, you'll figure it out soon enough. But you cannot tell anyone of these orders. They come straight from the General. No talking about this to anyone, under penalty of being shot."

Everybody jumped back at that expression.

"And make some noise. Pick up a shovel and stick it in the ground every once in a while. But don't shoot. We don't want to wake up our guests across the creek."

A soldier asked, "Ain't we gonna be able to sleep?"

"No, not tonight."

Groans came from the men. "That ain't fair."

Murphy said, "Here's what's fair. Tomorrow morning, you go home. Jackson, take that letter to your mother. All of you go home for a few days, a week maybe, no longer."

A soldier asked, "We still get our bounty, right?"

"Yes. I'll authorize it."

"What if you get killed?"

Murphy's eyebrows went up, then he returned to reality, a good question. "I'll authorize it before I get killed, all right?"

A soldier said to a comrade, "All right, that's fair." They all nodded in agreement.

"Go home for a while, then get back to the army, wherever we are."

Jackson had been watching this conversation the whole time, silent, thinking. Now he spoke. "But you won't be here, will you, Cap?"

Murphy's eyes twinkled with the familiar gleam that Jackson was accustomed to seeing. Murphy said, "See, I told you you'd figure it out."

Jackson's men stared in confusion. "What?"

Jackson turned toward his men. "I'll explain it to you later. Not a word to anyone."

Sounds of laughter came from a hundred yards west as distant soldiers finished up more of the whiskey. Murphy glanced over there, as did Jackson and his men. Murphy turned back to Jackson. "Oh, Jackson, one other thing."

"Sir?"

You know those men you gave the whiskey to?"

"Yeah?"

"You're in charge of them, too."

"Damn."

Murphy smiled and walked west.

Chapter Forty Two

Murphy approached a group of rowdy soldiers, next in line now that McKean's company had left. The men laughed heartily, taking pot shots at distance houses, buildings, and trees on the British side.

One American said, "Hey, did you see that? I hit that building over there."

Another replied, "What building? You can't even see them buildings."

"Yes, I can. I hit it, right in the side."

"How do you know you hit it? Looks to me you was just shootin' in the air."

"No, I hit it. I heard it. Smack. Right in the side."

"You heard it? Well, I didn't hear it. You couldn't hit a building if you was standing inside it."

The men all chuckled.

"You take that back! I hit three British up at the Run. You seen me. You wanna disport that, uh, disturb that... dispute that?"

"Yeah, I'll disport that. You hit three trees." He pointed across the creek. "Why don't you shoot that tree over there? I know you can hit a tree."

"Hush up! I'm telling you, take that back!" With his left hand, the solder pushed his antagonist in the chest. That soldier fell backward against their leader, Corporal Lamb, who was also pretty drunk. Lamb fell to the ground, unhurt, but the force of the contact caused both combatants to remain upright. They threw their rifles down and engaged in a shouting and shoving match, until finally they grabbed each other and wrestled to the ground, turning over and over to get the advantage of the top position.

Their comrades tried to tear them apart, but everybody was so drunk that they mostly just fell into a pile, laughing, even the two aggressors and Corporal Lamb.

Murphy walked up. Startled, Lamb saw him approach. "Whoa, an officer."

"It's all right, son. Who's in charge here?"

"I guess I am."

Corporal Lamb had trouble keeping his eyes fixed on Murphy and walking at the same time. He fell forward, but recovered quickly. Murphy stopped to let Corporal Lamb get his balance. The other soldiers gathered around, close enough to hear, but far enough away so that Murphy couldn't detect the heavy smell of alcohol on their breath.

What's your name, son?"

"Cor...Frul, uh, Corf-ru-ful, ah! Lamb. Cor-frul Lamb. Yea, that's it, Lamb."

Lamb smiled at his men. They laughed. Lamb staggered again. He steadied himself on his gun, propped into the ground like a crutch. His wobbly head focused on Murphy's many faces in his drunken eyes, but with effort, the images congealed into one. "Ah, Cap. There you are."

Murphy asked, "You boys been drinking?"

"No, not us, Cap. We ain't drinking." The corporal turned toward his men with a snicker, but it was a mistake, because he lost his balance again.

His men laughed. "No, sir, we ain't drinking. He's always like that." They laughed. The corporal laughed, too.

Murphy smiled to himself. The soldier repeated the process of regaining his balance and focusing his eyes on Murphy's face. Murphy waited patiently. The soldier smiled sheepishly.

Murphy pointed east. "You remember that corporal over there, Jackson? Remember, he gave you this whiskey?"

"We ain't got no (burp) whiskey, sir." The men behind laughed.

Murphy said, "He's a general now."

"What?" The men gasped.

Murphy said, "Corporal Jackson is a general now."

"Jack's a general? No, that can't be."

"Yes, it is. I just gave him his orders. He's in charge tonight. He's a temporary general, reports directly to Washington. He's going to give you some orders, and you'd better do what he says."

The men were astonished. "No, that can't be, not Jack."

"You will address him as 'General Jack,' or he has permission to shoot you."

The men turned to their right and stared in disbelief at Jackson's campfire. The shock of the news burned up a full ten percent of the alcohol in their brains.

Murphy enjoyed himself. He knew he couldn't send these drunken men on a twelve-mile march, they'd make too much noise. His plan was working out well.

"You men are assigned to stay here tonight. You'll do what General Jack tells you to do, or he has orders from Washington to, well, you know, pow!"

Murphy shouted that word so loud that all the men jumped back. "Oh, my God. I don't believe it."

"What did you say to me, soldier? You don't believe it, or you don't believe me?" Murphy was getting good at this eye-contact stuff. "Because either way, you're calling me a liar, and if you're calling me a liar, well, then, you know, pow!"

"No, no. I didn't say that." Corporal Lamb's head swirled in confusion. A soldier behind interjected, "No, he didn't say that, sir. He didn't mean that."

Corporal Lamb was dumbfounded. "All right. What do we have to do?"

Murphy looked at Corporal Lamb, and then at the men. They were not completely gone yet. Murphy estimated another three or four hours before they passed out, which should be long enough if they eased up a bit. "First, slow down on the drinking."

The men behind groaned. Murphy said, "little swigs only. You're going to have to stay awake for at least another four hours."

The men nodded reluctantly. Murphy looked at their campfire, a little dull. "Get some wood. Keep this fire going. If this fire goes out and you men fall asleep, you'll freeze to death from the alcohol."

"Oh, no." The men were relieved that this well reputed officer didn't confiscate their most prized possession, whiskey. In fact, he seemed to understand their need for its effect.

Corporal Lamb ordered, "Jimmy, Andrew, get some wood."

Two men took off south. Murphy looked at the rest of them, then at Lamb. "Can you make some noise? And keep making noise. Can you sing or something? What's that song, Yankee Doodle?"

Corporal Lamb called his men over. "Sure, we can sing. Boys, get up here."

Five men lined up as if they were behind the altar. The last soldier took his drink from the bottle and placed it gingerly on the ground. Corporal Lamb directed.

Lamb called out, "First verse."

The men's voices rose like a choir of angels through the cold air, to the tune of "Yankee Doodle."

> *Genr'l Howe He's like a cow,*
> *The King of all the porkers*
> *Tried to bed a girl who said,*
> *I don't do fat New Yorkers*

Murphy laughed. Other soldiers up and down the line heard the beautiful, familiar tune echo off the trees and the bridge in wonderful harmony. One of the soldiers hummed his note on the word "tried," creating a background chord, raised it up on the word "girl", then higher on "don't," and then joined in for the last word, "Yorkers."

British Corporal Lawrence walked up to the British bank. He looked through a spyglass at the Americans, filthy dirty, no shoes, ragged beyond belief.

 Lawrence yelled across the creek, "Hey Reb, how ya going to fight a war, you don't even have decent clothes."

The soldiers stopped singing. They peered across the creek to see who said that. Lawrence stood in front of a tree, invisible to the Americans that far away.

Murphy searched through the darkness for the source of the insult, but it was pitch black over there. Murphy called out, as loud as he could, "We don't put on our good clothes to butcher pigs."

The American sounds of digging abated. Mumbled conversations from the British ceased. There was silence on both sides of the creek.

Murphy yelled to the drunken men, "Get down." All of them hit the dirt.

From the British side, cannonballs ripped through the American lines. Nobody was hurt. American artillery responded from behind. Hundreds of muskets crackled from both sides of the creek. Another volley from British cannons attracted the attention of anyone who wasn't listening. American cannons replied with a loud boom.

Cornwallis rose out of a deep sleep. An aide rushed into his tent just as Cornwallis sat up in his cot. "What the hell was that?"

"Just a small skirmish, sir."

Corporal Lamb staggered up, laughing. "Second verse."

> *Colonel Rahl he took a fall*
> *and while the rain was pouring*
> *Genr'l Howe he found out now*
> *In bed he was a-boring*

Hundreds of Americans all along the Assunpink joined in for the chorus:

> *Yankee Doodle keep it up*
> *Yankee Doodle dandy*
> *Mind the music and the step*
> *And with the girls be handy*

Hysteria came from the American side as soldiers all up and down the line squeezed fantasy breasts, "handy."

Cornwallis said, "They'll sing a different tune in the morning," and went back to sleep.

Murphy walked away smiling. "Keep singing, boys, all night."

Chapter Forty Three

Toby sat on a box. Isaac lay on the ground on a blanket. Isaac said, "Whew. It's getting cold, isn't it?"

Toby had been sleeping, hunched over on the box. He woke up at Isaac's voice. "I suppose. Will you be all right? How's your arm?"

"This helps." Isaac drank from the whiskey bottle. "You know, thanks for getting me out of there. I wish I could shoot like that. You're all right. Sorry, for, you know, talking like I do."

"Aw, you did the same for me with the string on the gun. I got to tell Pa about that."

"Let's just keep that to ourselves."

"Ha. You shoot better when you ain't got a gun. Wait 'till the sergeant hears about that. Ha."

"Toby, you tell anybody that and I'll get some more string."

Toby laughed. "I guess we got a father again."

"I don't know. I don't know about that just yet."

Murphy came up. "So, how ya feeling? How's the arm?"

Isaac looked down at it.

"I don't know. I don't really feel it any more."

Toby said, "He's drunk."

Isaac adjusted the bandage on his arm and looked up at Murphy. "You know, Pa, I want to ask you sumpshin, sumpsin, sump...thing. Ah."

Isaac shook his head, as if that would drive the whiskey away. Isaac steadied himself. "I have to ask you. Do you still love Ma?"

Murphy asked, "I don't know. Is she still the same?"

Isaac and Toby glanced at each other, expecting the other to reply.

"Well, yeah," said Toby.

Murphy smiled, "Then I guess so."

They all laughed.

Isaac frowned. "Another thing, Pa."

"What?"

"When I crossed the bridge, I fell against Washing's, uh, Wash, uh, Washr... ing... son's horse."

"Easy, Isaac."

"Wait. The horse didn't move. Doesn't a horse always move when you touch it, at least look around? Shrwanson's horse did. I slid along the side of Wash... you know, his horse. It never moved, kept staring straight ahead, like the general."

"Well, it must be a pretty good horse. Or a pretty good general."

Isaac nodded satisfactorily and fell asleep. In the distance sounded,

> *Sweetie cried and cried that day*
> *She wouldn't let me go*
> *Cried so hard she popped her guard*
> *Her breasats heaving so.*

Laughter pealed from afar.

> *Yankee Doodle keep it up*
> *Yankee DoodleDandy*
> *Mind the music and the step*
> *And with the girls be handy*

Murphy looked at Isaac, asleep in the wagon. Toby sat on a box and studied the ground. The thoughts of the last few hours crept into Murphy's mind. He thought about Harry hanging in the tree. Satchel was dead. Jackson's a general now. Murphy worried the trick wouldn't hold through the night. He'd have to think of a way to straighten that out when the men learned the truth.

He thought about Jackson and Satchel, two brothers. Jackson took care of Satchel, but he couldn't prevent the inevitable. Murphy's eyes wandered to Toby, still staring at the ground, so young to be in a war. Murphy wondered if his sons would ever take care of each other like that, as Jackson did Satchel.

His thoughts drifted back to a simpler time. Maggie, ah, Maggie. Murphy thought about the arguing, the yelling, the gun pointing. Somehow, it didn't seem so important any more.

Murphy asked Toby, "How's your mother anyway, really?"

Toby was startled out of his weary trance. "All right, I guess."

"Is she?"

"Maybe tired, I think. We got two little ones at home. She looks really tired. I don't know, but she's all right, I think."

"Yes. She wrote me when they were born. I sent her a little something."
Murphy tried to lighten up the conversation, pass a little time.

"So why is she sending you to Allentown? You never explained that."

"Because of that soldier."

"What soldier?"

"A British man. He broke into the house. Grabbed Ma by the neck."
Murphy panicked.

Toby's face welled up with excitement. "Isaac and me pushed him,
Ma cut him, I think, with a knife."

"Oh, my God."

"Yeah, and he said he's going back there. Going to 'Stick her' with a
knife. He said that."

"Oh, my God, Toby. Who is he? Do you know who he is?"

"No, I don't know. He's just British. I don't know his name. Do you
think he'll go back there?"

Murphy sucked in his breath, deeply troubled. His eyes drifted away
from Toby. "No, I don't think so." Murphy glanced awkwardly at Toby,
intending to correct the lie, but fortunately Toby didn't notice the drift of
Murphy's eye contact. Murphy said, "We've got to find out who he is. I
can't let that happen to your mother. And I will not."

Instantly, three solutions flashed into Murphy's consciousness. A
maniac British soldier, probably a rapist, was after his wife. Well, ex-
wife. Solution one, could he find this soldier and kill him? That would
be the best plan. Solution two, could he perhaps post a guard around
Maggie's house, and she'd probably yell and complain and try and kill
them? Solution three, could he send a company of men over there, drag
her screaming out of her house to safety, along with the children, and
they'd have to disarm her first?

Maybe. Two and three would have to wait until circumstances
revealed themselves tomorrow. Solution one was the best choice, kill the
man. Murphy would work on it but keep the other options open.

Murphy changed the subject again with Toby. "I saw you shoot those
British at the house. That was very brave."

"I never shot nobody before. When I thought Isaac was dead, I, I don't
know, It didn't seem important no more."

"I know. It was a very brave thing you did. I'm glad to see you boys
are close. I'm so sorry I couldn't watch you grow up."

"We're not close. He hates me."

"No, not true. You're friends. I can see it. He's just a young man who
sees the world passing him by and he's afraid he'll miss it. You'll get there
too, some day."

Murphy followed Toby's eyes as they wandered toward Isaac.
Maggie's figure wandered into his head. He looked past Isaac into the
darkness beyond. The image of a young girl appeared in his memory, her

naked legs opened wide. She screamed. A tiny head protruded through the opening. Isaac had arrived. Murphy smiled at the thought.

"You know, I was in Philadelphia that day. I told you that, right?"

Toby racked his sleepy brain, distracted by the abrupt change in the conversation.

"What day?"

"When you were born."

"Yeah. You told me that, Pa."

"You were early. Couldn't wait to get here, could ya?"

Toby managed a fragile smile.

"Sorry, heard that before, haven't you?" Murphy sighed. "And now we're in a war." Murphy shook his head. "Isaac wanted adventure, and now you've both got it. What you've been through today should last you a lifetime. Not so with me."

Toby picked up on that, "What?"

"Well, I've never actually killed a man either."

"What? How can that be? You're in the army. You're an officer."

"True. I'm a highly competent, well respected staff officer."

"What's that?"

"I make sure everybody knows what to do. I make sure they have bullets and powder, but I don't shoot anybody. Even coming down from New York, I never shot anybody, not even today."

"Gosh. Are you afraid?"

"I think I'm more afraid of being afraid. I hope when a bayonet comes at me, I can be as brave as you were today."

Murphy continued, because Toby seemed interested. "You reminded me of Hand. That's something Colonel Hand would do, take out three British with two guns in one minute. We're lucky he was there today and not Fermoy. You, too. We're lucky you were there."

"And you. And the sergeant."

"Yes." Murphy got up. "I always thought I'd get into combat sooner or later, so I never worried about all the running around I do, but it's about things passing you by. Sorry to bore you, son. Try and get some sleep. We're leaving in a couple of hours. Good night, Toby. Good night, Isaac."

Murphy walked away, but Toby called him back, "Wait, Pa."

"What is it, Toby?"

Toby's eyes moistened. "I killed those men. I didn't want to, but I had to."

Murphy stooped down. He wiped Toby's eyes with his hand. Murphy grasped Toby's head and pulled it into his chest. Murphy rubbed Toby's head and looked across the river at the British camp.

"Ah, Toby. It's a war. You're a man now."

"I ain't a man. I'm only fourteen."

"Yes, fourteen. And a terrible thing it is for a war to force young boys to kill, terrible."

"They was going to kill Isaac. I had to."

"You did the right thing, Toby."

"Maybe they was fathers, like you, with boys like me and Isaac. I don't like to think about that. I killed them. I shot them." Toby cried fitfully. Murphy held him close.

"You know, Toby, I'm not a philosopher like Franklin. I don't know how to say how brave it was what you did today, except that you did the right thing. You saved Isaac's life."

Toby stopped crying. Murphy released him from his chest and rubbed his head fondly. "You truly became a man today. Never take abuse from anyone ever again." Murphy motioned toward Isaac. "Even from your brother. Although, I don't think you'll get that anymore, and I don't think he means to be that way. But you're a man now."

Murphy tried to lighten it up a little. "Hey, how'd you do that, anyway, take out those British? I saw that. I was fifty yards away, and I spotted you and Isaac running to the house, then I lost track of you. I saw three British run to the house, and then you're dragging Isaac out. What happened to the British?"

"I shot them from the railings. On the house. I put the guns on the railing, loaded, then held them at my side and waited for them to come." Toby stopped talking and stared eagerly into Murphy's eyes for the next question.

From Murphy's expression, Toby had the vague and comforting thought that maybe he was a hero, not a hero, exactly, but maybe he did well. He wasn't sure. His brain raced around and around, trying to reconcile killing those men with saving Isaac's life, and it wasn't easy. He decided not to think about it right now.

Murphy was surprised at Toby's resourcefulness. "Then what did you do?"

"I shot the left soldier first, then the right one. I had two guns."

"But there were three of them."

Toby became excited telling the tale. "I couldn't get the last one. I threw the gun at him, and then I ran. No, wait, I threw both guns. I don't know what happened then. I think Sergeant Swanson shot him."

"Damn. I wish I'd seen that. All I saw were three soldiers charging at you, and then you were dragging Isaac out. I wish I'd have been there." Murphy shook his head. "That was unbelievable. You go behind a house with three British coming, and you come out alone. I'm going to tell Colonel Hand about that."

Toby smiled. "Ya know, Pa, Isaac saved me too." Toby glanced over at Isaac to make sure he was still asleep. Toby whispered, "Don't tell Isaac I told you this."

Murphy nodded.

"Isaac shot the British, that guy I was telling you about."

Murphy was curious, "The soldier at your mother's house?"

"Yeah, yeah. Isaac shot him with a string on a gun."

Murphy felt a sense of relief. "What? So he's dead now?"

Toby frowned, "No, Isaac didn't hit him. He missed."

Murphy sighed. The weight of Maggie's safety was back on his shoulders.

Toby chuckled, "But wait. Wait'll you hear this. Ha. Isaac tied a string to a gun, to the trigger, I think. He pulled it. It went off. The British was scared. Ha. They ran away. Lawrence was so shocked. Whoa, wait, Lawrence. That's his name, Lawrence."

"Lawrence? That's the soldier? Lawrence? Are you sure? Is he an officer or anything?"

"I don't know. But that's his name. His soldiers called him that."

"What did he look like?"

"I don't know. Skinny little man, red uniform."

"How tall was he? Taller than you?" Murphy sized up Toby. "Never mind. Taller than Isaac?"

"Shorter than Isaac, I think. And a scraggly beard, a mean beard. Really mean. He was really mean to me. And Ma."

Toby leaned forward, eyes bright. He had the ear of someone who cared, genuinely interested in helping him exact revenge on the soldier who humiliated him and his mother. His young brain flashed back to the Trenton road, with Lawrence's bayonet sliding along his neck. Toby waited for the next question.

Murphy asked, "How old was he?"

"Really old."

"Can you be a little more specific? Was he as old as I am?"

"No, not that old."

Murphy smiled. He had a little piece of information. It was a needle in a haystack, but at least he knew the name of the needle.

Toby said, "Oh, and he had a patch over his eye."

"What?"

"Yeah, he only had one eye. He had a patch. How could he shoot like that?"

Murphy said, "Oh, my God, I saw him."

Toby asked, "You saw him? When?"

"On the Trenton road. I could have shot him right in the chest, right there. Oh, my God."

Toby asked, "Why didn't you?"

"It wasn't the right time. Damn. I should have taken the chance." Murphy shook his head at the lost opportunity.

"Are you going to kill him, Pa?"

Murphy stared straight into Toby's eyes, no lying now. "I don't know if I can do it, but I'm going to make sure he never hurts your mother. I promise you that, if I live, and if I don't, well, you and Isaac take care of her. You promise that to me."

"Yes, Pa."

"Good night, Toby."

"Good night, Pa."

Chapter Forty Four

Henry Knox moved silently among the guns in the rear of the American lines. He whispered orders, "Move that wagon out of there. You men, shhh, wrap those blankets around the wheels. Tie 'em up tight. You, go get some lamp oil. I don't want any squeaking."

A soldier spoke up in a plain voice, "Sir, why are we putting knickers on the guns?"

Henry put his hand over the soldier's mouth. He grabbed the back of the soldier's head and yanked the soldier's face into his big hand to stifle the words. "Hush." He stared at the other soldiers nearby, in case they got the same idea that they could speak freely in loud voices. The soldier struggled, unable to breathe against the force of Henry's huge hands, and no man could ever knock Henry Knox down from a standing position. Henry held the soldier's mouth and nose for a full minute, then he let the soldier go with a gentle shove backward.

The soldier gasped for air and recovered. "Damn." The other soldiers got the message.

Henry said, "Just do it, and quietly. We're moving out. No noise, no talking." His voice descended into a low whisper. "If these wheels make any noise, I'll have you carry these guns on your backs all the way to Princeton. You understand?"

The men nodded. Now they knew where they were going. They went back to wrapping the cannon wheels in cloth. Henry walked over to another group of cannoneers. Those men had seen the confrontation and hustled to tie cloth, shoes, shirts, pants, anything they could find, to the cannons' wheels.

Cannons, wagons, and men moved east. It was misty and cold. Many men had feet wrapped in cloth. The road was snowy now, but no mud.

The men lumbered along slowly. Officers gave orders silently. Sleeping men were awakened by their comrades, fell into line, and shuffled up the Quaker road. Sergeants pointed, whispering in hoarse shouts, "Go." Men acknowledged, moved through the fields, reached the road, and went east.

From the banks of the creek, a song drifted across the fields, to the tune of 'Twinkle, Twinkle, Little Star,'

> *Life is free if life's to be.*
> *Oh, please Jesus, care for me.*
> *Keep me safe and keep away*
> *All the harm that comes today.*
> *Through the darkness I can see.*
> *Now I know my God and thee.*

Campfires illuminated the bloody Assunpink.

Chapter Forty Five

Day Six, Friday, Jan. 3, 1777 2:00 a.m.

Toby, Isaac, Swanson, and his men got in line and reached the road. Isaac went off to the side and threw up, then crawled back to the group. Toby watched him come. "You all right?"

"I feel like hell."

"How's your arm?"

"It's killing me."

Isaac scanned the scene. "Hey, this is the road, Anna's road. Maybe I can get to see her again."

"You better not let the sergeant see you get out of line."

"You have to help me. I've got to see her. I'll die if I don't see her."

The army marched toward Princeton. Soldiers stumbled over rocks and tree stumps, hurt their feet, and stopped. They fell down, got up, and went on.

There was only a small sliver of moon tonight, not enough to illuminate even a single musket, just what the officers wanted to prevent their exhausted men from being seen by the British. That helped in a way, but the moon was also not bright enough to light up the ground. A faint ring of clouds surrounded it, making it glow even less luminous, just peeking out of the late-night sky, almost directly ahead, low on the southeast horizon.

Up forward, the road curved to the left. A group of men near the bend stopped abruptly. Several men behind watched the ground as they marched, paying no attention to the crowd in front. A chain reaction occurred as men smacked into those ahead of them. Twenty men spilled into the mud and off the side of the road. "Hey, watch that. What're ya doing?"

An officer hustled up. "Shhh. No talking." He straightened out the mess, but nobody moved. The army was stopped dead. The men sat down on the ground and closed their eyes. Many fell asleep. Eventually the line started to move again. Men got up and trudged ahead.

* * *

3:00 a.m. Friday, January 3rd.

At the middle of the line, the army moved so slowly that only a few steps per minute were necessary to keep the pace. The rhythm was monotonous. Men kept a light touch on a friend with a free hand and closed their eyes. They slept as they walked.

Other men fell off the side of the road, got up, and went back in line, a little more awake for a few minutes.

* * *

4:00 a.m.

Another stop, another, and another. A cannon off to the side of the road in the woods got the attention of several men in the middle of the line. Grateful for anything they could find to keep themselves awake, they rushed over to help retrieve it. A quick rest lying over the barrel brought some relief, then they hauled it back to the road and went on.

* * *

5:00 a.m.

The partial moon was half-high on its steady course west, intermittently obscured by a thin wisp of clouds. It was cold now. The warm sun wasn't due for another two hours. It was almost pitch black. The march was unbearable. Even if the sun came up, what were they marching toward, another disaster? The men dreaded the end of the march as they walked, sleeping. This could be their last night on earth, and it was a bad one. The snow turned red from the bloody feet of the soldiers ahead.

At the back of the line, the pace picked up a little. Toby, Isaac, Swanson, and his men moved more quickly up the road. Isaac got excited as they neared Anna's house. Isaac watched for anything he could recognize, a tree, a rock, a field, anything that would let him gauge the remaining distance.

Isaac looked behind him and saw Swanson plodding ahead. Isaac turned to Toby. "Keep an eye out on the left. Watch for the swamp, coming up."

"What?"

"Keep an eye out for the swamp. You remember the swamp, right? Tell me if you see it, to the left. I'm looking for the house."

"You can't do that. You can't go there. We'll get in trouble."

"Shhh. Go over there, to the left, so you can see better. Watch for the swamp."

Toby weaved among the other soldiers and ended up on the left side of the road, ten feet from Isaac. He looked right. Isaac looked left.

Good. Isaac nodded his head and whispered around the men in between, "Watch for the swamp."

Swanson heard muffled voices. "No talk."

Isaac put his finger to his mouth and addressed Toby on the other side of the road, "Shhh." McKean's men in between looked at Isaac and shook their heads.

Chapter Forty Six

Washington and Mercer sat on horses at the front of the line. Mercer said, "It's really bad. We've got the militia up front, the regulars in the middle, and the riflemen in the back. The guns are all over the place."

"I know, Hugh. I'm looking for a place to straighten it out. We need the regulars in front. They'll be the first to hit."

Mercer said, "You know, the boys said there's a field off to the right of the swamp. Maybe there."

"That's what I'm hoping for, coming up."

Murphy arrived on a horse, and Washington was glad to see him. "God, Murph, you have good timing."

"I just came from Greene a hundred yards back. He's wondering if the militia should be up front."

Washington said, "According to your boys, there's a dry field up here to the right. Tell Greene I'll get the militia off the road. Get the regulars to the front."

Yes, sir." Murphy saluted and went back. Washington and the troops came to a flattened cornfield on the right. Soldiers ten feet off the road to the left guarded the swamp.

Mercer ordered, "Halt. Militia, off to the right."

A militia soldier asked, "Why are we getting held back?"

Mercer replied, "You want to be the first into combat?"

The militia hustled into the field.

Washington said, "Hugh, I'm giving you the militia. Take the riflemen, too, and cover the rear. I'll take the regulars right into town. Get to the bridge and tear it down."

"Yes, sir."

The long line of marching men contracted inward on itself. The head, at Washington's location, relieved the pressure somewhat as militia filtered off to the right, into Anna's cornfield. They made room on the road for other men to come up. Men behind moved toward the swamp.

Washington peered through the darkness on the right. It seemed to be a deep enough place to hold the troops temporarily. He glanced down the Quaker road. Men came up quickly, a good thing, but not if he had nowhere for them to go.

Washington ordered a brigade of regulars, "Ahead, a hundred yards, then stop."

This was a perfect place to straighten out the troops. A cornfield to the right was just what Washington needed. Another few hours and they'd be in Princeton, too late if the right troops weren't in the right place at the right time. And the guns. Where were the guns? Washington hoped he wasn't making a big mistake here.

The regulars continued toward Princeton. The militia went to the right and into the field. Washington couldn't let the regulars get too far up, because they would be slaughtered if the British were in place and there were no reserves. Reserves, yes, such as they were, they were the reserves, the militia and a few riflemen.

Mercer maneuvered around some regulars and went back ten yards to direct the men into the field or ahead, according to their fighting skill. The best soldiers needed to be in front. Mercer had to try to recognize each brigade, regulars, continentals, militia, or riflemen. A group of continentals came up. Mercer pointed up the road, instructing them to follow the regulars and proceed toward Washington.

The regulars were excellent fighters, men who had enlisted for a longer time than the militia. The continentals were those men who were in for the duration of the war. There were only a few hundred of them. There was very little difference between the continentals and the regulars, except for the length of their enlistments.

Then there were the riflemen and the militia. The riflemen were shooters. They were not expected to engage in hand-to-hand combat and certainly not to receive a bayonet charge. Militia were temporary volunteers, young men who had other loyalties, mostly to their homes and families, men who would not fight outside of their own communities, and who could not be relied on to put themselves in danger.

Mercer faced south. "Militia, off to the right."

A group of militia went to their left, not right, slid down a little gully, and fell face-first into the mud of the swamp. Soldiers guarding the swamp heard the "smack" from a few yards away and came over to help. A guard shouted, "Get out of here." Mercer saw more soldiers following their comrades and put his horse in the way so the others wouldn't stumble into the swamp.

Mercer pointed to the cornfield, "Over there."

A militia sergeant said, "You said, off to the right."

Mercer bellowed, "Not my right, your right."

The sergeant mumbled, "Should've said so."

* * *

The field filled with soldiers. Officers steadied their men. Cannons arrived, got off to the right, slogged into the cornfield, and then went back to the road when the way was clear. Utmost priority was getting the line of men moving forward, with the right men in the right place. Mercer watched the men go past. Washington was a few yards north, directing the regulars to go up. He trotted back to Mercer. "Hugh, I've got to go up there and start heading for town. Take care down here, all right?"

"Yes, sir. I'll straighten it out."

Washington gave a final signal to Mercer before he joined the regulars up front, "Whatever happens, Hugh, take out the bridge."

"Yes, sir."

Washington turned his horse north. Before he went, he looked anxiously at Mercer, a general, confirmed by congress, proven, steady, brave. Hugh Mercer, a confidant, even a friend. The Braddock campaign twenty years ago flashed into Washington's mind. Mercer was there with him, both of them young men like those they now led. Washington hoped this wasn't a repeat of that disaster.

"Take care of yourself, Hugh. I need you."

"Yes, sir."

Officers directed the militia even farther into the field to get them out of the way of the cannons, now pulled back onto the road in the right place. The order of battle was regulars, continentals, artillery, riflemen, militia.

The men in the field glanced due east at a dark structure, unexpected among the trees and fields of the gloomy night. It was a small farmhouse, barely backlit by the partial moon. They didn't pay much attention to it until a tiny light flickered in a window.

* * *

Anna heard voices far away. She got out of bed and lit a candle.

A militia soldier nudged his companion as they walked deeper into the field, watching the candle.

Momma heard the militia talking faintly, far away, and got up, too. She lit another candle in the back bedroom and walked into the kitchen, trying to struggle awake. Anna looked out her window and saw figures standing around in the dark, misty, early morning distance.

The militia saw the second candle appear through another front window. The men raised their heads as Momma's candle moved through the house. They watched it shake and brighten as Momma moved toward Anna's bedroom in front. Somebody was walking through a house a hundred yards away. It was five o'clock in the morning. Somebody was definitely awake over there. The light of Momma's candle disappeared for a moment as Momma went into Anna's bedroom and put her candle on the sill next to Anna's.

To the militia, the two lights converged into a single pinpoint to create a unified, two-candle beacon. All the militia stopped now and watched the lights.

"Momma, I think the army's here. Maybe Papa's here."

Mamma peered out the window with growing nervousness and suspicion. Her right cheek was next to Anna's face. The two of them watched the shadowy movement of men entering the field.

The ragged militia stared at the distant house, hypnotized by the flickering pinpoints of light. They stood, sat, and whispered to each other. Too tired to sleep now, the slow rumble of the cannons behind them signaled a battle to come. The anxiety kept their heavy eyelids open.

The lights were fascinating, mesmerizing. They moved slightly as Anna and Momma switched positions. The men wondered who could possibly be awake at this terrible hour on this dangerous night.

Then the lights went out. Hope drained from the soldiers' faces.

"Momma, why did you do that?"

"If they soldiers, we no need them here."

"But Momma, it could be Papa. If he's here, he needs to find his way."

"He knows how to get here."

"Momma, please. What if he tries to come here and falls, or gets hurt, or something. Wouldn't you feel bad?"

"You no say that to me, Anna."

Anna hung her head. "I'm sorry, Momma. I didn't mean that. I'm sorry. But can't we do something? If Papa's here, I want him to come here."

Anna looked through the window again. The moon, forty-five degrees high and behind the house, faintly illuminated the hundreds of soldiers in the field. To the militia there was blackness where there was light before. Momma lit her candle again and placed it in the front window. Anna's eyes watered as she kissed Momma on the cheek.

The militia saw the single light reappear. They breathed better. There was hope after all, over there in that light, people alive, regular Americans. They hadn't thought about the regular people in a long time, except for their own families, and when they'd ever see them again. But there was a family over there, strangers, regular people, a hundred yards away, or somebody at least, on this dark, dreary, dismal, dirty, dangerous road to God knows where.

They felt better. The shock of the two lights, the creeping danger ahead, the moon above, the lights disappearing and then one coming back on, all these things snapped their fuzzy brains back to consciousness. They woke up.

At the house, Momma said, "Lock door. Get guns."

Anna went out of her bedroom to the front door, which was very close to her bedroom. She locked it and stayed by the front door, outside of her room. Momma stumbled through the house to the kitchen in the pale glow of a single candle shining through Anna's open bedroom door. Momma locked the back door and came back to the front of the house. Anna loaded two guns in the candlelight.

There were two more windows in the living room. One faced the field and the army, the other, on the corner of the house, faced west, toward Trenton.

Momma took the candle out of Anna's room and put it in the window facing the militia. She stayed low so the soldiers couldn't see her moving. She lit another candle and placed it in the window facing Trenton. The militia couldn't see that one because it faced away from them.

Momma said, "Come. We go to your room and keep watch." Momma and Anna went into Anna's room to the right, opened the curtains, and watched through Anna's window. Both clutched their muskets tightly and stared through the window from the dark room.

The militia saw the candle glow brightly in the front window. It didn't move. They stared and stared. No, nothing. Their thoughts drifted to the looming, almost certain peril, but they weren't sleepy any more.

* * *

Swanson looked through the trees skirting the right side of the road. Fleeting glimpses of a faint light danced in and out of the branches. He knew his house was there, but he became anxious because of the strange lights going on and off. He quickened his pace and looked at the road in front of him, clogged with soldiers inching along. He couldn't make any progress that way. He turned around and gave an order to McKean's men, "Keep going. I catch up later." McKean's soldiers acknowledged.

Swanson turned into the woods on the right. The trees were thin, but still a nuisance in the darkness. Swanson said, "You boys, come with me."

Isaac and Toby followed. It was almost pitch black, except for the faint light of the crescent moon. Swanson looked up now and again to see the candle far away and check his direction. He clutched a tree and scouted ahead, searching for anything familiar.

Isaac and Toby walked in Swanson's footsteps, Isaac leading, Toby holding onto Isaac's belt from behind. Isaac trudged though the sparse trees. He saw the flicker of light, turned around, and whispered to Toby, "That's Anna. She's lighting a candle for me."

"Aw, you're crazy. How would she know you're here?"

"No, no. It's her. I know it's her. It's a sign."

Swanson recognized a little dip in the ground a few feet away to the right, the shortcut. "You boys, get here."

Isaac and Toby followed Swanson deeper into the woods. Isaac could see that they were headed toward the candle, but he couldn't figure out why they were going there. Did Swanson see the candle, and he wanted to see who was there? It was very confusing. Swanson crouched low under a branch and stood upright in a small clearing.

"Here it is. This way." Swanson waited impatiently for Isaac and Toby to catch up. Beyond the clearing, a narrow dirt path led toward Swanson's house, through more woods. Swanson navigated it perfectly from memory. He stepped into the clearing and headed for his house.

Isaac and Toby noticed the trees becoming ever more thin. They saw an open field and Swanson moving quickly through it. Isaac ducked under a branch at the edge of the field, but clipped his left arm slightly on the trunk of a tree.

Isaac reeled in pain, but he didn't fall. He clenched his jaw fiercely to stifle a cry, then turned back to the woods and Toby. His eyes glossed over. Faint sounds of agony escaped from his throat.

Toby's eyes jumped open. "Isaac. Oh, no." Toby wished he could take some of the pain from Isaac. Not all of it. Toby knew he'd die if he took all of it, but just some of it, maybe half, to have Isaac suffer a little less.

Isaac clutched his arm and looked down at it. Blood seeped through the bandage and oozed between his fingers. He staggered against the tree.

"Isaac, we got to get you some help. We have to get to the house." The pain abated a little, so Isaac pushed away from the tree and walked into the field.

Swanson was fifty yards ahead, ignoring the boys behind him. He looked to the left and saw the militia standing around in the field, talking, fidgeting, waiting. Swanson strode deliberately toward his house, the western candle in plain view through the crisp air.

Isaac and Toby entered the field, then Isaac slowed, holding his arm. Swanson got closer to his house, and farther away from the boys. Isaac became faint, dropped to his knees, and barely avoided falling on his face and his bloody arm. Toby stopped and stood over him. Isaac turned his head and watched Swanson head straight for the house. Isaac nearly passed out, but the curiosity of why Swanson was going to Anna's house kept him conscious. Isaac thought instantly about Anna. That, too, diminished his pain. He said to Toby, "Wait a minute." Swanson just slugged along through the field toward Anna's house. Isaac called out to Swanson, "Where we going?"

Swanson never turned around, but replied, "To mein house. I get you fixed."

Isaac looked at Toby, then at the house. "Oh, no. It can't be, no. I can't believe it."

Momma heard the voices outside the corner window. "Stay here, child." She moved out of the bedroom, underneath the front window so none of the soldiers could see her, and looked out through the corner window. She picked up the candle and blew it out so she could see outside.

Swanson saw the candle move, then go out. No matter. He knew where his house was.

Isaac and Toby also saw the candle go out. Isaac mumbled, "I guess she doesn't want to see me." His heart sank. "We have to go back."

"No, we can't go back. You need help. Maybe her Ma can help you. She was nice, you know."

"What, nice? Where were you? She tried to kill you, remember? Owww."

Blood poured though Isaac's fingers. Isaac fell to the ground, faint from walking. Toby dropped to his knees, took off his coat, and wrapped the arm of his coat tightly around Isaac's wound. He held the makeshift bandage tight as Isaac stared straight up into the starry sky.

Isaac's eyes closed. Toby panicked. Swanson was almost to the house. Left was the field, too far to cross. Toby remembered the battle at Trenton, dragging Isaac backwards, and considered it, dragging Isaac across the long field, but it was too far to go. "Where's Pa?"

Anna came up to the corner window. Both she and Momma searched the darkness, anticipating a mob of soldiers to come to the house at any minute. Momma said, "I told you stay in there, keep look." Anna ignored her. They saw a man approaching, twenty yards away. Anna said, "I'm getting the guns." She slid on the floor underneath the front candled window heading for her room and the guns, but Momma grabbed her foot and dragged her back.

"Come here, girl."

Momma smiled at the figure coming toward them. "You no recognize that walk?"

Anna looked at Momma. Tears filled her eyes. She rushed to the door, ignoring the open window in front, where all the militia could see her.

Isaac sat up, using his good arm as a crutch. Toby asked, "Are you all right?"

Isaac said, "We can't go there. He'll shoot us. You too, if he finds out we stayed there."

Toby said, "Maybe they won't tell him. We have to get you taken care of. Maybe they won't say."

"We can't take a chance. Help me up. We have to go back."

"No. I don't think Anna will tell. We can get you fixed up and then get out. But you can't go staring at her or nothin'."

"I don't know as I can do that. I can't look at her?"

Toby shook his head. "No. You got to make like we was never there."

"All right. I'll try. But I don't think we'll even get to the house. He'll probably shoot us before we even get there."

Toby thought. "All right, how about, wait, listen. We go a little more up. We wait 'till he goes in. If he comes out with a gun, we'll run back."

Isaac considered the plan. "I don't know. I don't think I can run."

"Maybe you won't have to. I'll go behind. He'll shoot me first, then he'll be unloaded. You can get away."

Isaac smiled through his pain. "No, I'll go behind." Toby helped Isaac get up. They limped slowly toward the house.

Anna rushed out of the house and onto the front porch, Momma only a moment behind. Anna ran up to Swanson, jumped into the air, and threw her arms around him. "Papa, Papa." Swanson braced himself against the charge, then lifted her up with his strong arms and strode effortlessly toward the porch. Anna's legs kicked backward in the air. She squealed as Momma waited, smiling.

Anna kissed her father on the cheek as he carried her to the house, kissing her. He deposited Anna on the porch and gave his wife a big bear hug. They kissed.

Momma glanced up at Swanson's bandaged head. "Borg, hast du kopf geshaden?" (What happened to your head?)

"Aw, ist ein kleiner schnitt." (It's a little cut.) Swanson threw the bandage on the ground.

Isaac and Toby watched from the field. Toby whispered, "See, they didn't tell him. Let's go up."

Isaac said, "No. Maybe they didn't see us yet. It's dark, you know."

"How could your girlfriend not see us? She looked right at us."

"She's not my girlfriend. Don't you say that. You think she is? Shhh. They're moving." The boys stood perfectly still.

Anna hugged her father again, and then saw two figures over her father's shoulder. She stared intensely at them. "Isaac? Toby? Is that you? Isaac?" Anna rushed through the field toward the boys.

Swanson watched Anna run, and then turned to Momma. "Wast der Hölle? How she know? What goes on here?"

"They come here Tuesday night. I give them food. I say later."

Anna crushed Isaac with a hug and rubbed Toby's head. She kissed Isaac on the face, but her body smashed against Isaac's left arm. Isaac screamed. He grasped the sleeve of the coat that Toby had put there, now soaked with blood, and sank to his knees.

Toby knelt down next to Isaac, pulling the coat sleeve tight, trying to stop the blood. Toby said, "He's shot."

Anna stepped back in shock. "Oh no, you're shot. Oh, my God." Anna shouted to her mother on the porch. "Momma, he's shot. Oh, my God, Momma, he's shot." Anna cried as she reached down to help Isaac get up. Toby's bloody coat fell off of Isaac's arm. "Oh, my God, Isaac."

Anna and Toby helped Isaac struggle up. Swanson turned to his wife. "Greta, these boys of Captain Murphy. I need you fix him up."

Momma said, "Anna, get them in house. Boy, you shot too?"

Toby replied, "Not yet."

Chapter Forty Seven

Toby and Anna helped Isaac through the door and into the kitchen, where Anna held Isaac as Toby picked up his legs and laid him on the table. Swanson retrieved the two candles from the front room, came back, and held them over Isaac. Momma unwrapped the bandage, exposing a terrible wound. Toby held his mouth to stifle a pitiful yell. Blood spilled all over. Anna looked up at her mother, but Momma continued to unwrap.

Isaac clenched his jaw in pain. He looked directly into Toby's teary eyes, then turned to Anna, who held his arm tightly. Anna stared at the wound in disbelief and fear.

Isaac trembled. He didn't know that the wound was so bad, until now, seeing the faces of those around him, all but Momma, who slowly exposed the terrible devastation. Toby wiped the tears from his face. Anna turned her head so Isaac couldn't see her anguish.

Momma looked up at Swanson and motioned toward the cabinet. Swanson handed the candles to Anna, let go of Isaac's arm, and shuffled to the other side of the room. Momma said to Anna, "Hold close." Anna held the candles closer to the wound.

Momma mumbled, "Hmmm." She inspected the wound carefully in the dim candlelight and pointed, "Here." Anna moved the candles around to give Momma a better view. Only Toby held Isaac now.

Swanson, at the cabinet, took out a jar of salt and a brick of soap. He picked out a large knife from the counter, the very one that Momma had shaken at the boys on Tuesday night. Swanson also reached into the cabinet and took out two large candles, two inches in diameter. He used the knife to whittle a large bowl around each of the wicks, and then lit both large candles with a match. Back at the surgical area, Swanson placed the salt and knife on the table, next to Isaac.

Momma took the pot of hot water off the fire and brought it over. Isaac saw the pot. He mustered some courage from deep within himself and said, "You going to give me another bath?"

"Nein, too cold now. You stink, though."

Momma poked gently at the wound with her exploring fingers. She lifted Isaac's arm and examined the bloody exit wound, and then turned his arm backward and examined the entry point again, calculating the trajectory of the slug. She wiped some more blood off with her fingers.

"Oww!"

"That hurt?"

"Oww!"

Momma squeezed Isaac's arm at the location of the bullet wound with her thumb and forefinger. She gazed at the ceiling, using her fingers as eyes, feeling for the bone. "That hurt?"

"Oww! Yes"

"Good."

Isaac struggled against Toby. "No, no. I can't." He fought to get up. Swanson held Isaac down firmly. Toby turned his eyes away, crying.

Anna cried, "No, Momma, do you have to?" Toby broke down completely, crying fitfully into his hands. He turned his back on the expected cutting. Swanson reached over the table, squeezed Toby's arm, and spun him back to the scene. "Steady, boy, hold his arm." Toby settled down at the firm touch of a strong adult. Momma and Swanson didn't seem to be that concerned, only Anna, tears streaming down her face, although even she seemed to be more interested in the wound than in Isaac's pain. Toby concentrated on holding Isaac's arm.

Momma inspected the wound with the knife in her hand. Anna moved the candles for better illumination. She watched fearfully as Momma pushed some dead skin out of the way and wiped the blood. Anna said, "Oh, my God. Momma, are you going to... no, you can't!"

Momma looked up at Anna. "What, cut his arm off? Nein. Is not so bad. No hit the bone."

Swanson smiled. His battlefield triage had just been professionally confirmed. The bullet didn't hit the bone.

Isaac exhaled and looked at the ceiling. "Thank you, God."

Momma said, "Child, hold light here. See this? We take this away." Momma poked at a flap of skin hanging into the wound. Anna moved the candles closer, concentrating on the flap of skin.

Toby smiled and wiped some tears. "See, Isaac? See? It'll be all right."

Momma picked up the knife and sliced pieces of soap onto the table. She picked them up, threw them into the pot, and swished them around in the hot water.

Anna asked, "Momma, should I wipe the blood?"

"Yes, child. Keep blood out. Then I show you how we fix. Pay good."

Anna said to Isaac, "Hold these." She gave Isaac the two candles. He balanced them on his stomach and held them together with his good hand.

Anna gently wiped the blood off both sides of the wound, horrified at the damage she saw to Isaac's arm, but fascinated to see how Momma was going to fix it.

Momma took the wet soap and rubbed it against the wound, removing the scar and dirt with a cloth. She picked the arm up and did the same to the other side, where the bullet came out. Isaac screamed in pain. "No, please."

Momma said, "You want I cut it off?"

Isaac calmed down. He stared at the ceiling, panting.

Momma finished cleaning the wound. She took the knife in her hand and said to Anna, "Watch. We cut this flap, but not too short. We need cover hole."

Anna said, "I see. We cut off the bad part and leave enough for the hole."

Momma smiled. "Watch."

Anna watched closely. Momma cut the flap of skin with the sharp knife, carefully measuring its length so that it was long enough to cover the wound on the other side of the hole.

"Pull," said Momma

Anna pulled on the flap of skin to make it protrude beyond the hole.

"Good girl."

"Oww!"

Anna stretched the skin and held it in place. Momma cut off the ragged part. Anna released the skin and smiled with the satisfaction of a successful surgical intern.

Momma went to a cabinet and came back with a piece of string and a sliver of a shiny object. Isaac watched. His heart pounded. Blood poured out of his arm on both sides.

Momma wet the string with her mouth to form a point. She said calmly to Toby, "Boy, you stop blood." Momma slipped the string deftly through the eye of the needle.

Toby clamped the cloth tighter on Isaac's arm.

* * *

The militia outside were fixated on the glowing lights a hundred yards away. Swanson's two large, stationary candles in the back of the house threw shadows of the inside movement onto the ground, making the activity inside even more perplexing. The militia were wide awake now, watching the curious dream unfold in the farmhouse in front of them. They stared at the flickering lights, candles, shadows, movement, all a bustle of activity developing in front of them. Not a single exhausted militia man could take his eyes off the house.

Murphy rode to the back of the line, searching for Swanson. He came to McKean's men, just now entering the field.

"You see Sergeant Swanson?"

A rifleman pointed to the candle-lit house. "He went in there."

* * *

Momma hovered over Isaac. She said to Anna, "Now we sew him up." She poked the needle through Isaac's skin and caught the other side of the wound. She looped it off tight and poked another one through the skin, skillfully tying the knot like a professional dressmaker. Isaac tried hard to keep his whole body from shaking.

Momma said, "You stay still, you live. You move quick, I hit vein, you die."

There was a knock at the door. Swanson opened it. Murphy said, "Borg, are the boys here? Your men saw you come in here."

"Yes, come in, Cap." Swanson led Murphy into the kitchen where Momma continued her work. Isaac looked behind him, craning his neck as Momma pierced his skin another time. Isaac didn't feel that one. He saw Murphy and relaxed a little. Toby, still holding Isaac's arm, spotted Murphy behind Swanson and sighed in relief.

Momma straightened the needle for another plunge. She looked over at Borg and an American soldier next to him, open-jawed at the needle in the air. Murphy gaped at Isaac. Blood seeped from Isaac's arm.

Momma had never seen Murphy, but she knew who he was from her husband's descriptions and the circumstances. Momma smiled and went back to the arm with the needle.

Anna watched closely. She asked, "Momma, can I try?" There was a new doctor in the family.

"Yes, you try. I show you." Momma handed the needle to Anna, who took it gingerly, and fixed it between her finger and thumb. Momma said, "In here. Next to other stitch."

Anna moved the needle a little south.

"That right, go. Good girl. Then through. All right. Good. Pick up on other side now. Good. Good."

Anna struggled to get the needle through the other side of the wound, difficult to do with the blood gushing out on both sides. Momma wiped it away. Anna poked once, twice, but the needle still wouldn't go through. Isaac's scream swelled in his stomach, but not in his voice. He couldn't, wouldn't, let Anna know his fear and pain, but his heart pounded so loud in his chest that the blood spurted all over the table. The fear hurt worse than the pain.

Mamma wiped the blood again. She gently took the needle from Anna. "You do good, girl, but harder. Watch." Momma kept one eye on Anna and the other on Isaac as she plunged the needle through the wound on the other side. "See? We no pay attention to blood. We get good fix, then go through. See?"

Anna watched. She nodded her head, "Yes." Momma tied off the knot and ended with another loop. Anna studied the angle of the needle and the mechanics of tying the thread.

"You take." Momma handed the needle to Anna. "Start here, next to other stitch."

Anna took the needle and pushed it firmly through the skin. Isaac's eyes glazed over. Toby looked over at his father, who nearly fainted from the sight. Swanson sat in a chair and indifferently scraped the mud off his boots.

Isaac stared into Anna's eyes, those of his salvation, or the death of him if she made a mistake. Anna concentrated on the needle and getting it though the flap of skin on the other side. Murphy came over to the table, took Toby's hand, and moved it gently from Isaac's arm. Toby slumped down in a chair, glad to be relieved of this terrible duty.

Momma said to Anna, "I sew you father many time." Isaac's tears flowed, but he braved himself in the presence of his father and Anna.

Anna pierced the flesh on the other side of the wound and drew the string through. She smiled at Momma, "success."

Momma exclaimed, "Good girl. You make good doctor." Anna swelled with pride. "You tie off now, like I show you."

Anna took the needle, tied off the thread, and cut the loose string with her teeth. Anna beamed as Momma hugged her.

Momma pretended she didn't see Murphy standing there. Another loop of the needle, and Momma said to Isaac, "You know, you father favorite of my Borg. He good man, you father. My Borg write me on him. You pay good to him, you father."

"Yes, I know, I know. Oww."

Murphy held Isaac's arm with his right hand and covered Isaac's forehead with the other. The strength of Murphy's left hand against his head mitigated the pain. Anna took the candles from Isaac's stomach and held Isaac's good arm. She looked fondly at Isaac, then into the face of this strange man whom everyone seemed to know except her.

Swanson finished cleaning his boots near the door. He shouted over, "The stitch in time save nine."

Isaac said. "I've heard that. Oh, God, I should have known."

Swanson came over to the table. "Cap, this my wife, Greta. This Anna."

"How you do, Ma'am? Thanks for doing this."

"How you do, Warren. Borg say many good things on you. Thank you, take care of him."

"Not so. He takes care of me." Murphy looked at Anna. "And you're the famous Anna."

Anna blushed and turned her head.

Momma was done with the front side. "Turn him over." Isaac panicked. Anna nudged Murphy's hand away from Isaac's forehead. At the slight touch, Murphy moved his hand and motioned for Toby to come over and help. Anna took over at Isaac's forehead.

Anna said, "It's almost done, Isaac. Isn't it Momma?"

Momma gave an unassuring shrug, "Ya, sure."

Momma dipped the needle into the soapy water and swished it around. The water turned red. She glanced at her husband, who watched without the least bit of emotion. Momma recalled the many needles she'd poked through Swanson over the years. He never uttered a sound. But he wasn't a boy. Maybe Swanson never was a boy. They never had a boy, only Anna. No boys. All right, back to the task for Momma.

"Back-side bullet not so bad. We done in a minute. Two loops, no more."

Murphy and Toby turned Isaac over. The back of his arm was nothing but mangled flesh and blood. Anna wiped her eyes, but Isaac couldn't see, with his face pointing sideways. Toby stared in shock. Murphy averted his eyes from the wound. He looked over at Swanson for a sign of reassurance, but Swanson just watched the procedure as if it were a normal, every-day occurrence. Momma dipped the cloth into the bloody water and wiped the wound. She squeezed Isaac's arm with her hands and fingers. Blood shot out. It squirted onto the table and splattered Murphy and Anna.

Isaac screamed, "Aaieee!"

Anna turned away. "Momma, do you have to do that?"

"Yes, child, bad blood." She squeezed again, more blood. She reached into the gaping hole in Isaac's arm with her fingers and extracted a large flap of ragged skin. Swanson picked up the knife. He asked, "You want I cut it off?" Momma shook her head, "Nein. We need that. Make paste."

Swanson went over to the cabinet, got a bag, and sprinkled several ounces of flour into a pan. He noticed a big black bug running around in the flour, picked it out, and flicked it to the floor. Another bug, flick. He carried the pan and the bag of dry flour over to the table and set it down. Swanson cupped his hand, reached into the bloody pot, and dripped some water into the pan. He stirred it with his finger. Swanson knew the procedure. The mixture formed a paste. He set the pan down on the table next to the bag of flour and went back to the cabinet.

Momma spit on the needle to make it slide in more easily. She gently pushed it into Isaac's arm. Isaac was too weak now to object. She caught the flap of skin with the other side of the needle and looped it around.

Swanson came back to the table with a large towel and a jug. He put the lip of the jug to Isaac's mouth. "You want some?"

Isaac shook his head only a few inches, he was so close to passing out. He whispered, "No, makes me sick."

Momma smiled. "Almost done. Borg, come here."

Swanson came around to Momma's side of the table with the jug. "Now?"

"Yes." Swanson poured the whiskey on the wound. Momma sprinkled some dry flour onto Isaac's arm as Swanson held the pan of paste. With her finger, Momma scooped some paste out of the pan and spread it all around. Momma motioned to Swanson, indicating the two large candles in the kitchen behind her.

Swanson asked, "Now?"

"Yes, bring."

Swanson brought the two large candles into the room, carefully making sure the liquid wax didn't spill out of the large bowls he created. The militia outside saw two bright candles move through the house.

Momma said to Toby and Murphy, both holding Isaac's arm,

"Hold close." She took one of the candles from Swanson, held it over the wound, and poured the hot wax over the paste. Isaac screamed and almost ripped his arm away from Toby and Murphy, but they held it firmly. "Oww." Momma spread the paraffin around with her finger.

Swanson tore thin pieces of cloth from a clean fabric and bit the hanging threads off with his teeth. Momma ripped a long piece into small strips, wrapped the hole in a butterfly bandage that pulled both sides together, and then held the bandage hard so the paste would set. "Turn him over."

Murphy and Toby picked Isaac up and turned him over onto his back again so Momma could get to the entry wound. She turned Isaac's arm toward her and filled the entry wound with paste. "Hold him steady."

Isaac closed his eyes. Murphy nearly cried at what he knew would happen next. Swanson offered the second candle to Momma. She took it. The light of the candle glowed bright as it tilted backwards and the burning-hot wax poured into Isaac's wound.

Isaac couldn't even manage a cry. He was nearly unconscious now, the pain unimaginable. Spit dribbled out of his mouth and ran down his face.

The militia outside heard the faint cries from deep within the house. Murphy and Toby struggled to get a better grip on Isaac's arm. They kept it elevated as Momma fastened two more butterfly bandages to the wound. She took strips of cloth that Swanson continually provided her and wrapped the arm round and round. A quick needle through the cloth sealed the wound.

Momma announced, "Done. He be all right."

Isaac opened his eyes, breathed a heavy sigh, and looked down at his arm. Murphy wiped Isaac's forehead as Anna and Toby helped him sit up.

Anna asked, "Isaac?" She caressed his head. Toby ran behind Isaac in case he fell down, but he didn't. Anna looked at Isaac's big, fat, clean, white bandage fastened tight. "Isaac, are you all right?"

"Yeah. I'm all right." He moved his arm a little, and smiled thinly.

Swanson took the pot off the table and walked to the back door. Momma stopped him. "Where you go?"

"I throw this out."

"Not yet you do. Bring back here."

Swanson brought the pot of dirty water back to the table. Momma scooped the paste into it from the flour pan. She dipped the pan in the water and then wiped it with an extra piece of cloth. "Put there." Swanson took the flour pan, put it in a cabinet, and came back.

Momma dipped the cloth in the water and wiped Isaac's blood off the table, wringing it out frequently into the pot, swishing the cloth around in the bloody water and wiping the table.

Momma nudged Isaac away so she could get behind him. Isaac slowly swung his legs around. Toby and Murphy helped him get off the table. Isaac stood up. He looked at his arm again. "Whew." Murphy and Toby let go gingerly, expecting a collapse, but Isaac stood and steadied himself.

Momma wiped the table visibly clean. "Now you take out back." Swanson walked outside with the water and threw it into the yard.

Murphy said, "Thanks for doing that, Ma'am. You're an amazing person."

Isaac said, "Yeah. Thanks."

Momma turned away from the men and smiled. She strode into the kitchen with a face that could light up the room and a head that could hit the ceiling. She met Swanson coming back in. Momma took the pot from Swanson's hands, gave it a quick swipe with the bloody rag and put it back in the cabinet, ready for the next pot of soup. She threw the rag into a waste bag.

Isaac swayed, then stumbled. He smacked his good arm against the table to keep from falling. Anna yelled, "Momma."

Murphy grasped Isaac by the belt and propped him up. Toby held Isaac's shirt. Isaac staggered upright. "Whoa." His head wobbled.

Momma said to Anna, "Get chair. Sit him down."

Anna rushed over to the chair that Toby had fallen asleep in so many days ago. She dragged it behind the table. Toby released Isaac in his father's care and helped Anna drag the chair over.

Murphy eased Isaac into the chair.

Swanson said, "You do good, boy."

Murphy replied, "Unbelievable. Yes, you did real good. You all right?"

"Yes. It's going away now."

Toby said, "Pa, if I get shot, bring me back here."

Murphy said, "Yes, me too."

Momma came over to Isaac on the chair. Isaac followed her nervously, in case she wasn't done, because Isaac was prepared to challenge that if necessary. Momma hovered around the bandage with her fingers, examining it, pulling off a loose string or two here and there, but not actually touching the cloth, just fidgeting with the pride of her greatest medical achievement.

Swanson joked, "She easy on you. Not so with me."

Momma laughed. "Nicht zutrerffend (not true)." She smiled into Isaac's eyes. "He big baby, cry all the time." Isaac relaxed, relieved that it was all over.

Swanson said, "Nicht zutrerffend!"

Swanson's hearty laugh shattered the tension. Anna pulled Isaac's face into her breasts. Luckily, Swanson didn't see that, laughing up at the ceiling at the joke. Momma shot an admonishing glance at Anna, who got playfully embarrassed and gently pushed Isaac away.

Anna sat on the floor next to the chair and held Isaac's hand. Isaac glimpsed down at her beautiful hair, so stringy and wet a few days ago. He glanced away as Anna looked up again. Anna sat calmly at Isaac's side and surveyed all the people in the room.

Momma, almost a friend. Papa, still laughing, a "big bear," as Momma called him. Murphy, a good father. He seemed nice. Anna smiled up at Isaac. She wondered what Isaac would be like as a father. What about Isaac's mother? Who was she? Was she nice, like Momma? Would Isaac's mother like her? Then there was Toby, very young, but different in a way, too young for his age, and too old for his deeds. What to make of him? She smiled again. Anna wished that the war outside would just go away and it could be like this forever.

Sadly, it couldn't.

Murphy said to Swanson, "Borg, we're moving out in a few minutes."

"I figure."

"We're with the militia in the rear. The regulars will hit first."

Anna said, "Momma, the boys have to stay here."

Swanson stopped laughing. "Nein. No boys in my house with my daughter."

Momma and Anna turned to each other with a 'rather-not-tell-him-about-that-just-now' expression.

Murphy agreed with Swanson. "No. There could be British all over here tomorrow. If they find militia-aged boys here, well, they'll be safer with the army. You'll be safer without them."

"Momma?"

Momma agreed. "Is right. They go."

Anna released Isaac's hand. She got up from her crouched position at Isaac's side. Her dream was gone.

Murphy said, "Borg, our orders are to take out the bridge. We should be all right in the rear. You have any axes or anything?"

"Yes, I get them."

"We must have some, but I have no idea where they are." Swanson nodded and went outside.

Toby pleaded, "No, Pa, please. Not our bridge. We used to play there. Do you have to?"

"No, of course not, Toby. You can just stand there in the middle of it when eight thousand British come across from Trenton."

Swanson came back with an armload of axes and hatchets.

Murphy said, "Good. Toby, get them outside. Isaac, can you walk?"

"Yes, I think."

Anna took Isaac's good arm and helped him up. They walked slowly through the living room to the front door. Anna pulled Isaac to a stop. She tightened her grip on his arm and opened the door with her right hand, her left hand keeping a firm hold on Isaac. Even as she turned her eyes to the doorknob, she sensed in her left hand for any shakiness in Isaac's stance.

Isaac watched her and felt the pressure on his good arm. "I'm not a baby, you know."

Anna smiled apologetically. "Oh, I know that." Anna opened the door. As Isaac walked out, Anna murmured to herself, "Don't die, Isaac. Please don't die." Isaac didn't hear that.

* * *

A militia sergeant outside called to his men in the field, "Let's go. We're next in line."

The militia got up slowly, peering at the house. They couldn't take their eyes off it. The militia sergeant called again, "Get over here." The militia stared at the drama unfolding before them. Two figures came out of the house, now brightly lit by candles. The militia sergeant trudged into the field to get his men, but they wouldn't move.

A private spoke up, "Sarge, look over there." The sergeant looked at the house as Anna and Isaac came outside. Toby followed with the hatchets and axes in his arms. He dropped an axe and stooped to pick it up.

Anna turned Isaac around and kissed him hard on the mouth. Isaac wrapped his good arm around Anna and kissed her back, damned if anybody saw it.

Toby saw it. "You two kissing? Aw, Jeez."

Anna smiled, wiped some tears, and hugged Isaac and Toby together, and then rubbed Toby's head. "Take care of him for me, Toby, and yourself."

Murphy came out behind Swanson, along with Momma. Murphy didn't see the kiss, nor did Swanson or Momma. Murphy said to Swanson, "Let's get up."

The militia saw the kiss. They recognized Swanson's slow, stooped-over walk as he came toward them. They turned around, hustled off the field, and onto the road, but glanced backward often. Now they had plenty to gossip about for the next five miles into Princeton, two hours away, more than enough time to spread the word to anyone who would listen about the strange incident of Swanson and Murphy coming out of a local house in the middle of nowhere. The kiss only fueled their speculation. The militia were wide awake now. Murphy, Swanson, and the boys disappeared into the cornfield and rejoined the war.

A wagon appeared from the direction of the woods. The Swanson women turned toward the moans and groans and agonies of the wounded. Another wagon approached from the cornfield.

Momma said, "Anna, light more candles."

Chapter Forty Eight

The army marched almost due north and came to a crossroad. Washington and Henry Knox stopped at the point of a long line of Americans and faced the men coming up. The Quaker Road continued north toward the Princeton Bridge. The Sawmill Road went east and then curved north into Princeton. Washington pointed to his left for the column to proceed east, into town.

Alexander Hamilton marched by, his two guns pulled by strong but tired horses. Hamilton bent his back into the guns as he pushed from behind. He spied Washington and Knox on horseback to his left.

Hamilton straightened up and saluted, but he couldn't quite bring his hand up to his forehead, he was so tired. His arm went up in the air and came down. That action itself drained away more of what little strength he had. He tried again as he passed, and this time, he managed the full salute. His guns were getting farther away, but he turned around and faced Washington as he passed. Washington noticed.

Washington quickly returned the salute. Hamilton, relieved, caught up to his men and guns. He glanced nervously at his men, who, fortunately, didn't notice that he had lagged behind.

Washington remarked to Knox, "He's a good man."

"Yes, I know."

Hamilton shouted, "Keep 'em going, boys." Hamilton acknowledged in his own mind that many of his men, in fact, all of them, were older than he was. "Sorry, men. Keep going."

Another column of men saluted as they passed Washington and Knox, the men so weary they could barely raise their arms. The road was a little wider now, and easier to navigate. The sun, still below the horizon, faintly illuminated the road a bit more. The men marching to Princeton could finally stop focusing on the ground for the painful danger of stubbing a foot on a stone or a log.

The Quaker Road angled left, due north to the bridge. The sun hadn't yet graced the road with its warmth. Neither had it burned off the fog that made every yard seem like there was nothing but agony and death beyond.

The last of the regulars marched east toward town. A gap in the line brought General Mercer to the crossroads on a horse.

Washington said, "Morning, Hugh. How are you?"

Mercer replied, "All right. The militia are coming up." He looked behind him and saw shadows turn the bend in the dark distance.

* * *

Isaac held his arm as he rode in an ammo wagon. Murphy, Swanson, and Toby trudged along side. A single bird chirped out a two-note song far to the east, "whoo-weet." Five seconds later, there was another "whoo-weet." It was the only sound on the still-dark road at the rear of the American line, besides the normal trudging, sloshing, mumbling, whispering, swearing, and despairing of a moving army.

"Whoo-weet." Five more seconds and "whoo-weet." Toby listened to the bird as he marched, head down. He counted out the steps, "whoo-weet," two, three, four, "whoo-weet, two, three, four, "whoo-weet." He smiled, two, three, four. "Whoo-weet," two, three, "Whoo-weet. Whoo-weet"

Wait. Another bird a hundred yards to the east had replied to the first. There was silence for five seconds, then "whoo-weet," "whoo-weet" was the response.

Toby was startled by the break in the pattern. A crow made its presence known, loud and far away, "ca-cow." That statement woke up another hundred birds, "Whoo-weet, Whoo-weet, ca-cow." In minutes, a cacophony of bird talk erupted far to the east. Their symphony drifted toward the militia marching north as thousands of birds chirped out their morning songs.

Isaac groaned in the wagon. Toby pulled the blanket up to Isaac's chin.

Swanson said, "Sun's coming up."

Murphy shook his head, "Yes."

The column of militia and riflemen arrived at the crossroads. Mercer pointed north, sending the column that way. He gave an order, "Go up a hundred yards, then stop 'till I get there." The soldiers acknowledged.

Henry Knox recognized some stragglers from Sullivan's division, regulars who were supposed to go into town. Particular among them was Captain Joseph Moulder with two cannons. Somehow Moulder got mixed up with the militia.

Washington looked at the rising sun in the east. "Let's hope it's a good day, gentlemen." He galloped away, rejoining the regulars on their trek toward Princeton. Knox and Mercer watched him go.

Mercer cantered up the Quaker Road ten yards from the crossroad and stood off the road to the left, so the men could see him in the darkness.

Mercer wore a clean red and gold uniform, impossible to miss, even for his tired men. Henry Knox stayed at the crossroads and watched for other remnants of Sullivan's division.

Murphy, Isaac, Toby, and Swanson passed Knox and went north. Murphy saluted. Henry returned. "See ya, Murph."

Captain Moulder, the artillery straggler with the militia, struggled with his two guns. He was the last of the regulars to come onto the Saw Mill Road. Henry Knox watched anxiously as Moulder labored to turn the guns onto the road.

One of the guns had a broken wheel, so a soldier had to continually place a small piece of wood on the ground as the broken part came around. It was back-breaking work, bending over, following along, stooping down, pulling the wheel of the gun up at the circular break point. The soldier missed a break in the revolution of the wheel. The gun ground to a halt and careened two feet to the left. A friend took over. The original gunner straightened his back.

Knox asked, "Boy, you hurt?"

"No, sir."

Knox looked east at the regulars getting farther ahead. "Moulder, you think you can make it up there, into town? We need those guns. I can send a detachment back here to help you if you need it."

Moulder replied, "No sir. We'll be up presently."

Knox reluctantly left Moulder to straighten out his guns and trotted up the Saw Mill Road. Knox bellowed over to Mercer, only a few yards north.

"Good luck to you, Hugh."

Mercer nodded. Knox looked at the confusion that Mercer faced, militia, darkness, and a bad road, but it was getting light. Mercer only had to take out the bridge. It shouldn't be that hard. Knox turned his mind toward Princeton. He needed to find Hamilton, his best shooter with a cannon. Knox trotted off toward Princeton.

Mercer proceeded north up the Quaker Road. He was at the head of the long line of militia and riflemen, 350 men in all. He stopped 300 yards up and let the men go by. Some saluted, others didn't. They were militia. He was on the west side of the Quaker Road. "Keep going, boys."

Murphy, Isaac, Swanson and Toby came up. Mercer pointed slightly north, through the fog. He aimed his hand like a gun, squinting through the fog. Mercer said, "Murph, the bridge should be right about there. Get to the bridge and take it out. No matter what, take out the bridge." Murphy saluted. Men stumbled up the road. The bridge was a quarter-mile away, but the men couldn't see it yet, obscured by the fog, some thin trees, and the early morning darkness.

The trees that lined the Quaker Road were jeweled with a lustrous frost. The sun, just peeking from the east, now shimmered on their tops.

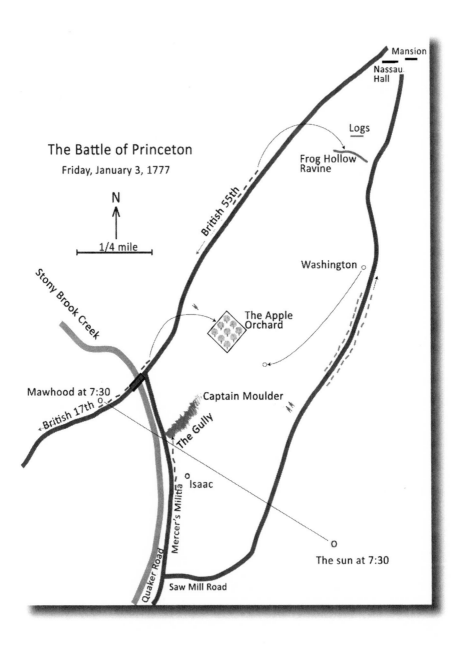

The Battle of Princeton

Friday, January 3, 1777

N

1/4 mile

Mansion

Nassau Hall

Logs

Frog Hollow Ravine

British 55th

Washington

Stony Brook Creek

The Apple Orchard

Mawhood at 7:30

British 17th

Captain Moulder

The Gully

Isaac

Mercer's Militia

Quaker Road

The sun at 7:30

Saw Mill Road

Chapter Forty Nine

The Princeton Battlefield was an open field of grass, gently rolling up to the northeast. A long, slow dip in the ground, a gully, took the field six feet below the average elevation going toward the bridge, and then rose back to normal at the bridge and the north road into Princeton.

It was as if an ancient giant, two thousand feet tall, lay there to rest a million years ago. His feet dangled into the cool Stony Brook Creek and his head rested on a pillow of land to the northeast, now a small apple orchard. The indent of his body formed the dip in the ground that Mercer's militia now approached.

Mercer led the troops almost due north toward the bridge, a quarter mile away. He searched through the thinning fog for a glimpse of the bridge. To his left, across the creek, a peripheral gleam of brilliant light caught his left eye, only a flash. Mercer spun his head toward it. He looked closely in the direction of where he thought the light originated, across the creek, in direct line with the rising sun to his right. He peered through the mist, trees, and fog a thousand yards to his left, but he didn't see it again. Mercer was worried.

The rear of a British detachment, four hundred strong, crossed the bridge and headed southwest toward Trenton. British colonel Charles Mawhood was 300 yards west of the bridge at the head the column marching to Trenton when, to his left, he thought he saw movement along the Quaker Road across the creek.

Mawhood studied the ground so his horse wouldn't stumble. He got off the road to the left and let some men pass by. He looked again, but there was nothing there. Another glance, and he saw something moving. Mawhood could just barely make out the forms of people going north, southeast of him. A British captain rode up. "What is it sir?

"There's troops over there, or something, I don't know. I thought I saw movement, over there." Mawhood pointed. The officer looked, but averted his gaze away from the sun. Nobody was there. Mawhood said, "Probably just some rebels who deserted, or a scouting party, still..."

Mercer was going north. Mawhood was going southwest. The front of Mawhood's line had just climbed a hill in the road. His men were a thousand yards north of Mercer, separated by the creek lined with trees on both sides.

Mercer saw what he thought was a thin line of soldiers, north and slightly to the left. It wasn't Mawhood, but the rear of Mawhood's troops crossing the bridge. With the fog and trees, though, Mercer couldn't tell if there was anything there or not, or who they were. He looked northwest to where he saw the gleam of reflected sunlight, but nothing was there now.

Mercer's 350 men marched down into the gully. He pointed his left arm north and slightly west, toward the bridge, so the men could see where they had to go, to the bridge. Murphy came up. Mercer lowered his arm. "Murph, There's something going on."

Murphy stopped. "Sir?"

"I thought I saw something, over there." Mercer pointed northwest, across the fields and the creek and left of the bridge. He motioned with his head. Murphy looked, but didn't see anything.

Mercer stared northwest as his men went into the gully. Last to enter were Swanson, his men, and Toby. Murphy spotted the bridge, becoming visible now with the diminishing fog. Mercer was clearly worried about something, but there was nothing to see.

"Sorry, Murph. Get to the bridge."

Murphy caught up with Swanson and Toby in the rear of the militia and went down into the gully.

* * *

To British Colonel Mawhood, southwest of the bridge on the other side of the Stony Brook Creek, the men he thought he spotted had just disappeared into the earth. He thought again that it was a scouting party, or deserters, or maybe the local farmers, or some women getting their daily water, or something. Even if they were rebels, they were gone. They probably ran away already, probably nothing to worry about.

Mawhood turned his horse around and trotted slowly back to the bridge, encouraging his men to keep going, an officer's ploy to let his men know he was in charge, their friend, and willing to risk his life in the rear for their sake. He glanced casually to his right now and again, southeast, for the men he thought he saw, but the sun was rising ever higher, and he couldn't look there any more.

* * *

The British army was the greatest army in the world and everybody in the world knew it. On equal terms, they had never lost a fight. Even outnumbered, they were a formidable opponent. Colonel Mawhood was one of the best the British had. His men were Highlanders, Dragoons, Royal Scots, Artillery, and Foot infantry. They'd known him for years, and Mawhood had never let them down. The nagging feeling that the enemy might be in his rear bothered a British officer.

Mawhood looked southeast again as he stopped his horse ten yards before he got to the Trenton side of the bridge. He let some more men get ahead. They moved very slowly, but picked up the pace as they passed him. They were the 17th, not famous for their speed. Mawhood grunted, "Hustle on." He glanced across the field one more time.

The laws of nature play terrible tricks on soldiers in war, and Charles Mawhood had just been taken in by the biggest one of all, the location of the sun. Fifteen minutes ago he saw a trickle of bodies marching north. The sun had just nudged over the horizon then. With the fog and the darkness, he could turn his eyes there and stare long enough to see movement. But now the sun was full faced above the trees. Mawhood couldn't look into the sun. That's where Mercer's militia were, in direct line of the sun, marching low into the gully, and blinded to his eyes.

With the bottom of the whole sun now off the ground, Mawhood held his eyes against its brightness. He saw more movement, well beyond what he saw before, a mile away, and almost due east. The sun was blindingly bright, but just to the left of it, in quick glances, avoiding the sun, Mawhood was astonished at what he saw. The Americans were here, in force, and going for Princeton. Mawhood had spotted the main army with Washington and Sullivan heading for town.

Chapter Fifty

awhood charged down the road in the Trenton direction. He yelled to the men he passed, "Turn. Turn." The men looked at him with surprise. Mawhood yelled, "Back. Get back. Back across the bridge."

The men of the 17th stopped. Toward Trenton, men heard the order to turn. They shrugged to each other, but they turned. It was an order. Mawhood saw the forward, western-most companies comply. He pointed east, toward Princeton, "Turn." He galloped east and crossed the bridge.

Just about to cross the bridge from the Princeton side was a single cannon drawn by horses, the last of the line moving west. The bridge was cluttered with men, all wearing heavy packs, but Mawhood plowed through them, yelling to the cannoneers, "Get off the road! Off the road! Get that gun out of the way!" Mawhood stopped on the Princeton side.

The cannoneers turned their horses into the field on the Princeton side of the bridge. The gun freed up the path for more soldiers. An officer galloped up to Mawhood. "What is it sir?"

Mawhood pointed to the column of Americans moving parallel to him, due east, but they were hard to see. The officer held his hand to his eyes to shield the sun, and spotted the rear of Washington's column. "Oh, no."

Mawhood shouted to the officer, "They're heading for town. Get the men turned. Intercept them. Wait." Mawhood calculated the speed of the two forces in a minute. "Wait." Mawhood considered, looking behind him at the 17th, and then toward the Americans. He peered closely up the road, expecting another of his regiments, the 55th, which should be on their way. He didn't see them yet. "I'm sending the 55th back to town. We'll make a stand at Frog Hollow. Bring the 17th up as soon as you can. I'll meet you at Frog Hollow."

The officer galloped toward Trenton, screaming, "Turn! Turn!"

The British were a nimble group. Hard as it was to turn a marching force, even if was only 400 men, they all had eighty-pound packs. Equipment, wagons, and horses had to get off the road to make way for the infantry. The British managed it quite well. A few mishaps took place as men marching west collided with those going east, but once everyone had their orders, it was a clean maneuver. They were the greatest army in the world. Mawhood's men were marching back to Princeton.

Mawhood rode into the gap between his two forces. At 650 yards from the bridge, 250 yards from the apple orchard, he spied his second regiment coming down, the 55th. The 17th ambled up slowly from the southwest. Mawhood rode up to the head of the 55th. An officer trotted down to meet him halfway. The officer was surprised to see men from the 17th coming up behind Mawhood.

"Sir?"

"Back up. Back into town. Get your men in front of the ravine, Frog Hollow. Get your guns up there. Send word back to the barracks. Prepare for attack."

"Sir? Attack from whom?"

Mawhood pointed east. Washington's troops were out of sight now, behind a rise in the ground, but Mawhood shouted, "The whole damn Rebel army, that's *whom!* Go. I'll be up shortly."

The officer turned his horse and ordered the column coming up, "About face, left front. Forward."

The soldiers and officers of the 55th repeated the orders as they received them, stopped and turned. At almost the speed of voice, the entire regiment turned and marched back to Princeton.

Mawhood watched them go. He worried about the troops in Princeton, and the supplies, guns, powder, shot, and food, everything the rebels needed to continue the war. If he could slow the Americans down long enough, he should be all right. His forces in town could handle the rebels, hopefully, until Cornwallis arrived with his 8,000 men. He wondered if the 400 troops of the 55th would be able to make it to Frog Hollow ravine in time to slow down the Americans.

His 600 troops in town would also need time to get their guns up. He had the 17th, coming up from the bridge, another 400 men. Mawhood had 1,400 men in all, including the detachment at Princeton, but they were not together.

Mawhood thought about the battle that was about to take place. He looked southwest to the 17th coming toward him, 300 yards away, and then back to the 55th marching quickly toward Princeton. Timing was everything. He called to the lumbering 17th, "Hurry up. Come up."

He continued working the battle in his mind. Washington was going for Princeton, that was obvious. It was equally obvious that Washington didn't know he was there, in his rear, or Washington would be charging across the field at the 55th. If the 55th could get in front of Washington and hold him long enough for Cornwallis to come up... No, they couldn't. And anyway, then Cornwallis would get the credit. Mawhood frowned at the thought.

On the other hand, Washington would probably blow by the 55th at Frog Hollow, but the 55th would retreat into town. When the rebels saw the Princeton guns, they'd hesitate. Mawhood mused at the fragility of the American force. If the 17th could come up in the exact rear of the Americans at just the right time, 400 slow troops, but excellent with the bayonet, the Americans would run like soup out of a broken pot. Suddenly, Mawhood wasn't so eager for the 17th to come up so quickly. He watched the 17th coming over the bridge and mumbled to himself, "Slow down, slow down."

Mawhood reveled at the glory in his mind. The Americans would face the Princeton guns and then run away as fast as they could when the 17th came up behind them. The rebels would collapse and scatter like jackrabbits, no doubt about it. It was classic.

The war would be over. He'd have defeated the entire American army with his small group of well trained, well disciplined, and superbly led forces, prepared, as always, to defend the realm with every ounce of their unlimited courage. They'd write military journals, articles, and critiques, like "Mawhood's Strategy at Princeton," "Mawhood Saves the Day," and "Have We No Other Mawhoods?" They might even write a musical, "Where Mawhood Stood." The name "Charles Mawhood" would be the talk of London. The ladies at court would be all over him. He'd bypass promotion to general and soar straight to knighthood.

The sun rose higher on the southeast horizon. Mawhood smiled to himself, "Ah, it's going to be a glorious day."

Alas, the fantasy was not to be.

* * *

The 17th regiment was strung out on the road, the lead just arriving at the apple orchard, the rear 200 yards behind them. Mawhood could see the bridge 650 yards away.

Mawhood looked south. Behind the 17th, he saw sticks, no, not sticks, they were gun barrels, coming out of the ground, hundreds of them, then hats appeared, dozens of heads, hats, soldiers, ragged soldiers, carrying guns, a whole force of... who? Who were they, and how could they be in his rear? They couldn't possibly be rebels, they weren't in the right place. This couldn't be happening.

* * *

Mercer's men emerged from the gully.

Chapter Fifty One

Mercer squinted through the diminishing fog. "Oh, my God." He saw the backs of hundreds of red coats marching obliquely away from him. They slanted slightly to the right, as the road curved that way. Mercer halted his line ten yards north of the gully to let more men come out.

He peered ahead, trying to figure out what the British were doing, marching away from him. They must have spotted Washington and Sullivan's troops heading toward town. Mercer knew he had to do something, but there was no way he could get in front of the British. They were 500 yards away and getting more distant every minute. Mercer would have to go northeast, south of that clump of trees, the apple orchard, in order to head them off, and it was unlikely that his men could get there in time.

Mercer shouted to the men behind, "Come up. Come up."

Murphy came out of the gully at the middle of the line with Swanson and Toby at his side. Murphy said, "Oh, no."

Swanson saw the long red line marching away. "Not too many. We go?" Swanson looked up at Mercer on the horse.

Mercer heard the broken words. "Yes. Go. Forget the bridge. Straight ahead." Then Mercer paused. "No, wait. Wait."

The men stopped while Mercer considered. He could see the forces were about equal. He had 350 men, and it looked to be about that number, maybe a little more, going northeast, away from him, but at least not a whole army.

Normally, a general would give a year's pay to be in Mercer's position. He only had to go north and he'd be in the enemy's rear. The British would have to turn to face him, almost an impossible maneuver in combat, especially on a narrow road. Mercer could destroy the entire British force just by being there. That's what Mercer's military mind told him to do, go north.

Mercer considered that option for only a fraction of a second. He had no more time to decide, and he did decide, instantly, because reality intruded into his military mind.

Mercer's 350 men were 300 militia and 50 riflemen. Both types of soldiers were absolutely worthless in this type of engagement. In an open field, or on an open road, the militia would run away first. The riflemen would fire once and then follow the militia as fast as they could. Or perhaps the riflemen would run first, with no time for another shot before the bayonet came. The militia would follow. It wasn't their fault, neither one of them, the militia or the riflemen. The militia weren't disciplined enough, and the riflemen had no bayonets. Neither force would be able to withstand a bayonet assault from experienced British troops.

With Mercer's force annihilated, the British would simply turn around and Washington and Sullivan would take the full blast of a whole British regiment in their rear, exactly what Mercer was now offered. The British could do it. His troops could not.

Mercer looked due east at the apple orchard. The end of the British line was almost at that clump of trees, but that's where the fight had to take place. Only the protection of the trees could keep his men from certain destruction.

Mercer said, "Murphy, shift right. Head for those trees."

Murphy and Swanson led the column to the east. Mercer sat in his saddle and encouraged the men coming out of the gully. He pointed to the orchard, "Go, go. Over there." Soldiers coming out spotted the sea of red uniforms moving up the road and angling away from them. The militia were not overly concerned, as long as they could make it to those trees. Mercer said again, "Over there. I'll be with you, boys."

British Colonel Mawhood was faced with a difficult decision. If he continued northeast and ignored Mercer, then Mercer would be in his rear. If he attacked Mercer with his even but better-trained soldiers, he'd leave Princeton exposed to the much larger American force, Washington and Sullivan.

Mawhood did what even an average British officer would do in this circumstance, and Mawhood was not an average British officer. He split his force. Mawhood yelled, to the men of the 55th, "Go. Get to the ravine. Double-time. Hold them until I come up." He turned around, shouted to the 17th coming up behind him, and pointed to the apple orchard, "Get to those trees."

Mawhood looked at the cannon that he had ordered off the road a few minutes ago. It joined the line of men rushing toward Princeton. "You. Get that gun back here, yes, you."

The officer at the gun stopped. "Sir? Shouldn't we be better served in town?"

"No. They've got enough guns in town. Get it back here. Down to those trees. Grape. Point it at the trees. Stay near the road." He pointed to a group of soldiers coming up. "You, there. Stay with this gun." Ten soldiers got off the road and helped point the cannon toward the orchard.

Mercer watched his men for a moment. Then he saw the front of Mawhood's line curve right off the road toward the apple orchard. The British cannon got off the road and loaded.

Mercer mumbled, "Oh, my God, they're heading for the trees."

Mercer galloped to the head of the American column, passing Murphy and Swanson, and stopped a hundred yards outside of the orchard. He pointed to the British, now just a little more than 500 yards away. He worried that the British would get to the orchard first. He hoped to slow them down.

"Charge. There."

The few militia at the front of the line looked at each other. Their faces showed they were not particularly good at charging. They proceeded reluctantly but quickly into the field, west of the apple orchard, northward, threatening the rear of the British force.

Fifty British from the rear of their line turned and marched south toward the approaching militia. Now there were two columns of British, moving parallel, one heading straight for the few militia, the other moving toward the orchard. The left-most British column was definitely going to be west of the orchard when they collided with Mercer's special group of militia. Mercer stuck with his plan, get to the orchard. He trotted toward the orchard on his horse, ushering his men to curve to the right. Both groups of British were too far away to fire yet. Mercer hoped he could get to the orchard before the British. "Hurry. Hurry."

For the militia plodding north, not nearly as fast as Mercer would like, the ground rose as slowly as the sun behind them. The British column of fifty men headed directly for them.

Mercer noticed the Americans coming up at an agonizingly slow pace. The British would take the high ground of the apple orchard for sure, especially if that British gun got in place, and it seemed as if it would. Mercer had to take the orchard.

The special militia force stopped, as Mercer expected them to. There was no way a dozen militia were going to charge fifty British, but the militia presence slowed the western British column slightly.

Mercer saw the militia look to their right. He knew the militia were trying to determine how long it would take the British to get to them with bayonets, and how long it would take themselves to get to the trees. The militia group shuffled east. To them, the math just wasn't right.

Mercer galloped over to Murphy, who was heading for the trees. "Murphy, take your men to the left. Take charge of those men over there. Cut off that British column. Just slow them down a little more so we can get to the trees."

"Yes, sir." Murphy said to Swanson, "Keep going." Swanson nodded and led his men to the apple orchard. Toby was in front.

Murphy tapped one of McKean's men on the back. "Shift left, over there." He pointed to the militia, west, and the British coming at them. The soldier complied, and thirty riflemen joined Murphy to intercept the British detachment west of the orchard. The rest of the Americans, 300 of them, headed quickly for the apple trees.

Murphy stopped his riflemen a hundred yards west of the orchard. The militia were glad to have some help because the British were coming straight at them. The rest of the Americans headed for the orchard, led by Mercer. Murphy said, "Get ready." The British charged fast. A hundred yards, ninety yards, eighty. The British stopped and fired. Their shots went high. Murphy yelled, "Fire. Thirty riflemen fired at the on-coming British. Some British fell, but they were clumped together, some in front, others behind them. The British in front were hit with three and four bullets each, dead, but a waste of bullets and time.

The British reloaded in place. They fired again.

The riflemen took even longer than normal to load, enough time to give the British a second round, and they fired. The British were too far away to hit, but the bullets came dangerously close. Some of the militia ran away south. After fifty seconds, the riflemen fired. Several more British fell.

Washington was a half mile due east. He heard the sporadic scattering of gunshots, looked to his left, and saw smoke rise above the trees in the direction of the Princeton Bridge. He assumed that Mercer had encountered a small guard at the bridge, and he was concerned, but at least he knew Mercer had made it to the bridge. He told General Sullivan, "Keep going."

Washington stopped as Sullivan's men went past. Washington listened intensely for more shots. The firing stopped for the time being. Washington thought, "He's got the bridge." Washington trotted slowly alongside the marching Americans. He had a nagging feeling, but everything was going according to plan. The only problem was if the soldiers in town heard those shots, they'd be alerted. Washington proceeded north, but stopped to just within calling distance of Sullivan.

The British facing Murphy rushed fast toward him and his riflemen and the few militia. To the east, the Americans entered the orchard. There wasn't enough time for Murphy's men to reload before the British were upon him. He shouted to his men, "Go, go. Get to the trees."

On Murphy's orders, McKean's men ran fast for the orchard. Murphy stayed in the field and reloaded for one last shot. A British officer shouted an order, "Charge." Murphy's bullet hit him in the head, his first kill of the war, the first kill of his life. Murphy sprinted with his unloaded gun to the orchard.

The British ran south. Murphy ran east to the orchard. McKean's men plowed over the fence and into the trees. Murphy got to the fence and climbed up, but a British soldier grabbed his coat. Murphy fell down, hard onto the frozen ground. The solider plunged with a bayonet. Murphy lunged away and scrambled up toward the fence. A blast from south of the orchard by militia and riflemen sent the remaining British back to the road. The British soldier instinctively ducked from the sound of gunfire. Murphy clutched the fence that surrounded the orchard and kicked the soldier backward with his boot. The soldier fell down against the force, got up, wiped his mouth, and ran back to the road.

Chapter Fifty Two

Of the many differences between the American and British armies, one became significantly apparent at this moment, at the Battle of the Orchard. The British were more skilful fighters, but the Americans could shoot. The British were more disciplined, but the rebels were more resourceful. The British could turn around and march in the opposite direction without asking questions, but the rebels had Washington. The British had the bayonet, the Americans didn't.

And then there was that other critical, intangible, subtle difference on this bright Friday morning and it existed nowhere but in the minds of the men who had to do the fighting. The British liked the open fields. The Americans preferred the trees.

The orchard was 200 yards from the road. The rebels were 400 yards from the orchard. The British got there first, a full ten minutes before the rebels came in from the southwest, but they stopped before entering the orchard. They just didn't like the trees. They preferred to be in a field where their cannons could support them.

The orchard was square, with the top corner pointing almost due north. A small picket fence surrounded it. The British cannon were at the top point of the orchard and fifty yards back, supported by ten troops. The rest of Mawhood's men lined the fence slanting away to the southwest, so that they were not in line with their own cannon. The British stayed out of the orchard for the time being.

The Americans hopped over the fence and immediately took cover in the south orchard behind the thin trees. They thanked God that they had made it to the trees.

Murphy and McKean's men entered the orchard from the west. Swanson, his men, and Toby came in from the south. Murphy was north of Swanson and the 300 militia who stumbled over the fence to get in. Mercer stopped his horse at the middle of the southwest side of the square, outside the fence.

As soon as the rebels entered the orchard, the British rose up and fired a volley with their muskets. There were no hits, except for some unlucky trees. Murphy was closest to the British. He called back, "Come up. Up."

The militia weaved among the trees carefully, unless that cannon went off and they weren't behind a steady apple tree. Murphy yelled again, "Get up. Come up here!"

Another British musket blast went high. Murphy stood up and aimed his rifle, as did the Americans in his vicinity. Militia and riflemen aimed together, although there was very little chance that muskets were going to do any good at a hundred yards away through a line of trees, or even rifles. An American volley hit nobody. The British loaded and fired from the road. Their aim was high again. Branches in the orchard got clipped off high in the air.

Murphy found himself fifty yards from the top of the orchard when he saw a British soldier at the gun light a match and hold it in the air. Murphy was unloaded. Almost all of the Americans were in the orchard now. Murphy shouted behind him, "Get down."

The Americans clung to their trees. Some dropped to the ground. The British cannon went off, with murderous affect as grapeshot filled the air. The tops of the trees were taken away by the shock of the blast, but the scattering iron reached low into the depth of the orchard, split the skull of a militiaman, and wounded three others. The rest of the militia ran south, away from the imminent death of another blast.

Swanson looked at his men. They were holding, reloading. He searched the orchard for Toby, whom he expected would be cowering on the ground. Instead, Toby stood and loaded. Swanson peeked around at the north side of the crotch in the tree that protected his head. Grapeshot had blasted away the bark. Swanson's eyebrows went up.

* * *

Washington heard the alarming crash of the British cannon to his left. He noticed smoke drifting up through the air a half-mile away, nearly due west, over the trees of the apple orchard. General Sullivan trotted up to Washington's position ahead. Sullivan stared in the direction of the apple orchard. Neither general could see what was happening there, only that there was smoke rising, cannon fire, and sporadic gunfire. Washington knew the orchard was almost a half-mile from the bridge, so the bridge was not being taken out. Also, Mercer had no cannons, so that was a British shot.

Sullivan said, "It's only a gun or two. Hugh can handle that."

Washington said, "I don't know. I'm going back. Take your men into town. Keep with the plan."

* * *

At the orchard, the British on their side of the fence maneuvered to get better aim. Three hundred British muskets exploded, followed by another volley from the orchard of American muskets and a few riflemen who managed to load in the short time. Both sides were shooting through fifty yards of trees. Even so, men on both sides fell.

The British cannon went off again, grapeshot, like the last time. The aim was lower now, and wounded three more rebels . Many rebels secretly stole away south to get out of the orchard and away from the danger.

Washington and Sullivan heard the second cannon blast. Sullivan said, "I'll send Hitchcock back."

Washington nodded and galloped west toward the orchard.

Chapter Fifty Three

Friday morning, the last day of the week it was, and Maggie Murphy-Sinclair was glad to see it arrive. She'd been awake since five in the morning, sewing some dresses she had promised to have ready today. At 7:30, she made some toast with a little jam for the children before they got up, an incentive to get their sleepy little heads out of bed.

At 7:50 she went into their room to wake them up. "Come, children, arise." She roused them from their sleep. "I have your favorite breakfast waiting." Maggie heard the faint pit-a-pat of gunfire out the window and turned toward it. She could tell it was coming from Princeton. Another crackle sounded very faint and far away. The children wiped their eyes and got up.

Maggie sat with the children at the table, the little ones devouring the toast and jam. "Mommy has a hard day ahead, dears, so come to the shop with me and behave yourselves. Then we'll do something special tonight."

Pit-a-pat, pit-a-pat, sounds of gunfire echoed from three miles away. One of the children strained to hear. "Mommy, what was that?"

"Nothing, dears, eat."

One child turned to the other, "Sounds like Toby is shooting his gun." The other child laughed.

"No, no. Don't say that. The boys are safe. They're just not here. They're far away."

Then came the boom of cannon fire. Maggie walked quickly to the door. At 8:00 Friday morning, unmistakable sounds of cannon reverberated through the house. Maggie opened the door and looked quickly toward Princeton. Another cannon blast made her put her bandaged hand to her mouth. "Oh, my God." She bolted the door shut and came back to the table, shaking, but recovering a little for the sake of the children. "They're safe. The boys are safe. You'll see them again, just not very soon. You have to be patient. You might be older then."

* * *

Anna tended to the wounded, some of them her own patients. Dozens of men and boys, some dead, occupied every square foot of the small farmhouse. Anna said, "Momma, I think this boy is dead. Oh, Momma."

Momma came over and put her arm on Anna's shoulder. She and Anna were both soaked with blood. Momma closed the eyelids of the young man. "Is all right, Anna. You do good." Momma motioned to the wagon driver to take the boy away.

The driver said, "Mrs. Swanson, we took some area in the back of the house. Is that all right?"

"Yes. Mark graves. Keep names."

The driver nodded and called another soldier to help take the body out back. A scream sounded from Anna's bedroom, where a real doctor sawed off a man's arm.

Anna broke down in tears. "Oh, Momma, there's so many boys, so young, it's so horrible."

"Yes, I know. You do good job today. You good doctor. You help many boys. Some live, some die. We do what we can."

"I'm sorry, Momma. I think about Isaac and Papa and Toby." Anna looked up. "Do you think they'll be all right? Please, Momma."

Momma replied, "And Warren. He take care you Papa." They all good men. We hope they be all right."

"Oh, Momma. Please don't let them die."

The clock chimed 8:00. Anna looked over at it. She remembered Tuesday night, New Year's Eve, when the clock struck midnight and she kissed Isaac. It was so different then, a happier time, and so few days ago. Everything was different now. The chimes stopped, and the faint sounds of cannon fire boomed from the northeast.

"Momma, what was that?"

A minute later, the sound of another volley reached the Swanson farmhouse, distinct enough to be heard over the groans.

"We wait, child."

* * *

At Trenton, aides gathered outside the tent of General Cornwallis. He came out of his tent and sniffed the crisp, smoky air, fastening his sword to his belt. "Ah, the smell of campfires in the morning, a fine day." The aides kept sheepishly quiet. Cornwallis said, "A fine day for a good fight."

Cornwallis walked to the edge of town. "Everything in place?"

An aide spoke up. "There seems to be a problem, sir."

"So, fix it."

"I'm afraid it's not that easy, sir."

Cornwallis arrived at the north edge of the field and looked through a field glass across the Assunpink Creek.

* * *

On the other side of the creek, General Fermoy came out of his tent. He stared across the water, 500 yards away, and saw 5,000 British soldiers, dozens of cannons, and bayonets everywhere. Fermoy looked left and right. Nobody was there. He stumbled back into his tent and reached under his cot for his whiskey. It was gone.

* * *

To Fermoy's right, Jackson and his men sprinted due south as fast as their legs could carry them, beyond the Quaker Road, through the hills, woods and fields. A half mile south, they splashed across a stream, plowed through a row of thick hedges, climbed a small fence, and fell panting into a clearing. They lay on their backs for ten minutes, looking up at the brightening sky. Jackson looked around to make sure his men were all there, and then finally got up. "Let's go." They all walked south.

* * *

Cornwallis lowered his telescope and glared threateningly into the eyes of his aides. They all turned away in shame. Cornwallis raised the glass to his eye again, furious at the sight. The American side was a shambles. Campfires smoldered, broken wagons cluttered the landscape, boxes and trash littered the field, and smoke blocked the upcoming sun. Even a couple of horses grazed in the deserted field. There were tents, hundreds of tents, but no movement. Cornwallis couldn't believe what he saw. Not a single American soldier appeared to be over there.

From far to the left, the faintest sound of cannon fire snapped Cornwallis back to reality. Another cannon blast from the Princeton direction finally got Cornwallis's attention. Washington was gone.

"Damn him. Damn the Fox. Get the men on the road. Double time."

Chapter Fifty Four

Isaac sat in the wagon near the road to the bridge. He saw his father and the other men disappear into the gully, but he couldn't see the British, a half mile away, obscured by the light fog. Then Murphy, the riflemen, and militia came out of the gully. The fog had cleared enough for Isaac to see the rear of red uniforms marching north. The Americans turned east and ran for the orchard. Isaac saw the head of the British regiment curve right off the road and head for the trees.

Isaac struggled to get up, but his arm hurt so badly that he slumped back in the wagon and gazed up at the sky. He propped himself up on his good arm, turned on his right side, and tried again to swing himself out of the wagon, but he needed his bad arm, and it was simply not available.

At the top of the orchard near the road, Murphy steadied the militia. "All right, boys, it's all right. There's not too many of them. We'll be all right."

A final ineffective volley by the Americans triggered the inevitable British response. Mawhood shouted from the road, "Charge." Four hundred British poured over the fence with bayonets pointing. They skirted around the trees like timber wolves, their eyes fixed on the American prey.

Murphy glanced over at his men, who now edged cautiously toward the south of the orchard. Murphy was at the point. He tried to steel his men, "Come on, boys, there's barely a few." The riflemen slowed their retreat and loaded, but it looked bad for them.

The British were forty yards away, then thirty yards, then twenty. At ten yards the British charged as fast as they could, south through the orchard. A couple of American muskets went off and smashed into the apple trees, but the British ignored the shots.

Murphy had only thirty men with him, mostly militia and McKean's soldiers. Swanson and Toby were with the rest of the Americans at the south end of the orchard. Swanson saw the British coming. He said to his men, "Load. Shoot good." To Toby he said, "You shoot, boy." Toby aimed his musket at the on-coming British.

At the point, Murphy couldn't get the ramrod into the barrel because his hands shook too much. A British bayonet came into Murphy's view, pointing at his stomach. Murphy swung the ramrod, deflecting the bayonet. The soldier careened to the right. Murphy slashed him in the head, backhand, with the ramrod. The soldier fell, but the ramrod broke.

Another British soldier charged from the left. Murphy shoved the butt of his rifle at him, hit him in the chest, and slashed the broken ramrod at his head. Blood poured out.

Murphy jumped out of the way of another bayonet. The soldier flew past. Murphy swung around and clipped him in the back with his gun. He ducked another bayonet coming at him from the right. One of McKean's men smashed that soldier with his musket butt and disappeared into the smoke.

Of the very few Americans in Murphy's vicinity, most had been stabbed to death, while others ran back or got killed in hand-to-hand combat as multiple British soldiers ganged up on them.

Murphy yelled, "Pull back. Back!" He took a new ramrod from a fallen rifleman.

A twenty-yard gap developed between Murphy's remaining men and Swanson's soldiers in the rear of the orchard. Murphy struggled south, panting, stopping to catch his breath, looking back, hugging the trees for protection, but British soldiers clogged the way. Another enemy soldier tackled Murphy from the front. Murphy slipped away, skitted along the ground, withdrew his knife from his belt, and plunged it into the soldier's side. Murphy gasped at the blood on his hand. He got up, put the knife back in its sheath and headed south. His men scrambled along side, but more British were already ahead. One turned and faced Murphy with the bayonet. Murphy ducked low and clipped the soldier's knees with his rifle. The soldier flipped backward. One of McKean's men fell on the soldier with a long knife and dispatched him with a vengeance. Murphy said, "Thanks," and helped the rebel up. The two of them were the last to get back, dodging the trees, running south.

Murphy spied Swanson and Toby. Murphy said, "Get out! Get out of the trees!"

Swanson recognized Murphy's voice, turned to his men and said, "Get back." Swanson's men ran to the fence at the south edge of the orchard.

Toby stood up and walked toward Murphy. The British were closing fast, but Toby didn't care. His father came toward him as Toby stood with a loaded gun, ready to face dozens of British with a single musket and tears in his eyes. "Pa!"

Murphy yelled, "Toby, go back! Go back!"

One of McKean's men grabbed Toby by the collar and physically dragged him away. The British rushed at Swanson's men. Behind them were Murphy and his few remaining riflemen, so Murphy was surrounded, although the British paid no attention to the few Americans behind them.

Hundreds more British came up in Murphy's rear. They plowed through the trees, stabbing at the retreating rebels.

A moving red-and-gold uniform attracted the attention of the British streaming south. They saw an officer on a horse to their right, outside the fence, next to a large tree. It was Hugh Mercer. A British soldier noticed the brilliant uniform. "Washington! There! Over there! Get him!"

All the British turned and veered to their right, heading for Mercer on his horse. The diversion gave Murphy and his men enough time to go south unmolested and get to the bottom of the orchard.

A British shot rang out. Mercer's horse tumbled to the ground. Mercer catapulted away from the falling horse, but his right wrist snapped as he broke his fall on the frozen ground. The British ignored the retreating Americans, jumped over the western fence, and charged for Mercer.

Mercer grabbed his sword out of its sheath and waited for them to come.

A British soldier shouted, "Surrender, you damn rebel."

Mercer said, "Not in your bloody lifetime."

The British crowded around Mercer in awe, thinking, "Is this the famous Washington?" They hesitated until a soldier declared, "It's Washington, that damn rebel!" Mercer looked up at them defiantly. He twirled his sword in his left hand to get a good grip, then jabbed it at the leading British soldier. The soldier jumped back and laughed.

A solider plunged a bayonet into Mercer's leg. Mercer screamed. He stabbed his sword in the air again and again. The British avoided the feeble blows and laughed again. Another bayonet went into Mercer's chest, but not too deep. The British wanted revenge. Mercer took another slash in the leg, another in the arm, then another in the other arm. The British preferred that Mercer bleed to death, not die right away.

Mercer released his sword and sank against the tree. The British turned to their left as the Americans poured out of the orchard. Murphy's soldiers reached Swanson, Toby, and the rest of the riflemen and militia. They all vaulted the fence and rushed south.

Murphy arrived at the fence, the last to go over. More British appeared from behind, ten yards away and coming fast. Swanson and his men waited for Murphy to come over, then all the Americans were in the field, rushing for the presumed safety of the other side.

* * *

Near the Saw Mill Road, rebel Captain Joseph Moulder dragged his wounded guns into place. He aimed them northwest, directly at the orchard.

Murphy spotted the cannons limbering up. There was no protection for them, not a single American soldier in their vicinity. If the British captured those guns, they'd turn them on the American retreat and it would be all over. But those guns could be their salvation. It was the last chance of slowing down the British onslaught.

"Swanson, get to those guns."

"No, sir, we stay with you."

Toby looked at his father, then at the guns so far away. "No, Pa."

Murphy screamed, "That's an order! Defend those guns! Go."

Swanson and his men maneuvered slightly to their right and headed for Moulder's guns. They were directly in Moulder's line of fire as the British came over the fence. Toby led the group and got to the guns first. Swanson trailed. McKean's men were with Swanson. Toby stopped at the guns, turned toward the orchard, and reloaded.

Swanson got to the guns and collapsed onto his hands and knees. He looked up at Moulder, "Sergeant Swanson (huff), First... (pant, huff, puff) Pennsylvania (pant) Riflemen." Swanson recovered his breath. Moulder heard the word, 'riflemen,' and smiled. His guns were now defended by ten riflemen. And Toby.

Hundreds of Americans poured into the field and ran directly into Moulder's line of fire. Moulder lit a match and held it high in the air with his right hand. He waved his left arm frantically right-to-left, "Get out of the way, get out of the way!"

The Americans saw two cannons pointing straight at them and an officer holding a lighted match. "Holy Jesus." They swerved to the left and right, plowed into the mud, and fell over themselves.

Murphy ran southeast toward the Saw Mill Road with the militia as the last of the British swarmed over the fence. Moulder waited, waited, and waited. The tension in his mind mounted as the fire on the match crept toward his fingers. He didn't want to hit the Americans, but he'd fire if he had to. He wiggled the match higher to give the militia a few more seconds.

Moulder, still holding his match in the air, turned to one of his gunners. "Shift right." The gun moved slightly to the right, where a group of ten British climbed the fence.

The British coming over the fence saw the two American guns 400 yards south, pointing right at them. They knew it was not at all a bad shot for grapeshot-loaded cannons across an open field. Even if Moulder missed, which wasn't likely, the American cannons had plenty of time to load and fire again. For the British, the trees now didn't seem to be such a bad place to be. They slowed their efforts to get out of the orchard and into the field.

The distance between the British and the Americans widened. Ten yards, twenty, thirty, the Americans were getting away as the British hesitated to charge across an open field in the face of those two menacing cannons. The Americans were almost to the Saw-Mill Road. Only a few stragglers were in the way of Moulder's aim at the apple orchard.

Moulder touched the match to the hole. Grapeshot soared into the orchard, taking down a half-dozen British. He touched the same match to the second cannon just as the heat seared his fingers. Another ten British fell. The British halted and reformed. Many sneaked back over the fence into the safety of the apple trees.

Moulder's men cleared the smoking residue out of the two guns with long sponges on sticks. They smashed in two more packets of powder and rammed in bags of grape. Without even looking at the slaughter, Moulder lit another match and touched it to the hole of the left cannon, boom, right cannon, same match, boom. The blasts took the branches off the south trees in the orchard, along with several unlucky British in the field who didn't have the foresight to go back. Moulder's gunners reloaded. All the British scrambled through the field to get back into the orchard, furiously smashing into each other to get to the fence.

Two of the soldiers who stabbed Mercer were still west of the orchard. They saw Moulder's cannons fire at their comrades. A cannon was a special prize in war. If they could capture them, they'd be heroes. Too bad. Swanson's men had arrived just as the British entrepreneurs planned their attack.

But a motion of pure-white cloth caught their attention a thousand yards south. A surrender offer? No. Isaac's bandage moved back and forth. There was a wagon down there, next to the meeting house, close to the guns, but far enough away that nobody would notice its being attacked. A wagon was almost as good a prize as a cannon, and there was a horse on it, as a bonus.

The two soldiers conferred with each other, then rushed toward Isaac's wagon. No other Americans were near Isaac.

British Colonel Mawhood's guns north of the orchard were worthless now, since they couldn't shoot through the orchard. Mawhood heard the sounds of Moulder's guns and knew he had to take them out if he were ever to win this fight.

Mawhood rode up to his gunners, "Right. Go right. Move."

The British cannon moved to the right and inched another hundred yards down the west fence to get a bead on Moulder's guns, a clear shot with solid ball unhindered by trees. It was only six hundred yards to Moulder.

Swanson watched the British sneak their cannon out from behind the trees, timidly, moving slowly west. His men continued to load and fire at the British in the orchard. Toby blasted away, his bullets falling harmlessly into the field. Swanson didn't fire any more. He kept his rifle loaded and watched the developing situation with the British cannon.

Artillerymen had a healthy respect for each other, especially when they were going cannon-to-cannon. But when it came to cannons supported by infantry, that was something to think about. The British gunners had orders to take out Moulder's cannons, but it might not be that easy. There were those Americans nearby in their dirty shirts, loose pants, and long, deadly rifles. Swanson was too far away even for rifles, but who in the British line knew that? Who knew how far a rifleman's bullet could travel across an open field on a clear morning with no wind?

Swanson pointed out the emerging British gun to his two best riflemen. They rested their barrels on the wheels of Moulder's first cannon and looked up at Swanson. "Sarge? We can't hit that far." Swanson said, "Aim high. Hit near." Swanson took aim from the second cannon. "Fire." The bullets disappeared into the air, or fell into the field, nobody knew. Now McKean's men took their turn. They rested their rifles on the cannons and aimed high, another game. Six more bullets sailed high, arcing up toward the British guns. The British heard the telltale arrivals whistle through the trees of the orchard on the left. One bullet hit the left cannon low on the wheel, did no harm, but frightened the British gunners into pulling the gun out of the way. McKean's men congratulated themselves.

Moulder's guns went off again. The British at the orchard fell to the ground and behind the fence to get out of the way. The field between the south orchard and the Saw Mill road was now almost completely clear of men as the British hesitated to charge into the guns.

Murphy struggled forward, the last of the Americans to come south. He panted heavily and trudged through the mud, looking nervously behind him. The British had stopped charging, but they were forming for another thrust. Murphy looked directly ahead, toward Swanson and Toby at the guns. To the right, he saw Isaac in the wagon. "Oh my God." Two red uniforms charged fast for Isaac.

Murphy stopped in the middle of the field. He loaded his rifle, more quickly than he ever had, brought it up to his cheek, aimed, and fired. One of the soldiers collapsed with a hole in his back. Murphy hustled toward Isaac as fast as he could run, but he was tired. He stopped at the edge of the field and reloaded, but there was no time to save Isaac. Murphy stared in horror at the scene unfolding before him.

Swanson and Toby watched Murphy running not toward them and the rest of the Americans, but to the southwest. Toby yelled, "Come on, Pa. Come on. Over here!" Swanson looked left to where he calculated Murphy was heading. He saw Murphy's victim fall, and then he saw Isaac in the wagon with the other British soldier getting closer and closer. Isaac was in terrible danger.

Isaac scrambled to the front of the wagon to get the loaded gun that Toby had provided. The soldier was only ten yards away. Isaac retrieved the gun and aimed it. He fired. He missed. The soldier stopped to get the momentum to plunge. He did plunge. Isaac watched the bayonet come at his stomach. There was nothing he could do about it.

A shot sounded from Isaac's right. The bullet shattered the soldier's left temple and blew his brains out the top. Murphy looked southeast. Isaac looked northeast. Sergeant Swanson raised his Kentucky long rifle in the air and reloaded.

Murphy turned left and joined the retreating militia, now almost to the Saw Mill road. Another blast of grapeshot from Moulder kept the British near the orchard, but they were not going to let a couple of guns keep them from victory. The British came out of the orchard and marched toward the road and the guns.

A lone figure on a horse galloped up fast from the east. Washington ran straight into the no-man's land between the militia and the British. Everyone gaped at Washington. British Colonel Mawhood gasped, "I can't believe it."

Hundreds of Americans arrived from the right, Hitchcock's brigade. They went behind Washington, mixing with the retreating Militia. Hundreds more Americans appeared, then hundreds more, and hundreds even more, until eight hundred Americans formed a long line from west to east facing the four hundred British. Washington sat on his horse, alone in the field between the two armies.

Washington shouted, "Fire!"

Both sides fired. A thousand bullets crossed the field. Smoke obscured everything. Murphy put his hand to his head and said, "Oh, my God, the General." As the smoke cleared, Murphy uncovered his eyes and saw the British running for their lives toward the orchard or the town, outnumbered now, and out-officered.

Washington spurred his horse after the retreating British, shouting, "It's a fine fox chase, boys." He slapped the British with the flat of his sword. They fell, or turned around with their hands up. Pursuing Americans picked them up. Washington kicked a defiant British soldier to the ground and galloped into the crowd of retreating enemy. The British who ran toward Princeton were all captured by the Americans before they got fifty yards. The cannoneers at the road abandoned their gun and slipped away across the bridge, Mawhood right behind them.

Mawhood paused on the Princeton side of the bridge and turned to look at the scene of his disaster. The field was filled with Americans. He spied Washington on horseback 700 yards away, near the fatal orchard of his career. American soldiers took the reins of Washington's horse and slowed it to a halt. Mawhood shook his head as he crossed the bridge west.

Chapter Fifty Five

A mile and a half northeast of the bridge, Sullivan's men headed toward Princeton. A hundred British soldiers ran westward from town toward the battle and went down into a ditch. The 55th, the four hundred troops that Mawhood had dispatched from the road at the orchard, curved around south and arrived at the ditch just as the Americans were a hundred yards away.

Frog Hollow was a low indent in the ground running about west-to-east, with steep banks on the American side, impossibly difficult for the Americans to cross, the British hoped. Five hundred British soldiers assembled quickly in the ditch. They threw away their packs and got ready for the American onslaught.

The British aimed their muskets at seven hundred Americans marching relentlessly toward them. Another thousand Americans were close behind. The Americans came within thirty yards.

A British officer at the ditch yelled, "Fire!"

The British fired. Six Americans fell, but now the Americans were in a sprint for the ditch. The British didn't have the thirty seconds needed to reload, and even if they did, they didn't have a thousand bullets. The officer yelled again, "Fix bayonets!" The Americans got closer every second. Hundreds of Americans ran toward the British. Now the Americans were at the west bank of the ditch. The officer shouted, "Pull back!"

The Americans went down into Frog Hollow without even slowing their pace. The British scrambled up the other bank, some of them turning around and facing the rebels with bayonets, but that was foolish. They perished from multiple bullets against impossible odds. Hundreds of other Americans arrived and opened up with muskets at point-blank range on the British in the ditch and those trying to get out.

The British who did get out ran fast to a stack of logs in their rear. Another two hundred British ran west from the town to reinforce them at the logs.

The British soldiers panicked and fired a premature volley. They missed. The British reloaded. The British officer surveyed the field. To his right, four hundred rebels were already behind him, heading for town, ignoring his position. Horses dragged two American cannons over there quickly. Alexander Hamilton ran alongside, spurring them on.

The Americans were like ants, all over, to the left, right, and center. They were Sullivan's division, two thousand strong, the regulars, and they'd had enough of this. They only wanted to swat this British force out of the way, go straight into town, get some food, and get some sleep.

The British officer at the logs watched them come with fearful anticipation. They were a division from hell. They were filthy dirty, with ragged hats, torn clothes, bandaged heads, and no shoes, but still they came. They came with hardened, dirty, exhausted faces, with stringy hair hanging down into their eyes. They slumped forward and marched slowly toward him like a wall of disaster about to crash. A couple of them fell as individual British fired, but still they came. To the officer, they were two thousand angry devils coming straight at him.

The officer looked left and right at his men. They looked up at him with pleading eyes. He took a handkerchief out of his pocket, attached it to his bayonet, and held it high in the air.

* * *

Nassau Hall, the center of the college, was five hundred yards north. An elegant two-story mansion stood to the right. Alexander Hamilton's cannonball plowed into the side of the building, burst through the outside wall, and smashed into a picture of King George hanging in a hallway. Another shot blew the outside bricks away and exposed the British inside ducking from the blast. It shattered tables, chairs, and beds, and came out the other side of the building. Hamilton's gunners reloaded.

White flags appeared in the windows and also from the mansion next door. Americans rushed up to Nassau Hall. Other Americans ran over to the mansion.

British soldiers emerged from the Hall in abject humiliation. Hamilton left his guns and walked up to the building. He kept a keen eye on the few British at the mansion to the right, but they were covered now by many Americans who marched the British over.

A single British officer came out of the front door of Nassau Hall as Hamilton approached. The officer frowned at seeing such a young American walking toward him. Other soldiers came out of the building and stood tightly packed, next to the door. Some of them had muskets. Hamilton took a chance and kept walking.

The British officer was five feet in front of his troops and held a pistol in his right hand. Hamilton spotted it from ten yards away and quickened his pace. He marched fiercely over to the officer, his heart pounding, not knowing if he'd be dead shortly from the pistol or from one of the muskets. He stopped in front of the officer within deadly distance of the British soldiers from Nassau Hall. He looked at the officer. "Drop your pistol, sir."

Noticing Hamilton's young age, the officer said, "I can only surrender to a superior officer."

"Put it on the ground."

The officer did. Hamilton took 300 prisoners.

Chapter Fifty Six

To the west, south of the bridge, Murphy, Swanson and Toby ran over to Isaac's wagon. Murphy got there first. He climbed up the side, grabbed Isaac's head, pulled it into his chest, and held Isaac's head for a minute. Isaac reached his good arm up and squeezed Murphy's shoulder. "Ah, Pa. I'm all right." Murphy released him and then climbed down.

Toby asked his father, "You think it's over?"

"Yes, I think so. You boys have been through a lot."

Toby said, "And you, too. I guess you're a combat soldier now."

"I can't believe how scared I was." He looked down at his hands, then up at Swanson. "My hands were just shaking. Then it went away."

Swanson said, "It get easier now."

Isaac said, "I want to write a letter to Anna, tell her I'm all right."

Swanson frowned at Isaac. "Ah, all right. You good boy. No can shoot, though."

Isaac grinned. "I don't know how to write a letter to a girl."

Murphy said, "Your mother can help you with that."

Toby asked, "We're going home?"

"Yes. I'll drop you off there. I expect the army will move north. I have to go with them."

Toby said, "I want to go with you."

"No, you're too young."

"But we're soldiers. The General called us that. He said that."

Murphy just shook his head.

Isaac asked, "Can you stay a few days with us? I mean, with us and Ma?"

"I don't know. That depends on your mother."

Isaac chuckled. "Wait'll she finds out we're all rebels."

Toby laughed. "She'll scream."

Isaac said, "No, she'll get a gun." They all laughed.

Visions of Maggie pointing a gun at his groin flashed through Murphy's mind. He smiled. "All right, here's what we do, Toby, you infiltrate from the rear and distract her. Isaac, take the right flank and wait for my signal."

Swanson smiled. "She's a wild one, eh? Like my Greta."

"Swanson, you take the left. I'll hold the riflemen in reserve. I'm going in through the front."

Isaac pleaded, "No, Pa, no. You'll be slaughtered. Oh, God, the blood."

"If I fall, you come in from the flanks. It's all I can do for my country." They all laughed.

Colonel Hand galloped up from the right. "Murphy, Mercer's bad. Get a wagon up there, then get some men and help take out the bridge."

"Yes, sir. Isaac, get out."

Toby helped Isaac climb out of the wagon. Swanson motioned for a rifleman nearby to guide the horse. The wagon lumbered north. Isaac shouted, "Wait."

The wagon stopped. Isaac struggled up to it and threw the axes and hatchets on the ground. Then he sat down on the road and held his arm.

Murphy said, "Toby, get those tools up to the bridge, then get away. Swanson, get your men behind and cover the bridge."

Toby grabbed the hatchets and axes and walked north toward the bridge, then stopped. He put the tools on the ground and went back to the wagon. He took Isaac's musket out and put the gun in the front of the wagon, making sure that Isaac knew where it was. Toby said, "Just in case." He walked back to the tools, picked them up, and headed for the bridge, six hundred yards away.

Murphy asked Isaac, "You all right?"

"Yes, I think so."

Toby was well ahead and moving fast, with Murphy and Swanson following. Isaac watched them all go as he rubbed his arm.

* * *

Men at the bridge worked to dismantle it. They untied the ropes and pulled hard at the railings. The men gratefully took the tools from Toby and hacked away at the ropes and logs. Toby found a free hatchet and chopped at the ropes on the western, Trenton, side of the bridge.

A log in the middle fell away into the creek. Toby danced on the shaky logs. "Whoa, Nellie."

Murphy saw Toby clowning around. "Toby, get off of there." He loaded his rifle.

Swanson said, "He no should be there. Dangerous. Bad bridge."

"I know. Toby, get back here now."

"Pa, this is our bridge."

"Toby, get out of there, right now."

Toby ambled off the bridge onto the Trenton side. He walked ten feet down the road and exaggerated a long, slow, follow-through salute. "So long, old bridge."

Murphy yelled, "Toby, get back here, now. Toby!"

Isaac saw the action at the bridge, far away. He picked up Toby's musket and fumbled with it as he looked around for some powder and shot. There was none to be found, but he couldn't hold the gun in one hand anyway, so it dropped to the ground. There was no way he could load it with one arm.

Isaac looked around for a knife, or a stick, or something that he could throw, anything he could use as a weapon. Then he noticed the soldier's gun, lying sideways on the ground. A small amount of black powder sprinkled the snow. If there had been powder in the pan, then the gun was probably still loaded. Isaac picked up the soldier's powder horn, sat down on the ground with the gun between his knees, and refilled the pan. He got up and moved slowly toward the bridge.

Isaac walked 400 yards, to a point on the road 200 yards south of the bridge. He followed the road that ran parallel to the creek, but he hadn't really walked since Momma sewed him up. The loss of blood took its toll now as Isaac became dizzy and slumped to his knees, but he steadied himself on his good arm and kept the musket level. He stared at the bandage on his bad arm, looking for leaks, turning the arm around to look underneath. There was no blood. Momma did a good job.

Isaac put the musket on the ground, lay down in the road on his back and waited for the dizziness to stop. He got up again and staggered up the Quaker road, carefully placing one foot deliberately in front of the other in case he should fall on his bad arm. Double images of the bridge appeared in his eyes. He focused on Toby, left of the bridge on the Trenton road.

Isaac sank to the ground again, not in pain or faintness, but just to make the images come together. He decided to stay where he was until Pa came to get him.

Isaac looked up at Toby ten feet west of the creek. He was shocked to see movement through the bare trees behind the hill in the road at the bridge, thirty yards behind Toby. He saw Murphy rushing up to the bridge.

Sergeant Swanson saw the movement also. "I get more men." Swanson took off to the southeast as fast as his lumbering boots could carry him through the muddy field.

Isaac got up. He stood in the middle of the road, watching Toby salute the bridge. Isaac shouted, "Toby, get away."

Toby looked right and noticed Isaac across the creek, far away, waving at him. "Hey, Isaac, look." Toby saluted the bridge again, laughing. He smiled for approval from Isaac across the creek. Isaac swung his good arm west-to-east.

Toby laughed. "What? What? I can't hear you."

Toby stepped forward onto the bridge, which swayed precariously. Men on the other side clamored to get off. Murphy wagged his arms in the air, imploring Toby to come across. Toby saw Murphy yelling, but he couldn't hear the words. He knew what they were, though. Toby said, "All right, all right, I'm coming." Toby moved gingerly farther onto the bridge.

From the Trenton side, two cannonballs flew overhead. One hit the mud on the Princeton side, the other splashed into the creek. A third cannonball plowed right through the planks of the bridge. Toby ducked. Another shot, and a wagon splintered to pieces in the field. The driver flew through the air. More cannonballs, and the south railing was hit. Toby turned his head and held his hands fast to his face to avoid the terrible splinters, like the ones the farmer gave him. He shouted across the bridge at Murphy. "Pa, help."

Murphy ran toward the bridge. A few other soldiers followed him with muskets, but they were eighty yards away. Another cannon blast hit the middle piling on the south side that kept the bridge out of the creek. Toby fell onto his hands and knees, holding on to the north-side railing.

The bridge screeched from the twisting logs rubbing against each other. Several logs in the middle came loose, dangled into the water, and fell ten feet into the creek. Toby danced among the falling beams, trying to maintain his grip and balance. The middle of the south side of the bridge was in the water, but both bank supports were still standing. The north side was intact. More logs fell into the creek.

Murphy arrived at the bridge from the Princeton direction. He put his gun down and tried to ease across the planks on the north side, but the bridge shook too badly from the weight, so he went back. "Toby, try and come across. Hold on to the railing. You can do it."

"Pa, I can't."

"It's all right, Toby. Just take it slow."

Murphy glanced behind Toby nervously, spotting the British now coming into view. Toby steadied himself on the very shaky north railing, turned around gingerly, and saw the British.

Lawrence spotted Toby alone on the shaking bridge. He ordered his men, "That one. Kill him." Toby heard the familiar raspy voice that he remembered on the Trenton Road, the same terrifying accent that threatened his mother five days ago.

Toby yelled to Murphy, "Pa, that's him!" Murphy looked into the face of the hated British soldier who threatened his wife and almost killed his boys. Murphy glanced at his rifle on the ground. If he went for it, he'd lose time. If he didn't, he'd lose Toby. It was better to get Toby off, then take care of Lawrence.

Toby turned violently in terror. He moved fast, too fast, on his hands and knees toward Murphy, so fast that the bridge twisted badly. "Pa, I can't make it." Toby stopped moving. The bridge stopped swaying. As the bridge steadied, Toby held on tight. He glanced behind him again at Lawrence and his men. They loaded.

Toby knew how long it took to load a musket. He had about thirty seconds, probably less. His mind flashed back to images of Isaac at Momma's house and the needle poking through the skin, the blood pouring out. Toby didn't think he could survive that. What if he was shot in the back, or the head? No needle could save him then, or hot wax, or even another bath. Toby glanced south, just on the off chance that Isaac could help. He saw Isaac struggling slowly up the Quaker Road.

Murphy said calmly, "Easy, easy. You're doing fine. Go slow. Come across. Toby, come across." Murphy looked behind him at the Americans coming up. He never saw soldiers move so slowly. Murphy shouted to them, "Come up. Come up!"

Isaac picked up his pace when he recognized Lawrence. Isaac got dizzy again and stopped. He fell on one knee, keeping his eye on the bridge. Lawrence's men finished loading and aimed.

Isaac shouted, "No, no. Toby, jump, jump!"

Toby looked west and saw the British stop and line up. They pointed their guns at the Americans coming up. Toby was in direct line between the British and the Americans hustling up to the bridge. The British fired to the southeast. Bullets plowed into the boards and ricocheted off the north railing. The Americans fired. Smoke filled the air. The British fanned out to the north of the bridge, away from the Americans, all except Lawrence and three other soldiers. They stayed twenty yards from the bridge on the Trenton Road and reloaded.

At the sound of the volley, Toby crashed into the north railing and fell down hard to get out of the way of the bullets and splinters. The north side of the bridge swayed farther to the north. The south side gave way altogether.

The logs dangled southward into the water. Toby hung onto the north railing as the south side fell. He lost the grip of his right hand and twisted backward onto the logs, looking down at the fast-flowing water, ten feet below. Toby was on his back against the few remaining logs, holding flimsily onto the north railing. His fingers held only precariously. His wrist would break if he didn't do something.

Toby pushed his left arm against the logs to turn onto his stomach and got a better grip on the railing. His feet fluttered in the air to get a foothold on the remaining logs, but there was none. Toby dangled from his left hand and thrust hard with his right hand to get a grip on the railing. Another thrust, no, it didn't work.

Murphy yelled, "Toby, Toby. Stop. Stop shaking the bridge. Be still, Toby, I'm coming." Murphy tried again to get onto the bridge. He saw Lawrence and three soldiers loading their muskets. Murphy on the east bank tried to physically push the bridge back into position, but it wouldn't move. He looked east at Swanson coming up. "Come here. Borg. Come up." Murphy backed away from the bridge and got ready to handle Lawrence and his men. Another shot and Toby would be gone. He ran over and picked up his loaded rifle. Murphy aimed at each of the men successively, first Lawrence, then the others, then back to Lawrence, then the men.

Lawrence's men recognized the unmistakable signature of a Kentucky Long Rifle, a narrow barrel and no clip for a bayonet, and certain death if that gun went off. One of Lawrence's men turned around, fell down, tripped in the mud, got up, and dodged trees to get away from the shot. The other two men aimed their muskets at Murphy, but protectively backed up behind two nearby trees. Murphy knew they couldn't fire walking backwards, so he ignored them and turned his rifle on Lawrence, but Lawrence ducked behind a tree so Murphy couldn't get a bead. Murphy shifted north to get a better angle.

Toby's wrist strained under the force of his weight. He lunged his body upward and reached high in the air one more time with his right hand for the north railing. He finally got it with just his fingertips. On his stomach now against the logs, Toby adjusted his grip with both hands. He pulled himself up.

The railing gave way with a loud crack. Toby brought the north railing down with him as the entire bridge collapsed, north and south. Toby slid down the logs into the dark, deadly water, and slipped beneath the freezing-cold Stony Brook Creek.

Murphy shouted, "Toby, Toby!"

Swanson came up and put his hand to his forehead, "Oh, mein God."

The Stony Brook Creek ran south. Murphy searched the water for signs of Toby between the logs, but he couldn't linger long, because he spotted Lawrence running over to his two men crouching behind the trees. Murphy's rifle drew a bead on Lawrence's moving, bobbing head. A tree branch prevented Murphy from firing, so he lowered his rifle and went south with the flow of the creek, searching again for signs of Toby. Lawrence got to his men at the trees, now ten yards north of Murphy.

Lawrence shouted, "Get over here." He snagged one man by the shirt and dragged the soldier up and toward him. Murphy aimed and fired. At that instant, the soldier in Lawrence's hand shifted and intercepted the bullet intended for Lawrence's head. Blood splattered all over Lawrence's face, but Lawrence was unhurt.

Lawrence turned and sent a musket bullet over the creek toward Murphy. He missed. Lawrence grabbed the other soldier and dragged him out of his safe spot behind the trees. The soldier got up and followed Lawrence south. Lawrence loaded as he walked, no danger now that he'd be shot by a slow loading rifleman. Murphy searched the stream for Toby, as did Lawrence on the west bank.

Murphy put his rifle on the ground and climbed down the bank into the water. He waded across the muddy stream through the freezing water searching for Toby.

Lawrence fired from the opposite bank, thirty feet away. The other British soldier took aim.

Murphy scrambled up the bank but slipped and fell back into the creek. The soldier's shot hit the bank where Murphy would have been. Murphy tried again to get out, but his footing failed, and he slid into the creek. A strong arm reached down the bank, seized Murphy by the collar, and dragged him up. It was Swanson.

Toby's head appeared above a log floating on the opposite bank. He stood up in the water, struggling to hold onto the log. The creek was only four feet deep. Lawrence and his man loaded.

Murphy called to Toby, "Come here, Toby. Come across."

Toby shivered uncontrollably. He clutched the log tighter. Swanson yelled, "Come here, boy."

Another bullet by Lawrence's soldier hit the log right above the initials IMTM. Toby slipped back under the water. Murphy climbed out of the stream with Swanson's help. "Get off him. Get off." Murphy ran and picked up his unloaded rifle. Swanson tried to determine which man, Lawrence or the soldier, would end up with a loaded musket first. Swanson could only take out one of them, but it was a guaranteed kill at only thirty feet with a rifle. Swanson aimed at the soldier and squeezed the trigger. The soldier dropped dead. Now there was only Lawrence. Murphy and Swanson moved south. They concentrated on where they expected Toby to be.

Lawrence on the opposite bank moved south with them. Swanson stopped. He poured the powder in, but he couldn't possibly complete the load quickly enough. Lawrence was getting farther south, but he was still slightly north of Murphy. Toby was presumably south, but no one could tell. Murphy proceeded south with an unloaded rifle. Swanson trudged behind, struggling to load while walking.

Toby's head reappeared. Lawrence pointed his loaded musket at Toby, only a few feet away.

Murphy yelled, "Get off him. Get off him, you son of a bitch!"

Swanson, twenty yards behind, had at least fifteen seconds left of reloading. He saw Lawrence point his musket. The aim looked just about right to Swanson's seasoned eye. Swanson hoped for a miss, but he was not optimistic. It looked as though Toby would be gone. He watched. Swanson slowed his loading procedure to make sure he had enough powder in the pan. He couldn't prevent the inevitable shot, but no matter what, Lawrence was going to die.

Murphy hugged the east bank, hoping to draw fire from Lawrence's musket. He aimed his unloaded rifle at Lawrence.

Lawrence yelled across the creek, "Ha. You ain't got no bullet in there, Reb."

Murphy shouted, "Get off him!" In a rage mixed with despair, Murphy flung his unloaded rifle across the creek, going nowhere near Lawrence. Lawrence watched the gun sail at him high in the air without the least concern.

* * *

Isaac's bullet hit Lawrence right in the chest. Lawrence fell face down into the creek and floated south. Murphy looked to his left. Isaac sat on the ground thirty feet away with a smoking gun resting between his knees.

Murphy plunged into the creek, waded across, reached underwater, found Toby's shirt with his right hand, and pulled him up. He dragged Toby across to the Princeton side.

Isaac reached down to pull them out of the water, but Swanson arrived and gently pushed Isaac back. "Take care that arm." Swanson pulled Toby out first, then Murphy.

Toby struggled to breathe. Face down on the Princeton bank, he coughed, wheezed, came alive, and turned onto his back.

Isaac asked, "Who says I can't shoot?"

Murphy replied, "Nobody now."

Swanson looked at Isaac. "How you shoot with bad arm?"

"I shot from the hip."

Toby sputtered and spat, "No you didn't, you liar. (Cough) Not at that distance. (Cough) You're lying."

"Well, Toby, just because you can't..."

"He's lying, Pa. (Cough) He couldn't shoot from there."

Murphy was relieved. "Not exactly from the hip, more like from the knee."

"You (choke) probably (spit) put the gun on the ground and pulled a string (cough)."

"Ah, Toby, I'll teach you how to do it someday."

Murphy looked at his two boys, safe now. He thought fleetingly about Jackson and Satchel, brothers who lost each other so young. Maybe Isaac and Toby wouldn't have to go through that. Not in this battle, anyway. Murphy suppressed a tear of joy. "Borg, I have to get up to Colonel Hand. You think they'll be all right?"

"Yes. I bring them along."

Murphy reached down and rubbed Toby's head.

Toby muttered, "Everybody's always rubbing my head."

Murphy smiled and went north, toward the bridge and the sounds of sporadic shots. On the slim chance that there would still be some fighting ahead, Hand would be there.

Isaac shouted, "Pa, wait."

Murphy waited for Isaac to catch up. Isaac paused, fumbling for words. "I can't stop thinking about that horse."

"What horse?"

"Washington's horse. At the Trenton Bridge. It never moved. And the General didn't either. They both just kept staring straight ahead."

Murphy understood now. He stared philosophically at Isaac. "And why do you think that is?"

"I don't know."

Murphy pointed to a log on the side of the road. "Sit down, son." Murphy sat on the log. Isaac sat next to him. Murphy looked east at the scrambling men, the smoky sky, and the wagons heading east. The smell of gunpowder filled the air. Murphy breathed deeply. The bright new sun was well above the trees to the southeast now.

"How's your arm?"

"All right, I guess."

"You want to know about that horse?"

"Yes."

Murphy adjusted his position a little and faced Isaac, gathering his thoughts. It wasn't easy, but an opportunity arose to talk to a son whom he hadn't seen in many years. Murphy paused nervously.

They both stared awkwardly at the smoke-filled landscape to the east. Murphy broke the silence, "It's a good horse."

"Must be." Isaac looked slantingly at his father.

"You know why I'm here, Isaac? No, don't answer that." Murphy looked down, then up, east. "I have a farm, a little hog farm. I left in June a year ago, eighteen months now. I haven't seen it since. I don't even know if it's still there. I have some neighbors taking care of it, but I really doubt if it's still there."

Isaac stared at Murphy, wondering what he was getting at, but also sad that he'd probably lost his farm. Isaac was curious as to why Murphy would so casually mention such an important loss. He listened closely.

Murphy continued, "It doesn't matter, though. It doesn't matter if my farm is there or not. It doesn't matter if I live or not."

Murphy coughed nervously. "All right. Sorry, son. The horse. You know what 'determination' means?"

"Yes, like, like you need to do something that's important and you can't stop 'till you do it."

Murphy was surprised at Isaac's eloquence. "Right. Gosh, good. Good thinking. Good way to say that. I don't know if Franklin could say that any better." Isaac smiled at the compliment.

Murphy gazed at Isaac admiringly. He hated what he did when he left his boys and Maggie. For a fleeting second his mind flashed back to the old house, the boys young and playful, Maggie always yelling for the three of them to "Stop shooting and get in here," when it got dark. It was happier then, a new land, new opportunities. It was hard, but happy.

Murphy shook his head. "Determination. That's the horse. Or more accurately, the General. The General's horse." Murphy cringed at the confusion he just caused.

"I see, Pa.

"Yes, thank you, for seeing. I'm not explaining it right. It's the determination, Isaac. Me, Swanson, the General, Henry Knox, and all the men who died coming down here. You know, Isaac, when you told me about that horse last night, I kind of dismissed it, but then I thought about it."

Murphy got up from the log. Isaac stood up. "I'm in the war, Isaac, and I may very well die. You're my son." Murphy kicked the ground, embarrassed for the greater confusion he was causing. "You know, Isaac, if I were a great person with words like Franklin, I could tell you a thing or two about that horse. And about determination. And about staring straight ahead when the enemy is coming right at you over a bridge, and they're shooting at you and ready to stick bayonets into your stomach."

Isaac listened.

Murphy said, "And if you're the General, well, that's not a very good place to be, on the bridge. All the generals I've ever heard about would be far away. I guess he just wanted to make sure we all got back.

"I'll tell you, Isaac, when I was in that field, and I saw the general on that bridge, well, I got a second wind. You were unconscious then, but Swanson and I carried you as hard as we could and as fast as we could through that field. I don't know. I guess I just wanted the general to get the hell off of that bridge. We have a great General here, Isaac. God protect him."

Murphy looked into Isaac's eyes. He expected Isaac to scrunch his face into confusion, but Isaac didn't. Isaac listened. He seemed to understand. Murphy breathed deeply at the relief. "You're my son. Isaac. And I love you dearly. And I want the greatest happiness for you, and Toby, and your mother, and everyone we fight for."

"And Anna."

Murphy smiled. "Yes, and Anna. But I will do everything I can, even die, so that my children, you, and your children, can be free."

Isaac nodded silently.

"I will not have you, and Anna, and Toby, and your mother live in slavery to a foreign government. I just won't do it, and I will gladly die rather than see that happen."

Isaac looked at his father with the determination that he defined before. Isaac said, "I want to join the army."

Murphy was caught off guard at the unexpected offer. "What? Oh, Isaac, I don't know."

"After my arm heals, will you come back and get me?"

"I don't know. We'll see." Murphy paused to consider the consequences. The army needed young men desperately, but this was his son. He could be delivering a death sentence if he agreed. Until now, Murphy only had himself to worry about, and that was hard enough to do. Now he was being asked for permission to watch his son die in battle, or in sickness, or in suffering.

But really, there was only one possible reply. Murphy said, "Yes, I'll come back for you. You have to learn how to shoot, though."

Isaac smiled. "Do you think we can win?"

Murphy thought for a moment. "Well, we've got that horse."

Murphy hugged Isaac and then went north.

Chapter Fifty Seven

Hundreds of Americans reached the eastern bank of the creek. They were north of the now sunken bridge. More Americans came up from the southeast. Bullets flew sporadically across the creek from both sides.

Colonel Hand was at the bridge. British Major Derring rode up on a horse from the Trenton road. Hand aimed his gun at Derring from thirty yards away, but Derring didn't see Hand yet. A bullet hit a tree dangerously close to Hand, who instinctively jumped back to avoid it.

Derring shouted to the men, "Cease fire. There's no bridge. It's just murder now."

Hand turned toward Derring as he heard the order. He lowered his rifle. "Cease fire."

Derring spotted Hand, dismounted, and walked up to the west bank of the creek. Hand walked up to the east bank. Derring waited for Hand to come up.

Derring asked, "When are you rebels going to learn how to fight a war like real men?"

"You don't like the way we fight a war, then get out of our country."

"You can't defeat the British army."

"No? Can your troops march all night in the freezing cold, half asleep, blood all over the road, just to get to the battlefield?"

Derring paused.

Hand asked, "Can your men fight two battles in eighteen hours and march twelve miles in between?"

"No. Not unless there's rum involved."

Hand laughed at the joke. "Ha. Yes, I know about that." Hand pointed south along the creek, to Isaac, Toby, and Swanson. "You see those soldiers down there?"

Derring looked south. Hand said, "That boy is only fourteen, but he can hit a moving target at thirty yards. With a musket!"

Derring peered through the smoke at the group of soldiers clumped together. Toby faced away from Derring, so Derring couldn't see his face, but he recognized Toby's small frame. He saw Swanson put a blanket around Toby. Toby reached his hand up for help. Swanson pulled hard and Toby rose to his feet and off the ground, standing now.

Derring said, "I know that boy. I delivered him at sword point to that maniac floating downstream. You will express my apologies to him, sir."

Hand replied, "Yes, I will. Good luck to you, sir."

Derring raised his arm to his forehead in a salute. "And to you." Hand returned the salute. Derring lowered his arm.

Derring turned and walked back to his horse on the Trenton side of the bridge. Hand watched him go for a moment, then strode east. Hand mounted his horse and paused for a moment. Derring took his horse's reins and pulled himself up, the two officers facing each other once more on horseback from twenty yards away. Derring saluted again. Hand returned. They pulled their horses in opposite directions and trotted away.

The Battle of Princeton was over.

Chapter Fifty Eight

Outside of Maggie's house, two children played with toys and looked up at three figures approaching. Murphy blocked their view of the boys, so the children didn't recognize their brothers yet. One child hopped up the steps and ran into the house. "Mommy, Mommy, strangers."

The other child watched the three men come. She recognized Isaac and rushed up to him. Isaac wrapped her up in his arms as she leaped, carefully protecting his bandaged arm. He kissed her affectionately. "Hey, how are ya, little missy?"

The child squealed, "Mommy, Mommy, the boys are back."

Still in Isaac's arms, the child reached for Toby. He squeezed her little hand, but Murphy got only a curious frown.

Isaac got a better grip on the child as the three of them walked up the steps. Maggie and the other child came out onto the porch. Maggie held her bandaged hand to her mouth. "Oh my God. Thank you, Lord. Thank you, dear Lord." Maggie stood on the porch in tears as her three men came up the steps.

Toby said, "Hi, Ma."

"Oh, Toby. Isaac. Warren? Is that you? Is that you, Warren?"

Isaac put the child down when they got to the porch. The child hugged Isaac's leg tightly. The other child grabbed Toby's leg the same way. Toby smiled down at them.

Maggie hugged both boys at the same time as she looked fondly at Murphy. Isaac winced. Maggie released them when she saw Isaac's arm. "Oh, no. Isaac, oh no, you're hurt."

"Sorry, Ma. I got shot. Toby saved me. You should have seen the little runt."

Maggie stared in horror at Isaac, then at Murphy, then again at Isaac. "You got shot? Oh, Isaac, what happened? Are you all right?"

"I'm all right, Ma. Anna's mother sewed me up."

"Sewed you up? What? Who's Anna?"

Toby snickered, "Isaac's got a girl friend."

Isaac said, "She's a girl. I need you to help me write a letter to her."

Maggie carefully examined Isaac's bandage and hugged him gently. "Oh, Isaac. I was so upset when you boys left. I shouldn't have sent you." She asked Murphy, "Is he all right? Warren, I never thought I'd see you again."

"Ah, Maggie, it's good to see you. Yes, he's all right."

Maggie cried. Murphy put his arms around her. She reciprocated by wrapping her arms tightly around him. "Yes, yes. Warren. Ah, Warren. Are you in the war? Were they in a battle?" She wiped some tears.

"Ah, what a battle. You raised some fine boys here, Maggie. You can be proud of yourself."

Isaac said, "Ma, I need you to write this letter. Let's go. She probably thinks I'm dead. Hurry, Ma."

"A letter, yes. Oh, Isaac, you know, the mail's very bad. I'm sorry. The war."

Murphy said, "I think I can persuade Sergeant Swanson to take a letter there."

Isaac said, "Yes, he can do that. He can do anything, Ma. Right now, Ma."

Maggie cried some more against Murphy's shoulder as the two small children hugged the boys' legs. They stared at Murphy suspiciously.

Isaac said, "He's our father."

Murphy crouched down and shook their little hands. The children looked away. Maggie smiled and wiped away some more tears. "Oh, Warren, I'm so sorry." Murphy stood up.

Maggie hugged Murphy again, more closely, then Isaac and Toby together, emotionally. She kissed each of the boys on their heads.

Toby said, "Ah, Ma, you can't kiss us no more. We're soldiers."

"No, you're my boys." Maggie turned back to Murphy. He wiped her eyes with his palms.

The five of them formed a circle on the porch, clockwise, Murphy, Maggie, Isaac, Child, Toby, and Child. Murphy sneaked his left hand down and touched Maggie's right hand. She clutched it tightly.

Maggie looked at Isaac, to her left. She put her arm on his good shoulder.

The child to Isaac's left touched the bloody bandage. Isaac admonished, "Careful there, Missy. I got shot."

Toby held both children's hands. The circle of contact was broken only by the child on Toby's left, Murphy's right. The child stared up at Murphy curiously.

Murphy gently squeezed Maggie's hand. She smiled embarrassingly. Murphy rubbed the child's head with his right hand to complete the circle.

He turned to Maggie. "It's all right, Maggie. We're all safe now."

Maggie said, "Let's go in. Come in, children, come in."

They walked into the house, Toby trailing. The child whose head Murphy had just rubbed looked up. "Is he our father, too?"

Toby rubbed the child's head. They all went inside.

Afterword

Congress paid the bounty.

General Roche Fermoy purposefully but foolishly burned down his own headquarters near Fort Ticonderoga in July, 1777. Thankfully for the American cause, he was allowed to resign.

General Hugh Mercer died on Sunday, Jan 12, 1777, in a private house on the Princeton battlefield, now a museum. Mercer County in New Jersey is named for him, as well as Fort Mercer, site of another revolutionary-war battle, and many streets, libraries, a college, and even an American super tanker. Mercer is mostly revered for being Washington's friend and confidant, always a strength for the great man in those troubling days. For what he did for Washington, we salute General Hugh Mercer.

Washington's weary men didn't have time to sleep at Princeton after they tore down the bridge. The British forded the Stony Brook Creek farther north and poured into town. There was little danger to the Americans, but Washington had to get his men out before the main British force arrived, and he did.

Washington marched his men north and camped at Morristown, NJ, where they were a formidable threat to the main British army in New York. Never again would "The Fox" be considered as anything but a very dangerous military opponent.

Catherine the Great of Russia heard about the Battle of Princeton and always wanted to meet the greatest man on earth, as the entire world perceived Washington. She died in 1796, never realizing her wish.

* * *

All of these situations are real, but didn't necessarily happen here. I had to borrow from other American wars. For instance, so little is known about the running battle of Trenton-Two, that most historians give it only a sentence or two, if mentioned at all.

There is a scene where an American rebel, Harry, is bayoneted in the trees. That might not have happened here, but it certainly did happen at the Battle of Baltimore, Monday, Sept. 12, 1814. The British didn't think it sporting for the Americans to be shooting at them from up in the trees, so when the Americans tried to climb down and surrender, the British bayoneted them. The Americans were discovered days later hanging upside down after the British had fled in humiliating defeat.

When Murphy yelled across the creek at Trenton, "We don't put on our good clothes to butcher pigs," that is a quote from a defiant rebel soldier in the Civil War. On Tuesday, Jan 20, 1863, after the North's disaster at Fredericksburg, the rebel replied to a Yankee's taunt of "Hey Reb, how you going to win a war, you don't even have decent clothes." The rebel yelled back across the river, "We don't put on our good clothes to butcher pigs."

Washington admonished the boys to keep quiet about the Quaker road, and Murphy added callously, "Or you'll do five years on a prison farm just waiting for trial." MacArthur said that. In the first days of the occupation he told his commanders, "Any soldier who so much as slaps a Japanese civilian will do five years in jail just waiting for trial." Later, passengers on a bus were astonished when an American soldier gave up his seat to an elderly Japanese woman.

The prologue is real too, with Americans giving food and comfort to enemy prisoners. A British officer was captured in Spain in the Napoleonic wars. He was marched through a French town, where the residents lined the streets and hurled rocks at him and his men. His captors had to hustle them away or they'd have all been killed.

The officer was exchanged, went back to London, spent some time with his wife, and ended up in Maryland in the War of 1812. He was captured again. He was marched through a Maryland town. The residents lined the streets. But this time, instead throwing rocks, they came out with food, fruit, water, and whiskey.

We know this because the officer wrote to his wife and asked, "And we're killing these people?"

The Battles of Trenton-Two and Princeton changed the world. Their importance can be summed up with Cornwallis's statement to Washington on Saturday, Oct. 20, 1781, Yorktown VA,

> *"You didn't win the war here on the Chesapeake,*
> *but on the banks of the Delaware."*

Kevin Montgomery, Chicago

We hope you have enjoyed Kevin Montgomery's book, *Six Winter Days*. If you have an interest in the early history of the United States, may we also suggest Gregory T. Edgar's novels of the same period, *Gone to Meet the British*, and *Patriots*. Both are available through multiple online retailers, including BluewaterPress LLC.

You may find more information on these and other titles at:

http://www.bluewaterpress.com

Patriots

The prequel to Gregory Edgar's *Gone to Meet the British*

The Battle of Bunker Hill, the first major battle of the Revolutionary War, is the backdrop of this story. Three teenage boys – two Americans and one British – learn that war is not the glorious adventure they thought it would be, and that their enemies are human beings after all.

Gone to Meet The British

The sequel to Gregory Edgar's *Patriots*

Gregory Edgar has once again produced an exciting story about teenagers in the Revolutionary War. This time, the autumn foliage and rugged mountains of southern Vermont and New York's Hudson Valley serve as the colorful backdrop for dramatic battles and unexpected romance.

CPSIA information can be obtained at www.ICGtesting.com
Printed in the USA
BVOW01s1344160414

350804BV00003B/205/P